CATCH OF A LIFETIME

JUDI FENNELL

sourcebooks casablanca

Published by Sourcebooks Casablanca, an imprint of Sourcebooks, Inc.

P.O. Box 4410, Naperville, Illinois 60567-4410
(630) 961-3900
FAX: (630) 961-2168
www.sourcebooks.com

Printed and bound in the United States of America
QW 10 9 8 7 6 5 4 3 2 1

Beth Hill—Your incredible generosity is staggering, humbling, wonderful, and so very much appreciated. I am honored to call you my friend.

Steph—Without your honesty and friendship, who knows where I'd be.

And, always, to my husband and children—Your love, support, and faith enable me to do this.

Chapter 1

THERE WAS A NAKED WOMAN ON HIS BOAT.

Logan Hardington shook his head and rubbed his eyes, but the picture didn't change. Lady Godiva was sprawled over a pillow on his deck, a navy blue blanket draped over the bottom half of the curviest ass he'd seen in a long while.

Long, blonde—almost yellow—loose curls tumbled over creamy shoulders all the way down to that blanket, the ends pooling in the dimples above her ass, some strands twirling along the visible portion of her cleft near the light blue markings of a faded bruise.

Shapely legs, one slightly bent, only a shade or two darker than the fiberglass boat deck, trailed from beneath the blanket, one small foot flexing in the soft morning breeze. A hint of upturned nose peeked from beneath the blonde jumble, pink lips pursed in sleep, slender fingers disappearing beneath her cheek. He wondered what color her eyes were.

And why she was naked.

On his boat.

Hungry gulls cawed overhead, but she didn't stir. The wake from McKye's charter jostled the *Mir-a-Mar* as the day's fishing tour set out, but that didn't rouse her either.

Oh hell. She was probably a drunk co-ed who'd followed some "sailor" home. He'd seen that walk of shame many mornings. Didn't these people think of the repercussions?

Logan looked back down the pier where his son, Michael, chatted with Tony as the wizened old salt chopped chum, and Logan smiled. Ah, the things he would have loved to have seen as a boy. The things he should have been able to show Michael from day one—

And would have if his ex-girlfriend had only mentioned a little thing like a pregnancy…

Logan tamped down the anger at Christine—who, according to his son, now went by *Rainbow* for God-only-knew-what reasons—and focused instead on the next female to make him wonder what men ever saw in women.

Then Lady Godiva moved and the blanket slipped to the side and Logan knew *exactly* what men saw in women.

But *not* what he wanted his son to see. No matter how much Logan wanted to savor the image.

"Hey, um… Miss." Logan hunkered down and shook one of those shapely legs.

She mumbled something and flipped her head the other way, a tangle of hair tickling his arm. Logan pulled his hand back and captured the curls as they slid across his palm. Silky. Soft. The way a woman's hair should be.

He blinked. What the hell was he doing thinking about her hair? She was naked, for God's sake, and his six-year-old was going to get one hell of a birthday present if she didn't wake up and cover herself.

"Miss, wake up." Logan shook her shoulder, glancing back to Michael. Thank God Tony had a ton of fish tales to keep the boy occupied.

The woman sighed, and her shoulder slid beneath his fingertips. Her skin was just as soft and silky as her hair.

He should not be noticing.

"Lady, you really need to get up." Not that getting up was a problem he seemed to be having. Christ. How long *had* it been if he was getting hard over the naked back of a lush?

Then she rolled over.

One lone curl encircled a taut, pink nipple.

Oh, boy...

No problem getting up now.

A naked woman... Right there in front of him. A naked goddess, more like. A gift from the gods just for him.

Except, of course, there was Michael...

Logan shook his head and reached for the blanket that had slithered to the deck atop some crushed shells and dried seaweed. Fighting with himself the entire time, he tossed it over her.

"What in the sea?" The blonde bombshell awoke as if she'd been tossed overboard, sputtering and spitting the blanket away from those perfect lips, the most incredible eyes widening above that mouth. The color of the sea... aquamarine. He'd never seen anything like them.

"Um, hi?" The corners of her eyes turned up along with her mouth. A dimple winked high on her left cheek.

"Oh." Logan cleared his throat. She didn't sound drunk. "Hi. I'm Logan Hardington." He rocked back on his heels. "Who are you?"

"I'm, ah... Angel. Tritone."

She was an angel all right. Straight from Heaven, via the bowels of Hell. A temptress. Flushed with the haze of sleep, innocence and sensuality stared at him from those ocean eyes, and she had the most delectable lips he'd ever seen. Slender arms clutched the blanket to breasts that spilled from the sides, leaving barely anything to the imagination. Not that he needed to imagine since he remembered every splendid inch of those heavenly delights. If this woman wasn't walking temptation, he didn't know what was.

"So, Angel Tritone, did you have one too many last night?" *Remember that, Hardington. No matter what kind of influence she'd be on you, she'd be a bad one on your son.*

Having to kick her off his boat definitely sucked. But he was a father now. A responsible, practical father who didn't fool around with sexy, naked women on his boat.

A horny, recently celibate father who'd *love* to fool around with this sexy, naked woman on his boat.

But who wouldn't.

Damn. This responsibility thing wasn't all it was cracked up to be.

Angel cocked her head to the side, curls spilling over her shoulders in perfect, centerfold-fantasy mode, and he had to work really hard to keep his groan from escaping.

"One too many what?" Her tongue flicked over her lips again in an unself-conscious and utterly sexy way.

He had to get her off his boat. For sanity's sake. Propriety's, too. Not to mention an impressionable six-year-old's. Logan stood up and held out his hand. "Never mind. Let's get you up and at 'em."

"At who?" She reached for his hand.

Logan forgot the question the minute her fingers touched his. Hell, he almost forgot his own name, and the six-year-old down the pier was fast becoming a distant memory.

Everything was becoming a distant memory, fuzzy and out of focus, because the moment her skin met his, everything else faded to black. Fire, hot and long and needy, sped through his fingers to every extremity, zipping along his nerve endings like a match to gunpowder; the heavy *thud* of his heart blocking out the call of the birds and the sounds of the marina.

Then she tugged on his hand to stand, and he had to steady himself so he wouldn't fall on top of her—but man, did he want to. Especially when the blanket slid down her body to pool at her feet.

"You're naked," slipped out. Since making that comment was better than falling on top of her, he wasn't too upset.

"I'm what?" Five-foot-nothing dipped her blonde head forward, the curls now caressing his wrist, one encircling his forearm, and Logan had to focus on his breathing. He'd never had such an intense reaction to a woman. Then again, he'd never seen a woman like this before in his life.

Pink stained her cheeks when she glanced back at him and, dog that he was, he compared the color to the tips of her breasts. Only for a second, but it was enough—her cheeks were lighter pink.

But the curls between her legs perfectly matched those brushing her hips.

"*Why* are you naked?" Oh hell. What kind of a question was that? "I mean, what are you doing here?"

"Sleeping?" She moistened her lips quickly, with just a hint of pink tongue—which was more than enough to get him thinking about that tongue…

"I gathered that. The question is why?"

"Oh." She ran her fingers through her hair, lifting it off her neck, and glanced toward the ocean. "Well, I was swimming, and… and there was a shark. Yes. A shark. And he was coming after me. So I climbed aboard your boat, and, and, well," she shrugged her shoulders and a few strands of hair fell across her breasts, one curling again on her nipple, "here I am."

Logan peeled his eyes off her breasts to meet her gaze. "Here you are."

"Yes."

A moment of silence followed. Well, silence between them. The gulls were making a hell of a ruckus. Logan cleared his throat, then picked up the blanket and handed it to her. "So, is there any particular reason you're naked? Where are your clothes?"

She gathered the blanket against her chest. Not that Logan needed help with that image or anything… "My clothes. Yes. Um. Well, I was swimming—"

Right. Skinny-dipping. "Alone?"

He was asking solely so he could get her off his boat and back where she belonged; that was it. No other reason.

"Not alone. There was the shark."

"But what happened to your things?"

"Oh. They're gone."

"Gone? Everything? Money, clothes, whatever? Somebody take them while you were swimming?"

She looked away again toward the ocean, her eyes blinking rapidly. "Yes. Everything's gone."

So he had a naked, destitute woman on his boat. And a six-year-old who'd be here any minute.

Logan reached into his back pocket and pulled out his wallet. "Look, I can give you some money. Get you a ticket back where you came from—where are you from?"

She licked her lips again and turned those stunning eyes on him. "Have you ever been to Kansas?"

"Me? No."

"Oh. Well, I'm from Kansas."

"You do realize you're a bit of a ways away from Kansas, right?"

She shifted her feet to balance on the rocking deck as another charter left the dock. "Yes. About four-hundred-and-thirty leagues or so."

Leagues? Only if she was swimming, and *that* he'd like to see from the middle of the country.

"So what are you doing here if you're from Kansas?"

"Studying."

"You're a student?" He'd figured her for a little older than college. Maybe she was a grad student.

And he cared, why?

She looked back at the ocean. "I'm… doing a field study for the summer."

Ah, yes. Older. "What field?"

"Biology. Maritime biology."

"Don't you mean marine biology?"

"Yes," she said, licking her lips again. He should probably get her a drink. "Of course. That's what I meant. Marine biology."

The boat rocked again and the blanket slid to the side, showing off her shapely leg in all its perfection, toes to thigh.

He should probably get himself a drink. Preferably a stiff one—

Not going there.

"So… where are you staying? I'll call you a cab." Anything to get her off this boat.

"Actually, I just arrived. I don't have a place to stay."

Logan was about to suggest a local apartment complex when he heard Michael yell, "Thanks, Tony!" and decided he'd worry about where she was going to stay later. Right now he had a six-year-old he didn't want to have to explain the birds and the bees—or naked women—to, so he yanked his T-shirt over his head and skimmed it over Angel's. Yes, it hung on her like a tent, but at least she was covered.

Not that it diminished the image burned into his brain, nor the incredibly hot vision of her in his clothing and nothing else, with her hair askew and that blush on her cheeks.

With his faded green T-shirt bringing out the green swirl in her eyes, the woman could be a mermaid come to life.

"Logan! Look what Tony gave me!" Michael ran down the dock holding up the perfectly filleted carcass of one of Tony's recent catches in one hand and keeping his baseball cap on his head with the other hand. From Michael's abrupt halt and the way his mouth dropped open, Logan knew the moment his son saw Angel.

Great. How was he going to explain this?

"Hey, Michael. Why don't you come say hi to Angel?"

What else was he going to say? *Come meet the*

naked student? The kid would be signing up for college tomorrow.

"But… how? What…?" The fish skeleton hit the dock and fell apart, but Michael didn't seem to notice. His eyes were glued to Angel.

"Hi… Michael? I'm Angel." Even her voice was beautiful—like a song dancing along the crests of the waves.

Oh, hell. Where had that fanciful thought come from? Logan never spouted poetry to beautiful women, preferring to keep every relationship real and out of the realm of fairy tale, though more than one woman had called him her Prince Charming. Usually right before he broke up with her.

"Ang… Angel?" Poor tongue-tied Michael. Logan could totally empathize.

"She's… um… a friend." One he'd just met, who didn't wear clothes and showed up out of nowhere, but the kid was six. It should fly.

"Your friend?" Okay, perhaps the incredulity in his son's voice indicated a need for more proof.

"Um… yeah." He focused on Michael. "She's new in town and was using the boat because she doesn't have a place to stay."

Michael's face perked up and he jumped aboard, adjusting his baseball hat. "Cool! Then she can stay with us, right?" He went right over to her and shook her hand. "Nice to meet you, Angel. You can be my friend, too."

That wasn't exactly what Logan had in mind.

"I'd like that, Michael."

There was that melodic voice again. Maybe she was

a singer. She certainly had the face to be a celebrity, and enough of them flocked to these beaches every year.

Meanwhile, his son was literally jumping all over the place. "So, can she, Logan?"

Can she what? There were a lot of things he wanted her to do—

"Can she stay with us? She can sleep in my room."

Logan tried not to laugh. Sleep in Michael's room? Logan didn't think so. If she was going to be sleeping in anyone's room—

"Michael, I think the guesthouse would be a better idea."

Angel smiled and Michael started bouncing again. "Cool!"

Shit. What had he just agreed to?

Chapter 2

ANGEL COULDN'T BELIEVE HER GOOD LUCK. SHE'D HIT THE crabpot!

Then she saw Harry's fin circling off the bow for the eighth time since she'd awoken and amended that. Luck had nothing to do with this; Hammerhead Harry did. And wouldn't it tweak his big ol' blockhead to know he could be helping her right into her dream job?

Served the shark right. Try to eat her, would he? Keep her stranded on a boat? Ha. Angel couldn't stop her grin. "Thank you very much for your offer, Logan. I'd love to stay."

"All right!" Michael bounced again—she couldn't wait to try that when she was alone—but his father looked a little green around the gills.

"Michael, I don't think—" The little black box on Logan's hip started playing music. He glanced at it and exhaled. "I need to take this call. We'll discuss Angel staying with us when I'm done."

Long legs carried him fluidly off the boat and up the dock, one arm swinging, head held high as he spoke into the box.

She had studied the way her brother Reel walked hundreds of times. He was the only two-legged Mer in their world, but walking was so different when Logan—Humans—did it. The lack of buoyancy on land made the flexion and extension of the muscles slightly different, requiring the ability to balance between two shifting appendages, the heel-toe rhythm, the contractions of his gluteus maximus…

"What happened to your tail, Angel? Is it going to grow back? Are you gonna stay here forever? Can I tell Logan that you're a mermaid?" Michael bounced beside her, his whisper loud enough to carry on the warm sea breeze.

Angel guided Michael to a pull-down bench behind the captain's chair, stepping on the lid of the catch box on the deck to make sure it was closed securely. No need for Logan to discover where she'd stowed away last night to escape Harry. Nor that Michael had seen her, helped her, and hid her. All under his father's unsuspecting nose.

She tugged Logan's soft shirt beneath her as she sat. She'd forgotten the nudity part of the transformation. Thank the gods Logan had thought so fast. "My tail will come back if any seawater touches it, so it's very important that doesn't happen around grown-ups, okay?"

Michael's little chest puffed out as he sat on the cushion next to her. "I'm the only one who knows about you, aren't I?"

Angel tapped the rim of his hat. "Yes, you are. And I wasn't even supposed to let you know, so we definitely can't tell Logan."

"Are you gonna get in trouble?"

So much it wasn't funny. Unless she could make this situation work to her advantage. "Not if we keep my tail a secret, okay?"

Yes, Rod, her brother the High Councilman, would be *so* proud of the lies.

Not.

Truth was, she wasn't either, but what could she do? Harry had been all about getting a Mer meal last night, and she'd been the only one around. So she could either have climbed aboard the fishing boat, or…

Or nothing. Harry or the boat. There was no other choice.

"Okay, I won't tell. I can keep a secret. Cross my heart and hope to spit."

That comment didn't make any more sense now than it had last night when she'd slipped on board just before dark. On the lookout for adult Humans, she hadn't seen the child, but he'd certainly seen her.

One thing about kids: they were infinitely more accepting than their adult counterparts—which was the basis of her plans for the Mer-Human Coalition her brother was forming. Michael had gone with the fact that she was a Mer and understood her need to stay out of sight of adults. He hadn't turned her in then, so she had high hopes he wouldn't do so now.

Not that she was condoning his lying to his father, but when it came to her life or a child's honesty, she was going with her life.

Still, The Council could bring charges against her for this.

If only Hammerhead Harry had kept to the truce agreement with The Council, she could have conducted her research without any detection, let alone face-to-face contact. All she'd been trying to do was monitor Human fishing practices, but the stupid shark just *had* to show up. Then she'd had to unload everything to the bottom of the sea so she could have a chance of outswimming him. There went all her notes, all her tools, and a lot of her self-respect.

But she now had the perfect opportunity to redeem herself *and* learn enough to earn the position of director of the Coalition she'd wanted in the first place.

All thanks to Harry—not that she'd ever tell him.

"I'm sorry I caught you last night, Angel." Michael unwrapped a small pink, rectangular item he'd pulled from his pocket, then shoveled it into his mouth. "I didn't mean to hurt you."

She stopped herself from rubbing the spot just above her big toe where Michael's fishhook had sliced into her fluke. First time in recorded history that a Human had actually hooked a Mer with a fishing line—and a child, no less. Without trying. She wouldn't be spreading that story around any time soon.

And, fish! That hook had hurt. But, ironically, it had been what saved her. She wouldn't have thought to use a boat to escape a shark otherwise.

"It's okay, Michael. Mers are fast healers, and you did save my life. Harry wouldn't come near me once you caught me." Sharks were more afraid of Humans in hunting mode than of going hungry.

Michael let the colorful wrapper flutter to the deck. "What's a Mer, Angel? I thought you were a mermaid."

Angel picked up his refuse and held it out to him. "Here. You shouldn't litter. It damages the planet."

"But it's only a piece of paper." He chomped on the substance… ah, chewing gum.

Amelia the pelican was a huge fan of the stuff, which she found on any dock, beach umbrella, or other surface where Humans congregated. Talk about damaging the planet.

"It's only a little piece of paper from you, Michael, but what if everyone did the same thing? Then there would be a lot of paper."

"Oh. Okay. I'll throw it in the trash." He took the paper from her and shoved it back in his pocket. That was a start.

"Good job." She patted his knee, curbing the desire to study it. She had her own knees now and could examine them all she wanted. She ran a hand over them, then extended a leg. Flexed it. Wiggled the toes.

"So what's a Mer?"

Right. Focus on the conversation. She'd have time enough later to study the workings of her legs.

"We are called Mers, Michael. Both male and female Mers. You Humans use the terms 'mermaids' and 'mermen,' not us." As for the *maid* part, well, that hadn't been true for *selinos*, but she wouldn't be explaining that.

"Mermen? There are mermen, too? Cool!" This time Michael forgot to whisper and—of course—his father was heading their way.

"Sssh!" Angel touched a finger to Michael's lips. "Remember, it's our secret."

Michael followed Angel's gaze. "Right. Our secret. But can I tell Rocky?" The little boy was back to whispering.

"Who's Rocky?"

"My pet raccoon. Well, he's not really a pet. He's a toy. I wanted a real pet, but Rainbow said no and I didn't ask Logan yet."

"Who's Rainbow?"

Michael grabbed the rim of his cap and tugged it lower until half his face was hidden. "Oh, she's my mom."

So Logan was married. Darn. She wouldn't have minded watching Human courting rituals. Oh well, beggars—and landed Mers—couldn't be picky. She'd be happy with what she got.

Then Logan reached the boat and she was very happy.

Logan Hardington was one fine-looking specimen— Human or Mer. Handsome face and warm, dark brown eyes below thick hair the color of a sea lion's pelt after a few hours in the sun. The light dusting of hair on his chest was a shade darker. Broad, tanned shoulders tapered to a taut abdomen where his black shorts rode low on his hips above long, well-toned legs. His face and lean, muscled body looked as if they'd been carved by a master sculptor.

Her sister, Mariana, who was a sculptor, would love to get her hands on him. Of course, Logan's wife might have something to say about that.

Here's hoping the wife didn't mind a houseguest.

Logan climbed aboard, and Angel took mental notes of which muscles contracted, the angle his upper body assumed to counterbalance the forward momentum, how his arms moved... If only she had her tablets to mark down these observations. Damn Harry.

"Hey, sport," Logan said, "I'm sorry, but there's a change in plans. No fishing today. I have to handle something with work. We'll go tomorrow." Then he looked at her. "As for you, Angel, I can drop you at the bus station—"

"But you said she could stay with us," Michael interrupted, hopping up from his seat and planting his fists on his waist. "I don't wanna watch TV anymore while you work. I want Angel to play with me. Why can't she be my babysitter?"

"Michael, hold on a minute—"

"Sit on a baby?" Why in-the-sea would anyone want to do that?

Angel didn't know how Humans cared for their infants since her sister-in-law, Erica, had remained on land for the birth of her daughter, but she would have thought that sitting on a baby was a bad idea. Showed how much she knew. Book studies could only get her so far. She needed real-life practicals, and this one had landed in her lap—and she actually *had* a lap.

But how had Michael gotten a baby? Her research showed Humans weren't capable of reproduction until the onset of puberty, the same as Mers.

Both males stared at her. "Don't you know what a babysitter is?" Logan asked while Michael giggled.

Obviously not what she'd thought it was. And, apparently, it was odd for her not to know what one was. "Of course I do. I was only joking."

Michael figured it out and managed to muffle his laughter, but she could see the questions behind Logan's eyes. She'd have to do a better job of fitting in.

"See, Logan?" Michael tipped the rim of his cap back. "Now you don't have to take off from work tomorrow. Angel can watch me. I won't have to go to daycare, and you can save the money. Rainbow likes to save money."

The child's smile was every bit as wide as Harry's, but full of lovely little teeth, a few spaces between them where the baby ones had fallen out. She wondered how many gold coins Matilda had placed beneath his pillow or if the Tooth Fairy Brigade only celebrated Mer tooth loss.

"Michael, that's not going to happen. Angel has more important things to do than watch you while I'm at work."

Ah. *Babysitting.* An odd phrase, but now completely understandable. Her people called it Mer-minding.

"Actually, I don't. My study doesn't take all my time." Not to mention, babysitting Michael would *be* her field study.

"See? She can!" Michael was now bouncing on both feet, his cap crushed between his hands, his thick auburn hair, so like his father's, flopping by his ears.

Logan was trying to glare at her over his son's head, but Angel purposely kept her gaze averted. She liked Michael's idea and didn't want to give Logan any ammunition for his argument.

Yes, Rod would have issues with this whole thing, but if he'd allowed her the opportunity to apply for the job she'd wanted, this situation could have been avoided. But Rod had spouted off about no more Human interaction by members of his family—interesting how he came up with that stipulation *after* he and Reel had both married Humans—and then Harry had pulled his idiotic move, so her fins were tied.

Besides, when she pulled this off and went back to Atlantis with firsthand information, she'd be the perfect candidate for director of the Coalition. Rod would *have* to give her the position—who better to work towards fostering Mer-Human relations with the goal to save the planet than a Mer who'd actually lived among them?

The Council would thank her for the leaps she'd made in advancing Mer knowledge.

If she didn't blow it...

"Michael, why don't you go see Tony so Angel and I can talk."

"I don't wanna." Michael puffed out his lower lip and crossed his arms. "You said I could have whatever I wanted for my birthday and I want Angel for my babysitter."

Logan looked ready to spit snails. Instead he rolled his eyes toward the heavens and scraped a hand across his jaw, the slight rasp setting Angel's skin to tingling.

"Look, sport, no offense to Angel, but I don't know her well enough to feel comfortable about her watching you."

She glanced away when Logan's eyes drilled into hers, and she hunched down in front of the little boy.

"Michael, how about if we do this on a trial basis? Maybe your dad would feel better about me babysitting if he spent the day with us. If he's happy with the way I look after you, we can discuss the situation then, okay?"

"But I don't want you to go away." The little boy's bottom lip trembled.

Angel couldn't help herself. She hugged him. He was no different from any other child she knew. "I'm not going anywhere, Michael. I promise."

Oh, hell.

Logan looked at the scene before him and tossed in the proverbial towel. First the problem at work, now this. He couldn't deny Michael the one thing he wanted for his birthday, but he also couldn't leave his son in the care of a total stranger.

It was a good thing he could work from home. He'd been doing it since Rainbow—*Christine*—had dropped Michael off with nothing but a note, a stuffed toy raccoon, a bag of tattered clothing, and a few children's books. What were a couple more days? Not the ideal situation, but school wasn't that far off.

"All right, Michael. If that's what you want, Angel can hang out with you while I'm working today, okay?"

"You're the best, Logan!" Michael wrapped his thin arms around Logan's thighs, giving him his first official Dad hug.

A lump formed in Logan's throat. What would it take to get a "Dad" out of him? Logan didn't know, but if caving in to babysitter demands was all it took to get a hug, he'd give the kid whatever he wanted.

He patted Michael's shoulders. No, actually he wouldn't. The hug was a nice perk, but responsible parents didn't give in to every whim and demand, even if doing so solved problems.

Not that he had any idea of responsible parenting given the pair he'd grown up with, nor the mother he'd inadvertently chosen for his son. Common sense said you couldn't give a kid everything he wanted, although he had to believe that giving in every now and then wasn't so bad.

He had wondered how he was going to be a single, working parent when Michael had arrived and had put Give Up Sleep at the top of the list. Visit a Dozen Day cares had taken priority for tomorrow. But now, with Angel around, those To-Do items were no longer necessary.

Then Angel stood up and smoothed his T-shirt down almost to her knees, and Logan had to yank his gaze from her legs. Actually, he *would* be visiting someplace tomorrow: a women's clothing store.

She stretched, and the T-shirt slid up her thighs.

No. Make that today. The problem at work could wait another hour or so while they found her something appropriate. If Angel was going to be around his son, a T-shirt wouldn't cut it. She needed clothing. Now. For his sake even more than her own.

Chapter 3

THE SEAGULLS WERE LAUGHING AT HER.

Atop a lighting fixture at the end of the dock, the birds started making noise the minute Angel stepped off the rocking boat.

They *could* cut her some slack. So she was a little unsteady. This was the first time she'd ever had legs, and disembarking a rocking boat wasn't easy. Not to mention, she was still floating over the fact that she'd pulled it off. Logan was letting her stay. She had an excuse and an opportunity to test out her plans for the Coalition.

Now she just needed to figure out how to pull off a disappearing act every other night to ensure the return of her tail so she could stay for more than a day or two. Much as she wanted to learn about Humans and get the directorship, she didn't want to sacrifice her tail to do so, which is what would happen if she had legs for more than two consecutive sunsets.

"How long have you had the boat, Logan?" She turned around as he climbed over the gunwale. "Do you use it often? Have you ever lived on it in the marina? The ocean? What does it run on? Diesel? Biofuel?"

Logan stepped onto the dock. "What's with the twenty questions?"

Damn. She had a bad habit of wanting to know the answer to everything right away.

"Oh, just curious." Then she tripped over some

loose mooring lines, and, on cue, the birds erupted with more laughter.

At least she stayed upright. As long as they didn't start speaking to her, she could pretend they were squawking that signature *caw* Humans found so annoying—and would find even more annoying if they knew the gulls were laughing at them. Seabirds just loved bathing-suit season.

Then her heel came down awkwardly on a hose some-one had left out and, this time, she couldn't manage to keep her balance and fell—right into Logan's arms.

Suddenly the seagull noise faded into the background. So did Michael's laughter, the creak of the boat against the dock, the motor of someone's charter leaving the marina, and all her twenty questions.

Everything faded into the background except the feel of Logan's arms around her. The flexing biceps beneath her palms. The tightening of his stomach against her chest. That delicious blended scent of sea breeze and man…

Angel looked up—he was so much taller than she was. So much bigger. Yet he wouldn't hurt her. She knew that. How she did, she didn't know, but some-thing… almost a quiet strength about him told her, in one instant, that she could trust him with her life.

She blinked. Now *that* was ridiculous. He was a Human. Humans were the *last* beings a Mer could trust. But when Logan raised her chin to stare into her eyes, Angel knew that wasn't true about him.

"Are you all right?" His voice was lower than before, the words breathless.

"I…" She licked her lips. Talk about breathless. She tried again. "Yes. I am." She tried to prove it by standing, but she wasn't exactly proficient with legs after such a short time and fell back against him.

Logan's head lowered.

Or did she raise hers?

Did it matter?

All that did matter was that his lips were just above hers and if she stretched a bit more—

"Hey! Come on!" Michael's voice broke into the moment.

Oh, gods. She'd been about to kiss him.

"Are you guys coming or what?"

Angel looked away. What had she been thinking? He was a *Human*, for Zeus's sake. She couldn't be attracted to him. That went against everything she believed in. All her scientific protocol and everything she wanted for herself. Hades, she'd broken up with her last boyfriend because he'd started getting serious. She didn't want that; she wanted to focus on her career. On the Coalition. On bettering their worlds. She didn't need to have an attraction to *anyone*, least of all a Human. Besides, Logan was married.

Wait a minute. What had *he* been thinking?

Or… maybe she'd just imagined it.

Yeah. That was it. She had to have imagined it.

Embarrassed, surprised, mad at herself, a whole host of emotions plaguing her that she didn't want to examine, Angel made a concerted effort to regain the use of her legs. Logan helped by steadying her—although *steady* was a misnomer because there was nothing steady in the heat zipping through her fingers, up her arm, and all over her body.

No. No. No. Mind back on your purpose here, Tritone.

"Thank you," she said, yanking her hand off him.

"You're welcome," he said, his voice still raspy.

"Hurry up!" Michael bounced on a loose weathered plank, hitting the beam beneath with a *thud, thud.*

Kind of like her heart was doing.

No it wasn't. That was just surprise. Embarrassment. She was *imagining* things.

Then Logan slid a hand under her elbow, and her knees got a little jellyfish-like.

She had one Hades of an imagination.

"Angel."

She really had to focus on walking. Legs took some getting used to. That's why hers were wobbly.

"Angel, do you want to make a call?"

Bird calls? Humans did that? Her research hadn't given any indication they practiced this old system of communication. Did they even understand the language?

"Um, all right. What breed?"

"Breed? You mean brand? Of cell phone? Does it matter?" He held his black box out to her.

Cell phone. Oh, crappie.

She stared at the black thing. She knew about the device, especially the mercury from discarded ones that leeched into the environment, but unfortunately, she didn't have a clue how to use one. She also didn't have anyone to call. Cell service wasn't exactly possible in Atlantis.

"Actually, there isn't anyone I can call. No one knows I'm doing this and, well, I'd rather keep it that way. They wouldn't approve, and if they heard what happened…"

Logan tilted his head to the side, studying her. "You want to prove something to them."

It wasn't a question, but it was so right on the currency that Angel grabbed it with both hands. "Right. They think I can't do this, and if not for that damn shark, I could have proved them wrong in a tailfli—in a heartbeat."

All of which was true—if slightly skewed.

Logan studied her another moment or two, his eyes narrowing, and Angel refused to remember how they'd darkened when he'd almost kissed her… or, rather, when she'd *imagined* he'd almost kissed her.

Oh, Zeus. Let it go already. If she wanted to be taken seriously in the Mer scientific community, the last thing she needed was to swim down that stream about a Human. With The Council's, and most of the Mer population's, prejudice against all things Human, her observations would be tossed aside as lovesick musings. She pulled her arm from his grasp—and ignored the sudden chill that raced over her skin.

"Okay, Angel, I know all about needing to prove yourself. But do you have any qualifications for child care? References?"

Oh did she. Sadly, they were all Mer-related. "One of my degrees is in child studies." Human child studies, to be precise, but she knew better than to make that distinction. "As for references, well, word would get back and that would defeat the purpose of not calling, wouldn't it? But I do have them."

"One of your degrees? How many do you have?"

Angel headed down the length of the dock to where Michael was impatiently waiting for them.

"Just three. Child studies, Humanol—um *soc*iology, and biology."

Logan's long legs caught him up to her quickly. "Hence the field study."

"Correct. Oh, and a minor in basket-weaving."

He stopped and grabbed her arm again, laughing. "Basket-weaving?"

"Yes. What's so funny about that?" This time she didn't need a reason to yank her arm from his hand. She'd worked damn hard to get her degrees. That course had opened up a world of information about textiles and early Human craftsmanship. "It's quite fascinating." She shoved off with the right foot, toes providing momentum. Or was it the ball of the foot? Damn, he'd made her forget the biomechanics.

"If you find basket-weaving fascinating enough to study it, as well as have the drive to earn all those other degrees, I might have you tutor Michael instead of babysit him." This time when he caught up to her, he didn't put a hand on her, thank the gods.

"Tutor? I don't think that would be—"

"Relax, Angel. I was only joking. Michael's looking forward to hitting the books when school starts."

Now it was her turn to stop him. "You hit books? Why?"

Logan's eyebrows went up. "You've never heard that expression?"

Oh, fish. She really had to watch her step—all of them. She plastered a smile on her face. "Now who's joking?"

"Touché. So, we'll work out a schedule for your field study and my work. Sound good?"

It sounded more than good. It sounded perfect. "Yes. Thank you, Logan. I won't let you and your wife down."

"My wife?"

"Rainbow? Michael's mother?"

Logan rolled those brown eyes. "Rainbow, that is, Christine, is certainly not my wife, and if she hadn't signed the birth certificate she pinned to Michael's shirt before she took off, I'd be hard-pressed to call her his mother. Trust me, Angel, letting *her* down is the least of your worries."

Michael stomped down the steps, his red sneakers flapping loudly on the planks. "Why do grown-ups always walk so slow? Rainbow never wants to hurry."

Logan muttered something about Rainbow being in a hurry to get out of town, but low enough that Michael didn't hear him.

Angel was sorry she had.

It was one thing to have to look at him clinically as a Human subject.

It was quite another to see him as a man.

Chapter 4

MICHAEL CHATTED ALL THE WAY OFF THE DOCK AND BACK UP the steps, with his father patiently responding, discussing anything and everything. Who owned which boat in the marina, why Tony cussed so much when he didn't think Michael could hear him, what they were going to have for dinner; the little boy never seemed to run out of questions to ask. It was both interesting and beneficial to listen to the two of them.

Interesting because Angel had wondered what Human conversations were like beyond Beach-Speak, the only dialogue she'd ever observed in the wild, and beneficial because it gave her something to focus on rather than that near-miss of a kiss and the fact that Logan Hardington was a man.

"You can ride in the back with me," Michael said when they approached the big, black vehicle. "Usually Rocky does, but he stayed home today. Rocky doesn't like boats."

She'd have to thank Rocky, because she'd always wanted to ride in one of these. The purloined Jet Skis and other small watercraft her professors had had them test in the middle of the ocean were nowhere near as interesting as wheeled vehicles.

She followed the little boy inside, mimicking his movements after he latched a belt across his chest and waist. She'd heard the reasoning behind buckling up, but, as a member of the ocean community, she had a natural aversion to being restrained by anything. But when in Atlantis… or, Florida, as the case may be.

"I never went to a beach before Rainbow brought me here," Michael said, brushing hair out of his eyes and readjusting his hat when Logan turned on the cool air.

Angel had heard about air-conditioning but the concept of a man-made breeze still stumped her—not that it kept her from enjoying it. The cold air reminded her of the body-surfing trip she'd taken with friends off the coast of Greenland.

If only she could write all of these impressions down. Her fingers were itching to get hold of the tools of her trade.

"We had lots of snow in the winter," Michael continued. "I'm real good at building snow forts. I bet you're really good at sand castles, aren't you, Angel? Logan and I made one, but it fell down. Will you show me how? I want to build the biggest one ever. And we can decorate it with fish and mermaids and sharks and seashells and everything."

"Sure—"

"And what about lunch?" The little boy barely paused to breathe. "Can we eat seaweed? How about clams? I've never had those. I bet they're good, huh?"

"Actually—"

"And tuna fish. Well, I've had lots of that and I really like it with mayonnaise but no relish. I don't like that. It's good with cheese sometimes and I like chips with it, but you have to have cranberry juice with it because orange juice tastes yucky and ruins everything. What do you want for dinner? Logan can buy us whatever you want. He got me a cheeseburger last night with extra pickles. I like pickles but not relish. How 'bout you?"

Angel caught Logan's eyes in the mirror he looked into occasionally. Those brown eyes had been so close and so warm when they'd almost kis—

No, dammit. She had a once-in-a-lifetime opportunity here—and since she'd become Immortal at some point, that was a really long time. She wasn't going to blow it for a good-looking guy. Logan Hardington was a Human *and* her ticket to the job she wanted more than anything. *A-n-y-thing*.

Luckily, Michael's chatter discouraged conversation between her and her *subject*. The little boy didn't need any encouragement to keep chatting, nor did he slip up and ask her about being a mermaid. He also didn't seem to require answers. A noncommittal *hmmm* from her every now and then was an invitation to keep asking.

She kept glancing out the windows, dozens of questions springing to her lips, but she didn't voice them. Logan would know something was up if she started asking about things he considered commonplace.

To her, they were anything but. The world looked so different from this side of the beach. The palm trees weren't quite as tall as they looked from the water, growing next to buildings that reminded her of the walls of an undersea trench. Streets were laid out just like Atlantis, but traveling them was so different. Back home, if she wanted to go to the next street, all she had to do was swim over the buildings, but here Humans had to maneuver around them.

Birds were the only ones who had the same kind of freedom on land as Mers had in the sea, where the shortest distance between any two points was a straight line, no matter the direction. It was an odd concept to get used to.

And there were so many vehicles. And the noises. The smells… The refuse. So many people walking alongside the roads. Weren't they worried about getting run over?

She looked out Michael's window. More of the same traffic. More palm trees, hedgerow after hedgerow of hibiscus and oleander, and… Wait.

"Is *that* a real sand castle?"

The biggest, most ornate building she'd seen so far stretched along a good portion of the road. Two staircases at the center swept up to a balcony that fed into double glass doors beneath an arched portico. Parapets and towers lined the roof and corners, with intricate scrollwork decorating the sand-colored façade. Three stories tall and almost as long as The Coliseum back home, with beautiful gardens out front, palm trees swaying in the breeze like sentries, the place *could* be a palace.

She'd seen remnants of sand castles Humans had made on beaches, some incredibly large and intricate, but she'd never heard of them living in one.

"How did they do that? How is it shored up to withstand hurricanes? Are there any more around here?" Where was her tablet, dammit?

The Council would love to hear about this. Think of the ease of construction if they could learn the secret to building with sand. No longer would they need to confine housing projects to the bases of islands. No more worries about the dwindling supply of Human torpedoes they'd confiscated for blasting through rock to fashion Mer homes. This would revolutionize home building.

Colonies could spring up anywhere on the ocean floor. Affordable housing was another thing she wanted to pick Humans' brains about since they'd done such an amazing (though others had different words for it) job of populating the planet.

Michael started giggling. "A sand castle? No, silly, that's a house!"

A house?

"They don't have anything like that in Kansas, I take it?" Logan glanced at her in the mirror again.

Right. Kansas. "Not that I've seen, they don't." And since she'd never actually been to Kansas, that wasn't a lie.

But it *was* one more gaffe on her part. Enough of them and Logan would rethink the babysitting position. Angel decided to keep her thoughts to herself.

Which, luckily, with Michael around, wouldn't be an issue. He picked right back up with his chattering—this time going on about sand castles he'd made—on the beach, with real sand—and Angel just sat back and let him talk.

Ten minutes later, Logan pulled up to a long block of stores, similar to downtown Atlantis.

What wasn't similar was the clothing inside the first store Logan led her to. Silk, cotton, rayon, spandex… all the fabrics she collected in their soaking-wet form were now hanging in front of her, a rainbow of color from wall to wall.

"You should be able to outfit yourself properly here, right, Angel?" Logan asked, reaching into his back pocket.

She wasn't quite sure what constituted properly,

although those dresses on the far wall looked good to her. But then she saw his wallet in his hand.

"Logan, I can't take your currency."

He arched an eyebrow. "Currency? Do you have another way to pay for the clothes? You can't go around wearing only my shirt. I'll take it out of your pay or something."

Angel stifled the guilt. She had plenty of diamonds in her vault back home. She'd get him one somehow.

"Thank you. I appreciate it." In more ways than he could know. She did not want to pass up an opportunity like this. Especially when she found a row of sequined cropped pants. She stroked a finger over the shiny faux-scales.

Clothing was a relatively new concept among Mers. Many still used their long hair for covering up or the shell-and-kelp method, but that was mostly the older generations. She had a wonderful collection of Human clothing at home from sale day at the Salvager Market, but it paled in comparison to this selection. Dresses, skirts, bathing suits, shorts, tops, pants… racks and racks of everything… She'd died and gone to Shopping Olympus.

Then she found a rack of tiny, silky shorts in vibrant colors and patterns with matching bikini tops next to them. She let the silky fabric flow through her fingers and over the back of her hand. It felt so different dry than when it was waterlogged. She loved her home, wouldn't give up the beauty of Atlantis for anything, with all the different hues of coral and patterns of brightly colored fish and the jewel-toned tails of her people, but fabric had a much better consistency out of the sea.

"*Blech*." Michael knocked his hat sideways. "Girl stuff."

"Girls like girl stuff, Michael," his father said, straightening the hat. "Someday you'll be glad about that."

"Nuh-uh. Girl stuff is yucky."

"Not if you're a girl." Angel reached in front of him for the perfect pair of purple shorts, a few shades darker than her amethyst tail, with delicate filigree like lace coral around the edges, then held them against the tops of her legs. "What to do you think of these?"

Michael shrugged his shoulders, but Logan turned the most interesting shade of red and walked away without a word. An odd garbled sound, but no word. Was that some Human language she wasn't familiar with?

Michael just giggled. "Logan still doesn't know you're a mermaid, does he?"

She shook her head. "No. And you have to remember not to say anything."

"I won't. I promise. I always wanted my very own mermaid. I hope you get your tail back soon. I liked it."

She was going to have to remind him about that word, *mermaid*. Mer. Period. As for the *my* part? She wasn't a pet, for Apollo's sake. "I like it too, Michael, but right now it's probably not a good—"

"Oh, that's a lovely style," said the Human approaching them, "but you're right, it's not exactly the best color for you. And I don't think a sixteen is the size you want." The woman took the garment and pointed to a selection beside her. "Here. This rack has your size. I would go with a softer color. Lavender, perhaps."

Logan arrived behind the woman with such a look

of relief on his face Angel might have thought he'd discovered Captain Kidd's treasure, except that wasn't possible because the pirate's bounty was on display in Atlantis, and Humans didn't know about it.

"Angel, this is Wendy. She'll help you with what you need. Michael and I have a few things to pick up. We'll be back in"—he looked at Wendy and pulled a small, rectangular piece of shiny plastic from his wallet—"an hour?"

Ugh. Plastic. One of her brother's reasons for starting the Mer-Human Coalition was to combat Humans' disposal of the vile compound. And now Logan wanted her to use it? Well, she'd use *all* of it so there'd be nothing left to contaminate the environment.

"I think we can manage to occupy our time," Wendy said, taking the plastic from him.

"I'm sure you will." Logan's smile thinned as he called a reluctant Michael to him.

"But I don't wanna go!" Michael took a step behind Angel.

A hurt look crossed Logan's face.

Angel couldn't have that. She was here to observe and report, not influence their lives. Coming between a parent and a child was forbidden in any world.

She put a hand on Michael's head and tilted it back. "It's okay, Michael. I told you I'm not going anywhere."

"You promise?"

"Of course I do." Especially since she didn't have a clue where she'd go or how she'd get there. "Now, go with your father and let me finish up here."

Logan smiled at her, and Angel had the oddest

sensation in her toes. They *tingled*. No one had mentioned that in any study she'd read.

"Okay." Michael stepped out from behind her and headed toward Logan. "But we're gonna come back real soon."

She certainly hoped so. She really had no other choice but to trust Logan when he said she was in Wendy's capable hands. It wasn't as if she'd be going anywhere without him.

"So, my dear." Wendy flashed the plastic thing again after Logan and Michael left. "Let's begin, shall we? Mr. Hardington said a complete wardrobe, and we might as well start from the inside out."

Angel really hoped a literal translation of that phase was not what the woman meant.

Chapter 5

THANK GOD SHE'D SAT IN THE BACK.

Logan rushed out of the boutique with the image of Angel's shapely, toned legs peeking out from beneath the hem of his shirt searing his brain and shooting straight to his groin. Yeah, as if the hardening of her nipples from the store's air-conditioning and that jumble of hair—not to mention the sexy lingerie she'd held against her body and that kiss they'd almost shared—had nothing to do with his condition.

God help him, he couldn't forget one single detail, and his body's reaction was making walking damn difficult. He angled away from Michael before adjusting his shorts, not wanting to contemplate what he'd be going through if she'd sat next to him in the SUV, those thighs inches from his—especially after watching them ascend the dock steps, then having her in his arms, almost kissing her… He'd been utterly relieved by Michael's seating arrangements.

And thank God for the store clerk. If he'd had to spend one more minute with Angel holding lingerie up to that body, it would have been the death of him. Even the hot Florida air felt cool compared to the way his body temp had soared when she'd done that.

Purple. *Jeez*. Might as well have been black lace. Or red.

"She's really cool, isn't she, Logan?" Michael hopped from sidewalk block to sidewalk block,

bypassing the cracks with the exuberance of the unin-
formed and innocent.

Logan had never done that as a kid. Hadn't known
it was something kids did, thanks to his unorthodox
upbringing—in the circus.

He would have laughed if there'd been something
funny about it. God knew, you couldn't get more unorthodox than growing up with carnies. A troupe—not
a family.

Logan settled a palm between Michael's shoulder
blades. "She's definitely cool, but I don't want you to
become too attached. She's going to have to leave at
some point." Sooner rather than later if he had anything
to say about it. For Michael's sake—and *his* sanity.

"Nuh-uh. She promised she wouldn't. Remember?"

"I know, but sometimes grown-ups say things they
don't really mean." How well he knew that. Firsthand.

Oh, sure, Goran and Nadia Harsányis, his "parents," had said they loved him, but then, they'd said
that to all the runaways they'd taken in. Even runaways' babies, like him. But it'd seemed to have been
more a way to get workers for their shows than any
idea of family.

Case in point: he'd been one master prestidigitator
until he'd realized that was all there would ever be for
him. A nomadic, itinerant, sporadic existence.

He'd wanted more. Roots. A sense of belonging
somewhere. Normalcy.

Life with the Harsányis troupe was none of those things.

He'd finally done his own running away at fifteen.
Run *away* from the circus. How ironic was that? Gotten
himself declared an emancipated minor, changed his

name, and worked his way through school, planning for the day when he could have a normal life.

He was so close. Partner in a venture capital firm that was on the cutting edge of green technology—life experiences providing as much of that education as college courses—judicious spending practices, friends, vacations, retirement accounts…

He'd only needed a wife to complete his vision. Enter Christine. They'd been on the right track for a few months, but then she'd broken out the incense and love beads, talked about joining a commune to practice her performance art, and he'd been plunged right back into that insane spiral again. Her name change was proof positive. He'd gotten out cleanly.

Or so he'd thought.

And now here was Michael. Logan was going to give the kid as much Normal as was in his power.

Michael jumped from one block of concrete onto another. At least his son was starting out on the right foot. And the left. Then the right… Logan allowed himself a small smile.

Then Michael landed on the block in front of him. "So Rainbow didn't mean it when she said I might not be here for long?"

Logan's smile disappeared. "She said what?"

Michael readjusted the baseball cap he hadn't taken off since he'd arrived and shuffled to another block, no longer paying attention to the cracks. He grabbed a crumpled piece of newspaper off the sidewalk and stuffed it in his pocket. "Um, she said you might send me away."

"What?" Logan reached for Michael's shoulder. "Where did she think I would send you?"

His son shrugged and pulled away. "I dunno. Wherever they send kids whose parents can't keep them. There are places, I know. She told me. She said they have lots of other kids and nice houses and good food and stuff, so it wouldn't be that bad. And I can bring Rocky."

Logan couldn't believe it. He didn't need this. First he had a son he'd never known about show up out of nowhere, then a complication at work, a destitute woman show up on his boat—naked—and now his ex had put the idea in his son's head that he wouldn't be wanted?

Logan wanted to kill her. He wanted to wrap his hands around her throat and choke the life out of her for even putting that idea in his son's head.

For not trusting in him enough to keep the child they'd made.

She'd *known* how he'd been raised. What he'd missed out on, growing up with the troupe and then later on his own. How he'd vowed never to do that to another person. One night, after too much wine and a sweet round of lovemaking, he'd opened up and told her about his shitty childhood and everything he'd overcome to get where he was.

Bad enough she'd kept Michael from him; now she'd dared question whether he'd keep his son? The anger and bitterness threatened to choke him, but Logan had to swallow it. None of this was Michael's fault.

No, the blame rested firmly on the shoulders of the woman he never should have trusted. Just add Christine to the list of people who'd let him down. It wasn't as if being let down was new, and Logan had gotten over being disappointed in people a long time ago, but he'd be damned if he'd allow anyone to disappoint Michael.

He opened the door to the next shop and motioned Michael inside. Ice cream was the perfect panacea for this conversation. The question was, who was he trying to make feel better?

"Rainbow was wrong, Michael. I'm not going to send you away. Isn't that why we have Angel? So you can stay with me while I work?"

"Cool!"

So, yes, it was cool that there'd been a naked woman on his boat. Not the optimum way to go about getting child care, but Michael liked her, she was well-educated and ambitious, and seriously, *anyone* was better equipped to watch Michael than the kid's own mother.

Aside from the fact that Logan had almost kissed a complete stranger in front of his son, maybe, finally, someone Up There was on his side.

Chapter 6

ANGEL WAS GONE.

Mariana swam through her sister's condo, making a mental list of what was missing: the slate tablets of notes Angel kept stacked on the desk in the study, the box of urchin spines she stored next to the Human perfume bottle of octopus ink, that bottle of octopus ink, and the sea-pak from the foyer closet.

The shutters were closed on every window, and clothing was strewn all over the bedroom, the Human shirts Angel had bought at the Salvager's Market floating atop the furniture in the soft current that wended through downtown Atlantis. This mess wasn't like Angel. She was a total neat freak about her "treasures," only getting maniacal like this for one reason.

Mariana somersaulted back to the living room. The sea stars were missing. The little colony of colorful echinoderms Angel had recently adopted from Rod's office usually spent the day wandering around the coral sculpture Mariana had designed for just that purpose.

She swam over to the kitchen sink. Yep. The herd of sea horses who roosted on the anemones in the window boxes were gone, too, as were the hatchetfish who lit the place at night. The transparent squid mantle that amplified their glow was now hanging empty from the ceiling.

Even the annoyingly deaf flounder under the front door had been missing when she'd let herself in. The fish was a stupid idea for a welcome mat, but that was Angel—all about helping the helpless.

Angel had gone on an expedition.

As sure as Mariana was swimming here, she knew that Angel had disobeyed The Council's orders and was off, somewhere in the ocean, meandering after Humans. It was what Angel did. The fact that it had been prohibited by The Council wouldn't have stopped her.

Zeus. Couldn't *one* member of this family stay away from Humans? First Reel, then Rod. Now Angel was swimming after them like a dogfish with a whale bone. What was so appealing about those bipedal land-dwellers? Mariana had yet to meet one worth endangering her life for.

She dove over the sofa, her flukes startling the sea cucumbers residing there into doing The Wave—poor things had so little to amuse themselves—and lifted the lid on the sea chest Angel used as a table.

It figured. Angel hadn't taken the harpoon.

Mariana took the monstrosity out, giving wide berth to the sharp point. Raised with stories of the damage these could do, she had a healthy respect for the Human weapon.

Which was why Angel should know better. No one set off into the wild blue under without one. Especially not alone. But Angel was so Hades-bent on proving herself, she'd probably considered her profession's tools more important than the one thing that could save her life.

Mariana wanted to hook her. Besides the fact that Angel could, at this very minute, be fighting off a shark or sailfish or orca without the harpoon, their brother was going to pop a fin when he heard about this. Gods knew, he already had enough stress dealing with the increase in iceberg calving rates; he didn't need this added mess.

And that's what it would turn into. Hades, they'd just gotten their parents off on the trip through the Seven Seas that they'd put off far too long. One hint of dissension among the Tritone offspring would have their parents Travel-Chambering home in no time flat.

And *that* was the last thing Mariana wanted.

Because, while her family waited for some sea creature to show up with Angel in tow, they'd all end up sitting around, kumbaya-ing in their parents' living room, and the conversation would turn, as it always did now that her brothers were happily married, to Mariana's work.

Mariana took the quiver out of the treasure chest and slung it over her shoulder. Let Angel have a fit that she was using this thing as Humans intended; Mariana didn't care. Her work wouldn't stand up to the family's scrutiny. Not this project.

That's why she had to get Angel back here—without anyone knowing her sister had been gone.

Mariana tucked the harpoon in the quiver, unable to repress a shiver as the sheathed steel slid against her skin. She worked with molten lava, so she was used to eruptions. Knew how to protect herself from getting burned.

But if anyone found out Angel was gone—or that Mariana had known and hadn't said anything—she wasn't sure she could manage the fallout from this one.

Chapter 7

ANGEL FELT LIKE A PRINCESS.

Okay, so, technically, since her family was royalty, she *was* a princess. But other than the occasional "my lady," the title didn't mean a hill of shells in her world. Here, though... wow.

Wendy must have melted that plastic with all these clothes. Angel *knew* it'd be fun to try on silky item after silky item, then put more on top of those. Swishy dresses, flowing skirts, lightweight pants, colorful tops. They were all so beautiful, like a tropical coral reef on a sunny day. That Humans could create such beautiful products said a lot about them—and gave her hope for the future.

And the shoes! Oh, the shoes. The flats came in so many colors, and Wendy had insisted she try on a pair for each outfit. Really, Angel hadn't needed much convincing. She loved the flamingo-colored sandals the saleswoman had said were the latest style. They were comfortable and looked so very pretty on her new feet.

And then, the high heels! All different heights, some thick-heeled, some as thin as an anemone tentacle. Made from cork and wood and even that loathsome plastic, decorated with sequins and braiding and bows... she was going to have to practice walking in them when she was alone. They were absolutely adorable. The saleswoman had suggested a pale oyster-colored pair for *casual* and a shiny pair of black ones for *evening*. Angel had never realized Humans changed shoes according to the time. All these neat things that came with legs. And firsthand experience.

With Wendy's help, she selected a white halter dress with a peek-a-boo cutout at the top of the bodice, criss-crossed with all the colors in Atlantis' coral gardens. It reminded her of home. Not that she was homesick per se, but Atlantis was so beautiful, she wanted that beauty with her on her first day in the Human world.

Angel followed Wendy to the checkout counter, anxious to see how the electronic equipment worked. She had one of these machines at home but hadn't yet been able to hook it up to an eel.

Harnessing the natural abilities of electric eels was one of the ideas she wanted to explore as director of the Coalition. Those suckers could generate a huge jolt if so inclined, but any time she'd approached one to test her theory, they'd turned their squared noses up at her and told her to take it up with their union rep.

They didn't even have an industry, yet they had a union. Slimy the eels might be, but they were ahead of the economic curve.

Wendy began scanning the items. The process, while fascinating, didn't give Angel the insight she'd wanted. Aside from taking the machine apart—and wouldn't *that* raise some eyebrows—Angel found she couldn't learn much by watching.

She learned better by doing. And now was the perfect opportunity to do something she'd wanted to do since Logan had woken her—experiment with balance.

She leaned her elbows on the counter and shifted her weight from one leg to the other, paying attention as she did so to the play of muscles, the pressure points on her feet, and how her toes reacted. She took one of the sandals off and did it again, mentally comparing the differences.

Then she lifted one leg, put it down, and lifted the other, thanking the gods no one else was around and that the countertop hid her actions from Wendy.

Until she accidentally knocked something off it. Great. Way to *not* call attention to herself.

Angel bent over to pick the object up, then realized that there was a plus to being clumsy. She could examine how her leg muscles and joints worked together as she reached down to pick up the leather-covered…

Book.

Full of paper.

Pages and pages of blank paper.

She loved paper, but it always disintegrated shortly after she got hold of it. Dollar bills, on the other hand, lasted longer and she could write all over them. If Humans would only make them bigger and less cluttered with minutiae, she'd use them for taking notes on her expeditions.

Like this expedition…

"I'd like to buy this, as well." Angel handed the notebook to Wendy. "And do you have a…" What did Humans call it? She couldn't very well ask for a sea-urchin spine and pot of ink. "A pen. Do you have a pen to go with it?"

Wendy held up a slim, blue stick. "Will this do, or would you like one from our designer collection?" She pointed to a rack at the end of the counter.

Three rows of the implements stood like tube

sponges, in all different colors and patterns. Some had spots, others swirls, others were solid colors. If Humans were so fond of colorful things, why weren't they more concerned with maintaining coral reefs?

Exactly the reason she was here. And why she needed the notebook.

Angel selected a green and blue pen that reminded her of Atlantian waters. "This one will do. And, actually," she selected a second pen and another book, "I'll take two."

Couldn't hurt to have a birthday present for Michael, and what better gift than a book to make notes in? She assumed Humans celebrated birthdays the same way Mers did, and if not, well then, she'd have two. They certainly wouldn't go to waste.

Wendy scanned the books and pens, placed them in one of the bags, then handed them to Angel along with that piece of plastic.

Why, it hadn't even gotten a smidge thinner with all the use the saleswoman had insisted they give it! Had Humans designed a hardier version of the non-biodegradable pollutant? Rod would be really annoyed to learn about this when he'd finally been making headway in the planetary cleanup department.

She was juggling the five bags of new clothes when the bells jingled again and Michael appeared on one side of her, Logan on the other.

"Here. Let me." Logan grabbed two of the bags, then signed the slip of paper the smiling saleswoman put before him. His eyes widened.

"You did say an entire wardrobe," Wendy replied.

"I did. Er, thank you." He reached for two more

bags. "Michael, you want to give Angel a hand with that last one?"

"Sure!" With something white encircling his mouth and dripping from an unidentifiable object in his hand, Michael reached for the last bag, but Angel decided she didn't want to risk the pretty garments and new notebooks to the mess.

"I've got it, Michael. Why don't you just enjoy… that… and I'll carry this."

"You wanna try my ice cream?" Michael held up the thing—ice cream. "It's peppermint."

"Michael, Angel doesn't want to get your germs." Logan held the door open for them.

Actually Angel *did* want to try the ice cream, but germs… she'd read a lot about germs. The microscopic vermin caused a lot of problems on land, many of which were a direct result of the overabundance of refuse Humans weren't conscientious about discarding. The Coalition's work would benefit both their races; that's why the Coalition was so important—and why it had to have the right Mer heading it.

Her.

A blast of hot air hit her as the three of them returned to the street-side pathway, and Angel decided that air-conditioning, for all its chemicals and energy usage, had some benefits. How amazing it was that Humans could control the temperature—which could explain why they didn't care what they did to the environment by doing so. But if they were clever enough to figure out how to control it, couldn't they also figure out a way to make the process cleaner and safer for everyone?

More Humans strolled along the pathway, some old, some young. She was mesmerized by how well several bicyclists wove through both Human traffic and the vehicular kind, amazed they could balance on two thin, rubber wheels. High heels would be enough of a balancing act for her; she'd forego the bicycles—especially the tires.

Those hazards were going to be one of the first issues she'd address. She'd convene a Sewage Reclamation Team to form a small island with tires somewhere in the South Pacific, then set the birds to the task of properly seeding it. Humans would get landmass, and Mers would have Oceanic Beautification: a win-win scenario.

White metal tables sat outside a restaurant, pastel umbrellas rising from their centers to shade the patrons. The soft *ding* of iced beverages harmonized with the *clink* of cutlery against dishes, so different from her world, yet so very similar.

"Can we get some more ice cream, Logan?" Michael licked his again, a dribble of white plopping on his shoe.

"I think one's enough." Logan's tone was stern, but the twinkle had come back into his eyes.

"A second won't hurt, will it?" Angel asked, winking at Michael. Another similarity between their worlds: children and treats.

"A *second*?" Logan arched an eyebrow at both of them.

"A second's cool! Let's go!" Michael ran ahead of them, stopping in front of another store, and pulled on the door. "I'm going to get creamsicle this time!" He dashed inside.

"What about you?" One of the bags Logan carried knocked into hers. "What's your favorite flavor?"

Uh oh. Potential trip-up moment. She pretended to search for something in her bag. "I like creamsicle, too." She pulled out one of the pretty undergarments. "Oh, phew. I thought I'd left this back in the store."

She thought she heard that strange garbled sound come from Logan again, so she risked glancing up, hoping she'd derailed the flavor talk.

Oh, she'd *definitely* derailed the flavor talk. That was no twinkle in his eye when he looked at what she held.

She glanced again at the garment. Ahhhh…

Wendy had said it was the perfect choice. Angel hadn't understood what the saleswoman had meant until just now. Well, okay, maybe she'd had an inkling, but clothing was a new concept to Mers and she hadn't really thought it would have that kind of effect on Logan.

Showed what she knew.

Stuffing the slip of fabric between the notebooks, Angel picked up the pace and almost walked out of the new shoes.

"So," she said, hiking the bag higher onto her arm and focusing on something else. What had they been talking about? Besides undergarments… "Do you like creamsicle? Or peppermint? What other flavors does Michael like? How old was he when he started eating it? Does he have it often?"

Yes, that's it. Think about the research. About the job she wanted. Focus on learning about their world—*not* whether or not Logan liked red undergarments.

Not that there was any question.

Thank Zeus, they reached the shop before Logan

answered because she needed to chill out, and air-conditioning could definitely take care of chilling out.

In more ways than one.

Okay, so maybe someone Up There wasn't on his side after all.

Logan opened the door to the ice cream parlor for Angel, leaning back to keep from touching any part of her or that bag.

She'd picked out red lingerie.

He'd actually given the saleswoman carte blanche—*and* his credit card—to outfit his son's new babysitter, and, between the two of them, a woman who was supposed to know fashion and another who had as many degrees as he did, they'd come up with red lingerie. It'd be ironically funny if Michael weren't involved.

Maybe this wasn't such a good idea. Maybe he should have just given her the money, bought her a one-way bus ticket, and told Michael she'd had to go home. He wouldn't have to worry about what she wore, what her favorite flavor was, how her hair felt on his skin... nor what it'd be like to kiss her.

Then Michael grabbed Angel's hand and tugged her forward, his smile almost bigger than he was, and Logan knew he wasn't going to ask her to leave. He couldn't break Michael's heart.

And hell, he was an adult. He could control himself. He'd proved it on the dock when he hadn't kissed her. He'd been planning to stop long before Michael's interruption anyway.

"Come on!" Michael was bouncing again. Bouncing

was, apparently, a good thing in a six-year-old—as long as there was no trampoline, sawdust, or audience as there'd been when he was six.

Angel slid past him, laughing, the scent of the tropics and something else clinging to her skin—like Logan wanted to.

Jesus. *Get a grip, Hardington—and* not *on Angel.*

He was in charge of millions of dollars at work—hell, he had a problem with eight million of them facing him when they got back. He certainly could handle an attraction to the babysitter without resorting to sending her away.

"Hurry up!" Michael ran to the counter, dragging Angel with him.

His son would be devastated if she left.

Logan sighed. That settled it. Put his libido in check and deal with this attraction in the only feasible way: forget it.

"Should I get creamsicle, Angel? Or do you think I should go for Moose Trail? I saw a moose once. Rainbow took me to a zoo and I saw lions and tigers and a moose. Little monkeys, too. They were hopping all over their cage. I'd be sad to be in a cage, wouldn't you?"

Angel slid her hand over Michael's shoulders, then under his chin, which she tilted back so that he was looking up at her. Such an intimate gesture between the two of them, as natural as if they were related.

But they weren't, and Logan, who was, couldn't even hope for anything so ordinary between him and his son. How had she managed it in the space of half a morning?

Maybe Michael really missed Rainbow.

Wouldn't that be a kick in the shins? The flake who'd all but dumped the kid and run was being pined for, while the father who was thrilled beyond belief to have his son live with him couldn't even get a "Dad" out of him?

"I think you're right, Michael," Angel said. "Being in a cage would be horrible. You'd have to wait for someone to feed you and talk to you, and you'd be stuck with someone else directing your life. It must be awful. I don't think I'd like to see those monkeys like that."

"It made me sad, too, like when Rainbow was in jail. She was crying when I went to see her with the social worker."

Logan's entire body froze. He couldn't have heard right. Rainb—Christine had gone to jail?

"When was this, Michael?" He worked very hard at keeping the anger from his voice.

Michael shrugged. "I dunno. It was only for a night and she bought me lots of tater chips and soda and ice cream before she went, so I didn't mind. She did, though. That's why she took me to the zoo. To show me what it was like and to tell me never to do anything bad so I wouldn't be locked up like the animals. And I never did."

Never. At six.

Christ. The kid had seen more of the bad side of life than Logan had at that age. Yet there Michael was, shrugging it off like water off his back. How much was bravado and how much was childhood ignorance? And how much was the futility inherent in being six?

"Well." Angel's voice was a bit too sharp, so at least she was with him on that subject. Good thing if she was going to watch his son—not that she could do a worse job than the child's own mother. He was appreciating her child studies degree more and more.

"Why don't we decide what ice cream we're all going to have? What flavor do you think I should get, Michael?"

It was almost as if she could read his mind. Not that it was too hard to figure out, but it boded well for her babysitting skills—which were obviously leagues beyond Christine's parenting ones.

Logan went through the mechanics of ordering and paying for the treat, even ate one of his own, but for the life of him couldn't remember what flavor he'd ordered. Not that it mattered, because he didn't even taste it.

With Michael and Angel discussing the merits of ice cream flavors as they strolled through the strip mall afterwards, the only thing Logan could focus on was that Christine had gone to jail and left their child in the care of a social worker. He couldn't believe it.

And he'd thought the *circus* had been a hell of a life for a kid. At least no one in his family had gone to jail, and no social worker had ever shown up. They'd also had more than potato chips and ice cream to eat—what the hell kind of meal was that for a child? Thank God Christine had come to her senses and left Michael with him. She obviously wasn't cut out to be a parent, but he… he was going to give his son everything he'd need to lead a normal, lawful life.

And if that included a well-educated babysitter who'd shown up naked on his boat, well, the money he'd just spent on her clothes was nothing compared to the security in knowing he had someone capable looking after his son.

Red lingerie notwithstanding.

Chapter 8

"ANGEL, WATCH THIS!" MICHAEL JUMPED OFF THE EDGE OF the pool in Logan's yard and did a half twist in the air before belly-flopping into the water. That had to hurt.

Angel clapped when he surfaced. "Good job! You almost made it all the way around that time."

"I'll get it. You'll see."

"I'm sure you will, Michael." She leaned back on the chaise lounge to watch him practice as he'd been doing since lunch.

Logan had disappeared into his study to handle some business, and she and Michael had had an interesting afternoon making paper animals with pages from his notebook, as well as figuring out how to make a peanut butter sandwich.

Between the two of them, there'd been enough peanut butter on their fingers that they hadn't needed the sandwich part, but Angel wasn't willing to pass up her first taste of *dry* bread.

"I'm gonna do a handstand, 'kay, Angel?"

"Go ahead." She hooked the pen on the notebook where she'd jotted her observations and impressions before lunch, then ran her fingers over the soft cover. She'd used a quarter of the pages already.

"Didya see me?" Michael popped up out of the water and shook the hair out of his eyes. It was the first time since she'd met him that he wasn't wearing his hat, though he had given it a place of honor atop Rocky on the other chaise.

"I did. Your legs were very straight."

"Cool. Now count how long I can stay under." He took a breath and ducked back beneath the surface.

Angel started counting and smoothed her dress over her legs. Such a cool feeling, to quote Michael. She hadn't bought many dresses at the Atlantis Salvager's Market, mainly because they weren't practical everyday wear in the ocean, but after being in this one all day, she might just have to spend a few hours on deserted islands wearing them. They made her feel so feminine and pretty, and Mers were, after all, accustomed to beauty. The oceans and the creatures in them, Atlantis, the reefs, their people... life was beautiful under the sea.

She looked out over the water beyond the stone wall surrounding Logan's backyard to where the rays of the sun sparkled across the tips of the waves that were gently rolling ashore. A pair of pelicans flew in shadow against the sunlight in the distance, one taking a sudden dive. A pod of dolphins swam offshore, their fins breaking the surface—

No. Those weren't dolphins.

They were sharks.

Hammerheads.

Harry.

Godsdammit.

Just like that, her peace shattered. For all she'd like to think that she was here for a greater purpose, the truth was that she was stranded here—all thanks to Harry.

And herself.

Angel sighed. Right. *She* was ultimately responsible for what had happened and where she was. Rod and The Council weren't going to let her forget that when she returned home—which was why she had to return triumphant.

She brushed her fingers over the notebook again. This would be her defense when she faced them.

"How long was that, Angel?" Michael sputtered as he surfaced, gulping in big breaths.

"Uh, thirty seconds, Michael. Good job! But I think you should to take a break."

"Yeah. That's a good record for today. Now I'm gonna see how long I can float on my back, 'kay?"

Angel hid her smile. How well she remembered that recuperative tactic from physical education class. "Okay. Go ahead."

She picked up her notebook and opened it to the page comparing Mer and Human offspring. Aside from the obvious differences of food, shelter, and legs, she hadn't listed much else. Treats, cajoling to get their way, being the light of their parents' lives… all the similarities supported her idea of using children to advance the purpose of the Coalition.

She clicked her pen to add Michael's flotation tactic and paper animals to her list when, "Could it really be? Angel Tritone?" almost had her jumping out of the chair.

She turned around. Then back. Who-in-Hades had said that?

"Psst! My dear girl!" Something small and brown waved green front legs at her from atop the wall. A lizard. An anole, to be exact, the brown coloring camouflaging him against the stone. He must have turned his limbs back to green to catch her attention.

"How are you?" The dewlap beneath his chin turned a vibrant orange as the green color slowly slipped over the rest of his body. "I'm Stewart. It's a pleasure to finally meet you. I've heard so much about your studies. Is this one of them? I could help, you know. I have been living amongst Humankind for quite a few *selinos*." Stewart's gesticulating hand moved as quickly as his words.

"They're not all as nice as this gentleman, if I do say so, and that child worries me. Why, before I ended up here, I'd gone through three tails at the hands of children. Three!" A shudder rippled down his body. "Vicious creatures, I tell you. Worse than any house cat. Well, perhaps not cats."

Angel glanced at Michael, who was happily spouting water from his mouth like a whale, and opened her notebook to shield the talking lizard. Bad enough Michael knew about Mers; the fact that animals could speak was just as top secret. "Hi, Stewart. I can't really talk right now." She motioned to Michael.

"Ah yes. *Bipeds*." Stewart gave her a thumbs-up with a tiny digit. "But I can be of assistance, you know. I've had extensive fieldwork in the strolling habits of Humans and ways to avoid them. Plus, I did my dissertation on escape tactics from the captivity their young find such delight in subjecting anoles to." He shuddered, a brown line of pigment zigzagging over his back.

"I'll take up residence in this lovely gardenia bush for the duration of your stay." Stewart shook his elongated head, then tapped the side of it with another bony digit. "But how silly of me. That won't be long at all, will it? You'll be leaving tomorrow because of that tail thing your kind has to deal with. I'm quite glad that doesn't apply to *anolis carolinensis*. I'd hate to think of my life being governed by tail issues. Whenever my tail becomes a problem, I simply leave it. How utterly horrifying to have to live your life according to your inability to do so. How *do* you stand it?"

The tail was nothing compared to Stewart's loud, godlier-than-thou attitude and the threat of her study being interrupted by an overzealous, self-important lizard.

"Hey, Angel!" Michael climbed onto the lip of the pool, and Angel flipped her hair back—and over— the stone wall, hiding Stewart from view. "Didya see me? Watch this!" Michael jumped in, shouting, "Cannonball!"

Funny. Mer children did the same thing off buildings in Atlantis—though they were usually *holding* cannon-balls. She'd add that to the list.

Stewart coughed behind her and *pfft*-ed the strands of her hair out of his face. "As I was saying—"

"Thank you for your offer, Stewart, but if you don't mind, the less interaction I have with wildlife, the less chance there is for one of you to slip up in front of the Humans and speak. Think of what that would do for your avoidance tactics around them."

Stewart stroked his pink dewlap, his eyes hooded. "Hmm. Good point. I'll just keep an eye out for any-thing interesting then and report in when I see it. Good evening, Your Highness." He straightened his tail, the tip turning brown first as he faded, limb by limb, into the background of stone. "Oh. A mention or two of my name in your report wouldn't be remiss, you know."

A mention? For almost breaking another Mer rule? Angel didn't think so. She'd be in enough hot water when she got back; she didn't need Stewart's help. She was about to tell him so when Michael popped up by the edge of the pool again, saving her from breaking that rule.

"How was that, Angel—oh cool! A chameleon! My friend Evan had one. Let's catch it so I can have a pet, too!"

Stewart mumbled something about heathens and children in the same breath as the tip of his tail twitched up—a sure sign he was ready to take off. While it was an idea Angel heartily endorsed, it wouldn't teach Michael anything.

"Michael, remember what you said about the monkeys in the cage? How you wouldn't like that?" She reached for the little boy's arm to stop him from rushing to the wall. "He wouldn't either."

"But I'd make it just like his home."

"Except he wouldn't be free."

"Oh. You mean it'd be like he was in jail?"

She hadn't meant to remind him about his mother, but no matter how self-aggrandizing Stewart was, lizards deserved the same freedoms as other beings.

And maybe, she grudgingly noted, even a mention in her report since he had—albeit inadvertently—brought about this lesson with Michael. "That's right, Michael. It would be like locking him up. And that's not fair since he hasn't done anything but walk on the wall. There's nothing wrong with that."

She uncrossed her ankles and put her feet in the grass, scooting to the edge of the chair. "So let's just enjoy watching him in the wild. That way you get to see what an anole is like, and he gets to live his life how he wants and do his part for the environment. Everyone's happy."

Michael licked his lips, his eyes darting from Stewart to her.

Stewart tensed, his tail inching higher, his back legs flexing...

"Okay." Michael shrugged. "He's kinda boring anyway. Just sitting there, looking scared. Besides, I'm gonna go play with my animals." With that, the little boy ran to the other side of the pool, grabbed Rocky, plunked the baseball cap on his head, then headed to the patio table for his paper menagerie.

"*Boring*?" Stewart's dewlap morphed to a brilliant red. "I'll have him know I've verbally sparred with the best and the brightest of the lizard world. I've—"

Angel managed to shush Stewart when she caught sight of Logan at his office door. She grabbed her notebook and opened it, once more shielding Stewart from Human eyes. After all the strange questions she'd asked Logan today, the last thing he needed to see was her talking to a lizard.

She could only imagine what he'd think of her then.

—◆—

Logan took one look at Angel and changed his mind again; someone Up There *was* on his side after all.

Having her here to take care of Michael while he'd put out those seventeen or so fires on the project was a godsend. Now the lead scientist was back on the job, R&D was on track, all the investors were happy with the results of the latest solar-chip testing, and he could relax and enjoy the rest of Michael's birthday.

Then Angel flipped her hair to the side, a curtain of golden silk flowing over her shoulders and Logan's relaxation took a hike.

Her hair was gorgeous and he simply could not stop wondering what it'd feel like falling across his chest. Intertwined in his fingers. Caressing his skin—

Hell.

He had to stop. She was here to help him with Michael and nothing else.

If only he wasn't aware of her all the time. Even with her nose buried in her book, something about Angel just reeled him in. Something called to him. Made him see her as a beautiful woman and not the hired help.

But she'd given no indication that she saw him the same way, and, really, the last few hours proved that he needed her here in a babysitting capacity, so he had to get his frustrated, testosterone-laden mind off her.

Deciding that checking what Michael was up to was the safer thing to do at the moment, Logan climbed the steps to the patio outside the kitchen. "Hey, sport. What are you doing?" He picked up one of the folded pieces of paper that was lying on top of a leather-bound notebook. "This is really good. It's a goose, right?"

Michael took the paper animal from him, unfolded it, smoothed it, then refolded it. "It's a swan. I taught Angel how to make it, but she didn't do it good."

Logan pulled out a seat next to Michael. "So where'd you learn to do that?"

Origami was a pretty impressive feat for a six-year-old. Logan let a little parental pride shine through. He may not have had a chance to help with the nurture part of making Michael who he was, but he'd been pretty dexterous with his fingers growing up. Michael had obviously inherited those genes from him.

"At the soup kitchen. Ms. Narita showed me."

Thank God Logan was sitting down. Unlike with the jail announcement. "What were you doing in a soup kitchen? Did Christi—I mean, Rainbow work there?"

Michael shrugged and kept his face lowered. "We went there a lot 'cause Rainbow said they cooked better than she did. They had ice cream, too. But not peppermint. When I get bigger I'm gonna work real hard so I can buy my own peppermint and have a big house to live in with a pet and Rainbow and everything." Michael put another bend in the swan. "See this? It can flap its wings."

The folded paper swan went up and down when he pulled on the tail. Logan took it from him to try it out, all the while trying to keep his shock at what Michael had said out of his voice. "That's really neat, sport. I'm proud of you."

He also ached for the child who'd had to eat in soup kitchens. Whose tattered wardrobe fit in a shabby pillowcase. Who was already planning to work hard so he could provide for his own mother—a mother who, while Logan was no longer her biggest fan, appeared to have gone to jail despite what he was beginning to suspect were mitigating circumstances.

But why hadn't she come to him? He would have helped.

"Logan?" Michael asked. "Can we have burgers tonight? On the grill? Mr. Ray made them that way once and they were good."

"Sure thing. Who's Mr. Ray?" Logan was almost afraid to ask.

Michael picked up something that looked like an aardvark. Or maybe it was a mouse. "The landlord. He used to give me hotdogs sometimes. 'Til we moved. So, can we?"

Logan would give the kid prime rib every night for the rest of his life if that's what he wanted. "Sure." He cleared his throat. "Would you like to help me make them?"

Michael looked up then. He even pushed the rim of the baseball cap back. Then he looked at Angel. "Can Angel help?"

Logan closed his eyes for a second. What was it about Angel that made Michael cling to her instead of him? She wasn't even related.

Then he looked over at her and knew why *he'd* cling to her—"Of course she can. Why don't you ask her?"

"Cool!" Michael hopped up off the chair and ran down the steps.

Logan opened the grill, unable to prevent himself from watching Angel smile as she took Michael's hand. She was one of the most beautiful women he'd ever seen, if not *the* most beautiful.

He turned on the propane and lit the burner, her laughter doing all sorts of babysitter-inappropriate things to his insides. He didn't know whether he should be grateful or worried that the sight of her had pushed thoughts of Michael's upbringing out of his mind. Then the setting sun backlit her dress as she walked toward him and Logan groaned.

Worried. He should be worried.

Every single curve. Right there. As if she weren't wearing a thing.

And, man, did he remember how she looked wearing nothing.

He eased the grill cover down, trying to concentrate on not burning himself instead of on her.

Why couldn't he get over the fact that she'd been naked? He'd seen naked women before. Okay, not strange ones on his boat. But the image of her would not leave him—and the dress only enhanced it, teasing him with that damn little cutout on her chest and covering curves he could probably draw perfectly. If he could draw.

"How about some help?" she asked, her hair falling down her back, the ends swaying by her hips.

Her smile was soft and beautiful; it reached her incredibly blue eyes, and her voice… It was so lyrical—

"Logan?" Michael tugged on his shorts. "Angel wants to know if we can help."

His son. Touching him. Asking a question.

Logan found saliva somewhere in his mouth and used it to form a coherent—he hoped—reply. "Dishes. We could use those." His arm even worked to gesture toward the table. His lips worked, too, as they returned the smile his son gave him.

"Race ya into the kitchen, Angel!"

And just like that, Michael and his touch were gone.

But Logan could still feel the warmth where their skin had met, and, in a way he'd never imagined, it filled his heart.

"He's a wonderful child." Angel's voice filled him in a whole other way.

He looked down at her. She was so small. Almost a

child herself—but not. A fact he couldn't seem to forget.
Or disregard. Or even *want* to disregard.

"Don't you think?"

Think what? Oh. Michael. He cleared his throat.
"Yeah, he is. I just wish I'd gotten to know him sooner.
Like six years sooner."

And he was admitting this to a total stranger, why?

"Angel, why don't you help him? The dishes are in
the upper cabinets and I haven't gotten around to child-
proofing just yet. They're pottery and heavy and if he
breaks them—"

"Aye, aye, captain." She kicked her heels together
and saluted him before hurrying inside.

He watched her all the way.

The fire crackled behind him and Logan laughed
at himself. He was acting like a teenager with his first
crush.

Too bad he'd broken up with Joanne last month. If
he hadn't, maybe he'd be a little better equipped to deal
with the wallop Angel packed, but Joanne had started
getting serious and he'd had to end it. She wasn't the
woman for him; he'd known that. He wanted a woman he
could envision having children with, and Joanne's idea
of motherhood was nannies and boarding schools. He
was *not* sending Michael away to any boarding school.

He'd always wanted kids. Wanted a traditional, normal family. One that included little league teams and
sleepovers. A family that had meals together as his
friend Drew's did. A family who read stories at bedtime,
vacationed in campgrounds, and went to amusement
parks. Joanne hadn't had the same vision.

So, he'd ended it, and when Michael had shown up,

he'd decided to put dating on hold. Bringing random women around wasn't in his son's best interests, nor was spending nights out on dates.

And then... enter Angel.

Something inside him thudded. What an entrance she'd made. Naked, gorgeous, and good with kids... could any woman be more perfect?

Except that she was his son's babysitter. Getting involved with her would be worse than the worst cliché—again, not that she showed any signs of wanting to be involved with him. So, for Michael's—and his—sake, he'd just have to suck up the frustration and live with it. God had given him two hands for a reason.

But why couldn't the new babysitter look like Marilyn Manson instead of Marilyn Monroe?

Chapter 9

MICHAEL KEPT CHATTERING SO MUCH DURING DINNER THAT Angel hadn't known whether to be relieved she wouldn't have to contribute to the conversation or to worry he'd accidentally blow her cover.

Actually, she'd almost blown it herself. Human food wasn't totally new to her, thanks to the occasional capsized vessel and the undersea wedding reception her parents had held for her brother Reel and his Human wife, Erica, complete with their favorite Human foods, but burgers hadn't been part of her experience.

She'd almost swooned when she bit into one. The combination of flavors and textures… And of course, the dry bread and condiments that hadn't been watered down… The burger was to die for. The flavors were so different. Stronger. Better.

And the beverages… She'd passed on the milk Logan had insisted Michael drink, but the iced tea was delicious. Fresh water, too, and even a sip or two of grape wine, so different from the kelp wine Mers had. What an experience for the palate. And the chocolate cake Logan carried out… it almost brought tears to her eyes.

She'd tasted chocolate before on the rare occasion and could smell the cake's sweetness. Charley, her father's advisor, could go on and on about the consistency of cake. She couldn't wait to try it.

"Should we sing?" Logan looked at her.

Sing? He wanted her to sing? Here? In front of his son? Usually when Human males wanted a Mer female to sing, it wasn't appropriate for children.

"You know 'Happy Birthday,' right?"

Ah. Right. She remembered that tune from Human Cultural Basics 101. "Of course I do."

Logan lit the candles on the cake, and Angel tried not to stare at the flames. They fascinated her. While temperatures in Atlantis were regulated by the heat of molten lava that flowed beneath the sea bed, flames were a foreign concept. She was going to have to experience this fire phenomenon up close while she had the chance.

She leaned forward, catching the hair that swept over her shoulder before it could catch on fire. She didn't want to experience it *that* closely.

Logan cleared his throat, and when she looked up, he quickly averted his eyes. "Ready?" he asked, his voice deeper than before.

Angel glanced down. The peekaboo hole in her dress gapped forward. That explained the throat-clearing. Thank the gods Logan was such a gentleMer—man. She pressed one hand against the bodice of the dress, tucked the hair behind her ear with the other, and sat back. "As ready as I'll ever be."

Logan cleared his throat.

Angel looked at him.

He looked back.

"Are you guys gonna sing or what? I want cake." Michael hopped up and down in his chair.

Logan cleared his throat again and spun so fast to look at Michael that Angel thought the man might fall out of his chair.

He tapped the rim of Michael's cap. "Ah, sure we are, sport."

He started the song then and Angel quickly caught up. Beneath her melody, he had a very nice voice. Tenor. On key. It could be a bit stronger, but that wouldn't take much work.

His lips formed the words properly—not that she was looking at his lips or anything—but perhaps he could lengthen that "you" note. His technique wouldn't take much tweaking. He breathed at the right moments, not straining to hit the high note, soft when he should be—

She suddenly realized she was singing solo. She stopped, mid-*dear Michael*.

"What?"

Both males stared at her, Logan with a strange gleam in his eye and Michael with a breathy, "You sing like an angel, Angel."

No, actually, she sang like a…

Siren.

Oh Hades. Her voice. She'd forgotten the effect it had on Humans. Especially adult males. Logan, his pupils almost nonexistent—the classic characteristic of Siren Song enchantment—was clearly under its influence.

"Uh." She cleared her throat and took another sip of that delicious wine. "I, um, that is… I guess I like to sing?" She shrugged her shoulders, going for nonchalant.

Big mistake. With the way her voice was working on Logan, his eyes went right to her breasts.

And wouldn't you know… they reacted. Now she knew what bras were for and was sorry she hadn't worn one, and, whoa, Michael should *not* be seeing that. She crossed her arms, then rested her elbows in front of her on the table.

"When do we eat it?" She didn't care if it was a stupid question. She raised her voice an octave and went off-key, going for a neutral expression to get Logan's mind off her. But if that look he wore was any indication, she'd say those stories she'd heard of Humans dying with smiles on their face after being lured into the depths by Sirens were true.

But what woman wanted a man bewitched by her voice into a conditioned response? Not her. A man should want her for her personality and mind first, *then* her body. This blind lust her enchanted voice created was just that... blind.

And the lust?

Well, okay, that was real. But only because of the enchantment of her voice.

Uh huh. And he hadn't almost kissed you earlier. Right.

Okay, fine. He wanted her. But she didn't want lust. She wanted love.

With a Human?

No, that's not what she meant. Angel huffed, annoyed that she was arguing with her subconscious while Logan's subconscious, conscience, ego, id, identity, whatever, had apparently gone into lustful hibernation.

"Yo-hoo... Logan... " She waved her hand in front of his face, praying to the gods that her nipples had gone back into hiding.

She glanced down.

No such luck.

And, tracking Logan's gaze, she saw that he'd noticed.

"Logan!" Michael walked around to his father. "What's wrong with him, Angel?" He turned his big, brown eyes to her. The worry in them affected her every bit as much as her voice had affected his father.

First she reminded him of his mother, then she scared the daylights out of him by hypnotizing his father. Some babysitter she was turning out to be. Logan would never let her stay now.

"Nothing, Michael. Your dad will be fine. Let's get him a glass of ice water. That should help."

She hoped.

Because while she had a vested interest in not seeing Logan as a man, he had no similar reason.

And that look in his eyes said he definitely was seeing her as a woman.

She was singing.

Harry lifted one side of his head out of the water. Oh yeah, that was Angel. The Dinner-That-Wasn't. And she had her sights set on that Human. Heh—true to form.

Sure, Mers could claim that they'd evolved from earlier times when everyone had the run of the sea, and demand that sharks do the same to qualify for that Representative's seat on The Council he was angling for, but when flipper came to fin, instinct won out.

The best part was, if she played up that angle and lured the Human to the water, the child was sure to follow, and Harry would get the best of both worlds.

Not only would he be able to capture Angel and ransom her back to The Council—his plan before she'd done the unthinkable and climbed aboard the Human's boat last night—but now he'd have two Humans to savor. Question was, which one should he eat first?

Ah, gluttony. Such a hedonistic pleasure.

But there was a problem. That boat.

Harry tapped the end of his head with his tail fin. That boat was too big for him to take on by himself.

Shit. He was going to need help—much as he hated to admit it. But the prospect of taking her hostage *and* getting a two-course meal was too much to pass by.

He gave one last look at the beach. Tomorrow night he knew right where she'd be.

He and the boys would be waiting.

Chapter 10

Angel couldn't get into the kitchen fast enough.

Logan's reaction freaked her out. She'd heard about the effect of Siren Song on Human males, but she hadn't expected it to happen like that. Didn't she have to *want* to mesmerize him with her voice for it to work? And that was definitely the last thing she wanted. Even if her toes *had* started tingling—

No. Really. She didn't want him to see her as anything other than Michael's babysitter.

"Angel, I wanna get some different paper." Michael turned his hat cockeyed on his head. "I'm gonna make more animals after cake."

"Um, sure, honey. Go ahead." Better to leave her alone to putter around the kitchen and try to regain her equilibrium—and she didn't mean because of her legs—than stand there while she was trying to pretend everything was normal.

Everything was *not* normal.

She grabbed a glass out of the cabinet, then turned on the faucet and ran her fingers beneath the water. Logan wasn't the only one who could use a drink of something cold. What was going on?

Well, she knew what was going on with *him*, but what had happened to her? Logan's gaze had sent shivers over her skin and ramped up her internal temperature. Oh she knew what it was; she just hadn't expected it. Not with a Human.

She filled the glass and drank most of the water in one swallow, then pressed it against her forehead, willing the coolness to have an effect. But when the French door opened and Logan strode in, Angel realized that water wasn't going to do the trick after all.

Not with that look in his eyes.

She set the glass down and backed up against the counter. "Logan? What are you doing here? We'll bring your drink out to you."

He didn't say a word.

Not one.

He didn't have to. The look in his eyes answered for him and Angel wasn't so sure she wanted to know what that answer was.

He gave it to her anyway.

In four strides.

That's all it took him.

Four.

Then he slid his fingers in her hair, pressed himself against her, and kissed her.

Really kissed her.

Mind-numbingly seductive, ravishing kisses.

He devoured her mouth, his tongue taking quick advantage of her surprise, and swept inside with a thrust so blatant her legs went boneless.

That didn't stop Logan. He slid an arm around her back and lifted her so her backside rested on the lip of the counter, making her the perfect height to return his kisses.

Return his kisses? She must be going craz—

Logan nudged her legs apart and suddenly her breasts were flattened against that hard, sculpted wall of his chest, her legs on either side of him, her swelling core demanding pressure, and Angel's breath disappeared.

Thank the gods Logan chose that moment to nip along her jaw, but Angel still couldn't catch her breath.

Then his tongue swirled in the soft spot beneath her ear, and she decided breathing was highly overrated.

Her head fell back and she reached for his arms to hold herself upright so he could reach... there... that...

Oh, gods... His tongue... it twirled around the shell of her ear, his warm breath sending goose bumps all over her. She wiggled on the counter, trying to close her legs, needing the pressure...

Then he pulled her against him even more, spreading her legs wider, and *there* was the pressure.

The long, hard length of him hit her at just the right spot. Her fingers curled into his biceps as he slid one hand beneath her backside to draw her closer.

She hadn't thought it was possible to *be* any closer.

Then she felt his shaft jerk between them and knew that there was, indeed, a way...

Angel opened her eyes.

Oh, gods. What were they doing?

Logan's tongue stroked the soft inside of her bottom lip and Angel knew *exactly* what they were doing.

Or rather, exactly what *she* was doing.

She was making out with an enchanted man.

Enchanted... and enchanting.

She tried to pull back. Regain her focus.

Logan was having none of it. With one hand still firmly beneath her backside, his fingers sending all sorts of riotous fires along her nerve endings, the fingers of his other hand opened wide across the back of her neck, his thumb angling her jaw just right so he could kiss her senseless again.

And, oh my, did he.

Angel closed her eyes, her body having given in before her mind, but oh, the sensations…

Her fingers curled again on his biceps, tugging him closer—if that was even possible—and her belly quivered when his tongue stroked hers. Her legs followed suit when his harshly drawn breath expanded his chest against her sensitized nipples and Angel couldn't stop a groan.

"Angel?"

Michael.

Oh, gods. Michael!

He couldn't see them. Not like this.

Angel squirmed, no longer groaning. No longer tugging on Logan. "Logan!" she whispered the moment his lips freed hers to once again trail over her jaw. "Logan, you have to stop! Wake up!" or whatever it was called.

Logan was a man on a mission. And that mission was the cord in her neck. His lips traced down it, soft, fluttery, just like her nerve endings, and if not for Michael's stomping on the steps, she might have gone with the sensations to see where they led.

But Michael Could. Not. See.

And just as importantly, she Should. Not. Do.

This time she put some *oomph* behind her actions and managed to separate them.

Logan looked at her with hooded eyes that were hotter than any fire, his chest rising and falling in a way her breasts were aching to feel. He reached out to caress her jaw and, for a second, Angel let him.

But when he took a step closer, she backed away.

This was all her fault and she was not going to damage a child's psyche because of her super-charged hormones, nor any hot, sexy, yield-to-me look in Logan's eyes.

She closed her legs—pressure at last—and managed to skirt around him off the counter before he could pin her there again.

She grabbed the glass by the sink and, having no clue what else to do because no one had ever discussed how to *end* a Siren's enchantment, tossed the rest of the water in Logan's face.

"What the hell?" Logan shook his head, water droplets flinging everywhere, but at least it did the trick.

She tossed him a towel just as Michael entered the room.

"I got colored paper this time," the little boy said, holding up the aforementioned paper. "Want to help me make a bunch of parrots? They're my favorite."

"Sure, honey." She made the show of adjusting Michael's hat on his head, but her main purpose was to prevent him from asking why Logan was all wet. She steered him toward the door. "Why don't you go set up on the table? Your dad and I will be right out. No peeking at your presents, though."

Michael smiled at her—a smile so like his father's that it took her breath away. "Oh, okay."

She waited until he was out the door before turning back to look at Logan—something she both wanted to do and dreaded doing.

How in Hades was she going to explain *this?*

Chapter 11

SHE HAD THE BEST BREASTS HE'D SEEN IN A LONG TIME.

Logan jerked his head. What was wrong with him? Ogling Angel's breasts? He should be shot. And as for pinning her up against the cabinets and mauling her, he ought to be drawn and quartered.

He wiped his face with the towel she'd mercifully tossed him and gave half a thought to gouging out his eyes. He'd never leered at a woman before, much less attacked one. She was a guest in his home. Michael's babysitter. Could he *be* a bigger cad?

He slumped against the counter and reached for the glass. Christ. Something had hit him like a tidal wave. There hadn't been a subtle thing about the staring he'd done. At her breasts, no less. The poor woman was looking at him as if he'd suggested he tie her to the bedposts. He couldn't blame her.

In another life, that idea would have a lot to commend it.

He shook his head. Something weird had come over him. Exhaustion maybe. The shock of finding Michael on his doorstep finally catching up with him? A naked goddess on his boat who sang like an angel and looked like a temptress? Who, at this very moment, might be wearing red lingerie beneath her dress? Hell, it was anybody's guess.

He took a swig of the water. Or rather, he tried to.

Nothing left.

That'd be because he was wearing it—and he didn't blame her in the least.

She started to fiddle with a few strands of hair. "Logan…"

"Angel, I'm sorry. I know that doesn't excuse my actions, but I honestly don't know what came over me."

She let go of her hair and gripped the chair in front of her, her tongue sneaking out to lick her bottom lip.

Actually, he *did* know what had come over him.

But that was no reason to act on it.

"I don't blame you if you want to look for another place to stay, but I want to apologize and assure you"—and himself—"that it won't happen again."

He hoped.

Her mouth fell open. "Wha…*what*?"

He laughed inwardly. She was going to make him say it. Well, served him right. What moron took advantage of a woman the way he had? You might think it'd been four *years* instead of four weeks since Joanne.

"That kiss. I was way out of line. I have no idea why I did it—"

She got this look on her face, and Logan realized he was digging a deeper hole for himself. Of course no woman would want to hear that the man who'd just been mauling her—quite pleasantly, there was no denying the truth in that—didn't know why he'd done it. She was gorgeous; he knew why he was attracted to her. He just didn't know why he'd gone all caveman on her.

"I mean, yes, you're beautiful, but that's no excuse for the way I behaved. I'm very sorry and you have my word that it won't happen again. Please don't leave. Michael really cares about you and he's been through a lot. I'd rather not disappoint him if it can be avoided."

"You think I'm beautiful?"

The funny thing was, she wasn't being coy. Her eyes, those beautiful sparkling tropical-seas eyes, were open and honest and guileless.

"How can you *not* know that you're gorgeous? Half the men on the street today almost tripped over themselves trying to get a look at you, and the other half were gay."

She blushed. Her cheeks were as pink as her nip—

Way to go, Hardington. Right back to being the lecher...

"Look, Angel. I'm really sorry. It won't happen again. Please stay."

She shook her head, the long blonde tresses that had sparkled in the setting sun with threads of burnished copper and gold coursing through them waved behind her like—

Jesus. What was *wrong* with him? He was waxing poetic? He must be getting sick. They did say kids were germ factories. Maybe Michael had given him some weird childhood illness.

One that makes you stare at a woman's breasts, attack her, then turn into Wordsworth? Keats?

"Logan, you don't have to apologize. I mean, I did kiss, that is, it wasn't all one-sided..."

Now she nibbled on her bottom lip, God help him.

"I think it's safe to say that I instigated it, Angel, and I'm sorry. Is there any chance we could move beyond this?"

She licked her lips again. She was trying to kill him. She had to be. No one could be that unconsciously sexy.

"Yes. Let's. I mean, after all, it is Michael's birthday. We don't want to upset him, right?"

He blew out a breath he hadn't been aware he'd been holding and put a palm on his chest where his heart was racing—and *only* because he'd been worried about hurting Michael with his utter stupidity—not any other reason. "Thank you. So… shall we head back out for cake?"

Angel nodded. "Yes."

If he'd planned it, they wouldn't have arrived at the door at the same time, but whoever Up There was having a good laugh at his expense certainly made it look that way.

He stepped back to allow her to pass, determined to act like a civilized, rational human being. It might be a little late, but he did know how to treat a woman. "After you."

She glanced at him, then tucked another swath of hair behind her ear, and headed toward the door. Logan was damned proud of himself for staying far enough behind her to resist the temptation to touch her as he followed her out.

Then she stopped in the doorway and turned around so quickly that the accomplishment evaporated. It was either touch her or knock her over, and the poor woman had already had enough manhandling from him today.

Luckily, he managed to stay upright, but he did catch hold of her arms to steady himself—not that it was in any way steadying. Especially with her hair now trailing over his arm.

What was *wrong* with him?

Angel took a few steps back out of the doorway and his grasp, and while, logically, he knew that was a good thing, he still wanted to pull her back.

"I hope that it's all right with you that I gave Michael a notebook and pen for his birthday." She did that damn lip-licking thing again that was beginning to drive him slowly and not so sweetly insane. "Everyone should have a special present on their birthday."

He knew what he'd like for his birthday—*Christ*. If only she wore perfume, he could attribute this fascination to it, but the scent of hibiscus clinging to her skin and the tang of sea-laden air and the gentle breeze off the Florida beach were enough to make a man go weak—

Oh hell. He was back to spouting poetry.

Logan cleared his throat, shook his head, bucked up his resolve and sucked it up—both his wayward thoughts and the sweet scent of Angel.

He yanked the door closed behind him a little harder than was necessary, rattling the panes. Good. Something else could be rattled. He leaned against the door and shoved his hands in his pockets, fully prepared to wait while she resumed her seat at the table on the patio. Then he'd sit as far away from her as possible and maybe—*hopefully*—get through the rest of this night with his sense of honor—what little was left of it—intact.

"That's fine, Angel, but it wasn't necessary. Having you agree to stay is more than enough of a birthday present." Lord knew, it was more than enough for *him*. "I mean, when we were out fishing on the boat yesterday, Michael said he wanted a mermaid for his birthday, of all things. If he only knew how I found you, he might even think you're one. Not that I want to tell him that, you understand."

Nor did he want to remember…

"But since a mermaid is out of the question, you, in Michael's eyes, are the next best thing."

———

Angel almost took a tumble. *The next best thing*?

If he only knew…

Good thing he didn't; he'd definitely want her to leave.

That'd been her biggest fear just now in the kitchen. On the countertop. That he'd somehow figure out she was responsible for him kissing her as if it were their last day on the planet.

But then he'd said she was beautiful.

Siren Song couldn't do that. It couldn't form opinions for the recipient. It only enhanced the chemical attraction—to the point of shutting down his inhibitions, obviously.

What had happened to hers was anybody's guess.

Zeus! Not only was Logan Hardington a fine specimen of a man, but she now knew *exactly* what that entailed. Down to every muscle-flexing, belly-quivering, nerve-shivering caress.

What was she going to do? Her study could be compromised by this attraction. If only she'd kept her mouth shut—well, okay, not during the kiss, but—

Wait a minute. Yes, dammit, that's exactly what she meant. If she'd kept her mouth closed all along—at the dinner table, during the kiss, now—her study wouldn't be in jeopardy.

Well, anymore than it was with all her questions…

"I think maybe I better leave." Before she went and did something she shouldn't.

Not *regret*; just *shouldn't*.

"Angel, wait—"

"You can't leave! You promised!" Michael's wail overrode whatever Logan was going to say as Michael came running across the flagstone patio. "You said you wouldn't leave me, Angel! You promised!" Michael wrapped his little body around her legs and held on tight.

Oh fish, she'd really messed things up.

"Michael." She tried to pry his arms off, but the child was stronger than he looked, especially being as upset as he was. Were tears salty enough to change her legs back to her tail? "Michael. Urchin, you have to understa—"

"Sport, Angel's not going anywhere."

"Huh?" Michael's bloodshot eyes blinked up at Logan.

Angel echoed the "huh?" She really *should* go somewhere.

"I said she's going to stay. Calm down."

Michael grabbed her legs even tighter. "But she said she was leaving. I heard her."

She should go. Michael was getting too attached to her and, gods knew, she'd been way too attached to his father not ten minutes ago…

Damn. She couldn't even muster the proper regret for that.

Logan tapped the rim of Michael's ever-present hat. "It's your birthday. What kind of party would it be if she left?"

"And she has to stay for ever and ever." Michael buried his nose so far in the folds of her dress that his hat fell off and Angel got another twinge in the vicinity of her heart. Different, but no less powerful, than the twinge she'd felt with Logan.

She put her hands on his shoulders. "Michael, I can't promise forever. No one can. But I'll stay as long as I can, okay?" Another thing she hadn't counted on in her deception—how her actions would affect the child she was introducing to her world in hopes of affecting change in his.

"But you have to stay until I'm all growed up."

Angel looked at Logan. She could use some help here.

"Michael, how about if we take it a week at a time," Logan said. "You start school soon, and Angel's working on a big project. She's going to have to go home at some point to present it. She has a family who will miss her, too. I'm sorry, son, but sometimes you can't have everything you want when you want it. Sometimes you just have to be happy with it when you have it. Let's enjoy Angel while we can, okay?"

Enjoy her?

He did *not* just say that.

From the quick grimace on his face when their eyes met, she knew that he had—and had made the same connection she did.

No no no. She was here on a mission. The Coalition. Her job. The fate of the planet. Big things. Major things. Things that should be leagues more important than an attraction to an enchanted Human.

Should be. But suddenly weren't.

"I can always come back, Michael." Okay, where had *that* come from?

Michael sniffled. "Promise?"

Somehow… "Of course I do. The world's not that big a place." Especially when The Oceanic Council had set up magical Travel Chambers throughout the oceans, including one not too far off this coast. And as director of the Coalition she'd have a license to return.

"Okay." Michael swiped a hand under his nose and glanced at his father before looking at her, his face growing somber. "Rainbow said everybody needs a family. That's why she sent me to stay with Logan. Does your mom miss you?"

Oh crappie. No wonder he didn't want her to leave.

Angel licked her lips and tried to keep emotion out of her voice. "My mom always misses me when I'm not with her, but I know she loves me and she knows that I love her, so it makes being apart easier. That's why you're lucky to have a dad, too, you know. More people to love you."

She pretended not to see Logan look away. Nor hear him when he cleared his throat. But she didn't look away when he hunkered down to eye level with the little boy.

"It's true, Michael. I'm the lucky one. It was the best day of my life when you showed up."

Michael wiped beneath his nose again then set his cap rim-forward. "Really? You mean I'm not ruining your life?" He even took a step toward Logan.

"No way, sport. Why would you think that? I've always wanted to have a son."

"Then why didn't you come find me before?

Rainbow said I was a compi… compacation and you don't like compacations."

The color drained from Logan's face. "Rainbow was wrong. She didn't know me very well if she thought I wouldn't want you around."

"So you're not going to make me leave?"

"I'm not going to make anyone leave. Not unless you want to."

Michael smiled then and let out a big sigh. "Oh, good. And Angel can stay, too, right?"

Logan met her eyes. "Yes. Angel can stay. For as long as she wants."

And there was the problem. Angel wasn't sure *what* she wanted.

She was, however, rather sure she knew *who* she wanted.

Chapter 12

THE CHOCOLATE CAKE WAS EVERY BIT AS DELICIOUS AS HER father's Olympian Advisor had claimed, and the smile on Michael's face when Logan presented him with a baseball glove—an object Angel had heard about but didn't really see the attraction of—was priceless. As was the ability to work beside Logan cleaning up the dinner.

Priceless? Angel almost dropped a plate at that thought. If her mother could see her now, *enjoying* chores.

Of course, the chores weren't what she was enjoying.

Something had changed.

Drastically.

Angel rubbed a spot on the plate a little more vigorously than necessary, forcing her mind back to the reason she'd stayed aboard ship last night. Well, the reason other than Harry, that is. This was all for the benefit of Merkind and the planet.

And if she kept telling herself that, she might actually remember it.

Then Logan's arm brushed her shoulder, and suddenly the fate of the planet took a backseat to what was happening here and now in the kitchen.

She stacked the plate on top of the others with a heavy *chink*.

"You okay?" Logan asked, taking the next one out of her hands.

"Um, sure. Why?" She reached for one of the glasses and started to dry it. Such an odd concept, drying things.

Logan set the plate down and leaned a hip against the counter. "Angel, I can't be the only one aware of the elephant in the room."

An elephant? Angel spun around. "There's no elephant."

She hadn't ever heard of anyone keeping an elephant as a pet in this country. India? Africa? Sure. Here? That was a new one.

"You've never heard that expression?" Logan flipped the dish towel over his shoulder.

Oh, Zeus. She'd done it again.

"I, um… well, yeah, but—"

"Angel"—he put his hand on her arm and just as quickly snatched it back—"I don't want things to be awkward between us."

Too late. "Okay."

"Michael will pick up on it."

"I know."

"So…" He picked up the dish again and started drying it. "Do you want to talk about it?"

Gods, no. "What's there to talk about? You kissed me; I kissed you; end of story."

It sounded good in theory. In her mind? Not so much.

"Right. End of story. It happened. It won't happen again. Everything's good." He said it as a statement, but his raised eyebrow was asking a question.

Could she let it go?

She had to. What else was she going to do? Sleep with him?

She almost laughed, but that wouldn't be appropriate. Or nice.

Or truthful.

Because the truth was, she was suddenly inordinately curious to see what sex would be like with him.

And not from any study standpoint.

Oh, Hades. She was in trouble—

"Angel, can you read me a bedtime story?" Michael, thank the gods, smiled at her from the doorway, his baseball cap skewed sideways *again*, just as his smile was again the image of his father's.

Angel tossed the dish towel on the counter. She didn't need to be noticing Logan's smile. Or the lack thereof as he looked at his son—the son who'd asked *her*, not him, to read a bedtime story.

Angel walked over to the little boy and knelt in front of him. "You know what, Michael? I'm really worn out. How about if your dad reads you one tonight, and I'll do it another night?"

The little boy lost the glow of hope and excitement, and maybe a tear or two worked its way into his eyes, but he didn't argue. "You promise?"

"I promise."

"Okay." He leaned sideways and looked at his father. "Logan? Will you read me a story?"

Angel heard the dish land on the countertop—louder than the one she'd almost dropped—but didn't turn around. She didn't even look up when Logan passed her with a quick squeeze to her shoulder.

"Sure, sport. Let's brush your teeth first, then we'll get you into bed. Do you know which story you'd like?"

Angel missed Michael's response as they left the kitchen, focusing instead on wiping the tears out of her own eyes.

Michael needed so much love. Logan needed to be the one to provide it.

And they needed help in bridging the distance.

Looked like her sojourn here would serve several purposes.

———

Wanting to distance herself from the Hardington men and the accompanying emotions, Angel decided to investigate the guesthouse Logan had opened earlier for her.

At the end of a brick path from the main house and overlooking the ocean, the three-room cottage was the perfect home-away-from-home for a displaced Mer. Whoever had decorated it had chosen the vivid colors of the Caribbean. Pillows and fabric in all shades of the sea dotted the white wicker furniture, and the pinks, yellows, greens, and blues of life in the tropics were splashed throughout the cozy living room and galley kitchen.

A bay window stretched the length of the bathroom wall, beneath which sat a freestanding tub with embroidered seashell towels draping over its scalloped edges. A hemp basket filled with bath products hung from a hook nearby. Painted in sand and coral tones, with tumbled marble flooring, the room reminded her of Atlantis. Just as welcoming and beautiful.

Although not as far from Logan.

She hadn't counted on a lot of this. Not the attachment to Michael, nor his to her, and certainly not her attraction to Logan.

Angel kicked off her shoes and walked into the bedroom. Another oversized bay window stretched the length of one wall, a long window seat before it. Shell- and sea creature–shaped throw pillows, again in the vibrant colors of the tropics, were scattered along the window seat's length and on the four-poster bed opposite it.

She gripped one of the posts and stared out at the unending ebb and flow of the sea.

He'd been enchanted; she had to remember that. His actions were not his own.

Hers, on the other fin…

It wasn't as if she'd never been attracted to anyone before, but they'd all been Mers. Hades, she'd *tried* to find one she could consider spending the rest of her life with, since her Immortality was directly dependent upon her getting married, but none of the men before Logan had affected her the way he did.

And she'd never been willing to compromise her desire for a love match with marrying for Immortality. The gods had made the crazy stipulation that women of the royal family had to marry before gaining eternal life, and she and her sisters had decided they weren't going to marry just anyone to get it. Eternal life was a long freakin' time to spend with someone, so they'd better love him.

Plus, their parents had a wonderful marriage, as did both of their brothers. The Tritone girls wanted their happily-forever-afters, too.

So she'd dated. And dated. And dated some more. She'd even lived with someone for a while, but knew now why she hadn't married him: there'd been no spark. Not like the one with Logan.

Angel curled a leg under her and sat on the corner of the bed. What was she going to do? The Council would question her objectivity the minute she returned home.

Hades, with all the sea birds on Poseidon's payroll, she was surprised she hadn't heard from one of The Council's winged spies already. Her brother had to know where she was and what she was doing.

What *was* she doing?

Angel took a deep breath. What she was doing was studying the Human race so she could become the Coalition's director. That was her primary focus and what she needed to remember.

And she needed to remember *why*.

Angel closed her eyes, that little stab of pain in her heart no longer catching her by surprise.

She needed the job for more than just saving the planet. Oh, she could kid herself all she wanted, but in moments like these when she was being honest with herself, she could admit it.

She needed to *be* somebody.

Someone special. Different from the rest of her family.

Fourth in birth order, Angel wasn't the oldest, the youngest, or the first girl, and with the arrival of her nieces and nephews, she had less than a penguin's chance in Hades of ascending the throne. She was just Angel.

A low beam of moonlight bounced off the mirror on the wicker dresser, flashing into her eyes, and she looked away, pulling a starfish pillow against her stomach.

Just Angel. How many times in her twenty-nine *selinos* had she heard that?

Oh, it's just Angel up to her strange studies.

It's just Angel bringing back yet another piece of Human flotsam.

It's just Angel wanting Reel to show her how his legs work...

She was sick of being *just Angel*. In a family of great achievers, she was low Mer on the pylon. Rod ruled their world. Reel guarded the vault that housed the economy's supply of diamonds from curious Humans. Mariana was becoming a sought-after artist, and Pearl had set every academic record there was.

But her... She was just Angel.

Just Angel.

She wanted to be Angel, the renowned scientist. Angel, the authority. Angel, the director of the Mer-Human Coalition.

Shaking her head, Angel got up and walked to the window. This study—this directorship—was her chance to be someone. She *had* to do it.

Angel squared her shoulders. Her whole life had been geared toward the study of Humans, and she couldn't let this chance slip through her fins.

Speaking of fins...

Angel looked at her legs, then glanced out the window. Not one shark fin broke the rolling plane of the water.

Here was something she could do and do right. Harry would expect her to be in those waves tomorrow night, and he'd do his damnedest to make sure she couldn't return—here *or* to Atlantis. So, if she wanted a prayer of staying longer—and being known as something other than Angel the Land-Bound—she could go into the water tonight. Thwart the pain-in-the-tail shark at his own game. She'd deal with the situation with Logan later.

Situation—ha.

Ah, well, denial could be good in times of stress.

Angel slid off the lacy yellow undergarment she wore so it wouldn't tear when her tail returned, but decided to keep the dress on until the last minute so she'd have something to wear for her return.

Denial or not, being naked around Logan definitely wasn't a good idea anymore.

—∿∿—

Logan shut Michael's door softly and took a deep breath as his fingers lingered on the doorknob. He and Michael had lain in the bed for over an hour, first reading the three train-themed books Michael had brought with him—twice—then talking about what it'd be like to ride on one.

Logan had had visions of Michael saying he and Christine had lived in one like those boxcar children. He wouldn't put it past Christine after the jail stunt.

But Michael hadn't said anything, and Logan hadn't asked. Frankly, he didn't want to know. Not now, while he was still mad/sad/upset about her having left their child with a social worker instead of contacting him.

Opening the French doors in his bedroom, Logan stepped onto the deck he'd built over the inlet to the Intercoastal on the north side of his property. His own peninsula. It'd been the biggest draw when he'd been looking for a home—protected waterway on one side, untamed ocean at the back, and a wraparound deck to enjoy both. Gripping the railing, he tried to do just that, letting the rise and fall of the waves calm him.

Even with all the craziness of his own unorthodox, itinerant childhood, his self-appointed parents had seen to the kids' education, and not once had the possibility of foster care raised its head. Oh, the Harsányis had had the ulterior motive of free labor, but they'd managed, in their self-serving way, to equip the kids with the necessary tools for success in life.

And he'd made it. More importantly, he had the security money represented and the sense of accomplishment in earning it on his own. He'd put enough away to never have to work again if that's what he wanted. He'd actually considered giving up his career after Michael arrived.

A light flicking off in the guesthouse drew his attention, and his gut tightened. If he *had* quit, there'd be no reason for Angel to watch Michael.

Warmth coursed through him as he thought of her there, on his property, in his home. Preparing for bed, maybe tucked in it, staring out at this very same view…

His thoughts went right back to their unbelievable kisses in the kitchen.

So much for tranquility.

Logan took a deep breath. He'd promised her it wouldn't happen again, and, to keep that promise, he had to stop reliving it. He'd never get that moment out of his head if he didn't.

He'd never get *her* out of his head.

But what was it about Angel that made all the other women before her fade into the background? And what the hell did that even mean?

Logan dragged his attention off the blue-shuttered window of the bungalow's living room, knowing perfectly well that, with the way the houses were arranged on the property, he had a view through the living room, down the hallway, and into her bedroom. And knowing perfectly well that he had no business remembering that—nor wondering about it. He tried to focus instead on the full moon rising in the night sky and what he was going to do about Michael.

A child needed a stable home. Emotional security. No one knew that better than he did.

Unlike Goran and Nadia, Logan was going to ensure his son had both.

Chapter 13

"ARE YOU OUT OF YOUR MIND?"

Angel heard the words the minute she felt something—no, make that some*one*—yank her beneath the waves.

And, fish! She didn't even have the full tail yet.

Angel twisted around, doubling back on herself, watching as amethyst shimmered along her lower half from her toes up, and she took her first aqua-breath just as her sea-vision returned.

Mariana was the tail-yanker. It figured.

"Let go, sis." As the last of her scales returned just below her navel, Angel flicked her tail to emphasize her point. Mariana still thought that because she was older, Angel had to listen to her. Angel had been trying to get out from under the big-sister thumb for *selinos*. When she was in charge of the Coalition, everyone would see her as an independent adult and take her seriously—at least, that was the hope.

Of course she had to *become* the head of the Coalition. Which she wasn't going to be able to do if Mariana got in her way.

A parade of skates flapped their wingtips as they swam by, their eyes bugging more out of their heads when they saw Mariana holding onto her. A baby skate fluttered over his mother to whisper in her spiracle while the mother shook her head—actually since she didn't have a neck, she shook her entire body—at Mariana. Angel could almost hear Mama "tsk-tsking."

Angel was right there with her.

Mariana let go, only to glare at the mother skate until the fish hustled her child away. Then Mariana crossed her arms over her shell-fillers—or rather, her breasts. Angel had decided that to pass as a Human, she needed to think like one.

And to have the time to get back to being one, this conversation had to be quick.

She kicked her tail and headed into deeper water where no Humans out for a late-night stroll in the moonlight could catch a glimpse of them. "What are you doing here, Mariana? And alone? The ocean isn't safe at night."

Mariana zipped up in front of her, and Angel had to stop swimming or bang into her. "I notice you're not too worried, Ang. Luckily we don't need to be. Amelia was flying by when you pulled your little climb-aboard escapade and she had Ernie threaten Harry about reporting him for going after you. Unlike Ernie, I would have just gone ahead and reported it, but, luckily, Harry got smart and hightailed it to bluer waters. Good thing I intercepted Amelia before anyone else did."

Mariana shoved her hands to her emerald-scaled hips. "I wish I could say the same for you. Going on an expedition? With a Human? *Really*, Angel? After specific orders from Rod to stay put? And *without* a harpoon. Honestly, what were you thinking?"

Angel mimicked Mariana's stance. Mariana was not going to intimidate her. "What I was thinking is that I'd start with a child and get *him* thinking about taking care of the planet. How does Rod expect his Coalition to get off the sea floor if we don't engage Humans in the conservation effort? Most adults are too ingrained in their ways to be open-minded about anything else."

Not to mention, they were always up for catching and studying a new species—a fact she wasn't going to mention since it'd only add magma to the well.

Mariana shook her head, her red hair swishing out around her shoulders. "You and your Human fixation. When are you going to let it go, Ang?"

"Let it go? Let it *go*?" Angel flapped her tail so quickly she churned the water into a small whirlpool and sent a school of silversides twirling off toward the Caymans. "Are you going to let your art go? Stop sculpting?"

"That's not the same thing, and you know it. *This* is dangerous."

Angel snorted. "Oh, right. And working with flowing lava is a swim in the reef. How many times have you been burned?"

"Is that what you want? To get burned?" Mariana shoved her hair back over her shoulder, but with the way the water was churning round them, it didn't stay. "Fine. Go beach yourself on a deserted island and lie out in the sun for too long, but for gods' sakes, don't do this, Ang. You know the penalty for letting Humans find out about us."

"Logan isn't going to find out."

It was Mariana's turn to snort. "Oh, right. Like the kid isn't going to say something. Not that it even matters. You tell one of them, you might as well scream it from their rooftops."

"Michael won't."

"Right."

Angel wasn't giving in on this. Attraction notwithstanding, she knew what she was doing here was the right thing to do. It was important to her. To the planet. Mariana wasn't going to win, not now. No matter how many times in the past her sister had managed to come out smelling like a hibiscus, this time, Angel had Right on her side.

"Look, Mariana. I know what I'm doing. I've studied them for *selinos*."

"Studying them and living among them are two different kettles of fish, Ang."

"You think I don't know that? Do you think I'm clueless as to what Logan would do if he were to find out I'm a Mer? I might not be Pearl, but give me credit for *some* brains, sis. Michael can keep a secret." Unlike the nosy pelican who'd sicced Mariana on her.

"So what do you hope to gain by this? Michael's a child. One child. He's not going to set the Human conservation movement on its ear or take the world by storm. How is that going to help you?"

If Angel had had any doubts—and she hadn't, not really, but if she had—Mariana's questions put them to rest.

She dove over her sister's head, angling toward the sea floor. "Mariana, where would the beach be without every grain of sand?" She grabbed a handful and let the grains sift through her fingers. "Sure, one little grain doesn't make a difference, but a beach has to start somewhere. Piece by piece, generation by generation, the grains pile up until there's a beach where none had existed before."

"So Michael is a grain of sand?"

"Exactly."

Mariana grabbed a handful and held it out toward Angel. "It takes a lot of grains to make a beach."

"Hey, I'm Immortal. I've got time."

"You're not Immortal yet."

Which took her thoughts right back to Logan's kisses in the kitchen…

Angel chose to focus on Mariana instead. "That's true, but I will be, and I have to start somewhere, Mare."

"Perhaps you ought to start with becoming Immortal before you worry about your metaphorical beaches, Ang. Have you made any progress on that front?"

Angel swam to the reef, skimming above delicate sea fans and avoiding the fire coral.

Progress? It depended on what Mariana wanted to call progress.

And with *whom*.

She wended around the sea plumes, startling a school of blue chromis who were searching for dinner, then caused a few dozen anemones to close up shop. She wished she could clam up, too. She didn't want to have this conversation.

"Or are you hoping this Human is your ticket to Immortality?" Mariana asked in her I-know-everything voice, catching up to her. "That's a really bad idea, you know. There are only three of us left to keep the bloodline a hundred percent Mer. I'm happy for our brothers, but we can't go around courting Humans. The magic would die out of our race in a few generations."

After seeing the dazed look on Logan's face when she'd sung, Angel wasn't so sure that would be a bad thing. She wouldn't expect Humans to want to do business with a race that could enthrall them with their voices.

And she wouldn't expect herself to want to be involved with a Human who'd *been* enthralled with her voice.

And yet, she was actually considering it…

Chapter 14

THE NEW ANGLE OF THE SUN THROUGH THE WINDOWS WOKE Angel too early the next morning. Unlike this bright, burning hit to her eyelids that jarred her awake in an instant, sunlight arrived differently in Atlantis: filtering through crevasses in the undersea cavern containing the city, bouncing off the golden walls and marble buildings, mixing with the refracted light of glowing magma to seep between her lashes and coax her awake.

The early-morning chirpings of robins outside her window didn't help matters either.

Stretching her legs and flexing her toes, Angel sat up on the bed with a yawn, realizing from the birds' startled looks that she was naked.

Again.

Blushing, Angel searched for the sheets to cover herself but had to settle for a pillow when she saw the twisted pile of bedding on the floor.

Why was she naked? Again?

Slowly, last night came back to her. Coercing cooperation out of Mariana had taken longer than she would have liked. It'd been catch-and-release there for a bit. Her sister was as tenacious as a game fish on a hook. Add in time she'd needed to dry her tail out to legs, and she hadn't gotten a lot of sleep. She'd been so bone-tired, she'd hardly been able to crawl into the bed.

Her nudity had nothing to do with that dream she'd

had of Logan covered in seawater and nothing else—well, except her.

Yeah, and she had some dry land in Atlantis to sell, too.

Angel got out of bed. Time to face the day and Logan. Now that the effects of Siren Song had had time to dissipate, things could be normal between them.

At least, that was the hope.

After a quick shower—not quite the same as a waterfall—Angel donned a set of new undergarments. She made sure to wear a bra this time and chose a pair of white capri pants—made in China, not Capri, which made no sense—a silky, Mediterranean blue, flouncy, half-halter top, and a pair of matching sandals. How much more fun it was to wear a full set of Human clothes than just the tops she normally wore. Maybe she ought to think about pajamas.

Once dressed, Angel headed up the stone path to Logan's lanai where another set of problems awaited her.

Should she go in the house? They hadn't covered this in her job description. What if both Logan and Michael were asleep? What if they weren't? What if this was something any other Human would know and she exposed herself by making the wrong decision?

"Well? What are you waiting for?" A flamingo raised her head from behind a hedgerow of hibiscus. "The kitchen's just inside and I watched him bring the groceries in a couple of days ago. He's got a few packages of prawns in there I wouldn't mind getting a hold of. What say you get me some of those and I'll keep your location a secret from your brother?"

"Ginger?" Great. Just what she needed. The laziest and most opportunistic flamingo in the Eastern

Hemisphere had just glommed onto her case study. And as for Ginger keeping a secret? Notsomuch. "What are you doing here? I thought birds of a feather flocked together and all that."

"Those Orlando chicks are too cliquey. Sometimes it's nice to be the only flamingo around." Ginger twirled her black-tipped beak, striking a pose that was ineffectual on females and downright ridiculous for anyone. Even a flamingo. To add insult to injury, the bird looked down from the back corner of her eyes. "So, what do you say? Prawns for silence?"

Angel tossed a swath of hair over her shoulder—so hard to get used to it hanging against her body instead of floating around her like kelp on a current. "I say that blackmail is a filthy practice, and if you're going to try it, you should first have a clean background. I know what you're doing with Roger, by the way. I think everyone except his mate does."

That took the stuffing out of the bird. Ginger deflated back to normal size and quickly set her plumage to rights. "Fine. You don't have to get snippy about it. I just wanted some prawns. Humans have taken all the good ones around here and I'm not a big fan of fish fry. It gets boring after a while."

"I know all about Human fishing practices, Ginger, among other things. That's why I'm here, and I'd appreciate if you'd keep quiet so I have the chance to make a difference."

"You don't want your brother to find out, do you?"

"I'd prefer if he didn't, but I'm a grown Mer. I'm allowed to live my life. If he does, I'll deal with it. But until then, I'm going to try to accomplish something."

"Oh? Is that what they're calling it these days?" The flamingo clacked her beak. "I *accomplished* something just last night."

Angel didn't bother dignifying Ginger's innuendo with an answer. She turned back to the door to decide what to do.

The decision was rendered moot when Michael came running toward her. "Hey!" he said, unlocking the door, Rocky dangling from his hand. His hat slipped backward, but he caught it before it fell off. "You still have legs!"

Angel glanced into the kitchen. Thank the gods Logan wasn't in sight. "I couldn't very well visit you with a tail, could I?"

"Sure you could. We could go swimming." Michael tugged her hand, and she had no choice but to follow him in. "Can you teach me to surf, Angel? I think it'd be cool. Rainbow said I'm too little, but I bet if you helped me, it'd be okay. 'Cause you can swim and all. And I beat Billy in the beststroke at the Y. It was in deep water, too. So? Can we? Go surfing?"

"Let's try something a little less dangerous today, okay, sport?" Logan said what she'd been trying to as he entered, his hair wet from his shower.

There was an image to make a girl's knees weak.

Then she got a good look at his toned legs beneath sand-colored shorts, the way his biceps stretched the sleeves of his navy T-shirt, the sexy way his hair swept against his collar, and realized she was in deep water. A few hours apart hadn't stemmed the tide of attraction she felt.

Thankfully, Michael's elbow bumped her and she refocused as the little guy turned the rim of his cap to the front before facing his father. "So what can we do, Logan?"

"Well, first, why don't we have breakfast before you go running off? You did just get here, you know." Logan pulled out a chair at the breakfast bar and motioned for her to take it without any of the sexy, hooded-eye thing from last night, nor a single hint that their intimate body parts had had a passing acquaintance with each other. Good. The Siren Song had worn off. She could breathe a little easier.

"I know I just got here," Michael replied. "But I didn't want to get in your way. Rainbow said you worked really hard to keep this house and I shouldn't make you lose it."

Angel didn't have to look at Logan to know how those words hurt. What mother would say such things to her child? What had Logan ever done to her to make her think that? Anyone could tell the man was thrilled to be a father just by looking at him.

Which she was determined not to do.

Being up close and personal as she'd been last night had been more than enough. Then there was that dream she'd had—

"So, what's for breakfast?" Probably not the best idea to invite herself to eat, but she caught the relief on Logan's face as the conversation changed direction. Then there was the smile he sent her way, and, well, best not to dwell too long on that.

Luckily, the meal wasn't all that different from what she was used to, but she shied away from dunking cereal in milk. She could have watered-down food any time at home, so she opted, instead, for the wonderfully fresh fruit Logan served and her first taste of bacon. Hot and crunchy, it became her newest second favorite thing about the Human world after wet, hot kisses…

Focus, Tritone.

She was trying to. Really trying to.

"So, what do you want to do today?" Logan put the last pan away and flipped the dish towel over his shoulder—and it stayed there.

Angel bit back the sigh. Fabric tended to float all over her condo; it was a real pain in the tail to keep the place neat.

And that was the only reason she was sighing.

"You don't have to work, Logan?" That too-familiar smile lit up Michael's face. "You can come with us?"

Logan lowered a glass of orange juice from his lips and shook his head. "I was taking off today to find day-care for you, remember? Since I don't have to do that anymore, the day is all yours."

"But I thought Angel was going to babysit me."

Logan's shoulders dropped ever so slightly. "Well—"

"I need your dad to show me around, Michael, you know?" Angel jumped in before Michael could hurt his father's feelings any more. "To tell me what you like to eat"—and pray it wasn't difficult to make since, although she might be a whiz with a magma grill and spatula, Human appliances defeated her—"and show me the house. That sort of thing."

"*I* can tell you what I like to eat. I'm six now, not a baby." Michael crossed his arms and jutted out his chin—and looked exactly like his father again.

"I was including Angel, Michael." Logan crossed

his legs and leaned back against the counter, his T-shirt tightening against his abdomen. "We can all spend the day together. What do you think?"

That got a smile out of the little boy. And the high-five to his dad got a smile out of Logan.

And a sigh out of her. Which, thankfully, she managed to keep very soft.

"Cool! Let's go see the manatees."

"Manatees?" *That* got her wayward thoughts off things they weren't supposed to be considering anyway. While Angel loved the gentle creatures—especially this coastal contingent who were the ones responsible for discovering the coup attempt against Rod a few *selinos* ago—she couldn't risk even one drop of saltwater reaching her legs. Not in front of Logan, and definitely not in public.

"Michael, I think I'd like to steer clear of the ocean for a bit, if you don't mind."

"Actually, Angel…" Logan addressed her directly, and silly her, she couldn't hide the shiver that action sent through her.

Good gods. What was wrong with her? She was a scientist, for gods' sakes. She should have some control over herself.

Yes, she'd proved that *so* well last night in this very kitchen … "The refuge is on the river," Logan continued as if there were no inappropriate thoughts diving through her mind. "The manatees are brought there for rehabilitation before being set free to find their way back to the open sea. We won't be anywhere near the ocean, and there aren't any sharks."

Sharks were the least of her worries now, but a river changed everything. Manatees could swim in both saltwater and freshwater, but freshwater wouldn't make her tail return. "Well then, that sounds like a plan. I'm in."

She would, however, have to make sure the manatees didn't blow her cover. The last thing she needed was them crowding around her and cluing the Humans in that something odd was going on.

Speaking of odd…

A quick flash of pink made her glance out the window. Ginger stared back with a pointed swish of her head toward the refrigerator.

"Betcha didn't know sailors thought that manatees were mermaids," Michael whispered loud enough for even Ginger to hear.

A beak-shaking, neck-undulating laugh caused the flamingo to fall off the one leg she'd been standing on.

"You don't say." Angel knocked the rim of Michael's cap down so he wouldn't see her glare out the window. Of course she knew that myth. Mers still laughed themselves silly over that bit of Human ignorance. Nothing against manatees, but when Mers could shift into sleek, graceful, *fast*-moving dolphins, why-in-the-sea would anyone think they'd choose a meandering sea cow?

"It's true. Logan told me. 'Course he also said mermaids don't exist." Michael broke into peals of laughter and Logan joined in, although obviously not getting the *real* joke.

Although the real joke was on her.

She could proclaim port and starboard that she was a scientist, that she had an agenda, that she was here for one reason and one reason only, but when Logan smiled like that, she was all woman—staring at a gorgeous man who had held her and kissed her and made her *want*…

"The sailors had probably been at sea for way too long if they found manatees attractive," Logan said when Michael left to get suntan lotion. "Still, you can't blame them. Who wouldn't want to believe in mermaids?"

"You would?" she asked breathlessly. Could it be that easy? Were Humans ready to accept that Mers existed? Was Logan?

Logan chuckled and lifted a glass of orange juice to his lips. "Well, sure. Who wouldn't? Beautiful, sexy women who whisk men off to deserted islands and make love to them all day? What's not to like about th—"

His eyes met hers and the glass hovered by his mouth, tiny ripples sloshing the juice around.

Was that look generated by Siren Song? Could it last this long? Or was that his honest-to-gods reaction?

Angel licked her lip. Oh yeah. She could see making love on a deserted island, no one around for leagues. The play of the surf and the sand against their skin—

Wait a minute. *That's* what he thought of her kind? How could he believe that? How could he *want* that? It made Mers sex objects. Not feeling, thinking people with hopes and dreams and aspirations and—

And she was taking this too seriously. Kitchen escapades aside, mermaids were obviously still a myth to him. A legend. A fantasy.

Oh to be his fantasy...

Logan cleared his throat and gulped a mouthful of the juice, his eyes suddenly focused on something outside. Angel hoped it wasn't Ginger trying to mime another command about the prawns. That was the last thing Logan needed to see.

Or...

She glanced down.

Okay, *those* were the last things Logan needed to see. Apparently bras weren't designed to be nipple armor. She'd have to make a note of that. When her hands were steady enough to hold a pen.

"Okay, let's go." Michael, thank the gods, bounded back into the room with all the exuberance and hormonal-fog-clearing ability of any child. "I'm ready."

He wasn't the only one.

Logan peeled his gaze off the panes in the French door and focused it on the white cabinets over the micro-wave. Then at the faded-denim curtain the designer had insisted he needed over the window. At the maroon-and-navy, rope-design tile along the top of the backsplash the same designer had insisted on.

It was no use. His eyes wanted to return to Angel. She looked like… He didn't know what she looked like in that outfit. *Perfect* was the only word that came to mind.

Her long, blonde hair—the soft, silky hair he'd felt trailing over different parts of his anatomy yesterday and wouldn't mind having along *other* parts of his body—hung to her hips, damp loose waves making him think of nights spent in wild abandon. Her face, with those rarest-of-color eyes, was breathtakingly beautiful. Her smile, so generous and quick, a Cupid's bow of a mouth and the dimple high in her cheek… the woman was utterly stunning.

And he'd had her up against the cabinets, devouring her with his lips and wanting to do the same with the rest of his body.

His gaze dropped to her breasts, round and full beneath her sexy top. He remembered *exactly* how her nipples had stood out against the dress last night, how they'd felt against his chest, and if he wasn't wrong, he could still seen their outline.

Nothing was designed to drive him to his knees quicker than the sight of her hardened nipples—except maybe it was that lip-licking thing she did. But normally he wasn't a breast man. If asked, he would have said the smile and eyes caught his attention first, followed by the rest of a woman's beauty, both inside and out.

He was going to have to amend that when it came to Angel. He honestly couldn't say what it was that drew him to her more. Of course, he hadn't had the benefit of seeing other women he'd dated naked before he'd started dating them—

Logan took a deep breath. It'd been damned hard to exorcise that image of her bare body from his mind last night.

"Are you ready, Logan?"

Michael looked at him with an expectantly hopeful smile.

Oh he was ready, all right, but he was going to fail in the father department if he didn't get his mind and his eyes off Angel.

"Sounds like a plan to me, sport." He tapped the rim of Michael's cap, praying he hadn't just agreed to something he'd come to regret. But from the smile on Angel's face and Michael's "*Cool!*" as he bounced out, it couldn't be that bad.

He couldn't get to the wildlife refuge quick enough.

If there was one thing guaranteed to cool his libido, it was the sight of nonmermaid-like, elephantine animals.

Harry swung his tail back and forth, lining up his troops a hundred meters offshore. The sun had crept over the horizon, beginning the countdown to sunset.

Angel's time on land was limited.

Harry knew it, and he knew that Angel knew it. And he knew that she knew that he knew it.

It made the anticipation that much sweeter.

"So how long do we have to wait here?" A.C., the most recent addition to the pack he'd recruited off the coast of New Jersey, didn't like taking things on faith, and the bad-ass attitude was starting to piss Harry off. The kid thought he knew it all, but then, the young always did.

Harry eyed the Hammerhead's pristine tail. For a self-titled tough guy, A.C. was short on battle scars. He'd had an entourage, which was what had caught Harry's attention in the first place, but the shark wasn't living up to his own press. Nah, Mr. A.C. Hammer could take that punk demeanor and stick a harpoon in it. Harry was the boss here. He called the shots, and if the kid didn't learn to take orders, he'd be out on his tail.

This time, Harry chose to ignore the punk. Let him know he wasn't as important as he thought.

"Okay, guys, here's the plan." Harry eyed the rest of the Hammerheads he'd assembled. Seven of the most battle-scarred, meanest bounty-hunting 'Heads he could find. "We're going in, in sphere formation, the opening closest to shore. That's where we'll herd her, but no one takes a bite."

"What the fuck?" A.C. added a swagger to his stroke. "I didn't sign on to be a shepherd."

"You'll be whatever in Hades I say you are and like it." Harry went snout to snout with the kid.

Harry's was bigger—and as usual, size mattered.

But the kid didn't back down. "So if we're not taking a bite, what are we going to do with her? She'll start singing bloody murder, and we'll end up with a feeding frenzy around us."

"You only get a feeding frenzy if you actually bite her, punk." Harry considered shredding the kid just to make a point to the others, but he'd recruited lean and couldn't afford to lose one member of the formation. Angel, for all her Human studies, was one smart Mer when it came to tactical maneuvers. All the Tritones were. Their father, Fisher, had seen to it.

Probably for just this reason. Sharks weren't known for taking direction well from Mers. Especially when the members of The Oceanic Council didn't give them one ounce of say in governing the oceans. Not even a seat on The Council. Even after Vincent had saved the day all those *selinos* ago—much as it pained Harry to admit it— he'd thought The Council would recognize the rights of *chondrichthyes*. But no.

"So what are we supposed to do with her?" Gianni, another recruit, asked.

Great. Just what the fuck he needed. A mutiny of the bounty hunters.

"She's our ticket in. The Council will realize we mean business."

"So we're not going to eat her?" Lou, a hunter lured out of retirement by the promise of a royal target, started frothing at the mouth—never a good sign. "Then why the fuck did you trawl me along, Har? This is bullsharkshit."

Okay, so maybe Harry hadn't exactly explained what this job would entail. But, dammit, he'd needed the best, and Lou was it. Too bad Lou had settled down to raise little 'Heads. But that's what you did when you landed a trophy wife apparently. Harry couldn't see it. Lou's mate had more air between her eyes than water, but hey, to each his own.

"Look, we can eat her, just not right off the beach. Give me some bargaining power, and if The Council doesn't cave, you each get a bite. But if we turn her into chum right away, we lose any hope of negotiation and will put ourselves on the endangered list. Fisher will be back in the hot seat and rally his troops out in full force, so let's not do anything rash."

"Rash?" A.C. rolled his eyes. "Rash was following you off on this wild grouper chase. I'm outta here."

Harry flicked his tail, propelling himself in front of the deserter. He inhaled enough water to inflate his gills to three times their normal size. He could do intimidating better than any punk kid.

"You aren't going anywhere. You signed on for this, and you'll finish it." Harry grinned, all of his teeth gleaming white. He knew because he'd paid those Spanish hogfish to do an extra good job. Intimidation could work wonders in a showdown. He wasn't about to get beat by this piece of floating garbage.

"Before this is over, The Council *will* acknowledge

us. They *will* hear us out, and they *will* pay attention."
He stared A.C. back into the lineup. "It's time we sharks
got what we deserve."

Chapter 15

THE MANATEES WERE BEAUTIFUL. ANGEL HAD ALWAYS thought so. So serene. Content to bob among the shoreline vegetation, these creatures never seemed bothered by anything. They took life as it came, floating with the waves, bumping into each other for comfort. Talk about babysitters. Any child of the sea was always safe in their care.

She still kept in touch with the herd her parents had hired to watch her and her siblings when they'd vacationed off this coast when they were younger. Matter of fact, she thought she recognized a familiar face or two, but luckily, by pretending to have a pebble in her shoe, she had the chance to ask the manatees to treat her as they would any other Human.

The birds, however, were another matter.

"Can you talk to animals? I saw that in a movie." Michael asked as a cardinal flitted down from the trees to tweet at them for the seventh time, swooping from one side of the path to the other, garnering her more interest than she cared for.

"Of course she can't, Michael," Logan said, swatting as the bird almost flew into his hair. Uh oh. It was a good thing Logan didn't understand the shrill chirps the bird sent him. "Doctor Doolittle is just a story. People can't talk to animals."

Well, actually they could. And she did. Sea creatures and birds. She could understand most languages but couldn't vocalize in all of them, so in the interest of interspecies harmony, all creatures capable of doing so used the universal language of English when not in the presence of Humans.

Thank the gods, though, that the cardinal hadn't lapsed into it, which meant her message had segued from the manatee community to the winged one.

It also meant that Rod would know what she was up to fairly soon if he didn't already. Oh, well. There was nothing she could do about it except get all her ducks in a row and give him one kick-tail pitch for the director's position.

The cardinal was overly tenacious. Probably the first time he'd seen a Mer, or maybe it was the royalty thing. While Angel was used to a starstruck attitude from youngsters and usually chatted with them to show she was just like them, she couldn't do that now. Now, she just wanted him to go away.

"He sure seems to like you, Angel." Michael pointed out what she hadn't wanted his father to notice.

"How about if we chirp along with him, Michael? Maybe he wants a couple of backup singers." And she could politely tell the bird he was causing her trouble.

"Okay."

Cardinal chirps were fairly simple and weren't really singing. If she kept her part short and sweet, her voice wouldn't have any effect on Logan or the other men around.

Thank the gods a warbler hadn't sought them out. Logan had already commented on the men falling at her feet yesterday; he'd definitely notice if dozens of them started following her around.

Roger knew that voice.

The crane lifted his red-topped head from the spilled popcorn in the garden by the penguin enclosure. He'd hate to be those poor, flightless birds. Sandhill cranes had such a better life—a life that was seriously in trouble if that was who he thought it was.

"I told you Angel was here." Ginger nudged him with her sexy beak. He loved the sensuous curves in it. "She's going to ruin everything, Roger. You have to do something."

He certainly did. He had a good thing going with Ginger. The wife didn't suspect a thing; after all, he agreed with her every time she laughed about what dodos flamingos were.

If she only knew what flamingos were capable of. Ginger in particular.

"I'll handle it. Don't worry your pretty pink feathers about it, Ginger." He ruffled his wings, girding himself for the task. "Why don't you head back to the beach? The Humans who work here are a little too interested in a free-roaming flamingo. We wouldn't want you to get locked up, would we?"

"Depends on who's doing the locking up, Rog." Ginger cocked her head with that half smile he loved.

He swatted her breast feathers. "Get going, doll. You're mine and no one else's. I'll take care of our interloper."

He knew just the fish to tell to get the job done.

Logan had to admit that having Angel around made life easier. Because of her, Michael was chattier, more outgoing, and more willing to hold his hand, so if he had to order his eyes off her curves every other minute, it was worth it.

Logan let go of Michael's hand so his son could hop along a low stone wall by the path, and he also—finally—let go of the angst he'd carried around for the past four days. Things had been so awkward between Michael and him. Stilted. Tense. Due, no doubt, to his cluelessness about raising a child and Michael's sense of abandonment by Christine, not to mention the "complication" thing Christine had probably scarred him with. Logan had tried to make Michael feel at home, to show him he cared, but the lack of good role models in his own upbringing had him second-guessing every decision.

Angel must have fared better with her parents; she knew just how to act with Michael. How to talk to him. To joke and tease and laugh and play paper animals with him. And how to get Michael to become comfortable with him. He owed her for that.

"Come on, Angel! You do it!" Michael scrambled up the steps cut into a flat-topped rock, sat in an enclosure that had obviously been designed for hyperactive six-year-olds, and patted the space next to him. "Sit here! You can see everything!"

Angel licked her lips. Again. Unconsciously sexy, yes, but she did it when she was nervous or unsure. Logan wouldn't have realized the reason except for the accompanying sideways glances she gave him beneath her lashes whenever she did it. Those, he couldn't help but notice.

She was giving him one now.

"Need a hand up?"

Relief sparkled in her aqua eyes. "Thank you."

He interlaced his fingers and caught her foot. It was small, just like her. And when he lifted her and she was so slight, protective instincts he never knew he had flared to life.

The adorable backside in front of him had something else flaring.

Then her hair brushed his face as she moved and Logan just had to inhale. Deeply. The floral shampoo he'd bought for the guesthouse mixed with the hibiscus that seemed to be her personal scent, and suddenly Logan wanted to bury his face in her hair like he had last night.

He remembered how it'd felt between his fingers, sweeping his cheek, trailing over his arms. How he'd wanted it wrapped around him with nothing between them…

"Come on, Angel. You're close!"

Michael said the words he'd love to utter.

And also reminded him where he was and what was going on.

What *was* going on?

Angel climbed to the top, and Logan watched the two of them sit there. She was a stranger. They didn't know her. By rights, Michael shouldn't be this comfortable with her. By rights, Logan shouldn't be this *un*comfortable with her.

So what was it about Angel that had worked this magic on him and his son?

"What are those, Angel?" Michael pointed beyond the trees toward something Logan couldn't see.

"Egrets."

"And that? Is that a chameleon?"

"No, sweetie. It's an iguana. It looks more like that anole from last night."

"Oh. And what about that?"

"A sandhill crane."

"It's awfully big. Is that why the trucks are called cranes? They're big, too."

"You know? I don't know. Maybe your dad does."

Two pairs of expectant eyes turned his way, and Logan smiled at them. At Michael because he loved him and at Angel because—

"Logan?" Michael's question stopped that thought at the same time a memory surfaced.

"Ridiculous." It was. He couldn't have those kinds of feelings for her. He'd just met her. And as for that memory...

"Logan?" Angel's voice wasn't the sweet one she'd used with his son. "You want to rethink your last comment?"

He looked at her, her hair shining like a halo around her, but her face was anything but angelic. "What?"

"That last comment. I think there's a better way to answer your son's question."

Answer Michael's question? He hadn't answered—

Michael's crestfallen expression said otherwise.

Oh, shit. *Ridiculous.* He *had* answered him—at least in Michael's eyes. And in Angel's, too, apparently.

"No, Michael, I didn't mean your question was ridiculous. A thought I had was ridiculous. It had nothing to do with your question. I think you're on to something. The birds were around long before the trucks, so, sure, that could be why trucks are called that."

It was a patchy repair job, but it seemed to do the trick. He got a halfhearted smile from Michael and a bigger one from Angel—and, no, he wouldn't dwell on her smile nor the thought that had prompted his *ridiculous* comment. As for that memory…

No way Nadia had been right. His fortune-telling mother was a master at inventing predictions. Nothing he'd ever seen growing up could convince him that she'd actually had psychic ability, especially when she'd come up with a prediction that he would fall in love with a woman from the sea.

Just because Angel had climbed out of the sea and onto his boat didn't mean Nadia was right. It certainly didn't mean he was in love with Angel either.

That's what he kept telling himself as Michael and Angel climbed off the rock. Nadia's prediction and Angel's appearance were coincidences.

He held out his hand, thankful Michael still wanted to hold it. But that was the only body part he was offering to anyone, anywhere. No more offering to help Angel up. No more brushing by her. No more inhaling her scent.

He didn't care what Nadia said. Falling in love with someone at first sight wasn't normal, and Logan was all about normal.

Chapter 16

ANGEL TOOK ONE LAST PASS BY THE MANATEE ENCLOSURE AS
they headed toward the park's exit. She'd loved seeing
everyone, but the fact that they were in pens saddened
her—and reminded her exactly what Humans were capable of. Oh, yes, this facility was for the animals' benefit, and visitor money enabled the caretakers to care for
the manatees, but other Humans weren't so altruistic.
That's why she was determined to succeed. For everyone's benefit.

The smiles Logan had given her today when she'd suggested Michael hold his hand were a personal benefit.

"So, Michael, what do you think of the manatees?"
she asked as they were departing, not dwelling on personal *anything* when it came to Logan. Well, trying
not to.

Michael wrinkled his nose. "Manatees don't look like
mermaids. Mermaids are pretty."

A smile replaced the thoughtful look on Logan's
face. He obviously found Michael's comment funny, but
Angel took the comment for what it was: a compliment.
"Perhaps not to you, but they're beautiful to other manatees. And they're very curious and gentle creatures."

"If they're so nice, why do they have all those marks
on them? The lady said people did that."

Pain speared Angel's heart. *This* was why she was
here. Why she'd stay as long as she could and do

whatever it took to get Humans thinking. And with Michael and other children asking questions, adults *could* learn.

"That's true, Michael, but people don't mean to harm them. It's just that manatees move so slowly, and not everyone pays attention when they're boating."

She raised her voice so others around them could hear her. It couldn't hurt to start getting her message out now to adults and children alike. "Sometimes it's hard to see what's happening in front of you if something moves too slowly. Then, by the time you do see it, it's damaged. You have to learn to be more careful in the future so you don't do it again."

"Sounds stupid."

"Michael, that's not a nice thing to say to Angel," Logan said, and Angel did admit to a thrill that he was defending her—not that he needed to. She knew what Michael meant.

Michael shot his father a very frustrated, eye-rolling, parents-know-nothing look. "Not Angel. *People*. Manatees live in the ocean and people don't so they should be more careful."

If only the adults could grasp that idea as quickly, her work here would be done. Then she wouldn't have to worry anymore about this attraction that was growing as the hours passed and what it could mean for her future.

A family walked by them going the opposite direction, the little girl swinging from her parents' hands. Michael's head whipped around to watch her as they passed.

Angel met Logan's gaze. Children weren't difficult to understand. Logan smiled at her and nodded. Together they raised their hands and swung Michael between them.

It took the little boy a surprised second before he realized what they were up to, then he shouted, "Cool! Again!"

"Sure thing, sport." Logan's laughter was as infectious as his son's.

And the effect of all that love and happiness made Angel late on the upswing. Michael's takeoff and landing ended up being wobbly, which made Angel stumble over her own feet.

Damned independent action.

She tried to regain her balance, but an exuberant child, new appendages, and the uneven surface conspired against her. Luckily, Logan had quick reflexes and managed to catch her. Again.

Tingles shot through her.

Again.

"You okay?" he asked, his eyes darkening.

Again.

And, this time, it wasn't—as evidenced by his widening pupils—due to Siren Song.

"Um…" What was the question? She was trying hard to remember, but the intensity of his gaze unnerved her. More like unraveled her. All her good intentions, all her arguments against feeling this way, all the reasons she shouldn't give one iota of consideration to leaning in and grabbing hold and pulling herself up against him, of wrapping her arms around him and reliving every second of last night and taking it to its ultimate conclusion—

"Angel?" Logan whispered, his fingers letting go of her arm but not moving away. Actually, he stroked her skin with the backs of his fingertips.

And maybe she did move a step closer.

Well why not? What was the big deal? Scientists

were people, too. She could keep her work separate from her private life.

Rod was going to be annoyed with her anyway. And it wasn't as if anyone had to know what she and Logan did. He was willing enough. It'd only take the smallest of movements to be in his arms and—

"Can we get some ice cream? I want Moose Trail this time."

And there was a child present.

Not to mention, a crowd. Plus Logan thought she was Human, was here to care for his son, and had tripped— and *not* because her legs were new appendages for her. Going into any kind of relationship merited honesty, and she was sure he'd have an issue with her tail.

Then a mynah bird flew above Logan's head, landing on the fence behind him, and her decision was made for her.

It was Rich, that son-of-a-Mer. Mynahs, and specifically *this* one, were the bane of Mer existence. Of all the birds who could let the catfish out of the net about their ability to speak to Humans, mynahs alone had the utter gall and deviousness to take advantage of Mer fears, always threatening to do it. Rich was the Top Bird in this neck of the woods.

The last thing she needed was for him to get an inkling of the battle going on inside her or to start talking to Logan.

From the way Rich was tilting his glossy black head, she had cause for worry. While rules were rules, Rich flew to his own tune; she didn't need him relating the current series of events to her brother or spilling the shells to Logan.

"I'm, uh, fine, Logan. Thanks." She straightened up,

using Michael's shoulder to steady herself and tried to pull herself out of Logan's grip without making it seem obvious. To him or the bird. Neither needed a clue about her feelings.

Logan's fingers tightened, and a quick scan of her face ended with his gaze lingering on her lips. So she licked them. Why? Oh, maybe because they'd suddenly become as parched as the South Aral Sea.

And they got even more so when Logan sucked in a ragged breath, his eyes narrowing.

He had really nice eyes. Deep and dark and intense. Eyes she could drown in—not that she could drown, but still—

"Logan? Can we? Get ice cream?"

Thank the gods for Michael.

The mynah snorted, which focused her scattered attention back where it needed to be because she really didn't need the mynah carrying tales to The Council.

One quick swipe of her tongue over her lips—and, yes, she couldn't help a brief smile as Logan's fingers tightened yet again— and Angel forced herself to break eye contact and step away.

"Ice cream sounds good to me." Angel glanced surreptitiously at Rich, who was shaking his head. That didn't bode well. "But first, why don't we see if we can find the facilities."

"What are fa-cil-i-tees? Are they like manatees?" Michael scrunched up his face.

"The restroom, Michael." Logan indicated an arrow pointing in the direction Rich was also pointing.

"But I'm not tired!" Michael stamped his foot. "I don't want to take a nap. I want ice cream."

Logan leaned down to whisper in his ear, then a smile spread across Michael's face. "Ooooh. Okay. Me, too."

Rich sighed, loud and put-upon, but took off anyway, headed in the direction they were going.

"I'll meet you back here," Angel said, finagling for a few minutes with the bird, waving until they were around the corner.

"What do you want?" she whispered as she skirted the door to the ladies' room and leaned against the stucco building.

"Your sister sent me."

"Mariana wouldn't send a mynah." Least of all the biggest mouth north *and* south of the Equator. Her sister had promised to keep her plan a secret for as long as possible; *this* species was not known for keeping anyone's secrets. The exact opposite, in fact.

Rich perched his wings on his hips. "Well she did, so live with it. Do you want to hear what I have to say or not?"

"Fine. Just keep your voice down. What is it?"

"She said your brother knows what you've done, but there's been some flare-up in the Middle East. Oil spilling by the bargeful, so the High Councilman is going to have to Travel-Chamber it over there. She gives you a few days for the reprieve and thought you'd want to know."

"Thank the gods for small favors." Oops. Angel cringed. She certainly didn't think the gods had caused an oil spill so she could accomplish her goal. That'd be placing too much importance on her mission from their point of view, and the last thing she wanted was any importance—or focus—put on her trip. Not to mention, any more environmental damage.

"Or you could thank *me* for delivering the news." Rich tilted his head sideways and nodded at the peanut vendor.

The bird worked for peanuts? It was cheap enough. She bought a small container with the change Michael had given her after he'd bought a soft pretzel—lovely, spongy confection—and poured a handful onto a bench.

Rich just looked at her.

Angel rolled her eyes and set the container there as well.

"Pleasure doin' business with ya," the mynah said.

"I'm all ready for ice cream now." Michael ran over to her, stopping quickly when he saw the bird so close to her. "Cool!"

The mynah lifted his head and, with half a peanut in his beak, mimicked Michael. "Cool!"

Michael then started a list of words, hopping up and down with every response from Rich. But Angel wouldn't put it past the bird to throw something else into the exchange, so she was happy when Logan said, "We should get going, Michael, if you want that ice cream."

The bird winked at her as they left.

Chapter 17

LOGAN COULD PUT THIS DAY ON HIS LIST OF GREAT ONES. Michael had obviously had a wonderful time, and Angel...

The woman was beautiful, knew a hell of a lot about the creatures the park rescued, and Michael obviously adored her.

And, Nadia's prediction notwithstanding, Logan was coming to adore her as well. He honestly couldn't say when he'd enjoyed a day—and a woman—more.

He followed Angel and his son across the parking lot and clicked the remote opener so Michael could climb in the car, wondering if Angel would sit in the back like yesterday, or the front as she'd done on the ride over.

Then she tossed her hair over her shoulder again and he wanted to ask her to sit up front. Right next to him.

Every time she'd done that today, every time her eyes crinkled with laughter or she'd sung with the birds, he'd found himself remembering last night.

"Angel." Her name slipped out before he thought better of it.

She reached the car and looked up at him with those expressive eyes. "Yes?"

"I—"

She did that thing again with her hair where it draped over her shoulder, dancing along her arm, a curl circling forward into the inside of her elbow. "What is it, Logan?"

It was powerful.

It was intense.

It was potent.

Different than last night, but no less compelling.

He slid his fingers up the path her hair had taken, feeling the velvet smoothness of her skin, hearing the slight catch of her breath that told him he wasn't wrong to do this. Seeing the quick, shallow rise and fall of her breasts that he wasn't feeling any guilt about looking at.

He stepped closer.

Her chin tilted, and she shook her hair again, sending more of the silky tresses sliding over his skin. "Is there something you needed?"

Oh, yeah. There was.

Logan leaned in.

—⁓—

Okay, maybe she could have rephrased that. But why, when his gaze was a physical burn on her skin?

He was going to kiss her.

Angel closed her eyes, half afraid she was dreaming this.

Half afraid she wasn't.

Today had been leading up to this. Every shared smile, every look…

And she couldn't blame it on her voice. Not this time.

Logan's hands closed on her arms. Lifted her up just a little. Enough to raise her to her toes. The ones that were beginning to tingle again.

His warm breath fluttered across her face, the scent of him surrounding her, blocking out the sweet smell of the jasmine nearby.

"Angel," she swore she heard him whisper, his lips just a breath from hers. So close she could almost feel them.

And then he stopped.

As if a door had slammed, she felt him pull back from the moment, and she opened her eyes.

His gaze met hers. His hot, intense, searing gaze.

"No," he whispered, and this time she was sure he pulled back.

She tensed. What in the gods' names did he mean by *no*?

His tongue flicked out to lick his lips and Angel thought she'd melt right there.

"Not like this."

Somewhere deep inside her, she found her voice. "Like this?" Deep, husky, shaky… but definitely hers.

"Here. In broad daylight." He shook his head. "After last night you deserve some finesse, and with Michael here," he nodded to the back seat, "it's not the right time. Or place." His fingers slid up her arms, caressing her shoulders, and Angel lowered herself back onto her feet. Back to the earth. The analogy made her want to cry.

But then Logan tipped her chin up so she could see his eyes. "When I kiss you again, Angel, it's going to be special. The right moment." He wet his lips again, his eyes doing a quick flick over hers. "Perfect."

She was melting again. As if she'd stepped into the ocean and her legs were turning back into a tail, sweeping the support out from under her, and she clung to him.

Perfect? Oh, she could go for perfect. The truth was, right now was pretty damned perfect. But if Logan wanted the moment to be more special, she could wait.

Because he'd said *when* he kissed her again, not *if*.

She could do *when*.

She *would* do when.

―――――

The setting sun's rays filtered through the blinds in Logan's office later that evening. When a streak of sunlight landed on the same line-item in the report he'd been looking at for the past half hour, he gave up. Shoving away from the desk, he finally admitted that he couldn't concentrate. On work, that was. Angel, on the other hand…

Yeah, he could concentrate on Angel.

Not that it was hard to do since she and Michael were right outside his office window, tossing a Whiffle ball between them.

All he had to do was look up for a front-row view of the beautiful woman he couldn't stop thinking about. She ran to catch the ball and her pants hugged that perfect ass and her gorgeous hair spilled down her back. Her laughter was as warm as the summer sun, her smile as sparkly as the waves, and Logan no longer gave a damn about the prospectus he was supposed to be taking a look at.

First she'd been naked, then he'd kissed her, now she was bending and moving and twirling and running outside his window like a beautiful painting come to life. And her laugh—every tinkling, musical note slid over his skin like scented oil, so heady he felt like a teenager again.

Jeez. He was back to spouting sonnets.

Thankfully, the phone rang.

"Hardington."

"Someone's working late." His best friend. The guy had perfect timing. "Or did the kid paint the garage with a gallon of ice cream? Get his head stuck it the stair rail? Decorate your truck with markers?"

"You'd love that, wouldn't you, Richardson?"

"Hey, then you'd finally get why I had to cancel on you at the last minute for the game. It's not like I wanted to miss box seats. Which, by the way, is why I'm calling. Can you get a babysitter on such short notice? I'd say Beth could watch him, but she took ours to her mother's. I'm lovin' the freedom."

"I can tell. You're enjoying it so much you're looking for someone to spend time with."

The window rattled, and Logan looked up. Talk about spending time with someone: Angel stood there, ready to toss a ball at him, her smile as wide and beautiful as the ocean behind her.

"Hey, come on, Logan. They're fifty-yard line. Can't get any better than that. You telling me you're gonna pass?"

He'd rather make a pass—"Yeah. I am. It's… well, it's a long story. Can't make it."

"Does this have something to do with a woman? There are only two reasons a guy is going to pass up fifty-yard line seats, and you aren't dead."

If she bent over in front of that window one more time, he just might be.

"Look, Drew, I gotta go. Call Randalls. He's always good for a night out."

"All right, but don't give me shit for not asking you. You were first on my list, Lo."

"Appreciate that." Even if he didn't believe it. He, Drew, and four other guys had been friends since the first project that had made them their money and reputations; someone was always available to catch a game or a bite with.

Angel made a grab for the ball before it hit the ground, but she missed and ended up sprawled on the lawn. He wouldn't mind catching a few nibbles of her leg.

"What about golf this weekend? Are we still on?"

"I'm going to have to get back to you."

Angel climbed to her feet and smoothed her pants over her ass.

"It's a woman."

She certainly was. "I'll call you, Drew."

"Uh huh. Good luck with that."

Logan hung up. He didn't need luck—not when he kept replaying the parking lot near-miss. How she'd closed her eyes and leaned in to him. Any sane man would have taken her up on it, but after the mauling he'd done the night before, his sanity was in question and, hell, they both deserved better.

This time, it'd be perfect. Without Michael and the public venue. He wanted to carry her up the stairs, peel those clothes off that enticing body he knew was underneath, and discover every erogenous zone she had. He wanted to hear her breath catch, see her eyes widen, then cloud with need. He wanted to touch every part of her, wrap her hair around his fists, trail kisses across those breasts that were driving him wild, plunge his tongue into her mouth and take all she…

Logan kneaded the knot at the back of his neck. He

was getting ahead of himself. Just because Angel hadn't made him stop didn't mean she'd be willing to take it to the next level.

Of course, he *could* always do his best to convince her…

Chapter 18

ANGEL CLOSED THE STORYBOOK AND SET IT ON THE NIGHT-stand beside the bed. "I had a fun time today, Michael." She handed him his bedraggled, stuffed raccoon.

"Me, too." Michael plunked the animal next to his pillow. "Angel?"

"Hmm?"

"Are you gonna be here tomorrow?" He made a big pretense of arranging the raccoon's paws just right, and his eyes didn't meet hers.

"Of course I will, Michael. I had a great time today." She almost reached out to tousle his hair but stopped herself. Yes she'd be here, but he was already so attached to her, she shouldn't encourage more. How would he handle it when she did have to go home? "I'll send your dad up, okay?"

"Okay," Michael mumbled.

"Good night." She pulled the covers over his shoulder.

"G'night."

At the bedroom door, Angel watched him slip his hat back on his head then settle down. One arm wrapped around Rocky, Michael curled the rest of his body around the toy and pulled the covers tight as if shielding them both from the outside world.

Angel's heart squeezed. How was *she* going to handle it when she had to go home?

She didn't want to think about it and turned off the light—only to have the blue glow of his nightlight remind her of her home. Even more than the waters of Atlantis, that soft light reminded her of her birthplace.

The Blue Grotto of Capri was one of her favorite places on earth. Most Mers were born there, in the turbulent waters during a storm when Humans had no access to the cavern. Oh, Humans thought it an inconvenience at the hands of the weather, but Poseidon monitored that area closely, knowing exactly when it was needed, and ensured his people would not be discovered.

She'd gone back many times during college to study Human visitors to the cave. They were always in awe, speaking in reverent tones about the grotto's beauty, some even jokingly claiming that the legends were true, that it was the home of Sirens, never knowing how right they were.

Those Humans who'd appreciated the gods' beautiful creation would want to save the planet. She truly believed that, and it gave her hope to teach them the error of their ways.

That's why she was here, first and foremost. That had been her dream ever since she'd seen that first Human all those *selinos* ago. It was the reason she'd studied and worked as hard as she had. To make a difference.

But it was going to hurt to leave Michael. *And* his father.

She clicked the door closed, then rested her head against it. She couldn't think about Logan. Not about how hard it'd be to leave. The Coalition was in its infancy. She was going to have her work cut out for her when she took office. There was an Advisory Board to assemble and all the committees. Mers to put in place within Human societies to work beneath the radar from that side, children to educate… Logan could only be a pleasant pastime. A temporary distraction.

If only there was some way he could be more.

She shook her head. There wasn't any way. Unless she was willing to break the cardinal rule of their society by telling him the truth, she couldn't have Logan and her world, too.

Regretting the reality that made it so, Angel turned around and—

Hit a wall.

And *not* the plastered kind.

The tall, dark, and handsome kind.

She didn't need to look up to know who it was.

But, somehow, just like last night, she couldn't seem to help herself.

She also couldn't help noticing that Logan didn't step back.

"I, um, was just coming to get you," she said. There. That sounded normal. Pleasant. Conversational.

Then Logan did step back and her tummy twinged. *That* wasn't normal. But it was pleasant.

Better than pleasant, actually.

"Oh?" Logan ran a hand through his hair.

"Um… yes. Michael. He's just about to fall asleep. I didn't want you to miss saying good night to him."

"Thanks, Angel. For putting him to bed and playing with him earlier."

"Oh, it's no problem. That's what I'm here for, right?"

"About that. Can we talk?"

Her heart sank. *Can we talk* was never good. She'd been wondering if there could be something between her and Logan, yet he wanted to "talk."

Color her embarrassed. She just hoped he didn't ask her to leave—especially now because she'd seen the tips of hammerhead tails offshore earlier. Knowing Harry, he wasn't giving up.

"Um. Sure. I'll wait for you on the lanai."

He moved past her and opened Michael's bedroom door. "I'll be down in a few minutes."

"You're in for it, you know." Ginger wriggled her serpentine neck through the yellow hibiscus hedge next to the lanai. "You've got a shiver of sharks just off the beach, slobbering all over the place, not to mention scaring every living thing into hiding. How am I supposed to get anything to eat? I still say you ought to raid the fridge for those prawns."

"Ginger, I'm not raiding anything for you. I've got enough troubles as it is."

What if Logan asked her to leave? Aside from the obvious worry about Harry, she would return home with nothing. A few dozen pages of notes weren't going to absolve her in The Council's eyes from coming ashore, and those observations certainly wouldn't give her the cachet she needed for the job.

Never mind what leaving Logan and Michael would do to her.

Angel kicked off her shoes and dropped into a lounge chair. The scent of hibiscus filled the air as the flowers neared the end of their one-day lives. She fiddled with one of the dying blossoms in the hedge next to her, feeling the correlation with her own life a little too closely.

"Troubles. Right." Ginger flipped her head upside down. "You don't know what trouble is. Living all high and fancy as a princess while some of us are left to survive on our wits. I'd trade places with you in a wingbeat."

"The difference between us, Ginger, is that all you think about is yourself."

"And maybe that's where your problem comes from. Do you really think you can save the planet? Honestly? And creatures say *I'm* vain."

Angel flicked the end of Ginger's beak to get her to leave her alone, and the flamingo undulated her neck as she backed out of the hedge.

Was that it? Was she vain to think she could do this? Was it an impossible task? Was Rod right? Was she destined to be *Just Angel* the rest of her Immortal life?

That she was questioning herself bothered her. Maybe she was going about this the wrong way; she didn't know anymore. It'd seemed like a good idea, but now...?

Now Michael's emotions were involved and so were hers and, Hades, she couldn't even manage to stick to her convictions about not falling for a Human.

Falling for—?

No. She was not falling for him.

She wasn't.

Really.

Angel sat up and smoothed her pants over her knees. There was a difference between wanting someone and falling for him. Huge difference. Life-altering difference. She hadn't fallen.

Had she?

Chapter 19

"ANGEL? WHERE ARE YOU?"

Logan. Angel's chuckle was half-groan. Talk about karma, the universe, whatever.

She swung her legs off the edge of the lounge and toed around for her shoes. "Right here, Logan."

He rounded the corner before she could get her second shoe on and stand, which left her gaze at thigh level. *His* thigh.

So not where she needed it to be.

She sprang to her feet—and teetered on the new appendages that were now at uneven heights, thanks to the one-shoe thing. Gods, when would she learn?

Then Logan reached out to steady her and didn't let go, and she figured she'd learned fairly well.

No no no. The job. She had to remember the job.

"Are you okay?"

If she could find her voice, she'd answer him. As it was, she could only nod.

"Oh. Good." He let go of her arms.

Thank the gods she managed to stay upright. Some learned scientist she was—cool, professional, able to maintain distance when dealing with her subjects—

Yeah, she was fooling no one. Least of all herself. Wanting, falling… Was there really that much of a difference?

"How about a walk on the beach?" He held up a white

plastic box. "I've got the monitor on in Michael's room so we can hear if he needs us."

"Oh. O...okay." Well, good. She was getting her voice back. That was a plus. Now if she could just get the tummy flutters to settle down, she'd be in good shape. Then Logan held her elbow while she kicked off the other shoe, and continued holding it the entire way down the flagstone path to the steps leading to the beach, all the while, her stomach was dancing the mambo.

It was a good thing they were going on a walk. As opposed to oh, say, hanging out in the kitchen...

A walk was harmless. It would give them a chance to get to know each other better. She could learn more about his world. Hear his thoughts. Practice walking on a new surface, and chalk it up to experience in preparation for her argument to Rod. It'd be a good argument.

So good that she almost convinced herself that was why she was going on the walk—until the cool grains of sand slid beneath her feet and squelched between her toes, and she had to grab Logan again to catch her balance.

When his warm skin met hers, and his muscles flexed beneath her fingers, her balance became seriously compromised as shivers ran up her arm, and toe-tingling became toe-curling.

Angel wasn't sure which rocked her world more off-kilter, the sand or Logan.

Or the wave that was headed right at her.

She hopped to the side to avoid it, glad she still had hold of him so she didn't go down—more than an embarrassment, that would have been a disaster. Her tail nondisclosure loomed large between them.

"So, um, what did you want to talk about?"

"You." Logan's voice swirled her tummy like high tide in an inlet.

"Me?" Her voice, on the other fin, sounded like a sick seal pup. She'd never squeaked before. It wasn't attractive.

Logan took her hand and headed down the beach away from the inlet on the other side of his house. "Me, too, of course."

"You?" Eloquent, wasn't she?

"And last night."

Her stomach did that squirmy thing again. "What, um, about it?"

Another wave flowed up the beach, a little too close to them for her liking, and Angel took another step to the side.

"You don't want to walk in the surf?" Logan didn't let go of her hand.

So she didn't let go either. "Not really. I saw some sharks offshore and would rather not tempt them."

"Sharks don't come onto shore, Angel."

"Well, you never know." Okay, it was lame, but what was she going to say? *I don't want to have my legs literally swept out from under me*?

Besides, the hand-holding was already doing a fine job with that, and she could only imagine what talking about last night would do.

"So, about last night." Logan kept his eyes straight ahead.

She knew because she kept stealing little glances out the corner of her eyes. "Yes?"

His grip on her hand tightened. "I promised you I wouldn't come on to you, yet today I did it again."

And how was she supposed to respond to that?

"But you didn't back away."

Oh. That's where he was going with this. "Um, yes… I mean, no."

Hades, she didn't know what she meant.

Logan stopped then. He turned to face her, his eyes searching hers. "Why didn't you, Angel?"

Angel's heart thudded. "I…"

A breeze swept around them, tossing her hair all around. Over her shoulders and wrapping it around her neck. Wrapping it around his. She reached for the bunch of hair that rested on him, but Logan beat her to it. He gathered the strands and swept them across his lips.

"Your hair is…" Logan's whisper melted into the sound of the waves. "It's beautiful."

And she melted into the sound of his voice.

Another wave slid onto the beach while the moment became supercharged.

Angel looked away first. There was something so honest in his gaze and, well, the guilt of not telling him the truth got to her.

But he'd never be able to fathom the idea of a Mer. No Human could. Mers had been relegated to myth status in their world, and that's where both races were comfortable with them being right now. She wasn't here to upset that balance. Just nudge it a little.

Still, she didn't like not being able to be herself with him. Her true self.

She gathered her hair, twisting it at the nape of her neck and knotting it over on itself, finding any place to look but at him. "Um, thanks."

Then he held out his hand and cleared his throat. "So… should we continue?"

Continue *what*?

She took his hand, knowing it wasn't the safest move on her part. Knowing she was going to have to answer his question—especially to herself.

But she knew the answer. She was attracted to him. She knew what it was like to kiss him. What he felt like pressed against her. The way his hair felt. The catch in his breath when she flexed her fingers against the back of his neck…

Oh yeah, they should continue. Because she wasn't going on a walk to learn anything scientific about Logan.

She was going on this walk to learn all about Logan for purely personal reasons.

The differences between them be damned.

"Son of a Moray!" Harry thrashed his tail. She was walking on the beach with the Human. Walking! And the sun was down! How in Hades was she doing this? By rights, the Mer ought to be running for the ocean, diving beneath the waves in a desperate attempt to get her tail back, but no. This Tritone was waltzing nonchalantly along the beach as if she didn't have a care in the world.

And A.C., damn him, was reminding Harry, port and starboard, that this was supposed to be a quick job. As if Harry needed the reminder.

He didn't know what she thought she was doing, but he knew he wasn't going to let her get away with it. She was the first royal he'd been able to get close to in recent months, and he wasn't going to let this opportunity slip through his gills.

He turned to Lou. "Keep an eye on them, but don't touch her. I want to check out a few things. I'll be back in the morning."

Somehow, some way, she'd slip up. And then he, and the guys, would pounce.

Chapter 20

"What do you mean she's on land? Still?" Rod swam from one side of the High Councilman's office to the other in what was sure to be record-breaking time, scattering the shoal of synchronized damselfish he'd hired for his wife's surprise party who were rehearsing in the corner.

Mariana backed out of her brother's way, bumping up against the sideboard that held busts of all the previous High Councilmen and almost knocking the newest addition off. She hadn't wanted to be the bearer of bad tidings for just this reason. She'd known Rod wouldn't react well.

Angel was so going to pay for this.

Mariana righted their father's likeness. "Yes, Rod. But she was in the water last night, so it's no big deal. She'll be back in before her time runs out."

Rod turned around, creating a strong enough whirlpool that the blennies snoozing in an alcove were sent twirling onto the coral beds on the ledge below. That had to hurt. "How do you know this, Mariana, when none of my informants knew where she was?"

She swished her hands to create a current to help the dazed fish back into their home. "It wasn't that hard to figure out, Rod. She'd taken her sea-pak and her notes."

"That was two days ago."

Mariana gulped. Oh, Hades. The crappie was going to hit the net now, for sure. Angel owed her. Big time.

"I spoke to her."

Rod spun around, this time disturbing the school of young sea horses who were trying to learn English. Probably not the best day for them to be here.

"You spoke to her? And you didn't think to bring her home?"

Mariana planted her hands on her hips, careful not to grip too hard. Scattering scales were a dead giveaway of tension, and she didn't want her brother to know how worried she was about this entire situation. For Angel's sake, Rod's, and her own. There was still the matter of her current project that she didn't want to come out.

"You know as well as I do, Rod, that you can't make Angel do anything she doesn't want to do. Especially when it comes to Humans. What is it about those beings that's so entrancing?"

Rod stopped swimming, and a strange look crossed his face. "You wouldn't understand."

Damn straight she wouldn't. And she never wanted to find out. But whatever the draw was, it got Rod to slow his whirlpool-inducing tail whips down to a soft flutter. The group of starfish holding onto the wall for dear life took a collective inhalation of relief.

"We need to get her back here."

"Good luck with that."

"I'm serious, Mariana. I don't have time for this. I should have left yesterday. We have to find some way to get her back. Soon."

"I'm serious, too, Rod. She's got it in her head that by doing this, she's going to find some magic formula to sell Humans on your idea of a Mer-Human Coalition for the betterment of the planet. You and I both know that's a long shot for some far-flung date in the future, but Angel's convinced she can initiate a change now by starting off with the children."

Rod pinched the bridge of his nose. "Gods save me from independent thinkers."

Mariana snorted. This from the guy who'd basically told the gods to shove it if they were going to take his throne away for marrying a Mer-Human Hybrid.

And he wondered where Angel got the attitude from.

"She needs to get her tail back here. Now. We'll work it out when I get back from the Middle East in a calm, rational manner, not like some rebellious teenager." Rod leaned on his massive desk—the work of some Human named Bernini. Did he get the irony, or was it just her?

"She better not hear you call her that, Rod." Frankly, Mariana wasn't too thrilled with the term, either. "She is an adult, you know."

"And as an adult she should know better. This exactly proves my point why she's not the Mer for the job."

"No, this proves that you're hogfish-headed about giving her a chance."

"What in the gods' names are you talking about, Mariana?" Rod gripped the sand globe on his desk, his eyes narrowing, and maybe… just maybe… he puffed up a little in size. High Councilmen could do that— become whatever size they wanted. Part of the package when one became the Mer ruler.

It was one big power trip, if you asked her.

"It's just that you've been interviewing everyone *but* Angel for this position. She's just as qualified, if not more, than many of the people you've interviewed." What was she doing defending Angel? Mariana didn't want her sister out there any more than Rod did, but, really, Angel deserved a chance at the job as much as anyone else, and for Rod to not even talk to her about it amounted to discrimination.

Rod dropped the sand globe on his desk, the water delivering it to the marble with a soft *plunk*. "Fine. Get her back here, and I'll give her the damned interview."

"An *un*biased interview."

"Whose side are you on, Mariana?"

Mariana swam up almost into his face. He might be the High Councilman, but he was still her brother. And this was their sister he was talking about. "Oh, I'm firmly on Angel's, Rod, make no mistake about that. You can't cut her out of the lineup because she's your sister and you don't want to lose her.

This time she was *certain* that he grew bigger. "That's not why—"

"Bullsharkshit." He didn't scare her. She was one of the few who would talk to Rod like this since he inherited the throne. Reel, of course, was another, but since he wasn't around much anymore, it was up to her to make Rod see reason. Even if she did agree with him on general principle.

"Of course it's why you're doing it, Rod." She flipped her tail sideways and floated away from him. "Look, we all have to live with Reel's decision to stay with Erica on land and have a mortal life span. You're not the only one it's hard for, you know. But you can't hold Angel—or any of us—too closely or you might end up pushing us away."

Rod lost the High Councilman demeanor he wore like a badge of honor, returning to normal size and resting his tail against the desk. "I know, Mariana, but…" He cleared his throat. "That doesn't make it any easier to accept Reel's decision. Or Angel's."

She flipped over and swam back to him. "He's happy with it, and that's what we have to remember. Give Angel a chance to do this in a way you can monitor, Rod. Right now she's off, unsupervised, getting into gods-know-what kind of trouble. Bring her back. Give her an interview, a fair hearing. That's all she wants."

Rod put his arm around Mariana and pulled her close. "How'd you get to be so smart, sis?"

She hugged him back. "It swims in the family. That's why we have to believe that Angel knows what she's doing."

Chapter 21

ANGEL DIDN'T HAVE A CLUE WHAT SHE WAS DOING.

Well, okay, she knew what she was doing physically, but emotionally? She was so in over her head here... Walking with Logan on a moonlit beach, him looking at her like *that*... she was playing with fire in a way she hadn't imagined.

The thing was, she didn't care—and how crazy was that?

They'd covered the basics on the walk: his childhood, his relationship with Michael's mother, his job, his life. She'd shared what she could of hers, glossing over some of the details, but the believability factor of her story proved her point that Mers could pass in the Human world.

Not that she'd include any of this in her argument to Rod.

They'd gathered shells on the walk back. She'd found a round piece of abalone that'd make the perfect necklace for Pearl, and Logan had found a piece of driftwood resembling a dinosaur for Michael. He'd shared the story of how Michael had come into his life and his anger with Christine for keeping his son from him and the hopes and plans he had.

But even though they'd talked about all of that, they hadn't addressed what was happening between them, or what had happened last night.

So now they stood at the top of the steps they'd

climbed down a while ago, that *something* now so much more than it had been. Something real and potent and pretty darn scary if she was honest with herself.

She didn't want to know so much about him. All the hardships he'd lived through, being on his own at such a young age, never having the kind of loving family she'd had, the tough, lonely life he'd pulled himself from to become so successful and such a caring father…

She didn't want to care this much about him. There was so much about Logan Hardington to admire. So much to respect.

So much to love.

No.

She didn't.

She couldn't.

It was too quick.

Too early.

Too soon.

Too wrong.

Too right.

Her knees buckled and she had to brace herself against the railing. Apparently Human legs weren't as sturdy as she'd assumed.

Or maybe it was just *her* legs that weren't sturdy.

She was in love with him.

"Angel?" Worry colored Logan's voice. "Are you all right?"

She shook her head. Of course she wasn't all right. She'd just had the wind knocked out of her sails by love.

And got it knocked out all over again when Logan scooped her up in his arms.

"Logan!" she squeaked again, dropping the seashells. Really—squeaking was not an attractive habit.

"Are you okay?" His brown eyes on her, she could see a few flecks of gold in them that matched the highlights in his gorgeous hair. She had the strangest urge to run her fingers through it.

So she did. She didn't think about it; it just sort of happened.

And so did the sharp breath Logan inhaled the moment her fingertips brushed the back of his neck.

As did the kiss that followed.

She didn't know who started it—didn't care. His lips were soft at first, for just the tiniest instant before he lifted her higher in his arms and deepened the kiss.

Angel couldn't think and didn't care about that either. She wrapped an arm around his neck and opened her mouth beneath his.

His tongue swept in and Angel moaned. Gods, he... Logan... was just...

She didn't have the words.

Logan didn't either. He growled in the back of his throat, the sound primal and possessive. Aroused. Male. And Angel felt herself respond.

Her breasts swelled, and she turned to press them against his chest.

Logan adjusted his hold on her, a move Angel only realized because suddenly he was cupping her bottom in a way so hot she'd have to be dead not to feel.

And oh, did she. In every cell of her body. Especially when he clenched one cheek, his fingers brushing the cleft between them. Angel felt her legs quiver, then go *completely* boneless this time. Thank the gods she was already in his arms.

She moaned then, and Logan released her mouth to skim his lips along her jaw, to the soft hollow beneath her ear, and Angel let her head fall back, shivering when the soft sea breeze caressed her moist skin.

But… wait. There was something—

He licked his way around the shell of her ear, causing her to shiver again, but he was right there to warm her, sliding his lips along her cheekbone to find hers again, his big, strong hand cradling her head, angling her just right, and she felt as if her heart was going to beat out of her chest.

She lost whatever thoughts had been trying to be heard and, frankly, she didn't care. She'd never been kissed like this by anyone but Logan. Never felt such feelings before.

She tugged at her arm that was trapped between them, trying to slip it around his waist, to feel the muscles clench and flex and tighten as he held her, but their bodies were too close. Dammit, she wanted to touch him as he was touching her.

Then his fingers slid between her legs from behind and she practically lost the capacity to think.

Oh gods, this was what she wanted. This. Him. Here. Now. It didn't matter who she was, who he was, what anyone would say. Logan was… he could…

Hades, she didn't know what he was or what he could, she just knew that she had to find out more. To know him more. In this way.

His tongue caressed hers, and her ability to breathe went the way of coherent thought.

"Angel," he whispered against her lips and she sucked in a big, shaky breath, his scent mingling with the salty softness of the night air. To Angel, it was like ambrosia—the nectar of the gods they hoarded so meanly. Now she knew why—if this stuff ever became available for public consumption, no one would ever get anything done. All they'd ever be thinking about wa—

"Make love to you."

Yeah. That.

"Angel?" Logan whispered her name.

He was asking her something.

Angel opened her eyes, trying to still the swirling emotions and thoughts and feelings rioting inside her, but when she saw the same emotions mirrored in his eyes—eyes that showed no sign of enchantment—she knew what her answer would be.

"Oh, Logan…Yes."

⁓⁓⁓

Logan never walked so quickly in his life; truthfully, he felt as if he'd flown. As if Mercury had put wings on his feet and zipped them both up to the bedroom.

He leaned back against his door, clicking it shut, fumbling to lock it and not drop Angel. She was so slight he could hold her against him with one hand, but he didn't want to stop touching her at all.

He also didn't want Michael walking in on them, so he managed to move quickly and without breaking the kiss he'd started halfway up the stairs.

She felt so good in his arms, her hair stroking him as if she were running hundreds of fingertips all over his body, and Logan groaned into her mouth at that image. He couldn't wait to have her under him and moving, naked, against him as she was right now.

He walked over to the bed and set her on it on her knees. She flung both arms around him, freeing that other arm at last. He hadn't wanted to be apart from her for even a moment to give her the use of that arm, but as one of her soft, graceful hands found the curve of his cheek and the other slid down his back, he realized that had been a mistake. One he'd never repeat again.

"God, your hair is so beautiful," he murmured against the golden strands that slid against his cheek like silk. Silk scented like her.

"Mmmm," she murmured, kissing his throat. Logan didn't know exactly what that meant, but he figured it was a pretty good response.

Then he didn't care what it meant because her tongue flicked across his Adam's apple and his breath caught at that very spot and he emitted his own "Mmmmm."

Definitely a good response.

Sliding his fingers through her hair, Logan caressed her neck and stroked down her back, remembering how sexy she'd looked with that blanket pooled at the base of her spine. He was going to kiss his way down to that very spot the moment he got her clothes off—though the way her hands were moving, it looked like his would be off before hers.

He had no objection to that.

Logan took a quick kiss to tide himself over the few seconds he needed to remove his shirt. Then he reached behind his head and yanked it up and off in one move-ment just as he had on the boat, only this time, there was no way he'd cover her with it.

"Oh gods…" she whispered against his chest, and Logan felt his nipples tighten.

Then she licked one while her fingers ran over the rest of his chest, feathering through his hair, down along his obliques, tracing down to his hip and Logan felt his knees tremble.

Ah, *that* was what had happened to her by the steps. He'd been so worried—

Her tongue trailed across his chest to his other nipple and Logan forgot all about that worry.

Now all he was worried about was coming before she got naked.

And with the ache in his groin, that was a serious possibility.

Logan speared his hands through her hair and urged her head back. Her tongue took one last twirl around his nipple, almost bringing him to his knees and Logan sucked in a deep breath. "Angel. Honey. Wait."

She glanced up at him from beneath long lashes every bit as golden as her hair, her lips plump and moist and pink. "Wait? Really?"

No, God, no. He didn't want to wait.

Logan closed his eyes. *Get a grip, Hardington.*

Oh he wanted to get a grip, all right.

"Give me a moment… to catch my breath."

Her smile told him he didn't have a moment.

Sure enough, she leaned forward and licked his navel, her eyes never leaving his. "Did you catch it yet?"

Her warm breath feathered over the trail her tongue had left behind and Logan shivered. Eighty-five degrees out and he shivered.

He also smiled. What a sight. Moist lips, an impish look in those gorgeous aquamarine eyes, her head cocked seductively, exposing the graceful curve of her neck, on her knees before him, her hands wreaking a fabulous kind of havoc everywhere she touched…

He cupped her cheek and drew her face to his as he bent over to meet her, her lips tasting so utterly delicious he thought this must be what ambrosia tasted like. That mythical nectar of the gods. No wonder poets called it that. An experience so heady and perfect it could only be divine.

He pulled back from the kiss, staring into her eyes, knowing he could lose himself in their depths. And while the thought was utterly terrifying, not being with her was more so. "I want you, Angel."

She smiled and its warmth was mirrored in her eyes. "I'm aware of that, Logan." Her straying hands told him she was, indeed, aware of how badly he wanted her.

She stroked him and Logan had to close his eyes and grit his teeth. It wouldn't take much.

"Angel," his breath was ragged, "are you sure—?"

"What do you think?" She undid his shorts and shoved them down his legs.

Alrighty then.

But she wasn't going to be the only one who got to play.

Sucking in another breath when her palm brushed the head of his erection, Logan slid his hands along the side of her shirt, finding the curve of her breast just as she wrapped her hand around him.

He rocked forward, trying to keep his balance.

Then she stroked his balls with her other hand and balance became a huge issue. "Oh, God, Angel…" He steadied himself on her shoulders, his eyes inexorably drawn to watch her hands on his body.

He sucked in a breath when she rolled first one, then the other, between her fingers, fondling him with just the right amount of firmness, playing with them, stroking them, as she swirled her palm on the head of his cock and her hair slipped over her shoulder to brush against his groin.

His knees were seriously demanding to be put out of their misery.

His cock was seriously demanding—period.

Logan didn't want this to end too soon.

Dragging in another ragged breath, he stroked her hair, trying to remember not to pull it. But it was hard, so hard, everything was hard…

"Angel…"

Thank God she stopped. He was one stroke away from coming.

"Yes?" She licked her lip again in that way she did and all Logan could think of was her doing that to him.

Later. They'd get to that later. Right now he wanted… oh, hell, he didn't know what he wanted. Only that it had something to do with her and being naked.

Hell, his shorts were still puddled at his feet.

He shook his head and stepped out of them, raising one knee to the bed, cupping her shoulder and sliding his fingers to the fastening of her shirt at the back of her neck, beneath that glorious hair, trying to show her what he wanted because he seriously doubted he could speak coherently at the moment. He was amazed he was capable of even semi-coherent thought.

The words, "Untie it," did manage to make themselves heard, and he exhaled when she let her top fall.

She wore the red lingerie.

Oh lord. Logan felt his blood race through his veins,

an utter rush of sensation and feeling and gratitude and lust and pure awe at how beautiful she was.

He fingered the delicate pattern of lace, just brushing her skin with his fingertips, hearing her breath go shallow. Watching her pulse flutter, seeing her nipples tighten, her breasts swell the fabric against her skin. He stroked the silk cup, his thumb unerringly finding the rigid peak at the center. It hardened and Logan couldn't help himself—he leaned down to stroke her through the fabric with his tongue.

Angel's breath caught and her head fell back, raising her breast to the perfect angle. Logan nipped at her with his lips, feeling himself grow harder, achingly so, and he nudged her backwards.

Angel went willingly into the pillows and cradled his head when he laid half on top of her, his tongue still playing with her.

He spread his hand wide against her stomach, enjoying the fluttery movements there as she tried to catch her breath, feeling the muscles move as she arched her breast into his mouth, as her legs slid apart, waiting…

Her shirt encircled her waist, and her pants stretched between her hipbones with enough of a gap for him to slip his fingers inside. A perfect invitation he wasn't about to refuse.

She moaned again, low and long. Beneath a small triangle of silk—red, he assumed—he stroked the curls that he knew matched her hair, wanting to feel them against his body, his face, his tongue.

Later.

Angel spread her legs wider, invitingly, and Logan slid his fingers lower.

She gripped his shoulders, her breath coming even quicker. "Logan, oh, yes, oh, gods, please…"

He nudged her bra down and circled her nipple with his tongue, sucking it into his mouth, totally unprepared for the sensation. She fit perfectly, as if she was made for him. His tongue stroked her, his fingers stroked her, and her body, well, it almost seemed to undulate like waves on the ocean beneath his touch.

She slid one of her hands up his back to tangle in his hair. "Logan. I want…" She arched against him, higher, her heels now on the bed, opening herself as much as her clothing would allow.

The hell with that.

Logan undid the front clasp of her strapless bra—a man surely invented that wonder—and shoved her shirt and pants down her legs. Angel pulled one leg free, kicking everything to the floor with the other.

Logan lifted his head. He'd been right. Her thong was red, too.

She looked like a goddess lying there on his bed, her hair spread out around her, some drifting across her stomach and chest, a nipple peeking from beneath it, moist from where he'd tasted her. Her lips swollen, her eyes dark blue with desire…

"Inside, Logan," she whispered. "I want you inside me."

He did, too.

With a jerky movement that he was too aroused to care wasn't suave, Logan braced one leg on the floor and grabbed a condom from the bedside table. Damned thing was too hard to open—

Especially when she reached out and stroked his cock.

His leg gave out and Logan had to brace himself so

he wouldn't fall on her. "You better watch out, Angel. We might not need this"—he held up the condom—"if you keep doing that."

"Oops. Sorry." She withdrew her hand. "I'll be good." Then she smiled that impish smile and shimmied out of her thong. "Or bad. Depends on what you want."

Logan dropped the condom.

Chapter 22

WHAT HAD GOTTEN INTO HER? ANGEL FELT AS IF SHE WERE watching someone else make love to Logan—and that wasn't something she'd ever done.

There was a lot going on that she'd never done. Who was this woman? She'd never been this uninhibited in her life. Never even thought to say the things she was saying to him.

And the red lingerie?

Ah, well, that saleswoman had known what she was talking about.

Logan straightened again, this time with the condom free of its packaging, ready to put it in place, and Angel was ready to let the Siren inside her free. She stroked him again, loving the sound of his breath whooshing out.

Loving him.

"You're killing me here, Angel."

Oh no she wasn't. She took the condom from him and rolled it into place, taking an extra long time so her fingernails could gently scrape along his length.

But Logan was having none of it. The minute she'd sheathed him, he knelt over her and began an assault on her breasts with his mouth, holding the rest of his body above her.

Angel squirmed beneath his strong, muscled body. Gods, she was used to the male chest, but something about Logan's and its light dusting of hair made her, well, *itch* to feel him against her.

Logan lowered himself onto her, taking his weight with his elbows as he pressed her breasts together, flicking his tongue from one breast to the other. Angel arched against him. There. That was one way to feel him.

He flicked his tongue again and her stomach contracted. Another part of her swelled. Angel didn't know how much more of this she could take.

Then he blew on her breasts and she had her answer. Not much.

She wrapped her legs around his back, settling her heels against the top of his backside, feeling the muscles there flex.

"Logan…"

He raised his head, those gold flecks in his eyes glittering. "God, you're beautiful."

"I'm also aching." Who *was* this woman?

He smiled and Angel decided she didn't mind the new her.

"Let me see what I can do." Logan rolled to the side, one hand tangling in her hair at the base of her neck and his other hand…

Oh, his other hand—

One long, hard, callused finger slid down her body, lightly brushing the underside of her breast, feathering over her abdomen, and tracing around her navel until, finally, he was *there*. Where every nerve was already alive and waiting for him. Where she was open and aching and wet for him.

"Here?" He smiled again, one eyebrow arching, and Angel couldn't find any teasing inside of her.

"Yes" came out in one long breathy, achy, pleading moan, and she twisted the sheets in her grasp.

Logan, gods bless him, took pity on her and stroked her, just where she needed him to. Flicked the tip of his finger just where she wanted him to. Groaned just how she liked him to.

Then pressed and stroked and swirled and dipped inside just as she craved him to.

The sensations were overwhelming, unlike anything she'd ever experienced before. *Logan* was unlike anyone she'd ever made love with and she didn't mean the lack of a tail. He took her higher, brought her to the edge but wouldn't let her dive off again and again, until she was one mass of needing, writhing, feeling nerve endings, panting and moaning, searching for something just beyond the next stroke of his finger, the next soft breath he blew against the sensitized skin of her breast, the next kiss he placed against her throat...

He flicked his tongue along her jaw, then along her bottom lip, and Angel tried hard to catch her breath—the problem being, she had no breath to catch.

His finger slid out of her body and he cupped her, his palm pressing against that most sensitive part of her, and she gasped, her eyes flying to meet his.

"You're incredible," he whispered.

"You are." She didn't know if she said it or simply mouthed the words, but by Logan's smile she gathered that he understood.

At least one of them did.

She had no idea why it was like this between them, no clue how one man could be so much to her, why he affected her like this, why she was willing to do this when common sense and everything she'd thought she'd wanted said it wasn't a good idea…

Because she loved him.

Gods, yes. She did.

The admission flowed into her, and Angel embraced it. This was what her parents, her brothers, felt and it was so right. She hadn't planned it, wouldn't have chosen it, but as he kissed her, she didn't care.

She loved Logan.

Then his finger stroked her long and hard and Angel could only focus on the sensations as that rising tide welled up inside her and she struggled again to breathe, to think, to focus, to see…

"Come for me, Angel."

She did. Shattered, pulsing against his finger as the dam of feeling flooded her, lifting her to the tips of the wave, tossing her into the trough, swirling her onto yet another rise. Cresting and plunging, swirling again… over and over, the feeling more intense than any vortex, more wonderful than anything…

Slowly she came back to reality and loosed the grip she had on the sheets as her breathing made it to somewhere in the vicinity of normal.

Logan raised himself above her, satisfaction tilting up the curves of his mouth. "Perfect."

Let him gloat; he was one hundred percent right. It had been.

She nodded. "You did say you wanted our next kiss to be perfect."

"Can't be more perfect than that."

"Oh, I don't know." She traced his lips with her

fingers. "Why don't you get down here and we'll see if we can make it even better."

"I like the way you think, lady."

She liked the way he moved, settling into the cradle of her thighs just where she'd demanded, the tip of his erection throbbing against her.

"Logan—"

"Angel—"

They smiled.

"Make love to me, Logan."

"My pleasure."

Maybe, but it was also hers. She tried to tell him that as he slid into her, but she was so filled with the wonder of him inside her—literally and figuratively— that she couldn't.

It was just so… so…

So *perfect*.

She *was* an angel—she felt like heaven.

Logan slid inside her heat and knew in that instant that this was right. What he'd thought he'd had with Christine at the beginning, what he'd thought this would feel like… he hadn't had a clue.

But with Angel, well, *this* was how it was supposed to be.

He slid out, then back in, smiling as she arched her neck, her eyes closing on a gasp.

He did it again… and so did she.

He liked watching her.

The third time, he dipped down to kiss her throat, inhaling the musky sweet smell of her and him and what they were doing. It made him harder, something he wouldn't have thought was possible.

Then she clenched him and he knew that it was.

God, she was perfect.

She swirled her hips and Logan almost came right then.

He captured her lips with his, not wanting to lose control. He slipped his tongue inside, stroking hers, tasting her.

She returned the stroking and Logan sucked on her tongue to match the rhythm of his cock inside her.

This time she moaned.

Logan threaded his fingers through her hair and knew he had to have it falling over him. There was just something so earthy and sensual about her hair, how it swayed when she moved, a curtain shielding her from him, giving him glimpses of what was behind it, tantalizing him.

Logan wrapped his arms around her and rolled over.

Those beautiful eyes of hers shot open. "What—"

"I need you on top, Angel. I want to watch you. I want to feel you move against me."

Her hair fell around them, brushing his groin, his thighs, his abdomen, and Logan groaned. It felt so good. *She* felt so good.

He fanned a hand on her stomach, his thumb stroking the curls between her legs, his little finger just below the underside of her breast. If she leaned forward, he'd be able to touch her there—

He wrapped a handful of her gorgeous hair around his other hand and tugged.

Bingo. She leaned forward.

But then he got another idea.

He filled both of his hands with her hair and tugged again.

She fell forward, her hair falling around them, her breasts right where he wanted them.

She smiled when he took one in his mouth.

And then she moved.

Good God! Logan almost shot off the bed. Her ass slid against his sac, her soaked, swollen flesh rubbing against him, and she arched her breast into his mouth on another long moan. Her hair swept his sides, fell across his lips, and desire shot straight from his balls to every part of his body. It was a wonder he didn't explode.

Actually…

Feeling his cock jerk inside her, knowing the end was near, Logan rocked into her.

She threaded her fingers through his hair, matching his movement with her hips in perfect harmony.

He released her breast and shoved a hand to the back of her head, dragging that sweet mouth to his, kissing her lips, parting them with his tongue, his other hand tangling in the golden hair that sensitized every part of his body it touched. Logan gripped her hip and surged upward.

Angel swirled her hips again. Just a little, but it was enough.

"Logan," she breathed against his lips and that was it.

Gripping both her hips now, Logan pounded into her until an orgasm more powerful, more profound, than any he'd ever had, rushed through him and he poured himself into her. As unbelievable as it sounded, as incredible as this entire situation was, something had changed inside him. Altered him. Realigned... *everything*.

He was in love with Angel.

—◦◦◦—

Moonlight from the far side of the room stretched along the wall and across the bottom corner of the bed with just enough light for Angel to see the shadowy outline of Logan's backside where he lay on his stomach next to her.

She wanted to run her palm over one muscled cheek but she was too tired to make the effort. Plus, he had his face buried in the hollow of her neck, and, frankly, she didn't want to move him.

She didn't want to move anything.

If she did, real life would come flooding back and she'd have to deal with it.

Right now she just wanted to *be*...

"Stay with me, Angel." Logan whispered.

Angel tensed. Stay with him? In what sense? What did he mean? Stay awake? Stay the night? Stay until Michael started school? Forever? What?

He rolled onto his side. "Angel?"

She looked at him. "What do you mean, Logan?" He had no idea what he was asking. None. And she wasn't sure she did either. Stay with him? That couldn't be an option.

Right?

The *thud* in her stomach said her heart didn't agree with her—the heart that had lived under the sea for the last twenty-nine *selinos*—and wouldn't he just love finding *that* out?

And then he smiled. That warm, feel-good, wrap-itself-around-you smile. He picked up a few strands of her hair, brushing the ends across his lips, then over her collarbone ever so softly, fluttering her already fluttering heart even more, sending shivers over her skin as he feathered her hair over her breasts, a soft stroke across her nipples, sliding down over her ribs, tickling her navel… and she sucked in a breath because somehow she'd forgotten to breathe.

Logan relinquished her hair and curved his hand over her hip, then up to her waist, gently over her ribs, sliding his hand beneath her, turning her so their gazes met. He looked at her as if he could see into her soul.

"I want you to stay, Angel. With us. I've never felt like this before. I don't really know you, yet… I do. It's almost… and I hate to say this because it's so cliché, but it's magical." His eyes traced her face, and his voice lowered. "You feel it, too, don't you? I know how crazy this sounds. I'm not impulsive, and I've never done anything like this before in my life, yet I know if I don't tell you this, if I don't ask you, it'll be the biggest regret of my life."

The biggest regret of hers would be if she said no.

Who was this new person inside her? This new her? Vamping it up with Logan was one thing, but this? Staying with him? Could she pull it off without him finding out?

Or… would she have to tell him?

"Logan, I… "

He kissed her, then rested his forehead against hers. "Sshh. It's all right. You don't have to answer now. I know it's sudden, but I had to ask. Had to let you know how I felt. We're in no rush."

True. The only rush she had was to get back in the water to ensure she could make this decision.

Because she might actually consider it…

She feathered the hair by his temple and met his eyes. "I'd like that, Logan. But you're right. It is quick. We'll just take it as it comes. Deal with things when the need arises."

He caught her hand and pressed a kiss to her palm— and the tingles started all over again. "That's fine, Angel. We'll make it work." He smiled that sly, devilish smile of his. "And as for needs arising…"

He pressed himself against her and there was no mistaking what need he was talking about.

Angel was all for meeting needs.

"Roll over," he whispered.

"Roll over?"

"Yes. Over." Logan nudged her hip. "There's something I've been dying to do."

She couldn't imagine what it was, but the look in his eyes—and the insistent poking at her hip—encouraged her to find out.

She rolled over.

For a moment, nothing happened. Then she heard the hitch in Logan's breathing and felt the barest brush of her hair against the base of her spine.

"God, Angel, I've been imagining this for so long…"

"We haven't known each other that long."

"Are you sure about that? I feel as if I've always known you." He kissed just above the base of her spine. "Your bruise is gone."

She stiffened. "My bruise?"

"Uh huh." When he kissed the exact spot, she knew

what he meant. That was no bruise. "You must have hurt yourself getting into the boat."

Actually, she hadn't, but she certainly wasn't going to tell him that he'd seen the royal birthmark that faded when she was out of the water.

"I was looking forward to kissing it and making it better." He did anyway—both kiss it and make *everything* better.

It was her turn for her breath to whoosh out. "You're doing a good job."

His lips curved against her skin. "You haven't seen anything yet."

She shivered in anticipation.

Then she shivered again when he kissed the base of her spine.

Then again when he moved to the small of her back.

And again, each time he kissed another vertebra, moving up her back, all the while circling the tips of her hair along the top of her butt and along the cleft.

Then his finger followed, stroking all the way down and between her legs just as his lips reached that sensitive area on the back of her neck.

Angel's lips fell open as she tried to take in more air. She tried. Really, really tried, but when his finger skimmed through her swelling folds to find the very center of her, she panted out what was left in her lungs.

Then his lips fluttered to her ear and he played with the lobe, his breath sensitizing her skin even more, and Angel didn't care if she never breathed again.

"You feel so incredible," he whispered huskily.

Didn't she know it.

She tried to respond, but that lack of air made it impossible, so she drew in as big a breath as she could possibly manage—if only so she wouldn't pass out and miss one moment of this.

Then he nudged her leg up and over his hip, his fingers playing there, finding every nerve ending, and she found enough breath to exhale.

"Like this?" He slid one finger inside her.

She nodded. A groan escaped… which was a major accomplishment with the sensations he'd created inside her.

"I know something you'll like even more."

She managed to turn her head enough to get a glimpse of his face. "I don't think that's possible."

He smiled, satisfied and cocky. "Trust me."

She did.

That simple; she did trust Logan.

Sliding his finger from her to press against her aching center, Logan rolled her onto her back, one leg splayed across his hips and he sat up to watch.

Open and aroused and exposed, Angel had never felt sexier. She pulled her knee up a little higher, her leg stroking him.

It was Logan's turn to groan.

Then he kissed her hip bone.

Oh she knew what his intentions were…

She couldn't stop the shiver. Or the rush of pleasure that swept over her and made her swell even more against his touch.

His eyes met hers, a question in them, but… not really.

They both knew the answer.

He skimmed his lips low across her belly.

Lower.

Then somehow, with a move she wasn't even sure she saw, Logan was there. Between her thighs, his fingers spreading her and his tongue claiming that part of her that was aching and begging for his attention.

Angel's other leg fell to the side as she offered herself to him.

Logan took. And took and took.

And gave and gave.

His hands slid beneath her to position her at just the right angle, his thumbs separating the folds, giving him unlimited access to every aching, needing, throbbing part of her.

His tongue swirled and Angel arched on the bed, grasping for the sheets, the mattress, a pillow... anything. Anything to grab onto as some semblance of reality while his tongue took her higher.

Aloft in a wave of sensation, her hips rose with each stroke of his tongue.

Then he slid one finger inside her—maybe two—and Angel felt the rush to the end begin.

Only Logan wasn't willing to end it.

He kissed the inside of her thigh, and her eyes flew open. She looked down at him, there between her legs, a satisfied smile on his face.

"Told you to trust me."

She could only nod.

Well, and raise her hips. She wasn't finished.

Nor was Logan, thank the gods. He lowered his head and began his assault all over again, this time nudging her legs farther apart with his shoulders, changing the angle, his tongue stroked her, and Angel knew it wouldn't be long.

It wasn't.

A few more strokes and Angel soared over the edge. She came against his mouth with a quaking, shuddering rush of pleasure and feeling and love that left her drained yet utterly and wholly complete.

So this was what it was like to make *love*.

So very different from having sex, and something she could no longer live without.

Somehow she'd have to make this work with Logan. Even though it meant telling him the truth—

She'd deal with that later.

"You awake?" he whispered against her belly, kissing his way slowly—too slowly—up her body.

She opened one eye—all she could manage. "Get up here, you. It's your turn."

Logan kissed her navel and dipped his tongue inside, one eyebrow arched her way.

"Again—I love the way you think, lady…"

Chapter 23

A RIBBON OF MOONLIGHT RIPPLED ACROSS THE PLANK FLOOR as if it were the calm night sea. Angel slid from beneath the sheets, too much going on in her mind to be able to sleep.

The clock's soft red glow said two twenty-seven. She needed to think and should have enough time to go for a swim, then get her legs back. She'd have to use the hair dryer in the guesthouse, but hopefully, she'd be able to crawl back beside Logan's warm body before he woke.

She smiled. Maybe crawling back in would wake him.

Her body tingled yet again, and goose bumps appeared—and they had nothing to do with the gentle breeze of the ceiling fan. They'd made beautiful music together, she and Logan. A symphony of sound and touch and taste, soft whispers, gentle sighs, the crashing crescendo of the final act…

There had to be some way to make this work. Her brothers had both done it, but Reel had wanted to live on land with his wife, and Rod's wife was willing to make the sea her home. She had to figure out some way to make it happen for her and Logan because he couldn't give up everything—he had Michael to think of. And she… well, she didn't know if she could live on land.

Then there was that mortal life-span complication.

What to do? What to do?

Two twenty-seven changed to two twenty-eight. What to do first was get herself into that water. The best place to think was in her natural environment.

She unlatched the lock on the door and squeezed through the opening onto the deck, glancing back at Logan. His shoulder rose softly in time with his breath.

"A few hours, Logan," she whispered, tugging the door closed behind her.

The moonlight trailed across the massive deck and over the railing to the blue water beyond. High tide had just started to ebb, and the soft waves lapped against the pylons in the inlet below, their crests breaking into hundreds of iridescent bubbles.

Angel looked out to sea. Not a hammerhead tail tip in sight.

Ha. Chalk one up for Harry's short attention span. She'd counted on it. Oh, sure, he could be swimming in wait in the deep, but she knew him. When she hadn't shown up before sunset tonight, he'd taken off in search of another meal.

But he'd be back tomorrow. Harry was nothing if not predictable in his anger at—and efforts to thwart—The Council.

To play it safe, she'd swim in the inlet. That was too close to Humans for Harry's liking.

Angel climbed over the railing, then braced her heels between the spindles. She took a deep breath—her last one of air for a while—raised her arms over her head and dove into the sparkling water.

The water hit her—cold, fresh. Alive. Her nipples tightened just as they had when Logan had rolled his tongue around them. Her legs shimmered as her scales slid over them, binding the two appendages into one, her skin drinking in the moisture. It felt so good to be whole again.

She twisted in her dive, feeling her flukes turn with her.

Whole again? But that's how she'd felt tonight with Logan. In his arms.

She'd felt whole. As if every part of her was where she belonged. No questions, no hesitation, no worries about anything, just him and her.

Her and Logan together.

Angel stopped swimming. It wasn't her tail that made her who she was. Was the lack of one what made Logan who he was? She loved him for him, and if she had to guess, she'd say he was feeling something similar toward her. Being with him was where she was supposed to be.

She laid back and closed her eyes, letting the ebb and flow of the water buoy her. No wonder she'd always been so curious about Humans. No wonder it felt right with him. She'd been searching for him. The two of them together were one, part of something greater than their individual selves. Add Michael into the equation, and she had a family and a chance to do what she'd set out to do.

She had a purpose.

She opened her eyes. That was it. No more questioning, no more wondering. She would do whatever it took to have all of it: Logan and Michael *and* her purpose.

She'd have to tell him the truth. Be honest. As much as it worried her, he'd have to see—after tonight—that it didn't matter that she was a Mer. He wouldn't possibly want her to get rid of her tail any more than she wanted him to get rid of his legs.

She looked at the beautiful scales, shimmering like the inside of an abalone shell in the moon shadow, all the shades of amethyst and violet and lavender sparkling through the water. Logan would like it. It was part of her, part of who she was, and once she told him the truth, he'd forgive her for the subterfuge. He'd understand.

Of course he would. He'd asked her to stay, made beautiful love to her; he felt something for her.

They'd work out the logistics somehow, but she would have Logan and her tail and show Rod that she could do the job she wanted. She, like her brothers, could have it all, and Rod wouldn't be able to say her observations were any more compromised than any decision he'd made since falling in love with Valerie.

Angel glanced skyward. A few more minutes, then she'd dry off, climb back into that warm bed with Logan, curl against him, and seize her life by the tail.

But first… she'd celebrate. Mer style.

She swam out of the inlet, keeping alert for any signs of Harry or his gang, but the other fish swimming around confirmed what she'd known. Unless the fish had a death wish, she was safe.

Angel swam along the ocean floor, gathering her energy. Skimming the sandy bottom, she made it to deeper water quickly, then kicked her tail to head skyward as fast as she could. Water streamed over her, her tail arcing beneath her and she lifted her arms over her head as she cleared the surface. Ah, the freedom as she exploded into the sky, somersaulting with joy as she dove back beneath the waves.

Again, she skimmed the bottom, flicking her tail to head topside again. This time, she arched backward and greeted the horizon upside-down, a perfect moonlit rainbow of color in her tail.

Again and again, Angel danced among the waves, wanting to sing her happiness, but that'd only invite trouble. Besides, the moon's trail had lengthened, and it was time to head back.

She flicked her tail and dove toward Logan's home, ready for the sea—and air—to be cleared between them. Ready to begin her life with him.

She couldn't wait to hear what he'd say.

Returning to the inlet, she swam toward the bank of the small beach there. She broke through the surface and brushed her hair off her face, shaking the water from her eyes just in time to hear what Logan *did* say.

"Son of a bitch. You're a *mermaid*?" He raked his hands through the hair she'd caressed less than an hour ago. "How is this even possible? How—*why* are you here? I have to believe it because I saw you—I *saw* you. Swimming and diving and doing whatever the hell it was you were doing, but... but you... you're not real. Mermaids don't exist."

Angel's heart sank faster than a ship's anchor. This wasn't how she wanted him to find out.

She swam closer to shore. "Logan, I—"

"Get back." He held up a hand as if he was warding off some demon's curse. "Don't come any closer. You... you're... you're a mermaid."

Her flukes touched bottom as the water carried her to shore. "But I can explain—"

"I doubt it, Angel." He cursed again, planted his

hands on his hips, and took half a dozen steps back. "Is that even your name? Or is it Siren? That would explain your voice—you hypnotized me, didn't you?"

"No. No, I didn't, Logan. Not tonight. And my name really is Angel." Her hands hit the sand, and she wedged her flukes in to move up the beach. If she could just show him—

"Yeah, well then God has a warped sense of humor. I thought you *were* an angel. Sent to me in reparation for all the craziness in my life, for my good deeds and honest living. That my mother had finally got it right." He snorted and threw up his hands. "Yeah, that's a good one. God, she must have had a field day with this. A fucking mermaid."

His eyes burned into hers. "And what do you mean, 'not tonight'? You cast some sort of spell on me in the kitchen, didn't you? That's why I attacked you. Talk about sick. Who do you think you are, Angel? And I actually asked you to stay with me? I must be out of my mind."

"But Logan, that's what I want, too." If she could just get out of the water and dry off, she could make him understand. She knew she could.

"Really, Angel. A mermaid and a human? Like that could work. You're a myth."

"But I'm not. And it could. It *can*. My brothers and their wives have—"

"There are more of you?"

The disdain in his voice stopped her explanations. She'd never felt the need to be ashamed of who and what she was. Why did his words make her feel she should be?

"So, what were you planning?" He started pacing. "Get me out on my boat, then carry me to the bottom of the sea, and do whatever it is your kind does to humans?"

"We don't do anything with Hu—"

"Or is there another agenda? Are you the advance guard, sent to prepare the way for a horde of mermaids to descend on land and take over?"

"Why would we want to take—"

"Or is *this* it?" He spun around and pointed at her. "Is this why I went against every grain of common sense and let you into my house? My life? My son's? You with your magical ability to make men crave you. Was any of it real?"

"Logan, of course it wa—"

"Dammit, Angel!" He ran his hand over his mouth and looked away. "Why? Why me? Why couldn't you find some other schmoe to work your wiles on?" He pinched the bridge of his nose. "All I wanted was a normal life with a normal wife. Instead I get… this. You. I was falling for you, dammit. You almost succeeded. And Michael. God, did you even *think* about what this will do to him?"

Tears choked her. "Logan, please, let me explain—"

His laugh was cold. "It's too late. I've already seen the tail. There's nothing that can explain *that* away."

"But, Logan, I… I love you."

Nothing.

Only the lapping waves made a sound.

He finally met her eyes. "I bet you say that to all the sailors." He turned inland. "Go away, Angel. I don't need this in my life. I don't need… you."

In half a dozen strides of those long, strong legs of his—legs that had walked beside her on the beach, carried her to bed, slid against hers—he strode up the stairs and back into his home.

And out of her life.

Chapter 24

"ANGEL?" MICHAEL KNOCKED ON THE FRONT DOOR OF Angel's house, then put Rocky on his shoulder so they could both look in the window. It was morning. She should be awake by now. He was.

"Angel!" He knocked again and lifted the front of his hat out of his eyes. He didn't see her. "Do you see anything, Rocky?" He lifted Rocky over his head, then stopped, snorting at himself. *Stooopid.* Stuffed animals weren't real.

'Course, Logan said mermaids weren't real, so you never knew what was real and what wasn't.

Like that lizard peeking over the edge of the roof. Even though he looked like a statue, he was real. And Michael really wanted him for a pet, even if Angel said it wasn't fair.

Was it fair that *he* never got anything he wanted? Even when Rainbow brought him cool stuff like ice cream and soda that he wanted, she'd had to go to jail.

Oh, yeah. That. Michael sighed.

Rainbow told him after that stealing wasn't right, no matter what, so he wouldn't try to catch the lizard 'cause that'd be like stealing him from his family.

He sighed again and scrunched his mouth sideways. Rainbow scrunched her mouth, too. Usually when his clothes or shoes got too small.

Michael looked at the new sneakers Logan had

bought him. These were cool. Red with racing stripes. And shorts that didn't have holes in them. He could actually put stuff in his pockets without it falling out. Like the shell he'd found. And the sand dollar.

Except... oh. Crud. The sand dollar got all smushed.

Michael put the broken pieces on the window ledge. There were five little white things inside that looked like angels, but one of them fell to the ground.

He picked it up. Angels weren't supposed to fall; they were supposed to fly.

And swim, too.

"Where *is* she?" Michael tucked Rocky under his arm and scratched behind his bestest buddy's ears. They both did their best thinking that way.

"You might try the ocean."

Michael raised Rocky's face. "Did *you* say that?"

Rocky didn't answer him. But someone sighed real loud.

Michael looked around. "Hello?"

"Oy vey." Whoever-it-was sighed again.

Michael scrunched his mouth sideways again. If it wasn't him, and it wasn't Rocky, and it definitely wasn't Angel, that meant...

He looked at the lizard.

"I'm impressed," said the lizard. "Most Humans don't even think to look at me. But then, I guess when you've seen a mermaid, conversing with a reptile is nothing extraordinary."

"Oh, *cool!*" Michael set Rocky down and tried to pull the stone bench over so he could climb up and talk to the lizard. Maybe even convince him to come live with him.

If the lizard wanted to live with him, then it wasn't like making him a pet, right?

"Here, here, don't hurt yourself." The lizard sighed again. "I'll be right down. But don't come too close."

And he was right down, too. He moved so fast, Michael couldn't see him for a few seconds, but then the lizard was on the window ledge, standing on one of the angels.

"I bet you catch flies really good," Michael said.

"Only when there's nothing else available. Do you know where flies spend their time?" Ripples went up and down the lizard's back.

"I'm Michael. I'm six. What's your name?"

"Stewart. And if you're looking for Angel, she's not here. You might want to try the beach. Give her a good shout. *With* the wind, not into it, if you don't mind. She should be able to hear you."

"You mean she went swimming?"

Stewart turned his head sideways and licked his tongue over his lips. "Well, duh. It is what mermaids do, after all." The lizard's eyes rolled at different times.

Cool.

"So run along down there and find her. You do that, and I'll get back to the nap you woke me from."

Michael picked up Rocky. "Okay. Thanks. I'm sorry I woke you."

The lizard started climbing up the wall. Cool.

"Just don't do it again. Oh, and I wouldn't mention that I spoke to you. The adults of your species never believe you anyway, and I've seen more children have their mouths washed out with soap—for gods-know-*what* purpose—than I care to. I don't need another one on my conscience."

"Okay. Bye."

Stewart grunted, just like Mr. Ray used to do after he came back from tying something on. Michael never saw what he'd tied, but he sure knew to stay away from Mr. Ray and not wake him up. The grouchy lizard was just like him. He wouldn't make a good pet anyway.

Michael hung Rocky on his back, wrapping his front paws around his neck the same way Logan did when he'd carried him into the manatee place. It was a fun way to ride.

He ran down the steps to the beach, trying to hold Rocky with one hand and the railing with another. Angel said it was 'portant to hold on, and he didn't want her to get mad at him.

The sand was cold and squishy, not like when he and Logan built the sand castle. He hoped the water wasn't cold 'cause Angel didn't buy a coat with all her icky girl stuff.

A wave got too close to his cool new sneakers. He jumped away and slid on a jellyfish. Logan told him never to touch one of those or they could sting him. He looked at the mushy mess. He didn't see a stinger. Not like a bee had. Bee stings hurt.

Another wave got close again, and he almost dropped Rocky. Michael looked around. Rocky wouldn't like getting wet. It made him soggy and sad.

He saw a big rock and put Rocky on it. Ha ha! Rocky on a rock! He made a joke!

Michael looked out to sea. Where was Angel? He wanted to tell it to her.

Well, Stewart said she went swimming, so…

Michael took off his new red sneakers and put them

on both sides of Rocky to keep him sitting up. Rocky fell over sometimes, and Michael didn't want him to get all sandy. Rocky didn't like sand. And Rainbow never let Michael take Rocky to bed with him if he was all dirty. Wonder if Angel would let him?

Michael took off his socks and put them on Rocky's paws in case he got cold. Then he walked down to where the sand got wet. The waves weren't very big but he didn't see her.

Stewart said to call her in the wind. That made no sense 'cause mermaids lived under the water. But Michael was smart. Rainbow always told him so, so he would call Angel where she lived.

He took off his hat, then with a real big breath, he stuck his head under the next wave and yelled, "Aaannngggeeelll! Where aaarrreee you?"

It sounded all garble-y. He hoped she heard him. Maybe he needed to try again.

———

A.C. heard him the first time. And the second. And the third.

Hades, the entire ocean probably heard the pup.

"Son-of-a-barracuda! Did you hear that?" He spun around, almost whipping Lou in the face with his tail fluke.

Missed. Damn.

Lou rolled one of his black, black eyes. "Yeah, I heard."

"She's gone. You want to tell me how she got by you?" Never mind that he'd been off getting some sweet tail from that *sweet* Abby… Zeus. Old guys. What a bunch of lazy tails. Thought that because they'd lived longer, they were always right. Ha. The reason they'd lived so long is that they didn't have a single *cojone* between them. All talk, no teeth.

Lou shut the eye without answering, and A.C. worked his mouth over his own teeth, feeling the flesh give way against the sharp spikes he worked so hard to cultivate. Sharper than broken coral, able to slice better than any sheared seashell, *this* was a set of choppers to be proud of. He wanted to put them to good use.

But Harry had said no. *Stay put, and keep both eyes on things.* Guess ol' Har forgot to mention that second part to Lou.

Well, ya know what? A.C. was sick and tired of listening to Harry call the shots. *Don't eat the mermaid, wait here, keep an eye out...* When were they going to get to the good part? And he didn't mean the gut. Or maybe he did. It was definitely better than an arm. Not enough meat there...

Fuck this. He was sick of swimming to someone else's tune—especially someone who wasn't even here.

He checked out the other Hammers. To a fish, they were all napping. *Napping*, for fuck's sake. Un-fucking-believable.

A.C. clamped his jaws shut. Shit. One of his teeth cracked loose. Damn it. Now was *not* the time to need a replacement. That always took a few days.

No way was he waiting here another few days. Matter of fact, he didn't want to wait here another minute.

"AAAnnngggeeelll!" the pup screamed again, this time in the air, thank-the-gods, since sound traveled so much better under water and the pup was loud enough to wake the dead—though obviously not sleeping Hammers who'd gone out for a late-night dinner and a game of Who Can Toss The Clam The Farthest. Ugh. Not even an octopus-tossing event. He'd head for the closest retirement reef before he'd let his life turn into *that*.

"AAAnnngggeeellll!" The pup was back to screaming underwater.

Hmmm…

A.C. glanced at Lou. Yeah, he was napping, too.

Well, Hades. He wanted *some*thing out of this waste of time. An appetizer was better than nothing.

A.C. switched into stalker mode—what he was known for. Silent but deadly, that was him.

He just hoped he could lure the pup far enough into the water to be able to grab him.

Chapter 25

HARRY SWAM BACK AND FORTH ALONG THE WALKWAY outside Ceto's Bahamian Palace, waiting for her guards to announce him. They'd probably shove a mouth guard in his jaw, too. The mother of all sea monsters was obsessive about her security.

Like he'd try to take a bite out of her. The gods might have stipulated what she could and couldn't do with her goddess powers, but some magic was stronger than none, and since he was a mere mortal, he wasn't about to test her. He didn't have a death wish.

What he did have was a hyper sense of justice. Sharks had been getting a bad rap ever since that ridiculous Human propaganda thirty-some *selinos* ago, giving *all* sharks a bad name, not just the Great Whites. He'd lost a lot of family members over the *selinos* to the hysteria Humans had created.

The annoyingly ironic thing was that Great Whites *were* rather bite-happy. Stupid idiots. Couldn't tell a sea lion from a Human… Now *all* sharks were paying the price.

Fine, then. Let the Greats make their own argument with The Council, but Hammerhead attacks on Humans were out of necessity, not stupidity. It wasn't as if Bipeds were so tasty that they were a sought-after delicacy. Most of them didn't have enough meat on their bones to make it worthwhile anyway. As for the angst that happened afterward… nah. Not worth the effort.

The Council owed them representation, but Harry had been beating that dead seahorse for *selinos* with no results. He was done leaving things up to protocol— and to the Fates. Gods knew, those "ladies" were fickle enough to find offense with anything.

No. He wanted this resolved in his lifetime—which was why he was about to propose something to Ceto he thought she'd go for. It never hurt to have a backup plan, and Ceto was his. Even though the bitch had kept him waiting the entire night and he'd missed Angel's late-night return to the sea that was all the talk around the cooler water, Ceto always got results.

Just like he would when he saw Lou and A.C. and the rest of the clowns who'd let Angel escape. Son-of-a-barracuda…

Thank the gods, Roger had had the good sense to let him know what was happening. It was worth every scrap of chum he could steal from those idiot Bipeds to pay the crane to keep an eye on things on land.

A pair of European man-o'-wars swung the white marble doors of Ceto's palace inward with their tentacles, the rush of water sucking any sea life strolling outside the gates in with him. Not that there was much. Ceto wasn't what anyone would call a good neighbor.

But Harry went along for the ride. Let Ceto have her power play; he was about to offer her a big enough opportunity she'd be bowing before *him* when all was said and done.

"The goddess will see you now," said a tiger shark. "This way."

Harry followed him down a long, domed tunnel decorated in abalone and oyster. Chandelier squid mantles, lit by hatchetfish and strung with pearls, dangled from the ceiling, making the whole place sparkly and girly. Ceto had invested heavily in her palace—taking the I-am-goddess-hear-me-roar thing a bit too seriously, in his opinion.

The tunnel opened into an amphitheater—which it had once been. Ceto floated—of course—on a raised dais made of glass, beneath which the most colorful of the local tropicals swam. Ionic columns held a canopy of sailcloth above her head. Probably stolen from one of her victims—she did love to live up to her Queen of the Bermuda Triangle reputation. Her chair was a sea sponge she'd bewitched into a throne for that very purpose. Ceto liked true creature comforts.

"Ah, Harry. To what do I owe the pleasure?" She swept a taloned—that is, *manicured*—hand before her, indicating the kowtowing area of the orchestra pit in front of her.

When the previous dynasty had ruled Atlantis, this building had been the *in* place. Full of hedonism and free spirits, it'd been their final corruption. The gods had reclaimed the throne for Poseidon's heirs and moved Atlantis under Bermuda, giving Ceto, he'd heard, the opportunity to get this place for a song. Literally.

Harry tried to keep the smile off his face. The orchestra pit. She was really overdoing it. But Harry went along with it. Sometimes playing to her vanity was the best offense.

"Good day, Ceto. You're looking lovely, as usual." Her malachite hair squirmed around her head, also as usual, and her twin tails shifted through the full spectrum of colors. The false image of relaxation didn't fool Harry for a second.

No one showed up at any of Ceto's palaces without reason. This wasn't a swim-by visit and they both knew it.

Harry settled himself in the pit as best he could while still managing to writhe enough to keep water moving over his gills. It was the one thing he hated about being a shark. Other fish could remain still, but sharks, for whatever reason, weren't granted swim bladders. If he stopped moving, he'd drown. Rumor had it that some ancestor had annoyed a god so severely that the god had forced this on the shark's descendants. Probably a Great White.

"Ah, Harry, such a charmer." Ceto motioned for one of her Serving Nautiluses to offer him a snack.

Harry didn't have as much luck keeping the smile off his face this time. The cephalopod acted as if Harry was going to take a bite of him. A little too self-important was that Nautilus. They were even worse tasting than Bipeds.

Harry shook his head, and the Nautilus left as fast as his gaseous escape mechanism—very appropriate term in Harry's opinion—would allow.

"Thank you for your hospitality, Ceto, but I'm here on an urgent matter."

"Oh?" The sea monster leaned forward, her shell-fillers almost spilling out of the Human top she wore.

He didn't get the fascination she had with their clothing. It tasted awful, was a pain in the tail to pick out of his teeth, and ruined the presentation as far as he was concerned. Still, whatever floated her boat.

Harry quickly explained his complaint with The Council, knowing he had a kindred spirit in Ceto, then mentioned Angel's escape and how she'd ended up on land. And the fact that she was now back in the sea.

"So where do I come in?" Ceto motioned for her personal Nautilus and took a handful of mussels off the platter he offered, crunching them one at a time. "I'm not setting a fin on land." She fluttered all four of the fins in question.

"That wasn't my plan. I want to capture her."

"So why involve me? Just go bite the twit." She snatched up a handful of prawns.

"How's Joey doing?" Joey had been the Human reward the gods had given Ceto during that whole Reel fiasco. Harry waited for her answer—and her reaction. Joey, he knew, could be a sore subject.

Ceto dropped the prawn that was halfway to her mouth. "Oh, gods, don't get me started." She shook her head. "He doesn't shut up. He's either complaining about the accommodations, barking about his rights—as if he has any—or screaming in pleasure. And, frankly, the screaming is getting on my nerves the most. The man is a selfish hog. Sure, he gets to enjoy it, but me? Pleh. The guy wouldn't find the Mariana Trench if I dropped him in it, let alone anything else. Some prize he turned out to be."

TMI, but the info fit with his plan. "So how would you like another one?"

"Another Joey?" Ceto's mouth twisted in disgust. "No thank you."

"Not Joey. Another Human."

Ceto raised one of her eyebrows, took a mussel off the platter, and ran it over her lips. "Go on." She cracked the shells between her teeth.

"Here's what I've got. I want to capture Angel and stash her here. Ransom her."

Ceto spit the shells at him. One hit him in the starboard eye. Great.

"Sorry, Harry, but I've done my time with The Council. They're still annoyed with me over my last infraction, in case you've forgotten. I highly doubt they'd be willing to give me another Human if I abduct one of their princesses."

"No, no. You misunderstand me, Ceto. I'll do the abducting. You'll just be loaning out your palace for a while as a holding cell. There's not much else in the ocean that will hold her. And you don't even have to be here. You could leave today, then I can bring her here, lock her up, and no one will be the wiser. Once my demands have been met, I'll release her."

"So where does the other Human come into play?"

"Angel is interested in one."

Ceto cackled like the witch she could be. "You're kidding."

He swung his head from side to side. "Looks like Fisher won't end up with any full-blooded grandchildren at this rate."

"Three out of five of his spawn are hooked on Humans. Ah, the delicious irony." Ceto popped another mussel in her maw.

"Right. So, Angel's interested in a Human. *And* he has a son."

"A child?" Ceto sucked in enough water Harry thought she might choke.

There was nothing Ceto wanted more in this world than a child. Human, Mer, monster… the race didn't matter to her since the gods had forbidden her to procreate.

"Yeah. Angel was singing to the Human and you know what that means. He's under her spell. So we'll grab her, and he and his kid will be right behind. You can have them in return for the use of your palace."

"And I can keep the child. Turn him even…" Ceto picked up a shrimp and studied him, waving the crustacean under her nose. "It could work…"

Oh, yeah. Ceto had taken the bait. He had her on board now.

Angel wasn't going to get away. This time, The Council would have to give in to his demands.

Or else.

Chapter 26

ANGEL DRAGGED HERSELF ONTO THE BEACH OF THE LAST deserted cay before Bermuda and plopped her tail in the sand. Forget heading home. She wasn't up for it. Physically, mentally, emotionally.

All she'd wanted was to prove to her brother that she had what it took to do the job. And look what her life had turned into...

Yeah, she'd proved something all right. She'd proved that she was so unqualified to do the job it was laughable, and worse than that, that she didn't know as much about Humans as she thought she did.

Great. Her degree, her thesis, her life's work... all of it wasted.

If Logan was too hardheaded to give her a chance to explain, well, then, no wonder the planet was in the shape it was in. Stubborn, prejudiced...

Oh who was she kidding?

She missed him like Hades. Last night had been perfect... Until she'd gotten out of that bed.

He'd wanted her; he cared about her. He'd said he was falling for her. They could have had something together. But she'd blown it.

A tear fell onto one of her scales, amethyst shimmering through the perfect, round drop until another splashed it away. Then another.

Tears. She was shedding tears for a Human.

She brushed them away. She was not going to cry over him.

But the tears didn't stop. Silent, heartbreakingly silent, they fell onto her tail, mingling with the saltwater, back into their element. As she was.

Gods. He'd been so disappointed. So... angry. So hurtful.

A crab came scuttling across the sand toward her, one of his claws waving as if she were here on a state visit. She shook her head and flicked her fingers to send him back where he came from. She wasn't up for small talk, and the fish carcass he was dragging held no appeal.

After taking an elaborate bow, the crab turned shell and ran away.

And, yes, so maybe she'd done the same thing, but could anyone blame her?

Especially after the way Logan had reacted. She hadn't tried to enchant him; how could he believe that of her? Last night had been so different from the kiss in the kitchen—didn't it mean *anything* to him?

Making love with him had been so perfect; how could it not be special to him? How could he not get beyond her tail to realize that? They'd fit together, their bodies in perfect harmony, creating music all their own. She hadn't sung a note. Love had made last night what it was. Wonderful. Special. Beautiful.

Another tear fell onto the back of her hand. How could he turn what had happened between them into something dark and ugly?

She picked up a handful of white sand and tossed it onto her flukes. So what if she was a Mer? She was a woman. One he'd felt something for, dammit. There was no faking *that*. What-in-Hades difference did it make if she had a tail? She certainly didn't look at him and say, "Oh yeah, he'd do if he could only lose the leg thing."

She sniffed back another round of tears. Why couldn't Humans accept people as they were instead of putting labels on them? Notice the similarities instead of the differences?

She flipped the sand off her flukes and washed them in the gentle waves, scrubbing at her eyes. Her amethyst scales were pretty, not something to be ashamed of, dammit.

Good thing she hadn't considered giving it up—especially not for him, the hogsheaded, stuck-in-the-sand, stubborn son-of-a—

Angel fell back to rest on her elbows and looked at the calm ripple of the sea's surface. The truth was, she might have.

Gods, what did that say about her? Half—if not all—of her life seemed to have been defined by conforming to others' views and expectations of her. Angel, the student? Check. Angel, the Human-crazy Mer? Got that covered. Angel, the two-legged babysitter? Yep.

Angel, who'd destroyed the veil of secrecy that had shrouded their race for millennia?

Sadly, that, too, was her.

She sniffled again. The thing was, they *were* her. All of them. But she was so much more than that. She was a compilation of life events and wishes and dreams and purpose and determination and...

And lies.

Yeah. That. She'd lied to him.

Her head fell back, and she closed her eyes. A liar. She'd been reduced to lying about who she was. Reduced to skulking around to find some way to wiggle into the job she wanted. Granted, Rod should interview her like he did everyone else, but she, too, should have gone about applying for the job like everyone else did—in ways not designed to break the rules and subvert tried and true Mer practices.

She deserved everything she'd gotten—or hadn't gotten.

She flung her arms out to her sides and fell back against the sand, the sun warming her, and she remembered Mariana's suggestion about getting burned.

The pain in her heart was more searing than any ray of the sun.

Gods… Logan. How could it have gone so wrong?

And Michael… She'd promised him she'd be there this morning, and now she'd made a liar out of herself with that, too. The poor kid had been through so much already…

A wave came out of nowhere to splash over her, salty drops sprinkling her face. Ah, the irony of the Universe flinging her tears back at her.

Okay, already. She got it. She should have kept to the original plan of observing and not gotten involved. It was all her own fault.

So what was she going to do about it?

Angel grabbed two handfuls of sand. Do? What *could* she do? Logan had made his point perfectly clear, and she was not a glutton for punishment. She wasn't going to do anything. That stupid conscience of hers could just take a permanent vacation some place cold. Like Antarctica. Angel didn't want to hear anything from it ever again.

Yet here she floated, moaning and giving up. Was that really what she wanted to do for the rest of her life?

Not really. But Rod certainly wasn't going to give her the job now, and what else could she do? She'd left her notes in Logan's guesthouse, and there was no way to fix this. Logan didn't want to listen; she'd lied to him and had—albeit inadvertently—bewitched him. He had a valid point. Several, in fact.

And Rod was sure to point out—not that he needed to because she was certainly aware of that fact now—that if she could screw up something like this, something so important to her, so personal, what did it say about her ability to handle the big-ticket items like world peace and interspecies integration?

No. She was done. She'd turn in her degree along with her aspirations and find something else to do. Salvage work maybe.

At least her Human knowledge would be good for something.

Chapter 27

COME TO PAPA! A.C.'S PRIZED TEETH GROUND AGAINST EACH other in anticipation—and this time he didn't give a flying fuck that a few broke off. Breakfast was about to be served.

"AAAnngggeeelll!"

Of *course* the pup had to be yelling underwater. A.C. wanted to clean out his ears. Too bad they were on the dorsal side of his head and he couldn't reach them. Hades. Didn't the pup have anything else to say? Another tone he could use?

If only he could surge in and grab him, but A.C. was still a few yards too far out, and the water was becoming too shallow for him to be able to function properly. And if there was one thing a Hammerhead liked to do, it was function properly. He was a veritable killing machine created by the gods. He hadn't missed any prey yet.

Except that Mer…

Yeah. Much as he hated to admit it, the fact that Angel had gotten away did count as a miss. Couldn't have that. He had a 100 percent EVA. Earned Victim Average. He'd put a lot of effort into it.

A.C. strummed his pectoral fin against the sandy bottom. How could he get Angel?

"AAAAnnnnggggeeeellll! I wanna come with you!" The pup splashed a few more yards into the water.

How handy was that?

"Hey, pup. I mean, kid." A.C. tilted his head sideways so the words would resonate above the water. Hammers were definitely *not* made to talk like this, but when you wanted something badly enough, you found a way.

"Who said that?" The pup stopped screaming. Finally.

Another handy thing was the fact that Human vocal chords were located in the neck, A.C.'s usual target of attack.

Although… Hmmm… Maybe he wouldn't eat him. Well, not yet anyway. If the pup—kid—cared this much about her, maybe she cared about him, too, and why *not* kill two parrotfish with one strike?

Yeah. He'd use the *kid* as bait to lure Angel out of her royal air bubble. Wouldn't *that* be a bait and switch? Mers were all about protecting the young—even Human young. He'd seen some perfectly fine cruise-ship meals pass him by, thanks to those damn altruistic Mers-turned-dolphins.

Dolphins. *Blech*. Mammal, or a Mer who'd turned into one for whatever idiotic reason they came up with, the result was the same: perpetually smiling, happy do-gooders. Made him want to puke.

The kid stopped moving and put a hat on his head.

Yeah, that ought to protect him.

Not.

"Angel?"

"No. Me." A.C.'s mind was churning along with the anticipation in his gut. He knew what he was going to do. And it was going to be a *b-eaut*. Everyone would be talking about this catch.

It really was a no-brainer to see why he was high on the food chain in every ocean. Instinct jumped in and saved him where indecision could have lost him this deal.

"You're… a shark."

Oooh, score one for the Human. "Yeah, I am. Problem with that?"

"Sharks eat people."

Only if they qualified as a meal. This pup was barely an appetizer. "Well, some do. But not all of us. And I can take you to Angel."

"You can? Cool!"

A.C. had absolutely no problem lying to him. A shark with a conscience was a skinny shark. Dead, even.

Besides he *would* take him to her. Right before he ate both of them.

The Human started heading in deeper. A little slower than A.C. would have liked, but it was progress—to both a gargantuan meal and one hell of a reputation. He didn't know the last time a shark had gotten a Mer.

"You really know where Angel is?"

Heh. He'd hooked the little sucker. "You betcha."

And then the sucker stopped. Two more feet, and *his* two feet would be A.C.'s.

"I dunno."

Gods save him from creatures with a brain—which would be why he put up with Abby. What that shark could do with only two brain cells…

"Look, kid. I can't hang out here all day. You comin' or what?" A.C. even turned a hundred-and-twenty degrees to make it look legit.

"How?"

"*How*?" What did he mean, how? It was the ocean. He was a shark. Was there really a question?

"Yeah. How? I can't breathe water like you and Angel can. I don't wanna get drowned."

Fuck. He hadn't thought about that.

A.C. scanned the area. He didn't see any boats around. No one to see him hauling his prize through the water and decide *he'd* make a nicer prize.

"Yeah. Okay. Whatever. You can ride on top. Climb on." The things he did for dinner. And lunch. And an appetizer... He'd savor every one of Angel's scales.

"Okay. I'm comin'." And with that, two little legs splashed through the waves, right toward him. A.C.'s mouth started to water.

The kid climbed aboard and grabbed hold of his dorsal. A.C. hoped none of the guys saw him acting like those stupid, Human-friendly dolphins, but then, they had no room to talk. They were just plain stupid. Besides, they were probably still asleep. Losers.

Still, A.C. wanted to hightail it out of there, so he whipped his caudal fin sideways—and almost flung his appetizer off in the process. He slowed down so the kid could hold on for dear life—such a futile gesture—because there was no fucking way he was gonna lose his ticket to a tasty Mer meal. This was like taking candy from a baby.

No. Make that, *making* candy from a baby.

Chapter 28

LOGAN WOKE UP WITH A HELL OF A HANGOVER. AND he hadn't even been drinking—how was that for *fucking sucks*?

No, it wasn't a hangover. He was drained. Physically from one of the best nights of his life—*before* her revelation—and emotionally… from, well…

The damn revelation itself.

She was a mermaid. A *mermaid*.

He wouldn't have believed it if he hadn't seen it with his own eyes. He almost wished he'd touched her tail—

No he didn't. She was a *mermaid*, for chrissake.

Mermaids were myths. Legends. Sirens. They lured ships onto rocks and sailors to their deaths by promising nights of deadly delight. Which she'd proved in that damn kitchen.

He *knew* something weird had been going on. He didn't attack women. No matter how gorgeous they were.

And yet, he'd *slept* with her. Was he out of his mind?

He had to be. She had to have cast some spell over him to make him fall—oh, shit.

Logan threw the covers off, one half of his brain calling him all sorts of idiot for even thinking what he was thinking, the other half terrified she *had* actually done something to him.

He looked down.

Normal. Thank God.

Tired and worn out, but normal.

Je-*sus*.

Logan dropped his head back on the pillow, his arms flopping to the sides, his hand curling into an indentation he found on his left. When he realized what he was doing, he yanked it away.

She. Was. A. Mermaid.

Logan ran a hand over his face. He needed a shave.

Hell, he needed a lot of things. A shave, a shower, a drink, and a trip out of town. Not necessarily in that order.

Michael.

Logan closed his eyes, groaning. How was he going to tell Michael about Angel leaving?

How was he going to tell Michael about *Angel*?

Uh, son? Remember when I said mermaids don't exist? Well, I was wrong. They do, and they're every bit as sensuous and desirable as the legends say.

Yeah. Not kid material.

Seriously, what was he going to tell Michael?

Kicking the rest of the sheet off, Logan groaned his way to sitting. He dropped his hands between his legs, resting his elbows on his thighs, chin to his chest, and took a deep breath.

And another.

Somehow he was going to have to explain to his son that the woman he'd come to care about was gone. Logan wasn't sure if that "he" referred to Michael, or to him.

Logan stood up. It didn't matter who it referred to. She was gone. It was over—and there was a mermaid swimming somewhere out in the water off the coast of Florida and he was the only one who knew about it.

As if anyone would believe him anyway.

He turned on the shower, the quick hiss of the cold spray hitting his skin with the brutality he needed to really wake up and get out of this fog. So, okay, he wouldn't be telling anyone he'd seen—slept with—a mermaid. Life could go on just as it always had. As it had before she'd shown up.

Ignoring the fact that the shampoo in his shower was the same one he'd stocked the guesthouse with—he was *not* going to remember what she'd smelled like—Logan poured some onto his palm, then rubbed it into his hair— a little too vigorously.

Good job on the ignoring...

He took a breath. Life *would* go on as it had before she'd shown up.

Except life *wasn't* the same, and she *had* shown up—

And he'd gone and fallen in love with her.

His eyes started to burn. Shit. He'd gotten shampoo in them.

Logan ducked his face beneath the spray, gritting his teeth against the pain.

In his eyes. The pain in his eyes.

Yeah, right.

Okay, so what? Yeah, it hurt. He'd never been in love with anyone before, not even Christine, and now, when he did go and fall in love, she was a freaking *mermaid*?

Talk about fucked up. And he'd thought the circus was bad. Wouldn't his parents just love to get their hands on her? The perfect sideshow.

Hell. That damn prediction of Nadia's. She'd actually been right.

But so what? There could never be anything between him and Angel. She was a *mermaid*.

Maybe if he said it enough, it'd start to make sense.

Blinking his eyes, Logan turned off the shower and grabbed a towel, scrubbing his face with it, trying to stop the pain.

If only it were that easy with his heart. How the hell did you fall *out* of love?

He wrapped the towel around his waist, tossed back a few aspirin, then headed to his closet. However you fell out of love, he was going to do it. He wanted Normal. Not the sideshow. Not a scientific anomaly or a legend come to life. Normal. Was that too much to ask?

Apparently it was, and now he had to tell Michael.

He was probably looking forward to that less than trying to get last night out of his head. *All* of last night.

Logan pulled on his shorts and grabbed a button-down off a hanger, folding the sleeves back on his forearms as he walked down the hallway to his son's room. Ten o'clock. They'd both overslept. No surprise why he had. But, Michael? Actually, that *was* surprising.

Logan opened the door. "Hey, Mi—"

The bed was empty. Great. *Real responsible, Hardington, letting a six-year-old get up for breakfast on his own.*

And he thought he could do this parenting thing, how?

Logan scratched his chest, then looked down. He'd buttoned the damn buttons wrong. And he wondered how he could sleep through Michael getting up? Obviously too damn easily.

Reworking the buttons, Logan headed downstairs, checking the kitchen and finding it empty. No cereal bowl in the sink. He opened the dishwasher.

Not there either.

He walked down the half-flight of stairs to the family room. "Michael?"

No answer.

Now he was worried.

Logan ran out the back and headed to the pool, dread pulling at him, weighing down his legs.

He jumped the gate and ran to the edge.

Oh thank God. No Michael.

So where the hell *was* he—

The ocean!

Logan ran across the flagstone path, down the steps, and onto the beach. Sand filled his shoes as he ran. He kicked them off.

"Michael!"

God, had Michael wandered down here? Had he seen Angel?

Had she taken him?

The thought punched him in the gut, and he stumbled to a stop.

Had that been her plan all along?

The thought sucked the rest of the wind out of him.

No. She wouldn't do that. She *couldn't* do that. Not after last night.

But what did he really know about last night? Hell, what did he really know about mermaids? They had to have gotten their reputation somehow.

Oh, God… he'd willingly brought her into his home. Set the stage for this…

Then he saw Rocky.

And the sneakers.

"Michael!"

The word tore from his throat, burning raw with regret as he fell to his knees at the water's edge.

Chapter 29

"Nice." Ginger tsk-tsked as she watched Logan fall onto the sand, then she turned to stare at the brown lizard sunning himself on the guesthouse's eave. "You really performed a public service this time."

The lizard didn't say a word.

Ginger sighed. "You do know I can see you, right?"

He still didn't respond, but one of his eyes rolled her way.

"Don't you go rolling your eyes independently of each other at me." She undulated her neck. "I call it like I see it. And you blew it, buddy. Big time."

The lizard turned even darker brown. That was such a neat ability, being able to change color. Too bad the only way she could do it was by giving up her favorite food in the world, shrimp. And even then, it took a while and she only turned white. White. Big flappin' deal. Thank goodness Roger adored her in pink, but still… It'd be nice to change for a change.

She took a step closer to the house. "Stewie, I really think—"

"It's Stewart." The lizard turned green with indignation.

Wonder what color he turned in envy? Ginger shook her head. She was stuck with pink, even in envy. "All right, *Stewart*. What were you thinking sending a child to the beach? Alone? Anything could happen. Take, for instance, that overblown hammerhead out there. He actually talked the kid into going along for a ride. What do you think is going to happen, hmmm? Didn't think about that, did you? Now you're going to have that kid's death on your bony little prehensile fingers. I hope you can live with yourself."

Stewart's tail twitched, and his hind legs bunched beneath him. "Hey, I can't help it if he's as bright as a gecko. He wanted to know, and he was waking the entire neighborhood. Do you *want* all the other Humans to find out about her? What do you think would happen when his father found the kid bawling his eyes out? The story would have come out."

"Look, you undersized dinosaur, the story already *did* come out. Logan found out about her last night. Was quite nasty about it, if I do say so myself."

Not that she'd been listening or anything. Well, okay, yes, she had been listening. But they'd had their little tell-all right next to her roost. She hadn't gone out of her way to listen in. Really, no one could have *avoided* hearing what they were saying.

That was her story and she was sticking to it.

Not that it was any of Stewart's business.

"You know, Stewart. If you'd kept your big ol' dewlap shut, Logan would have calmed the kid down and that would have been that. But, no. You just had to get involved, didn't you?" Ginger rotated her neck to get the kinks out. She really hated when animals did stupid things; it gave Humans the right to think *all* animals were stupid. "Now he *has* to go after her, and the entire Mer world is going to know that she let the catbird out of the cage, and all of Atlantis is going to be up in fins. Not to mention, you *know* how Humans are when it comes to their young."

"Something you obviously don't have a clue about." Stewart, the little smart-ass, leered at her. "Besides what do you care? I didn't know you were a member of the Angel Tritone Fan Club."

"Look, you komodo wannabe, just because I don't want to sit at home on any guy's roost doesn't mean I don't like kids. Or have a conscience. You just sent one off to his death. How can you *live* with yourself?" When would the dinosaurs stop trying to take over the world? They'd botched that job millions of *selinos* ago—had gotten themselves extinct to boot. Now their upstart ancestors were trying to do it again. Would the reptiles never learn?

"There's only one thing left to do." Seriously, birds were so much better equipped to deal with these kinds of emergencies—which was why they'd survived and the dinosaurs hadn't.

"You're quite right. There is." Stewart turned to face the other way, a co-mingling of brown and green over-taking his scrawny little body. "Go back to sleep."

On second thought, perhaps that color-morph thing wasn't the most attractive trait. "If I were you, Stewart"—perish the thought—"I might want to find another spot."

"What are you talking about?" Stewart asked, doing that independent eye-rolling thing again. That wasn't attractive either. Yes, she was very glad she'd been hatched a beautiful, lithe, seductive flamingo. "You don't eat lizards."

Heh. Let him sweat it. Well, only figuratively, since reptiles were physiologically incapable of that—another reason she was glad she was a bird.

"Correction, genius. We aren't *known* to eat lizards. That doesn't mean we don't."

Not that she'd come near him with a ten-foot beak, but he did deserve a little angst for the big angst he'd contributed to.

And now he turned so light brown that he was almost white. Ah, blanched with fear. She'd heard the term before but had never seen it put into practice. And it soooo wasn't attractive either.

Yes, Ginger, ol' bird, being a flamingo is where it's at.

That's why she was going to do what she was about to do. After all, the lizard caused it, but *she* got to be the heroine. Let those Orlando chicks eat their shriveled, old, gossipy hearts out.

She took a step forward, hiding her smile when he took a step back. "Listen up, *Stewie*. You need to fix this. Go find a storm petrel or someone who knows one. Get that bird in the air after Angel. She needs to know what's going on."

Hmmm… Who would play her in the movie? There weren't many Hollywood-ified flamingos.

Hey, *she* could do it. After all, who better to play her than her?

She'd show those Orlando babes a thing or two. There was a big ol' movie studio there. She didn't have to hang out at the marine park with them. Nuh-uh. Not her. She was headed for the bright lights and the big time.

Giving the lizard one last look, Ginger straightened the feathers on her crown, fluffed her back and then her breast to glam up for her trip, and took off down the beach to give Logan the low-down.

She just hoped he'd listen.

Chapter 30

LOGAN WAS GOING CRAZY.

That had to be it.

Michael's disappearance had sent him sailing over the edge of the cliffs of insanity because he was *standing on a beach, looking for a kidnapping mermaid.*

But what other choice did he have? The authorities would lock him up if he went to them with this story.

He should have gone to them with Angel.

A mermaid. Jesus Christ.

Logan dropped his head, pinching the bridge of his nose, willing himself to focus. Recriminations could come later. Right now, he had to find Michael.

So where did one begin to start looking for a mermaid? *Atlantis?*

"Hey there, good-looking." A female voice, sultry and sexy, came from behind him.

Logan looked over his shoulder. He didn't have the time, nor the inclination, to fend off some woman's advances.

But there was no one there.

Logan shook his head. He had to be hearing things. That went with Crazy, right?

He turned back around and looked out to sea again, shielding his eyes with his hand, hoping against all odds to see her there in the waves. At the very least, see her tail.

Hell. Her *tail*.

"I might be able to help you."

Okay, he did not imagine that.

Logan dropped his hand and spun around.

Again, no one.

He was really losing it because if anyone had been there, she would have frightened off the flamingo that was eyeballing at him.

Wait. *Why* was a flamingo staring at him? From six feet away? Why wasn't the bird scared of him?

"Yes, I'm talking to you." The flamingo's beak worked in tandem with that sultry voice.

Logan looked around.

A "hmmph!" came from the direction of... the bird?

That wasn't possible. Flamingos didn't speak English. In sultry, come-hither voices.

And mermaids don't show up in your bed either.

Logan's heart was pounding in his ears. He was having a stroke. A heart attack. An out-of-body experience brought on by his son's disappearance.

He took a few deep breaths, still staring at the bird.

"No, you're not going crazy, and, yes, I did speak." The bird took two steps forward. "So, can we dispense with the disbelief and discuss what you're looking for? I have a feeling I know."

"You... talk?" Logan was glad to hear *he* could talk. Apparently, hallucinations went with Crazy, too.

The bird could also sigh. Even roll her eyes.

It was a her, wasn't it?

"Yes. I talk. I also fly, but that doesn't seem to be all that interesting to you, and I promise you it's far more complicated than those airplanes y'all are so thrilled with. That's why your kind can't do it."

He would swear the bird was putting a sway in her step as she came closer. "What… why… are you talking to me?"

The flamingo dropped her head to the sand as if her neck gave out. She looked at him upside down. "Honestly, I don't know why I'm even bothering. You came flying down those steps like a bat out of Hades, and your first question has to do with why I'm speaking? Is that really the most pressing matter in your life right now?"

The bird had a point. Which was as bizarre as anything else in the last few days. Logan took another deep breath, then another, slid his hands to his hips, and tried to regain some semblance of sanity.

"You're right. That's the least of my worries. So… *Miss…*" What did you call a flamingo? "What do you know about my son?"

The bird picked her head up and stretched to her full five-foot height, beak in the air. "Ginger."

"I'm sorry, what?"

"My name. It's Zingiber La Fleur, but feel free to call me Ginger." She spread her wings and dipped her beak with a gracious bow, but the elegant image was destroyed by that name.

The bird had a stripper name. Would wonders never cease? Fine. Whatever. "Look, Ginger, it's nice to meet you, but I have to find my son."

She tucked her wings at her side again and picked up one of her bony legs.

"Yes, Logan. I know." She spoke to him as if he were a three-year-old. "But standing here on the beach isn't going to do you any good. He's out in the middle of the ocean. Where I suggest you hurry up and get to."

His hearing was going. First his mind, now his hearing. "What are you talking about?" Yep, sanity was gone.

The bird—*Ginger La Fleur*—sighed and did some weird twirling thing with her head. "Pay attention, gorgeous. Your son hooked Angel on your fishing trip the other day and helped her hide out in your boat. You brought her back. You let her live here. The kid got attached. So when you pulled your bird-brained move— No. Wait. Scratch that." She did, with her bony toes in the sand. "That idiotic stunt last night isn't even worthy of the name 'bird-brained.' When you pulled that slimy-like-an-eel move last night by kissing her off—and it was a kiss-off, don't think a bunch of us didn't see that PDA on the beach, by the way—she headed back home.

"Then Stewart, the brainiac, just *had* to tell your kid where she went, and a self-serving hammerhead showed up—and I'm worried that he will actually serve himself. Your kid hitched a ride out to the middle of nowhere with him. You know, you really need to have a life talk with the kid. Tell him all about the hazards of accepting rides from strangers, especially ones with fins—*mrrrmmph.*"

If someone would have told Logan that someday he'd find the need to muzzle a flamingo, never mind actually *do* it, he would have told that person to have his head examined. Now *he* was the one who needed to have his head examined.

"Can we just get back to what you said about a hammerhead?" he asked the flamingo—knowing he'd consider the insanity of that question after he had his son back.

She nodded her head.

"Fine. I'm going to release your beak." Another sentence he'd never have guessed in a million years that he'd say. "I want you to stick to the facts. What exactly happened?"

Ginger—good God—expelled an indignant, fish-laden breath. "I may not seem threatening to you, but I've got enough pounds of pressure in this beak to do some serious damage. Try that again, and you'll lose at least one finger, if not more. Got it?" She ruffled her feathers.

If he didn't need her, he'd tie a knot in that neck of hers. "Fine. Sorry. Now what about Michael?"

She dipped the top of her head onto her back, stroking the feathers, then did a quick zip by her knees before staring him in the eye again.

"I'm guessing the hammerhead told your son that he'd take him to find Angel and, for some reason, your son figured a shark was a safe bet. I don't know what you Humans teach your kids, but I'd *think* shark avoidance ought to be a mandatory school subject. Especially around here."

A shark? His son was riding a hammerhead shark? There weren't enough foul words in the English language to express what he was feeling.

Although, actually… he'd gone numb.

Michael was with a *shark*. In the ocean. Looking for a mermaid.

And he was talking to a flamingo… "Where did they go?"

"East."

"Thanks, Ginger." Logan took off at a run back

toward the steps. He had to get his boat out there and catch up with them.

"Hey!" the bird hollered from above him. Well that, at least, was normal. "Aren't you forgetting something?"

Logan didn't stop. "Forgetting something?"

"Yes. Usually the informant gets a reward."

An opportunistic flamingo. Which was better than any kidnapping shark. "Fine. Whatever you want. I'll get it when I get back."

"Or you can start by leaving your fridge open." She flapped her wings and beat him back up to his lawn. "I'll begin with the prawns and work my way to the scallops."

Hell, he'd give her an entire freezer's worth of the stuff if he got Michael back.

Chapter 31

ANGEL DECIDED SHE WOULD JUST LIE ON THE BEACH ALL DAY. Right here, at the water's edge. Listen to the waves, enjoy the tranquility, the solitude, and maybe then she could forget everything that had happened.

"You're kidding me, right? You're taking a *vacation*?"

So much for solitude. Who in Hades had found her here?

She lifted her head—only to have it snap back when her hair got caught under her—just like it had when she and Logan—

Maybe she'd cut her hair.

She rolled to the side and yanked the soggy mess out with a grunt, holding up her hand to block the sunlight that bounced off the water and into her eyes, blinding her.

"*Zeus*, Angel. What happened?"

Not that she needed sight to recognize that voice. Mariana. Great. *Just* who she needed.

"Nothing happened, Mariana." Unless you called your life's work going down the cosmic drain nothing.

Angel wiggled herself back into the water just to prove she was fine.

Maybe she could swim away fast enough so she wouldn't have to answer any questions—at least until she got back to Atlantis. Then there'd be *no* escaping

the questions. And the accusations *and* the disappoint-
ment *and* some kind of censure. And that was if she
was lucky.

"Uh huh. Nothing. Right." Mariana had trained for
marathons while Angel had been immersed in her studies, so it was no surprise she didn't get very far before
her sister was swimming beside her. "Last you told me,
you were all about living with Humans. One in particular, and I don't see him around."

Angel brushed the hair out of her face, trying not to
remember how Logan had played with it. That didn't
work well, though, since the whole awful story came
tumbling out.

Well, maybe not *all* of it. Some things were a little
too personal, even for a sister to know.

"You slept with him, didn't you?" Mariana asked as
they hit the drop-off to deeper water.

Then again, why even bother to try?

Angel did a swan dive off the edge, skimming past her
sister and hoping to lose her completely in the schools of
fish hanging around.

A wasted effort since Mariana caught up to her
quickly. These deeper-water basslets, though numerous,
weren't large enough to hide a full-grown Mer, and her
sister was as tenacious as a hungry octopus.

"So go back and talk to him."

"He thinks I'm a freak."

"So? I think you're a freak, and you still talk to me."

"Very funny."

"I thought it was. And it got you to smile."

Angel arched her eyebrows at her sister, then somersaulted beneath Mariana's tail, knowing the extra whip

she put on the end would churn the water and knock her sister off-kilter, if not flip her belly-up.

"Fine. Be that way," said Mariana, managing to keep herself upright even after Angel whipped again.

It figured. While Angel was *Just Angel*, Mariana was *Miss Perfect*. Always had been. She never found herself in these kinds of situations.

Of course, that could be because she actually followed the rules.

Yeah, yeah. Angel didn't need any lectures from her conscience. Nor a repeat of the waterworks. She wasn't about to dissolve into a puddle of tears—especially in front of Mariana.

"And it got a grimace out of you, too," Mariana continued, waving a passing barracuda away. "That's a reaction, at least. I don't need you moping for the entire trip back. I don't know what you expected, Angel, and frankly, I don't really care. You shouldn't have gone in the first place. You've annoyed everyone. Well, everyone except Mom and Dad. They don't know yet, but when they do, they won't be happy either. Especially since your Human found out you're a Mer."

Mariana cursed. "Gods, Ang. I came all this way to tell you Rod has consented to give you an interview, but I think that's the least of our worries now. I hope The Council will be as lenient with you as they were with Reel, but he, at least, had Erica with him. You left your Human out there with the knowledge. I don't know how they're going to react at all."

Did she really need this abuse? Angel waited for a dozen groupers to pass. Bad enough all of Atlantis had known Rod's thoughts on her career choice; she didn't need the whole Atlantic Ocean knowing about her disastrous love life, too. "I'm sorry you got dragged into this, Mariana, but I'm a big girl. I can take my lumps."

"If only it *were* lumps. You know the punishment as well as I do. Gods, Angel, I covered for you with Rod. Told him I'd talked to you, and that you knew what you were doing. That there was no way you'd fall for a Human. That you saw what it had done to Mom and Dad when Reel did and were too smart for that." Mariana snorted. "And now look at you. Mooning over a Human, of all things. What is it that has three of my siblings passing up perfectly good Mers for *them*?"

"Valerie is only half-Human." Not that you could tell anymore. Rod's wife had embraced her Mer half seamlessly.

"Semantics, Angel."

"No, actually, genetics."

"Don't get all professorial on me, sis. Save that for Rod and The Council. If I were you, I'd start thinking up my defense instead of getting defensive. And ways to get over him."

"Get over him? I don't need to get over him. Logan is a non-issue." That was what she'd tried telling herself back on the cay before Mariana showed up—too bad saying it out loud didn't make it any more believable.

"Sure. Okay. Whatever you say." Mariana swam past her, yanking the tip of one of Angel's flukes on her way by. "You forget. I know you, Ang. When you put your heart into something, you do it all the way. There's no way you're going to get over him quickly, and moping is only going to make it harder."

"And what do you know about it?" Angel kicked into action and tried to catch up.

"I've had my share of heartbreak. And even if I didn't, all anyone has to do is take one look at your face. Even a blind whale shark could tell something's wrong. I'd like to see you happy again."

So would Angel. That was the thing. She didn't *like* moping. She never moped.

She also didn't let people swim rough-shad over her, either—yet Logan had.

Angel stopped swimming. That's right. Logan had made his damning accusations, his pronouncement of how things would be, and she'd slunk back into the sea with a broken heart and a big ol' pity party.

What happened to her backbone? She used to have one.

Angel grabbed the hair that was floating around her like sargassum in a hurricane, perfectly mirroring her mood, and draped it over her breasts and tied it in the back like a Human halter top, but not.

She *did* used to have a backbone. And she wanted it back.

"Hey, Ang." Mariana dove into a somersault and headed back Angel's way. "Let's not go back to Atlantis just yet. A group of my friends are vacationing in the South Pacific right now. Let's join them. A girls' weekend. Or two. Relax, sun ourselves on a deserted beach, drink some fermented pineapple, have a grand ol' time. We'll just pretend this didn't happen."

"Really? And what are you going to tell Rod when he wonders what took you so long to bring me back?"

Mariana went for Innocent and I-Don't-Know-What-You're-Talking-About. "What do you mean?"

It was Angel's turn to yank on Mariana's hair. "Mare, I know Rod told you he'll give me an interview, but he has no intention of giving me the job. He told you to bring me home so I'd be where he wants me. Where he thinks it's safe." Never mind that he might actually have a point... "He's not going to let either one of us head out on some vacation."

"Honestly, Angel, where do you come up with these thi—?"

"It's all right, Mariana. You're just doing what our ruler commands. I get it. But, this did happen, and you know what? Logan *doesn't* get the last say. Fine if he wants nothing to do with me, but I'm not leaving until I do what I came to do. In for a periwinkle, in for a porgy, I always say."

And she did. She'd never done anything relating to Humans halfway, and she wasn't about to start with this. He might have hurt her—okay, no "might" about it—but she was a professional. She had an agenda.

Okay, so sleeping with him hadn't been on that agenda, and doing it—no surprise—hadn't been the best choice. She should have stayed true to her purpose and been that professional she'd prided herself on being.

Professional. Ha. Professionalism had gotten tossed out the porthole the moment he'd shown up.

Well, she wouldn't make that mistake again. The only way to fix her mess with The Council—and the problems with the planet—was to actually succeed in what she'd set out to do.

She did a quick back-arcing dive toward the coast. "Go without me, Mariana. I'm going back." She felt better just by saying it.

"To land? Are you crazy? The Council will definitely crucify you for this—and I'm scared they might actually do that. Trident and all."

"That's why I have to try, Mariana. I have to make something good come out of this."

Big words. But she was equal to them. Besides, what was her ego in relation to making the world a better place with harmonious interaction between their races?

Damn important, that ego grumbled deep inside her heart.

She ignored it. If she went that route, she'd be back on the pity party, and she did not want to go there. Time to focus on what she had originally planned. Get her life on an even keel and—

"AAAAAnnnngggeeellll!" A storm petrel dove into the water above her, his screech carrying downwards with impact.

The "even" part of that keel went bottoms-up.

"Ginger... A sea... Hike... Broken..." the bird garbled through the water.

Angel kicked toward the surface. She had no clue why the flamingo would go on a hike, and could only imagine what she'd broken, but screaming and *Ginger* never went well in the same sentence.

"Ang! Just where do you think you're—"

Angel broke the plane of the water before Mariana got the last word out. She scraped a few escaped strands of hair off her face and asked the petrel, "What about Ginger?"

The bird hacked out some water, then sucked in air, rustling his wings as he settled them against his back. "Ginger. Sent me. Tell you."

Angel nodded with the bird, willing his breathing to get back to normal. "What does she want?"

The bird nodded, then took another gulp of air. "She said… She said Hike went… shark."

"Hike?" That made no sense. Sharks didn't go on hikes.

"She said… Brogan… getting on his boat." Another couple of gulps went in.

The poor thing was really out of breath. He must have been flying as fast as he could. But the message didn't make sense—

"Logan? Do you mean Logan? Logan is on his boat?"

The petrel cocked the feathers over one eye at her. "That's what I said."

She wasn't going to argue with him. "Why does Ginger want me to know this?"

"Ginger?" Mariana appeared beside the bird. "Ginger's involved? Gods help us."

Angel shushed her sister while the petrel took another deep breath. "Ginger said Logan went after Michael and the shark, and she thought you'd want to know."

Angel held up her hand to stop Mariana's inevitable question. These were *her* Humans, and she was going to be asking the questions. "Shark? What shark?"

The storm petrel blew out a big, fishy breath. "Gods, woman, empty the water out of your ears. Ginger said that Michael went with a shark—*on a shark* were her exact words—to find you. Who the shark is, is still unknown. But when Logan found out, he jumped in his boat to go after them."

"The kid's with a shark? How in-the-sea did that happen?" Mariana could only hold back for so long.

What was that shark up to? Angel had yet to meet one who had any tender feelings for the Human race—other than as a tender meal.

And Logan knew? Great.

And, oh gods, Michael was with a *shark*.

"Logan's going after him?" Mariana continued her interrogation, and Angel was glad for the help because words were beyond her. "Why does this not sound good?"

"It's not." Ah, some words weren't beyond her. The fact that Ginger didn't know the shark worried Angel as much as the fact that a shark was involved in the first place. Ginger knew *everyone*, and if she didn't know this guy, that was even more trouble.

"Where are they?" She had to save Michael. She'd deal with everything else—Logan, her job, The Council—later. In the scheme of things, Michael's life was far more important than Logan's anger. Or her self-flagellation.

"Heading east was all I got out of Ginger," said the petrel. "Her beak was stuffed with prawns."

With prawns? Either Ginger had gotten into Logan's kitchen or…

Or what? Ginger had talked to Logan?

In the realm of possibilities, that was definitely one, because Angel would bet sand dollars to dorsals that Ginger knew exactly what had happened between her and Logan last night, right down to the humiliating scene on the beach. That bird did like her gossip. But the flamingo wouldn't speak to a Human unless she knew that he knew birds could speak—or that he'd seen a Mer. Angel could only imagine Logan's reaction.

On all fronts, she was in a sea of trouble.

But the bigger issue was… so was Michael.

Chapter 32

"ARE YOU SURE THIS IS WHERE YOU FOUND HER, KID?" A.C. circled the area again, changing the angle of his head to keep the kid's stubby little legs out of his eyes. The portside eye was more than a little irritated.

As was he. He didn't have a clue where Angel had gone, and any fish he'd tried to ask had taken one look at him—and his passenger—and had swum the other way. The little tuna-shits.

If he didn't have this stupid hitchhiker, he'd show them about swimming away from him...

Instead, he'd come up with another way to find her: let *her* find *him*.

The one plus to those scaredy-fish swimming from him was that they wouldn't be able to keep their gaping mouths shut. A shark carrying a Human on his back was sure to hit the gossip pools. All he had to do was float tight and wait for her to show.

The kid slid sideways on his back. "Yep, this is the place, but I don't see her."

Neither did A.C. But then, he was only working with one good eye.

He angled that eye downward. *This* was where the kid had found her? Why? What had she been doing here? There was nothing here. Not a *guyout*, not a mound, not even a pockmark in the earth's crust to take a nap in. Nothing. Nada. Zip. Zilch.

The kid slid again, and A.C. felt one of the little digited appendages leave his dorsal.

Probably trying to keep the stupid hat on his head. They'd had to stop four times to retrieve the damn thing, or the kid had started wailing.

When they'd recovered the hat the last time and the kid calmed down, he'd explained that his mom had given it to him before she'd left him with his dad. A.C. had wanted to tell the kid that he'd leave him too if he kept acting up like that, but he hadn't wanted to add crying to the wailing. Besides, he only had to put up with the annoying pup for just a little longer.

The kid grabbed hold of his fin with the other hand and tried to kick a leg onto his back, succeeding this time in damaging one of A.C.'s gills.

The Hammer rolled his good eye, then lowered his tail to get the kid back where he belonged. Not for any thought of being nice; more so that he wouldn't end up with a dislocated fin. This Mer better be worth it.

"Uh, Mr. Shark?" The kid tapped A.C.'s neck.

Good thing he was sensitive to vibrations, although this kid's squirming was sorely testing his patience. "Yeah?"

"Why is the water starting to turn in a circle like a potty?"

A.C. didn't know what a potty was, but circling water—especially here—could only mean one thing.

Fuck. He wasn't going to stick around to find out if he was right.

Giving a moment's thought to flinging the kid at the whirlpool to save himself, A.C. came up with a better plan. Escape first, but if he didn't make it, the kid could be used for something more than lunch, like saving his life for real.

"Hang on, kid." A.C. whipped his tail hard enough to do the quickest one-eighty he'd ever done—only to see every seabird within a twenty-mile radius head straight to shore.

Nah, he wasn't pinning his hopes on a kid.

Especially once the reprisal of the wailing started. No way were they going back for the hat. They'd never make it and the kid would be too dead to need the hat—and *not* because of him.

A.C. whipped his tail harder, but the water began to circle faster.

He ramped up his speed.

The water sucked him backward.

He strained to break free from its pull and had made it a few feet when the water changed direction and a voice he remembered all too well rose from the deep.

"Well, well, well, A.C. Hammer."

A.C. wasn't afraid of anything in the sea. Not Great Whites, not Bull Sharks, certainly not Hammerheads, not even Harry.

But her? She scared the shit out of him.

The water spun him around. There, in the middle of the vortex, with four obscenely pulsing tail flukes fanning out, floated his worst nightmare: the Denizen of the Deep and the mother of all sea monsters.

Ceto.

—∞—

Remembering Angel's warning about manatees, Logan kept the throttle low while navigating out of the marina, concentrating on something other than the huge fucking ocean out there. And hurricane season. And the *shark*.

He *would* get Michael back. There was no other option.

The shadow of a seabird passed over the front of his boat. A seagull.

Hmm...

Well, why the hell not? If there were such things as mermaids and talking flamingos, why not talking seagulls? What did he have to lose?

Logan leaned out from beneath the hardtop and hollered, "Hey! You! Up there!"

The bird didn't hear him. Or didn't understand him.

"Hey! Bird! Down here!"

A couple of boaters looked at him funny, but Logan didn't care. He wanted his son back, and if the gull could help, he'd ask. He didn't care how abnormal he sounded.

The gull swooped out of the sky and onto the windshield, wings still spread as it waddled up to the top and peered over, its pale eyes staring at him, beak clamped shut.

"Can you help me?"

The sea gull cocked its head sideways but didn't answer.

"You *can* understand me, right? You don't speak Spanish or anything, do you?"

The bird cocked its head the other way but still didn't say anything.

Logan felt like an idiot. "Great. I *am* losing my mind. I'm asking a bird for help." He shook his head and exhaled. Now what?

"That'll be *avian* to you, bub." The bird's yellow beak got a little too close to his nose, and Logan pulled back—and smiled.

"You *can* talk."

The bird nodded. "Yes. And how you knew that is going to be a topic of discussion at our annual symposium."

"Look, Mr. Avian. I don't have ti—"

"Actually, it's Mr. Gull. Taylor Gull."

"Okay. Fine. Look, I need your help."

"You need a lot more than my help. Try getting some manners." The gull hopped over and landed on the console, one webbed foot covering the compass. "So, what do you want and how did you know I speak?"

Logan didn't care for the gull's attitude but needed his help too badly to tell him to stick a clam in it. The bird—*avian*—would probably love to do it anyway.

He made one more turn, then they were heading for open water. "I met a mermaid named Angel and—"

"Ah, Angel!" The gull seemed to smile—could they do that?

Probably. They were able to do a lot humans knew nothing about. What was one more anomaly when they could think and speak?

"How is she? Did she get that Coalition job she wanted so badly?" The gull clapped his wingtips over the top of his back—another anomaly. "Ah, but of course she did if she's letting you see her. How wonderful. It's about time you Humans learned that you're not the only fishers in the sea. Mers were here long before your kind got a clue about the wheel. Beautiful creatures, Mers. And they don't eat *avians* either, though I do applaud your fellow citizens for not going after seagulls." Taylor resettled his wings and did a three-step tap dance off the compass. "So, what is it you need besides manners?"

Logan gritted his teeth and checked their heading. Ginger had said they were going east. He adjusted the wheel accordingly. "A shark kidnapped my son and I need to find them."

"A shark kidnapped your kid? Buddy, are you listening to yourself? Sharks aren't kidnappers. They're killers."

Logan couldn't even comment. A *killer*. As if he didn't know.

"So. You met Angel? I bet that's a story, huh? I mean, it's not as if you can just toss a line over and hope to catch one." Taylor brushed his beak under his wing.

"Actually, that's how my son found her."

One eye opened beneath the wing. "No shit?" He pulled his head out. "Wow. Talk about bad luck. So that's why she's talking to you, eh? What? Did you hold her captive? Try to sell her to science? I swear, you Humans would put the gods on display if you had your way. It's a wonder they let you inhabit the planet."

"Look, can we examine the theology of *avians* later? My son's missing, and I'm hoping you can point me in the direction of wherever the shark"—and his son—"went."

"Oh, is that all?"

Taylor flipped his head onto his back, then righted it. Logan had never paid much attention to that move before he knew birds could talk, but now... it was really annoying when you were trying to hold a conversation.

"So, can you?" Logan ground out the words, trying really hard not to lose it. Everything—his composure, his patience…

His sanity was already gone.

"Well, since you're a friend of Angel's, I'll see what I can do. Hang on."

With one flap, the bird soared skyward and, in another example of what-the-hell-had-happened-to-the-world, the bird put his wing over his eyes, shielding them, yet still managed to remain aloft.

Friend of Angel's? Logan thought about correcting him but decided against it. It was her fault this was happening in the first place—

But, actually, it wasn't. It was Michael's, if Ginger was to be believed. And who knew if a flamingo would lie? Certainly not him, and he'd thought he'd seen everything during his days with the troupe. Showed what he knew. The ironic thing was, those days now seemed normal compared to this.

Suddenly, in another what-the-hell-is-happening moment, hundreds of sea birds came barreling toward land, squawking and cawing in a massive cloud of wings and near-collisions. Taylor got lost in the throng as they flew over the *Mir-a-Mar*.

Then the gull dropped below the horde, his black-tipped wings flapping insanely to keep himself horizontal as he coasted around the back of the boat, landing on the seat behind Logan.

"Whew! That was close."

"What the hell's happening?"

"Something big. I couldn't get a straight answer out of any of them, but something is going on out there, just an hour or two up ahead. I'm betting that's where your shark and your son are. If you want to save him, you're going to want to turn 'er up full throttle."

Logan did.

And prayed he wouldn't be too late.

———~~~———

Angel never swam so fast in her life, not even when trying to outswim Harry.

Okay, maybe equal to when she'd been trying to outswim Harry for *her* life. But now that she was swimming for Michael's, even Mariana hadn't been able to keep up with her. She'd left her sister trying to catch her breath somewhere near Spanish Cay.

Worry fueled her. What had compelled Michael to get on the back of a hammerhead? Was he still alive?

She kicked harder and saw a pod of dolphin heading toward her from the east. Good. Dolphins were Human-friendly. They'd help her.

And then she saw who it was.

"Princess!" the head of her brother's Council Guards called out. "Your presence is requested in Atlantis—"

She didn't slow down. "Captain Brackmann, tell my brother I'll be there as soon as I can, but I have a job to finish first."

She was in trouble anyway; what was another infraction? She wasn't going to leave Michael out here. She was his only hope.

The dolphin swam up beside her. "I'm sorry, Your Highness, but my orders are to bring you in."

It was futile to argue. The Council Guards were trained to obey one commander and one commander only—the High Councilman. Her brother. Who could be one stubborn Mer and had a huge shell on his shoulder about her doing this in the first place. But she couldn't leave Michael.

She also couldn't outswim a pod of highly trained dolphins.

And then she remembered the final test all Council Guards must undergo before being accepted into their current positions: dolphin swim encounters with Humans. Her father had implemented those surveillance squads *selinos* ago. That training would bolster her argument—as would the fact that dolphins hated sharks.

"All right, Captain, but there's a Human child in jeopardy with a hammerhead up ahead. I want to save him. A *child*, Captain. We can't let the shark kill him."

The dolphin studied her.

"Really. Come with me to see for yourself."

The dolphin studied her some more, all the while keeping pace with her. "Fine. We don't need the balance upset any more than it already is. We'll follow you."

"Good. Let's go." Angel kicked her tail harder, and the captain whistled. Within seconds, all ten cetaceans were lined up behind her in perfect V formation.

The shark, whoever he was, was in serious trouble.

Chapter 33

A.C. WAS IN SOME SERIOUS SHIT.

"Ah, A.C. We meet again." Ceto swirled her finger in the water, and the whirlpool circled him closer to her, and, ironically, that stupid hat closer to him. "And *who* do we have here?"

"Do you know Angel?" the kid asked, leaning off to get his damn hat.

"Pipe down, kid." A.C. tried swimming backwards, but the current was too strong. So, *yes*, he'd planned to eat the kid, but at least he'd make the death quick. Painless even. Well, after that first bite. But Ceto? She was known for stretching torture out over eons. No one deserved that.

"I do know her, child," Ceto answered, her tails seeming not to move at all. Yet somehow she was closer despite A.C.'s attempts to get away. "Who are you?"

"I'm Michael." The lucky S-O-B actually got the hat *and* managed to stay on A.C.'s back. "I want to see Angel. She promised she wouldn't leave me, but she did."

A smirk settled on Ceto's lips as she met A.C.'s gaze. "Altruism, darling? How unlike you."

A.C. thought about playing it tough but knew he didn't have a prayer of getting away from her —not that he'd prayed in a long, long time, rest Mama's dear, departed, speared-by-a-Human heart.

There was only one way to deal with Ceto. Pander. At this point, he just wanted to get out of here with his life. "Yeah, well, you know... It's a kid. What are you gonna do?"

"Yes. That is the question, isn't it?" Ceto slapped the surface of the water, and a bloom of jellyfish rose around her.

A.C. rolled his eyes. Ouch. That portside eye still stung.

Just like the jellyfish.

He stopped the eye-rolling.

"I'll just relieve you of your burden, A.C. I'm sure you'd be much happier back in the depths. The sun does awful things to a shark's skin, I'm told." She wiggled her fingers at the largest jellyfish closest to her. "Concord, my majordomo, will escort you." She smiled at the kid. "Come here, child."

A long jellyfish tentacle snaked through the water, up under A.C.'s belly, then once around his tail.

Then another, this one circling in the other direction.

For the first time ever, A.C. wanted to stay on the surface. Knowing Ceto, if he went down, he'd never see the light of day again.

He tried another tactic. "Look, Ceto, the kid's mine. I'm sure we can come to some kind of reasonable arrangement if you get your henchfish to let go." He swung from side to side, but the tentacles held firm.

"But that would call for me to *be* reasonable, and whoever said I was?" She twirled her finger in a circle, and the *cnidaria* started winching his tentacle in—along with A.C. "As a matter of fact, I distinctly recall a time you told me I was most *un*reasonable."

Damn him and his stupid shoot-off-at-the-mouth

youth. He'd *had* to pick Ceto to challenge. It was amazing he was alive to be terrified of her.

And with good fucking reason.

His days were numbered.

Ceto lifted Michael off the idiot's back, encouraged to see there was no fear in the child's brown eyes. Not black like hers, but close enough. She wanted to pull him into her arms and hug him. Brush her lips across his forehead, stroke his hair, and hold him to her. It'd been so long since she'd held a child.

The Council and their foul rules. None of them knew what it meant to be the bearer of life. Not a single one. Yet they took that from her…

She'd never forgive them. All she'd ever wanted was to have a child in her life.

Michael was going to be that child.

He hadn't screamed when he saw her, proof that he was the one for her. Once she showed him where he'd live for the rest of his life, in a castle, surrounded by tropical fish and warm gentle waters, he'd be excited to stay with her.

"Hello, Michael."

"Hello. Where's Angel?"

Angel. Fisher's princess. The hope of Humankind, if the new Mer ruler's latest venture was to be believed.

And this Human wanted her.

It made Ceto sick to her stomach. The Mer was fully capable of bearing her own young. Angel didn't need this one. Ceto was going to make sure he wanted to stay here with her.

"Oh, I'm sure Angel will be along shortly. In the meantime, why don't you wait with me in my castle?"

Like sundial-work, the boy's eyes lit up. Didn't matter the race or the species, you offer someone life in a castle, and you got that same reaction.

"Oh, cool! Can I?" He kicked his legs in his excitement, one foot catching her in the rib.

Uncouth. You'd never see a Mer child doing that. Well, not that they had feet, but she'd never been kicked by a tail. He'd learn. They had lots of time.

"You certainly can." She pulled him close, unable to help herself, and brought her lips to his temple and her fingertips to his mouth, transferring the ability to breathe water into him in a way that wouldn't work with adults.

He smelled like a child. It'd been so long since she'd experienced such softness and scent…

"Where is it? The castle? All I see is water." Michael squirmed in her arms, and Ceto smiled against his hair.

"Close your eyes, Michael, and I'll take you to it."

"Don't do it!" A.C. whipped back and forth at the end of his tether, gnashing his teeth so hard some of them fell out. "You can't touch him! The Human's mine! Mine!"

Ceto flicked her fingers at Concord. He'd know what to do with the troublemaker.

She turned then so Michael wouldn't see Concord subdue the shark for transport to her dungeon. She circled her finger in the water, creating the funnel that would send the shark and the jellyfishes back to her home. They all disappeared with a soft sucking sound.

"Where's Mr. Shark going?" Michael asked, his eyes still closed as an obedient child's should be.

"He'll be joining us in the castle, but we'll go there a different way."

Conscious. Unlike the shark. He'd be lucky to make it to her home alive. Concord's venom could be deadly if not administered properly.

Ceto calmed her whirlpool before lowering them both beneath the surface. Oh, dear. She did so hope A.C. didn't receive an accidental overdose. She chuckled. No loss if he did.

"We'll all visit the castle together. Doesn't that sound lovely?" She patted the child's head, loving the fact that he was comfortable with her, when so many others hadn't been.

That proved it. He was hers.

Michael reached up to twist his hat across his forehead, then back, his lips going in opposite directions, but he still didn't open his eyes, the dear thing. Such a special child.

"I dunno. I'm not apposed to go with strangers."

Oh yes he *was* supposed to. "But I'm not a stranger, remember? I know Angel. We'll have fun. You'll see." Ceto picked up her speed and set off toward her second-favorite palace.

"But how will Angel know where I am? I don't know where she went. I wanna find her."

It'd be a cold day in the tropics before that happened. This one was hers. Let Angel make her own.

But Ceto had to get him to her lair. Then he'd see. She'd give him everything. "I know where she lives. I'll send a message to her. How's that?"

He wrapped his little arms around her neck and squeezed. His hat bumped her chin and drifted off in her wake. "It's cooool! Hey! My hat—wow! We're under the water! And I'm not drowning. Cool!"

It definitely was cool. And a gift—one most definitely *not* from the gods, but, surprisingly, from Harry. She owed him.

"I can breathe?" Michael's little face looked very perplexed.

Ceto soothed a hand over his hair because a mother should soothe her child. "Yes, you can. Because you're a very special boy."

"Rainbow used to say that. Angel, too."

Ceto didn't know who Rainbow was, but Angel wasn't getting him back.

If he was so special to her, she shouldn't have left him the first place.

Chapter 34

Seeing Logan's Mir-a-Mar racing through the water off to the northwest, Angel adjusted her angle of approach accordingly. Boats traveled faster than she could ever hope to swim so she didn't want to undershoot intercepting him.

"Captain, can you have one of your pod flag Logan down to let him know I'm here and ask him to stop?"

"Are you sure, princess? Having a dolphin break the Rule of Speech is a serious infraction."

As if that mattered with her list of felonies. "I'm sure."

The captain eyed her a bit longer, then whistled the order to the pod. One sleek, gray body dropped low, then sped off as the rest of them continued skimming the waves toward the boat, matching their speed to hers.

Angel was getting tired, but nothing was going to stop her from saving Michael. Why had he gone with a shark? Why had Logan let him? What had any of them been thinking?

A few minutes later, Logan's boat slowed. She hoped Logan was as receptive to her as he had been to the messenger.

He was waiting when she surfaced near the back of the boat. "What in the hell are you doing here, Angel?"

"I heard about Michael."

"Funny thing—so did I. From a talking flamingo. What do you have to say about that?"

"I'd say, thank the gods for Ginger and her nosy, fat beak, or we wouldn't have a clue where Michael was. Now, are you going to let me on board so we can find him, or do you want to waste valuable time arguing?"

"The only reason I'm doing this is so you can fix the mess you've created." He shoved the door open so hard it smashed into the boat behind it.

Angel caught it before it could do more damage on the rebound. There'd been enough destruction going around. She kicked her tail and landed back on the deck where everything had started, then closed the door.

It all looked so familiar.

If only she hadn't decided to stay.

If only she hadn't followed them in the first place.

If only Rod had given her the damn interview.

She hiked herself onto one of the pull-down benches on the side of the boat, willing the stabbing ache in her heart to subside. Would have, could have, should have… nothing would change the fact that Michael was at the mercy of a shark, and his only hope was her and Logan working together.

Logan did his part by heading back onto the bridge and firing up the motors.

Captain Brackmann breached next to her amid the churning water. "I'm trusting you, Princess." The dolphin dove into the water, then kicked out of it again. "Turn yourself in once you've recovered the child."

"I will," Angel called as the dolphin fell back when the boat picked up speed.

"You will what?" Logan turned around to ask, his eyes straying to her tail.

She couldn't blame him, but even though she

understood Human curiosity, it just made her feel so… well… *studied*. A specimen. Not like the woman he'd made love to—

Then again, she wasn't the woman he'd made love to, was she?

And hadn't she been studying him when she first arrived?

She shook her head. "Something I have to do for our ruler."

"You have a ruler?"

"Logan, let's not go into all that right now. I'm here to help with Michael." No matter how much it hurt her heart to see the distaste in his eyes every time he looked at her.

Gods, if only she could go back and re-do everything, she'd—

She'd do it the same way again. She couldn't regret loving him, but she sure as Hades would have spoken to Michael about not coming after her.

Logan stood up from his captain's chair and braced a foot on the box beneath it, his eyes alternating between her and the water in front of them.

"Oh, I don't know, Angel. I think the fact that you have a ruler might have something to do with this. I'm assuming he's a Mer—*man*, as well?"

Angel nodded.

Logan rubbed a hand across his eyes. "And Michael knew about you, didn't he?"

Angel licked her lip and looked away. "Yes."

"He caught you when we were fishing."

It wasn't a question, but she felt compelled to confirm it. "Yes."

"When I was in the cabin?"

"Yes."

"Your voice. It did something to me."

Again, not a question. "Yes, but only that time in the kitchen—"

"Why, Angel? Why didn't you just go back in when you got free?"

She looked up at him, standing there, wind whipping the hair she'd woven her fingers through, shirt stretching across the broad shoulders she'd laid her head on, the muscles in his thighs that had flexed around her now counterbalancing the boat's movements.

"Because I saw you," she whispered, knowing he wouldn't want to hear it.

"What?"

She cleared her throat. "There was a hammerhead in the water who threatened to kill me. It seemed like the lesser of two evils."

"For you, maybe. For Michael?" Logan turned back to the wheel and gripped it with both hands, his biceps straining the sleeves of his shirt. "He's out here, Angel. On a shark, so the seagull said—and don't think that's not freaking me out. Do you want to tell me why that is? How could a shark get Michael? Or can they walk on land, too? The folks at SNL would love to hear that, I'm sure."

He exhaled and ran a hand around the back of his neck, kneading the muscles there. "Morbid humor. That's what this is." He looked back at her. "And *why*? Where's the shark taking Michael? Why not kill him right away?"

She started to offer something comforting, but Logan didn't give her a chance.

"*Why* did you let Michael know you existed? *Why* did

you have to stay on the boat? Why couldn't you have stayed in the ocean where you belong and where none of us would be the wiser?"

No adult in this world would have believed Michael's story if it had come out. Adults never did. Eventually, Michael would have forgotten about her or have come to think of her as an odd dream he'd had as a child—after all, who didn't believe in mermaids and fairies and unicorns at some point in their lives? It had happened before. That was how the myths had started in the first place. Some Human had written down a child's recollection and called it a fable.

But this was no fable. And, yes, she was responsible. She admitted that.

She'd had her reasons, though. Good reasons. And no one could have known a shark would come along and disrupt them. No one could have foreseen any of this.

"Logan, look. You're right. I shouldn't have stayed that first night. I'd never planned to come on your boat in the first place, but Harry, well, he didn't give me much choice. He wouldn't leave. And then… well… You and Michael, you made me feel so welcome, and I'm trying to prove to my brother that Mer-Human communication is a good thing for the planet and figured the best way to start is with the children."

"But why *my* child?"

Because he was there seemed like such a lame answer, but the fact was, it was the truth.

"I never wanted to hurt you. Either of you."

"You should have thought about that days ago," Logan muttered, ramming a metaphorical harpoon a little harder into her heart. A little deeper.

"Logan, I can help you get him back." And she would. Come Hades or high tide, she *would* return Michael to his father.

Logan reached up for a metal bar above his head and hung onto it, his eyes focused on the horizon. "Good. And then I want you out of our lives. Forever."

Chapter 35

FIFTEEN MINUTES LATER, ANGEL SAW A SIGHT THAT MADE her blood run cold.

Floating on the waves, rim side up, was Michael's hat.

Logan saw it a second later.

He cut the motors, leaving one barely idling so he could steer alongside it. Then, leaping off the bridge and clearing her tail, he grabbed a fishing gaff to scoop the hat from the water.

The waves kept it just beyond his reach.

Cursing, Logan tried again—and almost ended up in the ocean.

Which was where *she* belonged.

Checking first for shark fins, Angel took matters into her own fins and dove over the side. Within seconds she had the hat, and two seconds later, Logan had it.

"Where the hell are they?" His skin blanched beneath his tan as he traced the rim of the hat, such stark pain on his face that Angel couldn't look at him. Not knowing she was responsible.

"I'll see what I can find out."

Ten minutes of searching the ocean floor and finding a fistful of discarded hammerhead teeth gave her a clue—as did the lack of sea life in the water around them.

There were only a few reasons every swimming thing would abandon an area. Environmental issues—which she could personally attest to not being the reason—or predators. There was no shark here. Not now. And even though one had been here, the sea life should have returned quickly once he left. But there were no fish or urchins or even plankton to be found.

Only one thing—one being—scared sea creatures into hiding like this. One highly disturbing and extremely possible reason, given their latitude and longitude.

Ceto.

It all made sense. The dearth of sea life, the proximity to Ceto's Bahamian Palace, plus that fact that a Human male, a child, and the opportunity to stick it to The Council were Ceto's trifecta.

It all made too much damn sense.

As did the fact that Harry had to be the one who'd helped her, though why Ginger hadn't recognized him was beyond Angel. Harry had a way of making himself known.

Angel surfaced with Harry's teeth in her fist, hoping the bastard would have to gum his food for the rest of his life—what little there was left of it, if she had any say.

She vowed to ensure she would. Especially when she saw Logan's reaction to her theory.

"A sea monster has my son," he growled in a low, deep, primal rumble, crushing the hat in his hand. He rested his palms on the side of the boat, his head hanging low. "Is he alive? Will she keep him alive?"

Angel swallowed. She didn't want to have to tell him this, but it was too late for regrets. The only way was to go forward. Save Michael. "Ceto won't kill Michael, Logan." Keep him locked in her home for the rest of his life, yes. But she wouldn't kill him. "I'm guessing she has him in her palace."

Logan looked at her then, the first time since she'd gone overboard. His brown eyes were almost black. "So where is this palace?"

"That way." Angel pointed. "Not far."

"Not far? There's nothing but ocean until we hit Bermuda."

She didn't say anything, letting his mind slowly come to grips with what she meant. In its own time. It was a tough concept for a Human to grasp.

"Underwater?" He was quicker than she'd thought he'd be. "Her palace is… She has my son *underwater*? She *drowned* him?" He staggered back out of her line of sight.

Angel kicked harder, going into a tailstand so she could grasp the gunwale and pull herself up to rest her arms on the side of the boat. "No, Logan. Ceto would never do that to a child. She loves children. She probably…" This was not going to go over well. It never did.

"She probably what, Angel?" Logan sat up.

"She probably turned him. Into a water-breather."

"She did *what*?"

Angel wanted to caress that worried look from his face, but only words were going to do it. "She made him capable of breathing water, Logan. It's not painful, and Michael didn't feel a thing. He's actually fine. Ceto won't hurt him."

"How the hell can you be sure of that? She's already done something to him. A water-breather? What? Does he have gills now?"

Angel bit back the sharp reply. He wasn't the only one having a tough time with Michael's disappearance. He didn't have to be insulting.

Mers—mammals—didn't have gills like fish. They—she—were higher on the evolutionary chain. Above Humans, even, but now wasn't the time to go into that.

"No gills. To Michael, it's the same thing as breathing on land. I doubt he'll even notice." She fluttered her tail flukes to get a better grasp on the boat. "And Ceto loves children."

"Yeah, she's proving that so well." Sarcasm dripped from his words. Sarcasm and bitterness. "Why do you people let her roam the seas, helping herself to children who don't belong to her?"

It wasn't as easy as locking Ceto up, but there was no time to go into Ceto's history now. Gods and goddesses, Immortals, powers… If he thought a tail was tough to swallow, he'd be blown overboard by the rest of what was in her world.

"Logan, I'm sure we're more frightened than Michael is."

Logan raised his eyebrows but didn't argue. "Fine. Whatever. But I can't sit around here doing nothing." He started pacing. "I'll call the Coast Guard. The Navy. They have heavy artillery." He stopped. "No, I can't. Not without telling them why, and the minute they hear 'sea monster,' they're going to think I'm crazy." He sat on the edge of the boat and looked at her. "*What* does she want with him, Angel? Why did she take him?"

"Ceto can't have any more children. The gods have forbidden it. My guess is she took Michael to raise him as her own. She's done this before."

"Of all the fucked-up—" Logan kicked the gaff, then shot back to his feet. "Let's go."

"Go?"

"Yes, go. Michael is *my* son and I'm going to get him. I have to do something, Angel. I can't just let her have him. So, can *you* do it? What she did? Turn me into a water-breather?"

Yes. She could. In direct opposition to The Council's orders and express wishes.

As if that would stop her. "Yes. I can."

"Good. Do it."

"Okay, but—"

"But what?" He grabbed the gaff from the bottom of the boat and held it before him like a sword.

Angel shuddered when she saw the sleek steel hook. That could do major damage. Problem was, she didn't know if they could get close enough to Ceto to use it. The sea monster was extremely cagey about security.

"Angel? But what?"

She tore her gaze off the weapon. "We need to be in the water."

"Not a problem." He took his shirt off in one fluid movement, grabbed something from a tackle box, shoved it and Michael's hat into his shorts pocket, then dove overboard to surface next to her.

"So how do we do this?" His hair was plastered to his head, seawater glistening on his eyelashes, and Angel didn't know that he'd ever looked so handsome.

Or so worried.

And that was her fault.

So she could either tread here and moan, or save Michael. No brainer.

Then she'd hie her tail to Atlantis to atone for her sins and pray to the gods that she'd even be able to pray because Ceto was going to kill her for taking Michael back.

Angel knew all of that—just as she knew what she was going to have to do.

"Angel?" Logan swam closer, his legs skimming against her tail when she lowered herself into the water.

She was going to miss him. "I have to kiss you."

"What?" His eyebrows arched. "Now? In case you've forgotten, my son is missing, and last night happened before I knew what you are."

The *what you are* hurt. Not *who you are,* but *what.* She was a *what* to him.

She was also the reason his son was missing, so she could put her injured heart and bruised ego on the continental shelf and get on with it.

"Logan, there's only one way you can get water-breathing ability."

He cocked an eyebrow. "Okay. How?"

Angel fluttered her fins to remain vertical and tried not to brush his legs with them. She didn't need him freaking out any more than he was about to.

"I have to kiss it into you."

Chapter 36

SHE HAD TO KISS HIM.

There were a million reasons for Logan to back away from that stipulation, chief among them that she was a mermaid. As much as he hated that fact, he couldn't deny that he'd wanted to kiss her last night.

Before he'd known.

And could, if he allowed himself, want to again.

But she was a *mermaid*. What would be the point?

There was no future for them. And even if there could be, he had Michael to think of. His son would have to lie to everyone he met because he couldn't tell anyone that his stepmother was a mermaid. Back-to-school night? "Oh, sorry, my wife couldn't make it. She's having her tail washed." Homeroom mom? "Sure, but the lemonade is made with saltwater."

Never going to happen. No and hell no. He wanted Normal.

A mermaid was *not* normal.

To bring that thought home, her tail brushed his legs. "Logan?"

And what the hell was he doing even thinking the word *wife* in relation to her?

"Are you ready?" She floated a little closer.

The kiss. Right.

"Yeah. Sure." He did want to save Michael from the

sea monster, after all—"Hold on a minute. Are you telling me that this… this… *thing* kissed my son?"

Angel shook her head. "Oh, no. For children, it's different. She just had to touch his lips with her fingers.
He's fine, Logan. Really. I'd bet my life on it."

Someone's life was riding on this. He'd start with the
shark's, then the monster's, then… well, he'd wait to see
what happened.

"All right. Let's get this over with." He steeled himself against the memory of last night.

Her mouth thinned to a straight line, and she glanced
sideways before swimming closer. A few escaped pieces
of her hair floated on the surface, flowing around them
as it all had last night, and Logan realized that her hair
was all that was covering her breasts. Breasts he'd
reveled in last night, licked and kissed and tugged on,
cushioned his head on—

Forgetting about last night was going to be harder
than he'd thought.

Because, in spite of everything, last night had been
all he'd ever hoped for, and, as much as he'd like to
forget it, when she licked her lips, when she touched
him, he couldn't.

Last night, making love—*being* with her, had been
amazing. Perfect.

Right.

Everything had been right with his world last night.
Her, Michael, all of it. But then she'd gone over the railing and his life had flipped upside down and backwards
every bit as much as she and her tail had in the water.

Then her lips brushed his, her breasts stroked his
chest, and Logan couldn't help but remember. Every

taste, every touch. Every silken, sexy caress of her body against his. How he'd responded, almost jumping out of his skin with need.

There'd been something magical with her last night— and it pissed him off no end that it was because she was a mermaid, with her mystical powers, and that damn man-luring ability.

He'd thought it'd been real. That he'd finally had a shot at what he'd always wanted.

Except that he'd *fallen for a mermaid*.

It was wrong. *So* wrong, but this… this didn't feel wrong. This felt like the polar opposite of wrong.

Logan couldn't help leaning into the kiss.

Then her arms slid over his chest to curl around his shoulders, her fingers feathering along his neck and her lips moved against his, her tongue pressing for entrance into his mouth, and, as naturally as breathing, he let her in, tasting that delicious, heady sweetness of her, welcoming it. Wanting it.

Wanting her.

Her fingers gripped his hair, and Logan slid an arm around her, pulling her up against him, slanting his head to one side, his tongue sweeping along her teeth, stroking her tongue, not caring if this was mermaid magic because it felt good. Too good. So good that he deepened the kiss.

Angel groaned when Logan bent her back over his arm. Her fingers tightened in his hair, and desire shivered through him.

He still wanted her.

He nipped at her lips, pulling the bottom one between his teeth, stroking it with his tongue, and she tugged harder on his hair.

Logan smiled around the next kiss he gave her, his hand plastered to her back, plastering her front against his. God, she felt so good. She fit against him just right, and her lips—God. Her lips…

He kissed her again, sliding his hand up to capture the nape of her neck, wishing he had some place to put the gaff so he could use both hands.

Wait.

Something about that gaff…

Angel tugged his hair again, but only slowly did Logan realize she was pulling him away.

He removed his mouth from hers and opened his eyes. More of her hair floated around her, a veil of gold, her lips swollen, pupils wide. A tremulous look filled her eyes, and Logan opened his mouth to say something—

He was taking in water.

And not drowning. Not even choking.

"Logan? Are you okay?"

He took a deep breath. Gulp. Whatever.

He was breathing water.

She'd done this to him. He'd gotten lost in that kiss, and all along, she'd been changing him.

She's a mermaid, *Hardington. Not exactly prime wife and mother material, no matter how you respond to her.*

Right. Forget that she'd been everything he'd wanted. That she had the power—both real and inherent— to make him forget what she was. He had to rescue Michael, and this mermaid magic sucked, as far as he was concerned. The sooner this was over, and he and Michael were on land, away from her and sea monsters and everything else, the better.

"I'm fine, Angel." He had to be fine. He dropped his arm to his side. "Where to?" He adjusted his grip on the grappling hook. Not as dangerous as a harpoon, and with his lack of willpower against Angel's magic, he didn't hold out much hope against a sea monster's, but Logan was glad he was holding it. God only knew what would have happened a moment ago if he'd had two free hands.

"Over there, Logan."

He followed where she pointed, amazed to see a building where none had existed before. It looked like something out of a fairy tale with turrets and balconies and rows of gothic windows decorating its pink façade. A reef wound around the exterior with every color of coral he'd ever seen, and some he hadn't. Gray obelisks flanked a massive set of white marble doors and sea grass covered the top of the structure; thousands of colorful tropical fish floated among the gently fanning tendrils, a soft, almost indistinguishable murmur drifting along the current.

"Along with the ability to breathe water, you can now see and hear things that other Humans can't." She flicked her tail and headed toward the building, repositioning her hair. "And not to freak you out, but you'll hear fish talking, too."

A stingray fluttered along the sandy bottom beneath him, a sea anemone on its back, waving its tentacles as if to emphasize a point.

Logan swam after Angel. "Fish talk, too?" Hmm, his voice sounded normal to him.

As if on cue, a pod of dolphins raced up to them, and one answered that question before she did.

"Princess, I—"

"Princess?" Logan almost shouted. "Now you're a *princess*?"

"I've always been a princess, Logan. My father was the High Councilman."

As if that explained anything. Logan had a headache.

"As I was saying," the dolphin continued, "I advise against this course of action."

Angel didn't stop swimming. "I understand, Captain, but I have to do this."

Princess? Captain? The dolphin was military? Angel was royalty?

Jesus. There was a whole other world down here that mankind knew nothing about.

"We can't come with you, Your Highness."

"I know." Angel arced gracefully back around to face Logan. "I can't help dolphins remain under water any longer than they already can, Logan, so it'll just be you and me. Are you sure you still want to go?"

What was his choice? Leaving Michael to the sea monster's mercy and Angel to defeat it by herself? "Hell yes, I'm coming."

The dolphin nodded toward the surface. "We'll wait there for your return."

Angel thanked the dolphins and set off again, swimming over a sandy mound rising from the ocean floor. At the peak, a sea cucumber sneezed and the starfish that was inching up the side answered, "Gods bless you."

If Michael weren't missing and the situation so dire, Logan was sure he'd never believe what he was seeing. But the fact that he was swimming next to a mermaid, understanding fish and dolphins, hearing an echinoderm sneeze, well, Logan was finding his worldview severely skewed—and severely screwed. "Is there *any*thing that doesn't talk?"

A crab saluted him from the opposite side of the sand mound, and Logan returned the gesture before realizing the thing was a crab. A pincer-bearing, toe-grabbing, butter-dippable *crab*.

"Not really," Angel answered.

Logan wanted his old life back. His old ignorance. Where the craziest thing in his world was the ex-girlfriend who'd changed her name to Rainbow and dropped a heretofore unknown child on his doorstep. Not some new world order where fish talked and mer-maids frolicked. Where sea monsters stole children from their fathers who were just trying to raise their kids in a safe, sane, normal world.

It wasn't lost on Logan that Rainbow's hippie life-style was the one that would offer Michael the more normal childhood at the moment—or that *he* was the parent who wasn't able to.

But, by God, that was going to change.

Chapter 37

THE PINK CORAL-COVERED BUILDING WHERE THE SEA MONSTER was holding his son morphed from fairy-tale charming to dungeonesque the closer they swam and as Logan surveyed the lay of the... *land?*... around it.

Other than the terraced coral garden in front, only aquamarine water surrounded them—and comparing the color of the water in this hellish place to Angel's eyes would be an abomination.

"We need to find somewhere to lie low so we can scout the area, Angel. That... molehill, crab heap—whatever—back there isn't going to cut it."

"There's no reason to." Angel stopped swimming when he did. "And no way, either. All of Ceto's palaces are set up with open space around them. There are guards in every tower monitoring arrivals. She already knows we're here."

Son-of-a-bitch. "So your plan is to go straight in. Meet her face to face. In a position of power." Bluffing.

"Unless you've got a better idea?" She started swimming again.

Well, hell. He was a decent poker player—and it wasn't as if they had many choices.

Or did they?

He tugged one of her purple flippers. "We both don't have to go, Angel."

"Yes we do, Logan. You don't know Ceto." She

turned somber eyes on him. Eyes that had lost that sparkle she'd had since he'd met her—which was as much a tragedy as Michael being inside.

No. No it wasn't. Michael was the focus of this expedition, and Angel's eyes be damned.

"Ceto knows we're here. This is her territory. She knew the moment you stepped aboard your boat in the harbor, the minute The Council Guards showed up. Nothing goes on in these waters that she doesn't know. We can't sneak up on her, so it's better to go in under our own power and deal with her in an even swimming pool than have her send out her henchfish to round us up and herd us in."

He didn't like it, but obviously he had no choice. At least he'd brought the hook. And the knife. "Fine. Let's do this."

When they were twenty yards from the palace, the massive doors opened. Silently, slowly, the swirling water sucked everything in the immediate vicinity inward. Effective. Ominous. Deceptively innocuous.

Unlike the battalion that awaited them.

Logan clamped his jaw shut as he saw the army of horror treading just inside. Barracuda lined up in formation with a row of morays behind them, and a sawfish swam beneath the contingent like a colonel inspecting his ranks. Logan had the uncomfortable feeling that that was exactly what the fish was doing.

This was where his son was being held?

"*Princesa*." One of the barracuda broke rank and swam to Angel, a little more in her face than Logan was comfortable with, but Angel held her own.

"Mato, please tell Ceto we're here to see her."

"You think she doesn't know?" The fish writhed back and forth so much like a giddy two-year-old that he was either happy, high, or hooked.

Logan wanted it to be the latter. He gripped the gaff tighter.

"And you." The barracuda swam over to him, his eyes narrowing as he got too damn close for Logan's liking. "Get rid of the weapon. It won't do any good around Ceto anyway."

Logan had figured that, but he wouldn't hand it over until Angel nodded. He didn't like feeling naked and vulnerable. Good thing he still had the knife. Did fish know enough about clothing to check pockets? He hoped to hell not.

Luck was with him—if he could call any of this luck—and he made it in without a pat-down, though the fish had asked him about Michael's hat, smirking when he saw what it was.

"Yeah, you can keep that. It's not as if you're going to drown the goddess with it."

Goddess? Talk about delusions of grandeur.

They followed the deadly fish down a long corridor, unusual chandeliers hanging from the ceiling, an ancient hall of horrors that, somewhere, housed his son.

Logan steeled himself against the pain. Michael was in here. Beneath the water, probably scared and wondering where he was. Logan wanted to kill something, starting with the barracuda and working his way through every last moray before moving on to the sea monster.

He didn't want to imagine what Michael was going through. The terror, the abandonment… First, his mother dropped him on the doorstep of a father he'd never known; now a shark had brought him to this watery pit.

Logan exhaled a long stream of water—something he didn't want to dwell on. He'd get Michael out. Then he'd take him back on land and give him the most normal childhood he could—find his son a two-legged stepmother, buy a dog, build a picket fence around his yard. No more of this mermaid shit.

Hell, he'd move inland. Kansas even. Somewhere away from the ocean and the memories. Away from the possibility of any of this ever happening again.

Angel swam around the ninety-degree turn at the corridor's dead end after the barracuda as if she knew exactly where she was going. As if they were invited guests. Not like they were here on a rescue mission that could get ugly.

Or become a battle to the death.

But how ironic was it that Angel, a mermaid, a mythical creature said to lure men to their deaths, was on a mission to save his child?

No.

He couldn't think like that.

They were in this predicament *because* of her, and he was not about to romanticize it. There was no future with a woman who was half fish.

Although she hadn't been last night…

Logan shook off the thought. Last night was over. Today, the future, were what counted.

He followed her around the bend, taking note of each turn they made, identifying marks in the similarly decorated corridors, the view from the windows, and gearing up his internal compass to keep track of where they were and how they'd gotten there.

Lobsters lined the next corridor, antennae angled as if they were cadets offering a military salute—or making sure he and Angel stayed in line.

"Logan, whatever you do, get Michael out of here, okay?" Angel whispered when the barracuda rounded another corner.

"Of course I will. What are you talking about?"

She glanced around the corner, then back at him, tension etched onto her face. "Just trust me. I know what I'm doing."

"Let's move it, *Princesa*." The barracuda's toothy snout preceded the rest of his deadly body back around the corner. "You know how she doesn't like to be kept waiting."

Yeah, well, Logan didn't like having his son kidnapped, but then, you didn't always get what you wanted.

But he was about to. He fingered the knife in his pocket.

The sea monster was going to get what was coming to her.

Chapter 38

THE CORRIDOR OPENED INTO A CAVERNOUS ROOM, TIERS OF seating descending to a stage carved from stone and marble. Massive columns held up a scallop-edged roof, sea grass or kelp or something draped from it like curtains. One side was tied back—with an octopus? The other side flowed away from the stage in the current, and stone statues lined the concave back of the stage—

But they weren't just any statues. No, those looked like…

Logan blinked. Easter Island faces?

A cloud of jellyfish circled above the statues with synchronized pulsations, their tentacles swaying from side to side as a swarm of different-colored morays dodged in and out in an other-worldly allemande left.

A large dais made of glass sat at the center of the stage, and on it…

On it was the most amazingly horrific creature Logan had ever seen.

The sea monster. Only… she didn't look like a monster.

She didn't look like anything he would have thought a sea monster looked like. Like a giant squid or something. Not this green-haired version of Mae West.

A Mae West with two tails.

Two tails. One green, one blue. Fins tapping against giant clamshells below the dais as if they were footstools.

Receiving plates of… food… as if they were a tribute.

She didn't look monstrous, but she'd taken his child. That, alone, put her in the death-is-too-good-for-her category.

Sharks flanked each side of the stage where she held court, and sawfish patrolled in front of her, their double-sided bills looking way too lethal for his son to be near. The lionfish standing sentry on the edge of the dais didn't lessen his concern.

Where was Michael? What had the beast done with him?

The sea monster looked out from her throne, a hideous smile on a face that could be beautiful, but wasn't. Bitterness chilled her eyes, and sarcasm crooked her mouth. An almost palpable anger tightened her shoulders, causing her jaw to clench so tightly he thought she'd shatter her teeth.

Then she laughed—a deep, husky cackle—and it skittered all over his nerve endings in an Oscar-worthy Wicked Witch imitation—an apt description. All she needed was the pointed hat and a wart.

Too bad she didn't melt in water.

She laughed again and, as they descended the steps, Logan saw what she found so enjoyable.

In the depression in front of the stage—an orchestra pit if they were on land—the array of tropical fish picked up the tempo of their… dancing? Swirling so fast they should be dizzy when they finally stopped. A pair of stingrays flapped their wings, turning in circles above the fish, and crabs and lobsters clacked their pincers in a bizarre balletic choreography around the outer edge of the performance. A pair of neon green moray eels undulated across the stage, writhing themselves into and out of a series of knots.

"Oh, cool!"

Logan froze. Beside him, Angel did, too.

Michael.

"Get moving." The barracuda shoved him from behind, then circled around to lead them down the stairs.

Logan didn't need anyone to lead him. His son was here.

He stepped onto one of the stone seats, trying to see where Michael was, but Angel grabbed his hand and pulled him down. Or her up. He didn't bother to figure out which it was.

"Logan, listen to me. You can't hope to get out of here alive with Michael unless I distract Ceto. I plan to, but if you hear any rumbling whatsoever, just grab him and get out."

"Rumbling?"

The barracuda looked back, his lower jaw slung forward, the spikes he called teeth glinting in the light from more of those same chandeliers as were in the hallway. Logan took a step down the stairs.

Angel didn't let go of his arm. "Ceto was a goddess at one point, and while the gods took away most of her powers, she still retains a few—one of them being the ability to cause seaquakes. The Mariana Trench didn't dig itself, you know. I shudder to think what she could do with this building, so you have to grab Michael and get out."

Oh he fully intended to. "What about you?"

Angel glared at Ceto. "Don't worry about me. I'll meet up with you afterward."

No she wouldn't.

Angel knew *exactly* what would happen when Ceto got that angry.

But she had to fix this. She was the reason Michael was here and she'd get him out alive if it was the last thing she'd ever do.

The reality was, it probably would be.

Chapter 39

LOGAN DIDN'T KNOW WHAT ANGEL PLANNED, BUT HE'D MAKE sure Michael was well out of harm's way.

"Cool!" reverberated again in the light current.

Logan leaned off the bottom step to follow the sound and saw Michael clapping and smiling as colorful fish darted in front of him. He looked anything *but* scared and injured. Angel was right. Ceto hadn't frightened him.

Thank God for small favors. He glanced at Ceto. He wouldn't be thanking her, however.

The sea monster met his gaze, and an eerie smile slid across her face. She nodded to the four makos at the edge of the stage. Two flicks of their tails put them on either side of Michael.

The witch glanced at him, her message loud and clear. Don't say a word, or she'd hurt his son.

Logan ground his teeth and reached for Angel's arm. They had to figure out how to get Michael free before they went any closer.

"Michael, why don't you go with my friends back to your room?" asked Ceto. "The oysters are there, ready for us. I'll be along shortly to play pearls with you."

"Can I be a cowboy?"

Surprisingly, the monster smiled a genuine smile and her voice even softened. "Of course. Brutus, let him on."

On a shark. Logan would have taken off after them to

intervene if the sea witch hadn't looked up at him again. And licked her lips.

He knew that look.

Thank God for the knife in his pocket. It was something, at least. But if she ordered the makos to harm Michael, he didn't know that he'd be able to get to him in time. He and Angel had to play this carefully.

Except that Angel decided to pull her arm free and kick her tail hard enough for her wake to send him staggering back onto the stairs as she zoomed over to face the monster.

"Hold on, Ceto," she growled.

Great. What was she up to?

—⁓—

Ha, good. Angel hid her smile at surprising the old witch but let that small victory buoy her. Gods knew, it might be the only win she got as this played out.

Even then, success wasn't a sure thing, but she had to try something. She'd seen the expression that had crossed Ceto's face when Logan appeared. The sea monster was nothing if not predictable. Not that it was all that hard to recognize Ceto's hungry look—especially because Angel felt the same way toward him.

So now she had two Hardington men to rescue.

"Hi, Angel!" Michael waved as she swam closer, and Angel couldn't help but return his smile. "Look what I have! Isn't it cool?" He held something up: a four-foot-long moray eel whose bite could be deadly if Ceto released it from the stupor she'd lulled it into.

A quick glance at the smile playing on Ceto's lips and the fingers tapping on her now black-scaled hips confirmed that she would, if pushed, let the eel do it.

Or… *would* she?

Ceto had lost her last child in the battle with Reel. The Council had given Joey to her to keep her amused and kept tabs on her destructive activities where Humans were concerned. Angel herself had seen the reports. There'd been no "rescued" children from shipwrecks the sea monster had caused, so Ceto was still childless.

While that made her that much more desperate, it also meant she wouldn't hurt Michael.

Logan, however, was a whole different story.

Oh, Ceto would let him live, but in a capacity he definitely wouldn't appreciate. And one Angel didn't want to imagine. She'd heard stories of Ceto's Humans and they weren't pretty—and neither were the men when the monster was finished with them.

And she'd just left him alone…

Son-of-a-Mer! She wasn't in the same league as the ex-goddess when it came to being calculatingly evil.

Angel swallowed very carefully. Ceto's eyes were on her, and Angel didn't want the sea monster to see her sweat.

She straightened her spine. Time to do this.

"Hi, Michael." She swam up to him slowly, not wanting to let Ceto know exactly how much this child meant to her.

"What took you so long?" Michael set the moray in the seat next to his and got to his feet. "Wanna ride a shark with me?"

Brutus bared his teeth in a gruesome, Mer-killer smile.

Angel wanted to drown him. And Ceto. Too bad the last wasn't possible.

"Maybe later. Are you okay?" She couldn't help

asking, though she did refrain from dragging him to her to make sure he was. He was breathing, talking, and not scared; she didn't want to jeopardize any of that.

"I'm kinda bored. Ceto doesn't like to play hide-and-seek."

Angel did smile at that. She *bet* Ceto didn't like having a child run and hide from her.

"Or we could play baseball." He looked around, the quick motion sending him spinning. Which got another "Cool!" out of him. But then he stopped spinning, and his face fell. "I forgot my baseball glove."

"You can play with it when you get home."

"Okay, but you know what? I lost my hat. How am I gonna play baseball without it? Rainbow gave it to me for frembrance so I won't forget her. She said I'm the only one who's gonna frember her when she's gone."

The woman should have thought about that before she left him. If she had, none of this would be happening. But Angel couldn't blame this on Rainbow. It was *her* fault for over-swimming her bounds and, therefore, up to her to fix it.

"Michael, why don't you show your father around outside? Ceto and I have something to discuss."

The sea monster left her cushy *holothurian* throne at that and headed toward them. "I don't think so, Angel, but nice try—"

"Logan's here?" Michael whirled around, spinning once more. "Where?"

"Right here." Logan appeared at the opposite end of the row, and Angel heard Ceto gasp.

Whether it was because the monster had been too focused on Michael to see Logan swim across the theater or because she recognized the murderous rage on his face, Angel didn't know. Nor did she care. She'd use either to their advantage.

But first she had to get Logan and Michael away from Ceto.

"Michael, your father has something for you." She glared pointedly at Logan. *Get him out of here.*

"What is it?" The hopeful expression on Michael's face gave her some hope of her own. Surely the gods wouldn't let Ceto win? Ruin this child's life just because *she'd* made a bad judgment call?

"We found your hat." Logan held it up and, like a magnet, Michael was by his father's side, shoving the cap on his head.

Ceto was not happy. She motioned for the makos to surround Logan and Michael. "Instead of going outside, Michael, why don't you take your father to play pearls? I'm sure he'd love to see your room, and I'd like a little time to speak with Angel." Ceto sang the *suggestion*, her eyes on Logan, as her hair undulated like over-sexed eels around her shoulders and her tails rippled red and orange like flowing magma from the tips of her flukes to her hips. Subtlety was not Ceto's strong suit as she tried to ensnare Logan with her Siren Song.

Good luck with that.

Logan took a step toward her and took a breath. "Ange—"

"Logan, take care of Michael." Angel couldn't let Logan speak or Ceto would know her enchantment didn't work because Angel had gotten to him first. Who knew that the birthday-song debacle would end up saving him? Humans could be enchanted by only one Mer.

"And, Ceto, I wouldn't get rid of all your guards if I were you."

Ceto smirked. "But you aren't me, are you, Angel?"

"No, thank the gods. I'm Angel Tritone, daughter of the previous High Councilman and sister of the current one. I know exactly who I am. The question is, do you?"

Not that Rod would want her using his position to fix her screw-up, especially since she'd disobeyed direct orders, but one sure thing about her brother was his loyalty. As far as Ceto knew, a High Council contingent could arrive at any moment, which would put a kink in whatever she thought she was going to do.

Thank the gods, The Council, and everyone else who'd so put the fear of the gods into Ceto, the sea monster called back three of the sharks, leaving Brutus, the biggest, to guard Logan and Michael. Still not ideal, but it did give Logan a fighting chance.

And she meant that literally.

"I know who you are, too, Angel! You're my bestest friend and you're a mermaid!" Michael laughed before turning to Logan and reaching for his hand. "See, Logan? I told you they were real. And I bet Santa Claus is, too. But not the Easter Bunny. Somebody would catch a giant rabbit and make him a pet if he was. But I wouldn't. I didn't even try to catch Stewart, 'cause Angel said it wouldn't be nice to be in a cage, and he's kinda weird anyway."

Brutus snorted and herded them toward the corridor on the left, directly opposite from where she and Logan had entered. Not where Angel preferred, but as long as they were moving away from Ceto, they had a chance.

"You wanna see the oysters, Logan?" Michael kept up his chatter. Gods, she'd miss that. "They're ugly, but they have really pretty pearls inside them. I even found a black one, but Ceto said that that one was too little to play with. I want to find a pink one."

As they reached the corner, Brutus too close behind them for Angel's liking, she heard Michael say, "I want to give it to Angel, 'cause she's a girl and girls like pink. 'Cept Rainbow doesn't. She likes blue, but I don't think they make blue pearls. What's your favorite color, Logan? I like red the best, then blue. We had lots of blue stuff…"

Logan glanced at her as they turned the corner, but Angel pretended to misinterpret his *don't do anything foolish* look. She'd do whatever it took to make sure they got out alive.

"He's not going to leave here." Ceto's voice was right behind her.

Fluttering just the tips of her flukes, Angel turned slowly.

Ceto floated forward in all her evil glory, her twin tails pulsing that hideous red she was so fond of, her malachite curls backlit by the hatchetfish lights like some Hades-inspired crown. "You shouldn't have come."

Angel crossed her arms, shaking with anger, but she knew Ceto would think it was fear. "You didn't leave me a choice."

Ceto slid a stray curl away from her face and tucked it behind her ear. "You don't need this one, Angel. You're more than capable of producing a brood of your own. Something, in case you've forgotten, that I am not permitted to do."

"Ceto, I understand your pain, but—"

Ceto's tails flared like a flash of fire, then went black. The remaining makos scattered out the archways at the far side of the chamber. Angel didn't blame them.

"No one understands." Ceto advanced on her. "Not you, with your youth and your beauty and your virile, handsome Human. Not even your brother. I would have expected him to get it since his wife has begun spawning their own. Those old cronies I'd hoped Rod would have had the good sense to replace on The Council don't understand either. They never did. No one understands."

Actually, Angel *did* understand. But Ceto's losses didn't justify her actions. And they certainly shouldn't enable Angel to feel any softening toward the sea monster. There was no softness in Ceto. Not when it came to what she wanted.

"Ceto, let him go. Let them both go. They aren't yours, and they don't belong here. They need to be back in their world."

Ceto's hair flared out as if an electric eel had slammed into her, the curls almost straightening in her anger, then recoiling like a spring. The fairy basslet dance troupe dispersed as quickly as the makos had, leaving her and Ceto alone in the giant theater where the sea monster's words rang off every stone surface.

"*Belong*? You're one to talk. You were on *land* with them, Angel. Tried to pass as one. I'm supposed to back off from something that's my right while you upset everyone else's natural order by communing with them? I don't think so, little girl. I've had it with the half-assed generosity of The Council. Joey Camparo is no prize, let me tell you. I want a child, and since they've refused to allow me my own, I'm taking Michael."

"Take me."

"What?" Ceto's curls stopped mid-bounce.

"Take me instead."

"An interesting offer, Tritone, but you're hardly child material any more. If you'd made that offer twenty-five *selinos* ago, we might have had something to talk about."

"No, Ceto. I don't mean as your child." Angel straightened her back and took a deep gulp. "Take me as your hostage."

Chapter 40

LOGAN ROUNDED THE CORNER INTO A WINDOWLESS CORRIDOR lined with the broken remnants of a dead coral colony on one wall, and cooled, pitted lava on the other. He was almost out of earshot when he heard Angel's offer.

Hostage.

Angel was offering herself as Ceto's hostage in return for Michael.

He didn't know whether to rush in and save her or hightail it out of there—until Michael's question gave him the answer.

"Why isn't Angel with us, Logan? She's coming, right?"

Logan's heart squeezed, both at the hopeful expression on his son's face and the knowledge that Angel was *not* coming with them.

Hadn't been planning to, obviously.

Logan couldn't let her sacrifice be in vain. He had to get Michael out of here.

"She'll be along when"—if—"she can, Michael," he whispered, urging his son toward a light at the far end of the corridor, trying to block out the generosity and unselfishness of Angel's act and focus on thwarting their shark guard and the bitch who'd put them in this spot to begin with.

He couldn't throw away this chance Angel had given him. A parent was supposed to protect his child. The child's welfare came first—a fact Christine hadn't realized, but one Angel instinctively had.

She was trading her freedom for his son's life. Of all the selfless things to do… She'd knowingly put herself in Ceto's power to give them the opportunity to escape.

He tried to remember why he'd been bothered that she was a mermaid. Hell, the kid's own mother hadn't been that unselfish and she was human. No, Christine had dumped Michael when the going got too tough, but Angel…

He was a fool. He never should have told her to leave last night. He should have seen beyond her tail to the person she was. To the good-hearted, loving, giving woman residing in that body—tailed or otherwise.

He'd get Michael out, then find some way to help her.

"Okay. I guess." Michael tipped the rim of his baseball cap lower on his face and dragged his hands along the rough lava wall. "When's that gonna be?"

"I don't know."

"Let's move it along, Humans." The shark's breath preceded his words and Logan didn't want to focus on what could cause such a stench.

The daylight got brighter. Somehow they'd have to make a run for it. Logan surreptitiously checked the corridor behind him—and saw four hundred pounds of fish filling the darkness there. They obviously weren't going back that way. Their only chance was through whatever was up ahead.

Logan looked forward. Plant life grew along the wall, which meant direct sunlight. Conceivably then, they had a straight shot to the surface, but what awaited them in between?

They had to get away from the mako and, preferably,

without witnesses. Logan wasn't exactly looking forward to hand-to-fin combat with the big fish, let alone with any of the guy's buddies.

He slid his hand into his pocket and grasped the edge of the knife, his thumb straying to the blade-release mechanism. The knife wasn't that big, but still, a well-placed blade could bring down a shark.

It could also put his arm in bite range. And Michael in harm's way. But makos were some of the fastest swimmers in the shark world; he didn't have much choice if they had to make a run—swim—for it. He'd rather any confrontation be on his terms.

Something swam by outside, passing through the daylight, casting its shadow onto the wall. He had to act before any other sharks showed up.

Logan squeezed Michael's shoulder to get him to stop, needing the least traumatic way to do this for his son—and the deadliest for the shark.

"Get moving, *friend*." The shark butted Logan in the back with his bullet-shaped snout.

That was the opening Logan was looking for.

He pretended to stumble and shoved Michael away with one hand while whipping the knife out with the other, engaging the blade, and spinning around to shove it between the mako's eyes in one maneuver.

Someone Upstairs was looking out for him because the shark's eyes glazed over without him uttering a sound. The embedded knife effectively stopped any bleeding, so they were home free on alerting the entire Caribbean, and the water carried the dead fish gently onto the corridor floor where it looked like ol' Brutus had decided to take a nap.

The fact that he was belly-up against the wall wouldn't necessarily be a good detail to point out to a six-year-old.

"Hey, Logan." Michael did a somersault into a handstand before righting himself. "Didya see my handstand? Were my legs straight? Angel said I was real good at handstands. What do you think—hey. What happened to Brutus?"

"He, uh… He decided to take a nap." Logan swam over to Michael and swept his arm around his shoulders, turning his son around so they were facing the bright light at the end of the tunnel.

Mission accomplished. Now they had to escape those tower guards Angel had mentioned.

Another shadow flickered on the wall.

This time, Logan recognized the shape.

Lifting Michael, Logan pushed off the lava wall and swam to the arched window. One side of it was wide enough for him to squeeze through.

He hoped.

He looked outside to make sure that shadow wasn't a trick.

"Hey, cool! Dolphins!" Michael waved. "I like dolphins better than sharks. They smile."

And, more importantly, they were on their side.

Logan took one last look down the corridor. Past the dead Brutus and into the inky darkness. Angel was back there. With at least three other makos and a sea monster who'd once been a goddess.

He had to save his son. That's what Angel wanted.

"How about we go meet them, Michael?" Tucking Michael's hat in his pocket, he grabbed a piece of broken coral and smashed the window, then cleared the debris as best he could and helped Michael through, garnering several nasty cuts when it was his turn. But they were free. In a manner of speaking.

Judging the distance between the towers and the dolphins, Logan kept an eye out for the tower guards. He and Michael should be able to make it…

"Yo, dolphins!" Michael, who had no idea of their predicament, waved so hard he floated off the wall, only to start swimming toward the mammals.

Logan didn't have long to wait before the first bull shark wiggled through the window on the southernmost tower.

Shit.

Logan shoved off the wall, scooping Michael in his arms, and kicked his legs for all he was worth.

He looked back. The bull shark was closing in.

Then another one swam over the top of the building.

They weren't going to make it—

The dolphins dove down in formation, one taking Michael on its back, two others lodging beneath Logan's arms, and carried them off, the speed in their powerful tails putting much-needed distance between them and the sharks.

Miles later, sides heaving, the dolphins circled together. "Where's the princess?" the captain asked.

"Still there." Logan kept his voice low, not wanting Michael to understand the seriousness of their situation.

"You *left* her?"

He tossed Michael his hat, then steered the captain away. "She gave herself up as a hostage so we could escape. I couldn't risk my son."

"Your son's safe now."

All thanks to the woman who was down there, facing God-knew what. He wanted to go back. But the sharks… Michael…

No. She'd given up her freedom—possibly her life— to save Michael's; Logan wouldn't jeopardize that. Angel wouldn't want him to.

But he couldn't just leave her there. "Can you distract the sharks?"

"What?" The captain's toothy grin opened in shock.

"Can you distract the sharks? And take my son to safety. I'm going back."

The captain closed her mouth and nodded. "We can, and we'll protect the child. It's a very courageous thing you're doing. Thank you and gods-speed, Human."

Logan didn't want to leave Michael, but what choice did he have? He couldn't leave Angel down there.

He wrapped Michael's arms around a dorsal fin. "Hold on tight, okay?"

"Okay. Are we gonna race?"

"In a little bit. There's something I have to take care of first. Now hold on, I'm counting on you." He tucked Michael's hat into the waistband of the boy's shorts, then dropped a kiss onto his temple. "I love you, son."

Michael's smile appeared, the gap between his teeth reminding Logan of the discarded shark teeth Angel had found and what she was facing. He definitely couldn't leave her to the sea monster's mercy.

"I love you, too, Log—Dad."

The dolphin arced then, tail rippling the water, and Michael headed to shore with half the contingent, while the other half took off back toward the palace.

Dad.
He'd finally gotten the Dad.
And Angel wasn't around to hear it.

Chapter 41

"HOSTAGE?" CETO TAPPED HER FINGERNAILS AGAINST HER lip, her tails now alternating between red and orange.

Well, at least Angel had brought the threat level down. A red tail wasn't much of an improvement, but it beat black. A black sea-monster tail was never good.

"You know, that could work." Ceto started circling her. "Although I did try that with your brother, but he and his *Human* managed to get away."

Angel had heard the story enough times that she knew it by heart. She also knew she was signing her own death warrant by saying what she was about to, but she had to do this to save the men she loved.

"You put Erica in a regular room, Ceto, not a cell. She was able to get out and free Reel."

"Yeah, who knew a Human had that many smarts?" Ceto's tails flared, then went back to being black. "I'll never make that mistake again. I had a new bedchamber specially made when The Council and I hammered out the deal about Joey. He hasn't gone anywhere."

According to Erica, Joey's ex-girlfriend and Reel's wife, it wasn't a surprise that Joey hadn't, nor, frankly, anything to be upset about.

"So, you're suggesting I hold *you* for ransom until The Council permits me to procreate again?" A soothing aquamarine color panned across Ceto's tails, and her curls relaxed to soft ringlets around her shoulders. The sea monster almost looked pretty.

Then she turned sharply and the curls sprang back into tight coils, the tails went dark purple, and her eyes narrowed. "How long do you think that's going to take? Rod is one stubborn Son-of-a-Mer and I'm not exactly a fan of having another female around."

"I'm sure Rod will want to meet with you as soon as he learns what's happened, Ceto. But you have to let Logan and Michael go. What's one child in the face of being allowed to have as many as you want again?"

This time, when everything softened on the sea monster, she did look pretty. "Oh, to hold one again, to feel its soft, cuddly body against me." She smiled, and for the first time since Angel had known her, it reached her eyes. "There's nothing like it. Nothing at all. Their unconditional love…"

She sighed, and her tails turned the palest shades of pink and blue. "Children are one of the things the gods have managed to do right. They don't judge you or care what you look like or what other people think. Everything is new through their eyes, everything such a wonder and so exciting. Anything is possible. They bring such hope. Hope for a better world. Hope that you can do some good yourself, you know? That you can love them and guide them, then set them forth in the world to carry a part of you with them, biologically or otherwise. They have the possibility to do and become so much. To touch others." She leaned back against the stage, her flukes fluttering. "There's nothing like having a child, Angel. Nothing at all."

Ceto closed her eyes, and her arms cradled an

imaginary infant, and for a moment, Angel felt sorry for her.

"But those bastards took that away from me."

There went that moment.

Ceto's eyes flew open as her tail turned as black as the deepest part of the deepest ocean, her eyes as hard as cooled magma, and her hair as twisted as any whirlpool she'd ever spun in her Bermuda-Triangle mood.

"Yes, I do think your ransom idea has merit, Angel."

"So you'll let them go?"

"Let them go? Come on, Angel, I may be a softie when it comes to children, but I'm not stupid. The only way to ensure your compliance is to keep them locked away. Once I get what I want, you can have what you want. If I don't get it, well then sorry, you don't either."

"You old bitch—" Angel lunged toward Ceto, but at that moment a tiger shark zipped into the room.

"My Goddess! It's Brutus. He's been knifed!" The shark was practically in a frenzy.

"Knifed?" Ceto growled.

Knifed? Angel felt a glimmer of hope. *That's* what Logan had grabbed from his tackle box.

"Yes. In the corridor. And the prisoner has escaped with your child."

Escaped! They were free! Angel wanted to twirl, she was so giddy.

And then suddenly, she *was* twirling. Only this time, it wasn't because she was giddy.

No, this time, it was all Ceto's doing.

—⁓—

Logan heard Michael's squeals of laughter as the dolphins carried him toward land. Thank God his son didn't have a clue about what he'd just gone through. He should come out of this unscathed.

Provided his father could bring Angel—and himself—back.

He was halfway to Ceto's palace when the first rumble shook the sea.

Two more kicks, and the dolphins who'd gone ahead of him reappeared. "Human, we have to evacuate!"

"Evacuate? Are you crazy? She's still there!"

"There's nothing you can do. You have to come with us! That was Ceto and you have no idea what she's capable of!" The captain motioned toward the surface. "Come on!"

"But Angel—"

"The princess is fully aware of what's happening down there. There's nothing more you can do for her."

Another rumble sounded, and the water began churning.

"Human, you don't have much time. You've heard the stories about the Triangle?" Logan nodded. "Well, now you're seeing it in action. We need to go now if we hope to outswim it. Hold onto my dorsal and I'll get you out of here."

Logan stared at the palace, then at the dolphin. The calm captain had a wild look in her eye... and Michael was still in the water.

He had no other choice.

He reached out for the captain's fin. "Let's go."

The dolphin kicked them toward the surface, angling back toward the coast as another rumble sped through the sea, this time bringing the water with it and circling around on itself.

The beginnings of a giant whirlpool.

They cleared the surface then, and another dolphin swam up next to the captain. "Hang on to me, too!" he called and they took off with Logan between them.

Logan couldn't look back. He'd failed her. She'd given up so much for him and Michael and he hadn't been able to save her.

What was he going to tell Michael?

How would his son deal with this?

How would he?

Chapter 42

A week later

"WHEN IS SHE COMING BACK?" IT WAS THE SAME QUESTION Michael asked him every night.

Logan set the beers down on the hall table outside Michael's bedroom door. His son shouldn't see him drinking.

He shouldn't *be* drinking.

But it made thoughts of her so much easier to take.

No. Not easier. Less difficult. Bearable.

Almost.

"I don't know when, Michael." That was the same answer Logan gave him every night. "Do you want to talk about it?"

Michael slouched further under his covers, the stuffed raccoon falling on his head from atop the pillow. "I dunno."

Which meant *yes* in kid-speak.

Logan pushed the door open and walked over to Michael's bed, nudging his son's legs over so he could sit. "I'm sure she's fine, Michael."

"Do you think Ceto put her in a cage like Joey?"

"Joey was in a cage?"

Michael had told him about the friend he'd met there, this Joey, but this was the first he'd heard about any cage. It made him shudder to think of what he and Michael had narrowly escaped.

Only… Angel hadn't.

"Yup. It was a big room with a bed and everything, but with handcuffs on the bed and bars on his door. He kept asking me to get him out, so I don't think he liked being in there."

Logan didn't know which revelation to react to first. A bed with handcuffs was not an image he wanted Michael to have in his head. Logan hoped Michael would forget about it after a while, but Logan wouldn't. Ceto was one sick son-of-a-bitch. No, scratch that. Make that one sick bitch.

And he'd left Angel down there.

"Angel said being in a cage would be yucky, so I hope Ceto didn't do that to her."

Logan did, too. But, God, this was just tearing him up. He'd left her in the depths with that sea monster. In a whirlpool that had sucked everything around it straight down.

She couldn't have survived that… could she?

And if she had, *was* she a prisoner?

"And A.C. was in a cage, too."

As far as Logan was concerned, the damned shark that started this nightmare could rot in that cage for all he cared. Hell, that was too good for the fish, but Michael had cared about the shark. Had sung the hammerhead's praises about finding Angel until Logan couldn't bear to hear anymore.

They'd had several chats about not accepting rides with strangers—or sharks. Logan had considered taking Michael to see someone professional about the ordeal, but who'd believe him? Worse, they might find something wrong with *his* parenting skills and he'd end up losing his son. No, so far, Michael seemed to have adjusted well—other than pining for Angel.

"I know you miss her, Michael."

"She promised she'd stay with me," Michael said half under his breath.

"I know. But sometimes, even when we want to, we can't keep our promises. She might not be able to come back." Logan didn't want to contemplate *why* she wouldn't be able to.

"Like Rainbow?"

Another woman he didn't want to think about. His relationships needed a serious overhaul. A flighty woman with zero parenting skills and a mermaid. His life was as much a circus now as it'd been growing up.

He would probably do best by his son to remain single. After all, he hadn't exactly had the best role models and would probably do a better job alone than Goran and Nadia had done together. As long as he stayed away from mermaids...

He squeezed Michael's leg through the covers. "Rainbow will come back someday."

Probably when Michael turned eighteen and was an adult who'd be able to support her, but Logan realized he was going to have to hunt her down before that. She couldn't abandon their son.

Michael reached for Rocky and tucked him against his chest so tightly that if the animal were real, he'd suffocate. "Nuh-uh. Rainbow said she couldn't come back. That's why she gave me the hat. For frembrance. 'Cause she had to meet someone."

"Meet someone? Who?"

"I dunno, and she didn't want to talk about it. Mr.

Ray said it was about a big sea and Rainbow didn't really want to go. Then he laughed, but it wasn't a funny laugh. When Angel comes back, can she live in Rainbow's sea? That's why I wanted a mermaid for my birthday, so Rainbow would have a friend."

Logan's blood ran cold. "She had to meet someone about a big sea?"

"That's what Mr. Ray said."

The big… C?

Oh, God. He'd misjudged her. Christine hadn't abandoned Michael out of selfishness, but self*less*ness. She'd spared their son the agony and worry of watching her go through cancer—and dying from it, by the sound of it.

She'd given Michael to him because she wasn't going to be around.

Logan blinked back the wetness that sprang to his eyes and inhaled a deep, shaky breath.

Hell. He'd misjudged her. And Angel, too. Badly.

Logan cleared his throat and leaned over to kiss Michael's forehead, putting the baseball cap back in place afterward. "I think Angel would love to live in Rainbow's sea, son."

If she'd somehow survived Ceto's.

He had to find out. He had to give Michael something to believe in. Both women couldn't be lost to his son. Or to him.

"Night, Logan."

Logan. "Dad" had lasted until Angel hadn't shown up that next day.

"Good night, Michael. I love you."

Michael murmured something. He always did.

Never clear and never loud, but Logan chose to think of it as a "Me, too." The pretense helped him sleep at night.

So did the beers he picked up when he walked out of Michael's room. He headed down the hallway, through his bedroom without a glance at the bed he hadn't been able to sleep in, then onto his deck.

Again.

It was a damn familiar and painful routine.

He sat on the decking and stretched one leg out in front of him, the other bent so he could rest his beer arm on it, dangling the bottle against his thigh, swirling the contents around after each swig.

Six nights now. Six nights on his deck, staring out at the silvery water.

Alone.

Between Christine's—no, *Rainbow's*, he owed her that—illness and Angel's disappearance, well, Logan wasn't quite sure where to begin his penance.

He'd have to see if he could track down Christine's family, though the effort would be futile at best. She'd been a free spirit and hadn't claimed any ties to anyone or anything—something they had in common since he hadn't liked claiming his. It was why he hadn't blinked when he'd read her note about Michael—it fit her perfectly.

As for finding her now… She and Michael had lived so many places, according to Michael, that he didn't have a clue where to begin. And with that baseball cap for "frembrance," she obviously didn't want him to. Michael—and he—would have to remember her as they'd known her, not as she was at the end.

Life was funny that way. You were born, you lived, and you died, with only the memories held by those you left behind living on.

Water murmured against the pylons below as he raised his beer in the moonlight, toasting Christine and thanking her for finding him. For giving him his son. Promising her that Michael wouldn't forget her. Michael needed those memories just as…

Well… just as Logan needed his.

He rested his arm on his knee again, the bottle brushing his calf. He hadn't thought about his parents in a long time. Made a point of not thinking about them, actually, but that wasn't fair to anyone, himself included. Who was he but the sum of his experiences? No matter how much he'd like to claim otherwise, he wouldn't be who he was today if not for where he'd been.

Logan took a long swallow of the beer, remembering his family and how he'd wanted a normal life back then. How he still wanted one, but what, really, was normal?

Take Angel, for instance.

A part of him wanted to take her all right; the other part remembered that she was a *mermaid*.

And yet, in her world, she was perfectly normal. Things he found new and odd were commonplace to her. Yet she'd adapted to his world, had lived among humans, and no one had been able to tell the difference.

But she's a mermaid, his subconscious argued.

He knew that, yet he couldn't get her out of his mind.

Did that mean he was out of his?

She has a tail.

He knew that, too, but her tail didn't stop him from remembering how she'd looked in this very same moonlight, in his bed. The way she'd made him feel, the way she'd made love to him. How she'd laughed with Michael, and how Michael had played with her. It hadn't mattered to his son what she was; he loved her for *who* she was.

Logan took another swig. *Who* she was…

He'd found her journal and read the entries. An invasion of her privacy, true, but after she'd sacrificed herself for their freedom, he'd wanted to find out who she really was.

He remembered the look she gave him before Brutus had ushered them out of Ceto's theater. She'd been determined—even knowing what would happen. And when the whirlpool had hit…

Logan leaned his head back against his house and closed his eyes against the memory, but it wouldn't go away.

The dolphins had kicked against the current, until, at last, they slipped from its pull, exhausted and worn out, drained both physically and emotionally, knowing that they'd failed her. They'd *all* failed her.

He'd thought about calling the Coast Guard to look for her, but, really, why bother? He certainly couldn't tell them they were looking for a mermaid, and no human could have survived that whirlpool. The official reports said it'd been spawned by a 6.2 quake. According to the experts, the epicenter was an uninhabited area of the ocean—one that included no pink coral buildings, no sneezing sea cucumbers, and no saluting crabs. No Angel.

But Logan knew better.

Had she survived? Was she still with Ceto? Was she a prisoner?

What the hell could he do about any of it?

He stared at the moon. Bright and full, it cast its glow on the wave tops, seemingly on the exact spot where they'd gone below the surface.

He had to go back out there. See for himself. Help her, if it wasn't too late.

Then an elongated, graceful silhouette flew across the moon, pink wings glowing in the moonlight, and he got an idea.

Logan jumped up and waved his arms. "Ginger!"

The flamingo glanced over, then changed her course, fluttering to a landing on his deck.

"Well, hello again, gorgeous. I don't think I've ever had a Human summon me by name. I hadn't thought your kind was into interspecies relations, but I'm told it can be kind of kinky." She circled her neck in that weird, back-scratching, leg-rubbing way. "So, what do you have in mind?"

Not what she did. "Angel was out there. In Ceto's palace when the quake hit."

The come-hither grin on the flamingo's face disappeared. "Yeah. I heard. Must have pissed the old witch off something fierce because Ceto rarely quakes the sea like that in the Triangle. It causes way too much interest and stirs up all those old myths. Ever since The Council started docking her for the cost of the cleanup, interest is the last thing she wants. Well, *that* kind."

Ceto was not who he wanted to talk about. "What else have you heard? Is Angel okay? Did she survive? What do you know?"

"Whoa. Hold on there, hotshot. What's it to you?"

Logan's hand shot out to grab the bird by the neck,

but he thought better of it. "Prawns for the rest of your life."

"Now you're talking." The flamingo tossed her head backward, then brushed it along one wing, giving him a look with just one eye. "So here's the skinny. Her brother—you know, the ruler of their world? She's with him in Atlantis. Rod takes care of his own. Unlike *some* people I could mention." She glared at him, then flipped her beak up. "So, there you have it. The chick is safe and sound, deep in the bosom of her family."

"But how is she? Is she injured?"

"Weren't you the one to tell her to take a long dive off a short pier? Why do you care?"

Because he did.

As simple—and as complicated—as that.

And he didn't just care.

He loved her.

He… loved her.

But he sure as hell wasn't going to let Ginger be the first one to find out.

"Ginger, how is she?"

"She's fine." The bird fluffed her wings. "Well, for the time being anyway."

"What does that mean?"

Ginger cocked her head to the side, and Logan could swear she arched an eyebrow at him—except flamingoes didn't have eyebrows. Or maybe they did, hidden under their feathers. Nothing would surprise him these days.

"Ginger."

Now she rolled her eyes. "Fine. She's fine. For now. Once they get done with her trial, however…" She shrugged her… shoulders?

"Trial? What's she on trial for? She saved our lives."

Ginger swung her head around and straightened her neck to full height. "More like, what *isn't* she on trial for? That Mer broke so many rules, they went through six urchin spines writing the warrant. She'll be lucky to ever see the outside of a jail cell again—and she'll be lucky if that's the *worst* they do. A pity, but then, I guess what goes around, comes around."

Ginger switched her weight atop her bony legs like a little kid needing a restroom, giving him another come-hither look from beneath her lashes. "Now, had she stacked her karma with good deeds like, oh, I don't know, doling out scallops, her fate might be different."

He had no clue what the bird was talking about beyond "jail cell." They couldn't put Angel in jail. She'd sacrificed herself for Michael. That wasn't criminal; hell, she was a hero.

"How do I get to Atlantis?"

"And then there's—what? You want to do what?" The bird undulated her neck in a pink figure eight. "Atlantis? What? Did you suddenly fall head over fins in love with her? Oops, never mind. You don't *have* fins. My bad."

"Ginger, how do I get there?"

Ginger sighed. "You're crazy, aren't you? Do you know what happens to Humans who try to sneak into Atlantis?"

He didn't want to know because that wouldn't change his mind. Besides, he wasn't planning to sneak in. "Ginger, where is it, and how do I get in? I want to provide testimony at the trial."

The bird's head dropped to the deck with a *thunk*, then she shook it and raised it on a wobbly neck, as if the bones had collapsed. "Uh uh. I wouldn't stick my neck out for her, if I were you. You might want to consider picking up and moving inland. Maybe find a cave to hide out in for the next few centuries, 'cause going there? That's suicide."

"Would you tell me for a side order of scallops to go with those prawns?" Everyone had their price.

And that was Ginger's.

Her neck straightened and her eyes narrowed. "Daily?"

"Once a month."

"Once a week and you've got yourself a deal."

"Done."

And then she told him how to find the lost continent.

Chapter 43

THE NEXT MORNING, LOGAN STOOD OUTSIDE A YELLOW AND red tent. They'd gotten a new one.

A permanent one, according to the sign on the gate: *The Flying H Family Circus.*

Family Circus. The irony wasn't lost on Logan.

"You really lived in a circus?" Michael held onto his hand, the baseball cap tilted back just far enough that he could look up without it falling off.

"Yes, I really did." In another lifetime. And one he was now going to subject Michael to.

But he didn't have a choice. He wasn't about to take him along to find Angel, and Rainbow... well, Rainbow had enough on her plate at the moment if he could even find her—and he didn't have time to look.

His... parents were the best choice he had. He'd never starved, and Nadia had always been there with a big hug whenever he'd gotten hurt. She'd taken care of him when he'd been sick, asked how his day was. Right now, he'd have to be happy with that for Michael. God willing, this would only be temporary.

"This looks cool. Let's go in." Michael was back to bouncing. Logan had missed that.

He hadn't, however, missed the musty hay smell that greeted them when they opened the tent flap. Nor the Hungarian curses filling the arena where the net held the four fallen flyers while the trapezes swung madly above them. Good thing Michael didn't know Hungarian.

"Can I do that?"

"Not right now, Mi—"

"Hey, you!" One of the flyers flipped over the edge of the net, his accent as thick as the sawdust below—and just as familiar. Goran was still at his old tricks. "No audience 'til four. You come back then."

"Hello, Goran."

His father was in his seventies, yet he still had the tightly muscled body of an athlete who practiced every day, hour after hour. Logan remembered it well.

"Who are you?" Goran rested a foot on the ring and shoved his hands onto his hips, the same way he had when any of them had put the raising of the big top in jeopardy.

"It's me, Goran. Lacko." God, that was a name from the past.

"Lacko?" For once the guy was speechless, and the look of surprise added years to his face. "You came back?" He stepped over the ring and held out his arms. "You brought your child?"

A lump settled in Logan's throat. Open arms. Just like that, Goran accepted him back with open arms.

He nodded and met the old man halfway in an embrace that wiped out the years and much of the baggage Logan had carried with him for so long.

"Lacko, your mama, she's going to be so happy." The gruff guy who'd demanded a lot from him stood there with damp eyes and a firm grip on Logan's shoulders. "We'll go to her, yes? With the little one."

Goran tilted Michael's face up, the baseball cap hitting the sawdust. For once Michael didn't complain.

"Ah, this one. He looks like you. Full of mischief, but good. You were a good son, Lacko, eh? Now you're a good father, I think."

The praise did more for Logan's soul than he would have thought. A good son. When he'd felt anything but, both before he'd left and afterward when he'd faced the world on his own.

He'd been so ashamed of where he'd come from, yet now… This was what it was all about. Family. No matter if they shared the same DNA or not. Goran was welcoming him home.

"Come. Let's go. These three, pah! They practice without me. They need it."

With the flip of the hand Logan remembered so well, Goran commanded the others to get back to work, then headed to the rear entrance of the tent where the caravan Logan had called home waited.

<hr />

Logan let the flap fall in place behind him as he left the big top hours later, feeling as if a huge weight had been lifted from his shoulders. And not about Michael's safety, though he was confident in that.

"But, Papa, I can climb higher." Logan smiled at Michael's plea. How well he remembered saying the same thing at that age.

"You prove to me you do this right, then you go higher. Not before." Logan mouthed the words as Goran said them, remembering them as well.

His father had finally put down roots. His brothers, now grown men with families, had taken over the management of the family business. Aunts and uncles and cousins… they were all so entwined Logan couldn't ask for a better place to leave his son, especially since they'd accepted Michael—and him—unconditionally.

Goran, Nadia, his brothers and sisters, they'd all been glad to see him. Not one had begrudged him taking off when he'd been a teenager, other than for the scare and sorrow he'd put in Nadia's heart.

Being a parent himself, Logan didn't think he could ever make it up to her, but he promised them—and himself—that he'd visit often.

With what he was about to do, however, he hoped he'd have the opportunity to make good on that promise.

Chapter 44

"He's asked about you." Mariana shut the door behind her with a swish of her fluke and set a tray of food on Angel's bedside table.

Angel rolled over on the mattress and looked at her. "He has? Who'd he ask?"

"Ginger."

Angel groaned. "Great. That bird doesn't like me."

"True." Mariana dipped a piece of shrimp in the mango puree. Ginger *didn't* like Angel—which was why the bird had been more than happy to share that little bit of gossip with *her*. The bird knew the news would make its way back to Angel. But rubbing saltwater in the wound only hurt on land. In the sea, things were different.

And about to get a whole lot more different if Mariana could pull it off.

"So? What did Rod do when he heard Logan was asking about me?" Angel took the shrimp and popped it into her mouth.

"Rod doesn't exactly know."

Angel sat up and flicked her tail over the edge of the mattress. "Why not?"

Because Mariana didn't want to get her sister's hopes up or jeopardize her plans. "You said yourself that Ginger doesn't like you. She came to me to gloat."

Angel flopped back and punched a starfish pillow—who squealed.

"Oh, sorry, Jenny." Angel plumped the starfish back up, then stuck her on the wall. Jenny suctioned herself there. "So, what did Logan say?"

Mariana nudged Angel's tail out of the way and took a spot on the bed. "When Ginger told him you were alive, he wanted to come to the trial. To testify."

Angel sucked in a boatload of water. "He can't. They'll kill him."

"Or you."

"No, Mariana. No. I won't have him risking his life for me. What about Michael? Who'll take care of him? You know The Council. They won't let a Human out alive."

Exactly what Mariana had thought.

But still… if he was volunteering… and wasn't that what Ginger giving him directions to Atlantis had been all about? The flamingo thought she'd hurt Angel, but Mariana hoped it'd be the way to set her sister free.

"But Angel—"

"No." Angel pushed off the bed, swam to her closet, and started rummaging inside, tossing clothing all over the place. "Look, I knew what I was getting into when I started this. And I certainly didn't risk my life for him to lose his. It was pure luck that I escaped the implosion and collapsing roof at Ceto's palace. Otherwise any talk of Logan coming here would be moot."

Mariana swam over and started picking up Angel's mess. "But see? Your survival could be divine intervention. The gods staged that oil spill so Rod wouldn't be able to convene The Council until today. They wanted you to live."

Angel snorted. "If the gods had wanted me to survive so badly, they would have allowed emergency Travel

Chamber usage to go anywhere I wanted instead of only one direction—home. I'd be in Florida with him, instead of facing a death sentence, and, again, this would all be moot." She held up one of the Human shirts. "What do you think of this one?"

"I think you're nuts."

With him. Angel's choice of words spoke volumes… though not the kind The Council would want to hear. The Tritone family had lost enough of its members to Humans—which was Rod's argument against Angel going in the first place.

But Rod had fallen in love and no one gave him grief about it. Hades, he'd even earned his High Councilman position because of it. Why couldn't Angel have the same chance—both at life and love?

Much as it pained Mariana to imagine her sister *out there,* with a Human, it was better than the alternative.

Angel picked an oyster off the serving tray. "Why am I nuts? It's a pretty top."

"It's from *Humans.* Rubbing The Council's face in your transgression isn't such a good idea when facing them for your life, Ang. You're going to set them on their tails before your lawyer even opens his mouth."

Angel popped the oyster in her mouth, then spit the pearl from it across the room into the Ming vase Mariana had found for her graduation. The pearl made a nice tinkling sound as it circled down to the bottom.

Mariana made a not-so-nice gurgling sound. "You don't have a lawyer, do you?"

Angel shrugged. "Why bother? I've already been tried and convicted anyway. Figured I might as well save this family and the citizens the added expense. It's not as if I have a prayer of getting out of this. I mean, I *did* talk to Michael. I did turn Logan."

"Zeus, Ang. Do you have a death wish or what?" And what did it say about Mariana that she was going to attempt to save Angel's life with a move that could very well put her in the same boat? But, Hades, she wasn't going to let her sister go down without a fight.

"Of course I don't. But I'm not going in there to apologize, Mariana. I did what I'm accused of, but with good reasons. First and foremost, let us not forget Harry was all over my tail. Was I really supposed to just tread water and let him get me?"

Mariana could argue that if Angel hadn't gone in the first place, none of this would be happening, but she wouldn't. She'd *thought* Angel's lawyer would come up with a compelling argument, but obviously her sister was going to ride her seahorse into the sunset on this one.

Mariana couldn't accept that.

"I did the best I could. I even got some useful information out of the experience." Angel pulled the top over her head.

Mariana piled the clothing Angel had tossed onto an odd piece Angel had collected. A spinning wheel. It looked more like an instrument of torture to Mariana. She'd heard the stories about what that needle could do. "Is that information enough to save your life? Because I can't watch it, Ang. I can't watch them do that to you."

"It might be if I had it with me. Unfortunately, I left the journal back at Logan's, so who knows?" Angel's breath hitched and her voice lowered. "But I'm certainly going to try."

Finally, the emotion Mariana knew was beneath all the bravado. Angel was as scared as the rest of the family—which was why Mariana couldn't just lie down and rest on the bottom.

She didn't hold out much hope for Angel's argument, but if The Council heard the words straight from the Human's mouth, perhaps then they'd listen.

And allow Angel to live.

Chapter 45

LOGAN CHECKED THE COORDINATES GINGER HAD GIVEN HIM, then looked overboard. Somewhere down there, beneath the island of Bermuda, Atlantis waited.

He dropped anchor, wondering how much damage that did to the reef, but if this all played out like Ginger had outlined, that would be the least of his worries.

Grabbing his scuba gear, Logan scanned the area. A perfect Bermuda day. Sunny with wispy clouds. Logan could see for miles. A pair of boats were well beyond shouting distance, and others farther past them. Windsurfers sailed near the shore, and that party cruise had been headed north. He'd rented the boat for the week, so it wasn't expected back until then, and no curious Jet Skiers were around to take note of how long he'd be gone. His arrangements were either good subterfuge or suicide.

He hoped it wasn't the latter.

One more look at the map and the coastline confirmed that he was at the right spot. Ginger had even mentioned the area off the bow where the greens of the shallows meshed with the blues of the deep in a ninety-degree angle.

Time to do this.

His ability to breathe under water had disappeared the day after he'd stepped back on land, so Logan had to don scuba gear. He made sure to include a knife—something he'd never again be in the sea without—then slid into the temperate water around the island and hoped to God this worked.

And that Ceto wasn't lying in wait for him.

Ginger hadn't been able to find out any information on what had happened to the sea monster. Logan hoped that meant she'd been crushed beneath thousands of pounds of marble, coral, and statues, though he wouldn't mind getting a shot at her.

A kaleidoscope of tropical fish surrounded him—small, large, darting, meandering, chasing each other all over the coral reef—and the sea was suddenly more alive than it'd looked from above. Sea fans, anemones, corals... They were just as colorful as the fish swimming among them.

Bermuda was beautiful; it only made sense that Atlantis would be here. Sense in a there-really-are-such-things-as-mermaids way.

Logan swam out to where green water met blue, wondering how he was going to do this. Ginger had told him where Atlantis was but not how to get in. Bermuda was a cave-diving tourist destination; there had to be some trick to getting inside the submerged city, or Humans would have found it years ago.

Suddenly, the largest school of jacks he'd ever seen surrounded him, clumsier than he remembered ever seeing jacks. They bumped his shoulders, his head, his tank, his mask...

They were trying to tell him something.

Damn. If only he could breathe under water, he'd be able to understand.

But ... Wait. Angel had said that every fish spoke English.

What'd he have to lose at this point other than his dignity? And since there was no one around to risk even that, he took a deep breath, then pulled the regulator from his mouth.

"I need to get to Atlantis," came out as a series of bubbles and mumbles, but it was enough to catch a few of the fishes' attention.

He tried again. "I'm looking for Angel, the mermaid. She saved me from Ceto."

Bubbles appeared from the fish. Answers to his questions?

Sadly, he couldn't understand them, and whatever charades they started to do got lost as his mask fogged.

Damn change in air pressure. People weren't supposed to speak under the sea, so why should the mask be designed for it?

Cursing—which only fogged it up even more—Logan shoved the regulator back in his mouth and ripped off the mask. He was going to have to go to the surface to clear it.

Logan kicked his flippers to head up—

Only to be grabbed by something from below.

Chapter 46

Angel swam into The Coliseum to the murmurings of the assembled members of Atlantian society. Octopi, eels, fish, crustaceans, Mers, Council members. They were all there, every stone seat in the circular building filled.

A public lynching.

The gold walls of the Atlantian cavern were bathed in the glow from the massive magma wells ringing the circular building. A gently waving, multihued carpet of every species of anemone known to Man and Merkind covered the marble floor, while thousands of sea beings stared at her with antennae, eyes, or some version thereof.

A convened Council used to intimidate her, having all the pomp and circumstance of an entity that dated back thousands, if not millions, of *selinos*. But now that The Council was convened for her, interestingly, she wasn't intimidated.

Seriously, what more could they do to her? She'd almost cost Michael his life with his father, had almost cost Logan his life, period, and she'd broken the cardinal rule of the Mer World. This trial was a no-brainer. Everyone knew the punishment for letting Humans know about Mers. It was the same as turning a Human—which she'd also done.

Death.

Funny how she'd never thought the law would apply to her. After all, she was a member of the royal family.

Eligible for Immortality. A scientist preparing for the role she would play in Atlantian government to help better their world.

How clueless she'd been in her altruism.

Rod floated behind the coral table at the far side of The Coliseum with the rest of The Council, including his wife, Valerie. The rest of the Tritone family—Reel and his wife, Erica; Mom and Dad; her younger sister, Pearl—sat in the seats behind The Council. Everyone except Mariana. Her older sister was taking this harder than any of them.

It warmed Angel's heart but also added more guilt to her shoulders.

From a purely scientific standpoint, however, it was interesting how she was thinking more about her family at this moment than about herself. But then, she had an almost disembodied detachment from the trial. As if she were outside her body, but… not. For some reason, she could muster no horror at these proceedings, no worry, no anxiety. It was as if she'd already consigned herself to death.

But then, *hadn't* she when she'd gone on her field study in the first place?

No matter how the trial played out, she couldn't regret saving Michael. And Logan—mustn't forget Logan.

As if she could.

But The Council, Rod… they'd regret it. This. Whatever sentence they handed out, they'd regret because Rod was right. Human and Mer futures were destined to be linked, and the Coalition was that bridge. How did Rod hope to get the program up and swimming if Humans weren't aware of them? Mers were going to have to clue Humans in at some point…

Rhetoric was what they'd call that argument, but it was the only one she had. She wasn't going to die a martyr.

Hades, she didn't *deserve* to die. She'd been trying to *help* their world. Besides, Rod had broken a rule, too: the one about the High Councilman not marrying someone who wasn't a full-blooded Mer. His wife was a Hybrid, yet he hadn't cared. He'd decided to marry her and had done so, rules be dammed. How was what she'd done any different?

Well, other than the fact that her transgression threatened the entire Mer world.

True.

But then, so would the Coalition if it wasn't handled correctly. And if Rod didn't appoint her director, it wouldn't be handled correctly.

The current proposal, and The Council's working model, was to approach Humans on diplomatic terms. Deal with their governments. Set up a United Races governing body. But it wouldn't work. They had to start with the children. Make the changes from the ground up. Go to the Humans who were most likely to accept them—never mind *believe* in them—instead of those who would want to eradicate or study them.

The current model was doomed to fail if The Council wouldn't listen.

And with Humans then knowing of their existence, what would happen to Merkind?

Chapter 47

SHIT SHIT SHIT SHIT SHIT!

Logan kicked his feet, trying to free the one that'd been caught, all the while paddling his arms towards the surface.

The creature, whatever it was, let go and Logan swam for all he was worth, managing to grab his knife. Now if only he had his mask on so he could see the thing coming.

He wasn't waiting for it to attack again; the boat wasn't that far away.

He cleared the surface and headed toward it, only to almost crash head-on into a—

Mermaid.

Right in front of him. Long, flowing red hair and a sparkling emerald green tail. Almost as beautiful as Angel.

No one was as beautiful as Angel.

"I'm Mariana Tritone. Angel's sister." The woman's voice was almost as lyrical as Angel's, but it didn't affect him at all. "Do you really want to help her?"

It spoke to how far his reality had shifted when he entered into the conversation as if it were completely normal. "Yes. She saved my life and my son's. I owe her." Not to mention, loved her, but he wasn't sure how they'd take his defense of her, let alone a declaration of love.

Hell, he wasn't sure how Angel would take it. After what he'd said to her, he wouldn't blame her if she never wanted to see him again.

The mermaid stared at him, then nodded. "What I'm about to do goes against every law we have. I want you to understand that. I can't promise the outcome. If you come with me and The Council rules against you, you could very possibly be giving up your life for my sister. Still want to come?"

Logan had made his peace with that when he'd made his peace with his family. Michael would be cared for, but he could never live with himself if he didn't do this for her.

"I'm in. They can't prosecute her for this. There were mitigating circumstances."

Angel's sister shook her head. "You don't know The Council. But I want to save my sister, so I'll take you." She reached for his hand and drew him closer. "Since Angel already turned you once, I just have to give you a quick kiss so you can come with me. Ready?"

He'd had a lot of practice pulling miracles out of a hat when he'd been on his own, and look how far he'd come. He wasn't going to give up now.

"Hell yes, I'm ready. Let's go."

Chapter 48

"THE COUNCIL WILL COME TO ORDER."

Angel straightened her shoulders as Rod banged the whalebone gavel on the slate he'd recently had installed on the table. Some morbid part of her would say that he'd wanted it so his proclamations would toll like a death knell, but she was ignoring that part.

"If the Accused will approach The Council."

Feeling like a condemned prisoner—which was what she was, actually—Angel swam forward. Protocol dictated that she approach in an upright fashion, but when one was fighting for one's life, protocol could be damned.

"Angel Tritone?" Her brother looked incredibly imposing behind that table. And also incredibly sad.

Another black mark on her conscience.

"Yes." Proud of herself for betraying no emotion in her voice, Angel fluttered her flukes to be at eye level with him. With them. All of The Council. Rod, Valerie, Santos, Henri, and Thorsson. She hoped her two family members wouldn't condemn her, but the other three… They'd been opposed to Rod's plan from the beginning. She couldn't see them helping her out.

But she only had to convince one to flip to have a majority. Just one.

And if she couldn't… well, she wanted each one to look her in the eye before condemning her to death.

"You are charged with two counts of revealing your-self to Humans, one count of turning a Human, one count of disobeying Council orders, and one count of creating a natural disaster. How do you plead?"

This formality was a joke. They thought she'd fall in line.

Ha.

"I'm not pleading, Rod."

"What?" Santos smacked his tail against one of the table supports. "What do you mean, you're not plead-ing? This is a trial. You must make a plea."

"Well I'm not. There were special circumstances, number one being that I didn't get a fair shot at the Coalition director job due to prejudice and discrimina-tion on my brother's part. If I'd been treated fairly, I wouldn't be in this position."

"That's no guarantee you would have gotten the job, Angel." Rod wiped a weary hand across his face. "Nor does that absolve you from what you did."

Angel planted her hands on the table, a move so egregious that only a condemned Mer would try it. "True, but I shouldn't have had the need to prove myself just for an interview, Rod. You can't use your fear of losing the rest of us against me. If we fall in love with Humans, then we do. It's a risk you're going to have to take, no matter who you send on land with your Coalition. You can't control people's feelings."

She backed off the table and crossed her arms. Still eye level with The Council, though. "So, no. I'm not pleading anything. If you want to hook me, you're going to have to do it yourselves, but someone has to help

Humans see what they're doing to the planet, and your way isn't going to work."

"I say we hook her."

Well, she could kiss Santos's help goodbye.

Henri nodded, and Thorsson was about to speak when Rod held up his hand. "Fine, Angel. Tell us your vision for the Coalition. Get it off your chest, then we'll get back to the charges."

That was a concession she hadn't seen coming.

She brushed some hair off her forehead, then locked her hands behind her back.

"To start with, we need an Advisory Board—one that includes Humans."

The collective gasp wasn't unexpected. "You've made a start on the garbage cleanup, Rod, but there should be a Sewage Reclamation and Recycling Team." She shared her idea about discarded tires as the foundation for small islands and reiterated the sad statistics everyone knew regarding sea creatures' deaths by the ingested plastic particles that never broke down—so aptly named *Mermaid's tears* by Humans themselves—as well as those infernal six-pack plastic rings that were equal-opportunity strangulation devices. Mammal, fish, fowl—those rings were deadly.

"I want to appoint an Alternate Energy Commission to examine other types of power. Eel and wave, for starters. Maybe something with migratory fish like salmon. Humans are doing things with solar and wind. We need to share our knowledge.

"We also need to start with the children, Rod. Not the adults as you've proposed. Adults don't handle change well." Current company included, but she figured it wouldn't be a good idea to antagonize them. "But we can begin now. That's the beauty of this. Start with the children. Teach them. We've got how many representatives in those swim experiences and aquariums around the world? Let them take the initiative.

"Little by little, as those children grow to adulthood, their society's consciousness will change. We'll infiltrate instead of instigate. Subvert versus confront. Let them think they came up with the ideas. Then, when the thought of Mers is pervasive enough, accepted enough by those who've had actual encounters with us, *then* we implement your face-to-fin dialogue."

Santos pressed his palms on the table and raised himself to full height. "This is exactly what we tried to tell you, High Councilman, when we first learned of your sister's whereabouts. Mixing with Humans in their environment is not a good idea in any capacity—neither the occasional rogue Mer nor an organized Coalition. Humans aren't ready for us, and freethinkers like the Accused will only stir up trouble. I say we put an end to this Coalition idea and focus on keeping the Humans out of the waters."

"We aren't letting sharks have representation, Santos," Valerie said, the half-Human side of her obviously taking offense.

"I agree with Santos." Thorsson's deep voice vibrated through the water. "This is why the Coalition is a danger to us, High Councilman. Dissention, disagreement… We have laws for a reason. They've governed us for the past two millennia and put to rights a system that had previously swum amok. The gods were not happy with Mer behavior and let us know in no uncertain terms. I say we hook Angel as a violator of the laws and as a lesson to those who think differently."

The debate carried over to the spectators. Angel tried to hear if the tide was running in her favor, but there were too many opinions and too many voices.

Until one rose above all the others.

"Or," said that voice, "Angel could marry me."

Chapter 49

MARRY?

Every head, eye spot, and antenna swung toward the doorway.

Angel couldn't have heard correctly.

And then she saw who it was.

Logan?

As gorgeous as the last time she'd seen him, Logan swam into the Coliseum, Mariana right behind him.

Oh gods. What had Mariana done? The Council would crucify him—and she did mean literally. No Humans except her sisters-in-law had ever witnessed a convened Council, but they were married to members of the royal family.

"Who are you, *Human*?" Thorsson's last word rasped across the silence as tightly as his clipped beard swung against his chin.

All the beings in the arena followed Logan as he walked—yes, walked, on two legs, every bit as tall and strong and proud of his heritage as he had a right to be—toward The Council.

He didn't utter another word. Not until he reached her.

"Hey," was that word.

Then he hugged her. Chest-to-chest, thigh-to-tail, arms-wrapped-around-her hug and, omygods, it felt so good. She'd never thought she'd see him again—

And then he kissed her.

Right there, in front of everyone.

Everyone, who'd suddenly gone quiet.

Tough. Let them eat kelp. She hadn't lied to Logan. In Mer form or with Human legs, she was in love with him and The Council could stick that in their collective crawl and stew on it. She was going to enjoy this moment.

It might very well be her last.

She slid her arms around his neck, then gave a good kick of her tail so she was fully in his arms, as involved in the kiss as he was, showing him—there, in front of everyone—just what he meant to her. Let them talk. She didn't care. If she was going down, she was going down with a smile on her face and love in her heart and the man would finally understand that what she felt for him transcended their differences.

"Ahem."

Those two syllables reverberated loudly enough to catch her attention.

Logan's, too.

He pulled back, his eyes never leaving hers. "So. *Will* you marry me, Angel?"

Gasps now filled The Coliseum, but Angel didn't care. She didn't care when the gasps escalated to mutterings, nor even when they went to full-out bitching and complaining.

All that mattered was that Logan had asked.

"You bet I will."

And then Logan was back to kissing her and Angel didn't give one flying fish who was outraged.

Until Zeus *poofed* onto the scene.

Chapter 50

ONE SECOND LOGAN HAD THE MOST BEAUTIFUL WOMAN IN the world in his arms, and the next, he found himself face to fin with the biggest merman he'd ever seen.

Not that he'd seen all that many. His eyes hadn't focused on anyone but Angel from the moment he saw her.

This newest, bigger, badder version of merkind clasped him on the shoulder and conjured a chair out of thin air—water.

"Have a seat, son," he said, steering Logan into the chair. "You, too, Angel." Another chair appeared next to his, and Angel floated into it.

Logan grabbed her hand. He wasn't about to let go. Her sister had said marriage was the only way out, and Logan was all for it. And not just to save her life.

"Zeus, Sir." Rod, one of the two brothers Mariana had pointed out before he'd set foot in The Coliseum, nodded at the newcomer—*Zeus*, of all people—from behind the table. "To what do we owe the honor?"

Zeus approached the bench, shaking a finger at Rod. "You're smart, Rod, but I bet even you didn't see this one coming."

The merman glanced at Mariana, who was trying hard to keep a smile off her face. Looked like she'd known what she was talking about.

Zeus turned to face him. "By the way, Logan, it's

mer. Capital M and no *man* or *maid* after it. Just Mer. Your kind added the suffixes."

Wow. Logan thought he'd been prepared for anything, but Zeus? An honest-to-God Greek god? Here?

Then he looked around. Mermen—no, Mers—all around him, fish and eels and barracuda sitting next to each other, not a snarling maw in the crowd. Nothing should surprise him.

"Actually, it's 'honest-to-gods.'"

Logan looked at Zeus. "Sorry?"

"Gods." Zeus walked toward him. "You thought, 'God.' I prefer you use the plural, otherwise, when I return to Olympus, I'm going to hear it from Hera. And Aphrodite *and* Poseidon *and* Eros—especially Eros. They've accused me of getting too big for my toga on occasion, and singling myself out from the rest of them tends to get their Irish up. Or rather, their Greek." He patted Logan's shoulder. "Okay? From now on, it's 'gods.' Lower case, plural. Keeps everyone happy."

The guy… *Zeus*… swam back to the head table while Logan just stared at him.

"So," Zeus thrummed his fingers on the table. "I'm sure you're all wondering why I'm here. After all, we gods bowed out of your adjudications *selinos* ago. Close to two thousand, I believe." Rod nodded. "Right. Well, you see, we've obviously been following this case closely, due to your predecessors. Pontus and his heirs didn't manage their Human interaction well, as we all know."

"What's he talking about?" Logan asked Angel. Mariana hadn't told him this part of their history.

"The previous dynasty treated their reign as one long party and got too involved with Humans. The gods got fed up with the destruction that caused and cleaned house. That's when my family took control," she whispered back.

"We gods decided that an impending marriage necessitated some intervention on our part." Zeus looked back at Logan. "So, son, do you care to tell us why you've suddenly decided that life with a Mer is preferable to the *normal* one you so craved on land? Is this some contrived plot to tug on the heartstrings of the assembly? A hope for a celestial pardon?"

Zeus planted his hands on either side of the chair, his face inches from Logan's. "Or is this a ploy to make the ultimate sacrifice as a means of earning Immortality and escaping death?"

Logan took a deep breath. Of water. Funny how that didn't bother him anymore.

He met Zeus' gaze, then slowly pushed on the arms of the chair and rose. Zeus grudgingly allowed him to stand.

Every eye in the place was on him.

Logan didn't care.

He brushed past the god to face Angel, her beautiful eyes both worried and shining with happiness. He reached for her hand, then dropped to one knee.

"Angel, I love you." He said it loud enough for everyone to hear. There would be no misunderstanding on anyone's part. Especially not hers. "I have since our night together. Probably even before. I love how you laugh, how you sing, how you make everyone around you feel special and good and valued. I love how you are with my son, and I love how I am when I'm with you."

Tears filled her eyes, and he had to clear his throat.

"I know I said awful, hurtful things to you that night. I was an ass. I didn't mean them. I was just so… surprised, and—"

She put a finger on his lips. "I know. I should have—"

"No." He shook his head and inhaled that special blend of hibiscus that was all Angel. "You shouldn't have. There was no easy way to tell me. I behaved badly. But I want to make it up to you. And not because you saved my son. Not because you put yourself in danger. Not for any of the reasons Zeus said." But he *had* used Mariana's knowledge of Immortality to his advantage. It'd been the only way, and one he'd embraced wholeheartedly.

"I want to marry you because I couldn't live another day knowing you were suffering. That I'd never see you again. Whatever it takes, if I have to give up living on land or only see you occasionally, I'll do it." He stroked her cheek with his other hand, then cradled it and ran his thumb over her lips. "I love you Angel, and I want to spend the rest of my life with you."

—⁓—

There wasn't a dry eye in the place—oh, that's right. They were underwater.

But Angel knew tears when she felt them, and they were what was sliding down her cheeks. And what she tasted when she kissed Logan. "I love you, too," she whispered against his lips. "I never lied about that."

"Then it's settled." Zeus clapped his hands and a giant golden abacus with different colored pearls floated in front of The Council.

Angel looked past Logan as Zeus swam over to it. What was the head god up to?

She caught Mariana's smile before her sister tucked her chin to her chest and draped her long hair in front of her face.

She had a feeling Mariana knew exactly what Zeus was going to do—and she had a feeling she was going to be eternally grateful to her sister.

"In the system of checks and balances that we use On High, two negatives—" the god slid two small black pearls to the side—"equal a positive." He slid a pink pearl on another row.

"Angel offered herself in Michael's place. Knowing Ceto as we all do, that was certain death." He slid one of the black pearls back toward the middle. "Then we have Logan. Mortal, Human Logan who dared to venture back into Ceto's palace to save the woman he loves. Again, almost certain death." The other black pearl slid home.

"Two sacrifices." He tapped the one small pink pearl. "One positive left." Then he slid the pink pearl back.

"The precedent's already been set. Noble sacrifice earns Immortality. Reel will testify to that."

Angel looked at her brother, who held his wife's hand to his lips. Reel had earned Immortality for saving Erica's life, then declined it to spend the rest of his with her.

"And if someone's Immortal, they cannot be hooked, killed, or destroyed. Which is how Ceto survived her own seaquake. She and I had a little *chat* after she slithered out of that trench she buried herself and half the continental shelf in. I believe I've put the child issue to rest with Ceto. She's on indefinite community service at Artemis's orphanage."

Zeus brushed his hands, and the abacus disappeared. Then he raised his hands, palms down, toward where Angel and Logan sat, and closed his eyes. "So, by the power vested in me, I now bestow Immortality upon you, Angel Tritone, you, Logan Hardington, and any progeny thereof."

He opened one eye, then the other, nodded, then clasped his hands behind his back, and faced The Council. "Rod, I believe all that's left for The Council to do is decide a fitting punishment since a death sentence is now a non-issue."

Thorsson tossed up his hands and Santos grumbled something.

Henri, however, had something to say. "Humans are the worst punishment I, personally, can imagine. Filthy air, crowded living arrangements, ignorance of other civilizations... I say we give Angel the job she so desperately wants. Talk about a fitting punishment. And marriage—especially to a Human—is just one more shackle."

Not in her mind. To her, Henri couldn't have given her a better punishment. Logan, Michael, and the freedom to do what she wanted.

This trial had turned out better than she'd ever expected.

―᚜᚜᚜―

Hera was waiting for Zeus when he returned home.

"You just had to do it, didn't you?" She crossed her arms and tapped her foot beneath the saffron toga he'd given her for Mother's Day.

Zeus grabbed a bottle of ambrosia out of the icebox

and wiped it across his forehead. "It was fascinating, sweetheart. They're finally flexing their Free Will muscles. It's only taken them two millennia."

Hera huffed and walked over to her prized hyacinths. She picked up the spritzer and watered first the purple, then the pink, then finally, the white. His wife was a creature of habit. In some things. "I knew you wouldn't be able to simply observe. You just had to play *deus ex machina* to the hilt, didn't you?"

One of her habits was to keep his feet firmly planted in the clouds.

He took a swig of the ambrosia. "Don't get your laurel leaves in a tither, Hera. Logan found a way around the statute with no help from me. Give me a little credit for knowing my creations. I just showed up to bestow the Immortality. Besides, you can't tell me you don't love a good happily-ever-after."

Hera's spritzer hit the window ledge.

"*Whose* creations?" She turned her head so slightly that the long braid down her back barely swayed, but it was all the more effective for its lack of movement.

Oh shit. "Um, *our* creations, dear. Ours."

She nodded and picked up the spritzer. "That's better. So, you gave Ceto something to make her happy and keep her out of trouble, and you saved a Mer, a few Humans, and their civilizations."

"Don't forget coming up with a fitting punishment for those two sharks." He tried to keep Smug out of his voice, but Hera knew him too well.

Surprisingly, his wife laughed. "Yes, sticking A.C. and Harry in a Human aquarium was a stroke of genius. How long will they be there?"

Zeus let Smug out. "I figured five *selinos* ought to teach them a lesson. Three if they're on their best behavior."

Hera sniffed. "That I'd like to see. So, what's next on your agenda?"

Zeus picked up the latest edition of *Natural Geographic*. Easter Island. Hmmm. Every so often Humans revisited the origins of the statues. He wondered what Mariana thought of that.

Smart girl, that Mariana.

"I think we ought to take a vacation." He thumbed through the article to the map and ran his finger across the twenty-seventh latitude, west of South America. "How does Chile sound?"

Chapter 51

LOGAN WAS GLAD ANGEL DECIDED ON LEGS FOR THEIR wedding day. And the morning after—if only for the fact that she looked utterly magnificent straddling him.

Her skin glistened in the warm Caribbean sun. The pineapple-and-hibiscus-scented breeze wisped her golden hair around them, and the rhythmic arrival of the surf on the deserted island beach set the tempo for their lovemaking.

The twilight ceremony last evening hadn't been his idea. If he'd had his way, they would have been married in Atlantis immediately after the trial, but Angel had specifically requested a land wedding with all her family… and no tails. It wasn't enough that she'd finagled both the job she wanted and had him—by virtue of his experience with green technologies—appointed to her Advisory Board, she'd wanted to make a statement about bringing the sea and the land together via their marriage.

The earliest the wedding could be pulled together, tails shifted into legs, and Michael brought over had been last night. Logan hadn't let Angel out of his sight for one minute between the verdict and the wedding.

And what a sight she was: naked, sexy, with that glorious hair cascading over her shoulders, the ends caressing him wherever they touched. Logan realized he'd found paradise. Anywhere Angel was, was paradise—and he didn't care that he was waxing poetic again. Those poets had been onto something.

Logan reached for her hips, her deliciously silky, naked hips, and slid his palms down her thighs as she straddled him. "You know I really don't mind the tail, right?"

She tossed her hair down her back. "Now? You want me to have a tail now?"

"Well, no. Not now, obviously. But later. You don't have to sneak off like you did before."

Angel blew against his throat, then traced her tongue up to swirl around the shell of his ear, little puffs of her breath warming him more than the sun ever could, and one of her hands found his nipple. He sucked in a breath. She'd discovered just the right way to do that for just the right reaction and had been using that weakness to torture him for hours.

Not that he was complaining.

"I know I don't have to, Logan, but if it's all the same to you, my tail is the last thing I feel like thinking about right now."

He smiled. Oh, he didn't mind thinking about her tail...

He ran his hands back up her thighs and around to knead her backside, pressing her down onto him a little more, gratified to hear her groan, "That's not fair."

"Tell me about it." He did it again.

"That's it, buster." She wiggled in that sexy way she'd discovered drove him wild. Which it did all over again.

Angel, in all her naked beauty. Even more gorgeous than she'd been on his boat. She was his, and he could look and touch and savor all he wanted.

He didn't give one damn that she was a mermaid.

Mer. Whatever. She was Angel, she was his, and she was free because of his love.

She tossed her hair, this time to the side, where it drifted against his hip, a sensation so erotic it almost made him come. Then she did that tongue thing again below his Adam's apple, her nipples stroking his chest, and Logan didn't know how much longer he could hold out.

"Are you trying to kill me?" he murmured between a sigh and a groan.

She kissed the underside of his jaw, her breasts flattening against him, the slick wet heat of her enfolding him. "I can't, remember?" She did that thing against his throat again. "Unless you want me to stop?"

"Hell no," he growled, urging her to sit up, then angled her hips up just a bit... right there... that was it...

Logan spread his hands across her flat belly, his thumbs meeting where she pulsed against him, and he stroked her.

"Oh gods, Logan..."

"Oh gods, Logan, what?" He slid one thumb along her swollen flesh until he reached the spot where they were joined, then slowly stroked upward.

Angel's breaths came faster. Shallower. Her skin flushed just enough to be noticeable, and even the sun couldn't match the heat they were generating together.

She ran her tongue over her lips in that way he loved, her eyes almost closed, and moved against him. Against him, on him, around him, everything he saw, touched, smelled, wanted, it was all Angel.

He stroked her again. "Come for me, sweetheart."

The words themselves had power, but it was the tiny

hitch in her breath that wound her around his heart. It was as if they'd been created for each other, every part fitting so perfectly…

He'd been an idiot to tell her to leave. A fool to think anything made any difference for them. Here was where he was supposed to be. With her.

"Oh, Logan." She changed her position, now falling back to brace her hands on his thighs, opening herself up to his touch, wet and hot and ready. Her hair slid down her back, falling between his legs with an erotic simplicity that stole his breath. A few strands drifted between her breasts, down to where he touched her.

"Don't ever cut your hair, Angel." He grasped a shank of it behind her, threading his fingers through it, and tugged gently.

Framed by the window and silhouetted against a sky the color of her eyes, she arched her back, her breasts swelling, nipples tightening, and Logan ached to run his tongue over every inch of her.

He stroked her again and she shuddered. She was achingly beautiful. Natural. Breathtakingly and elementally so. The very essence of a woman.

He shifted beneath her, knowing she'd feel him inside her, and stroked her again. Her eyes flashed open, then he used the tips of her hair to trace the spot where her trident tattoo had been—one more piece of the magic that was Angel.

"Do that again," she breathed, her tongue flicking against the corner of her mouth, and his cock responded with the same movement inside her.

She rocked back, her breasts heaving as she took a deeper breath.

His thumb circled on her and she moaned, her inner muscles squeezing him.

Using his palms, he lifted her off him, just enough that she protested, only to press against her swollen flesh and make her cry out.

"Oh gods, Logan, yes… I'm almost… I… please…"

Sweat glistened on her body, and the heady scent of ocean and Angel and lovemaking filled the air around them. Logan slid his thumb down a little farther, all the while circling, using her own wetness for the perfect amount of friction.

Perfect. That's what she was.

She squeezed her legs around him, trembling, and her inner muscles contracted, sending spasms of need spiraling through his body, tightening his balls, and he knew it wouldn't be long.

He dug in his heels and thrust into her, pressing down on her hips as she contracted around him again, his thumb still circling, her breasts rising and falling before him, eyes half-closed again, her tongue tracing maddening circles on those sweet pink lips, her breath coming faster, harsher, her fingers biting into his thighs as her inner muscles quickened.

"Yes… yes… oh… my… Logan…"

Shudders stronger than any earthquake wracked his body as they came together, the sensations more powerful than any whirlpool.

The love they shared greater than any differences the gods had created between them.

"I love you," he had to whisper, wrapping both arms around her slender form, feeling the fragile bones in her back yet knowing how strong she truly was. Strong enough to take on the world's worst monster for him. "Forever."

And, thanks to Zeus and her love, it truly was *forever*.

Chapter 52

"ANGEL? LOGAN? WANNA PLAY BALL?" MICHAEL'S shadow fluttered on the filmy netting draping their honeymoon cabana door. Private island getaways didn't need doors—unless one expected a six-year-old to make an appearance.

Logan helped Angel smooth the sheet on the bed, then checked himself in the mirror. They'd had to scramble into their clothes when Mariana had done the first loop around the island. Good thing Angel's sister had a big set of lungs—half the Caribbean had probably heard her warn them Michael was on his way.

One more reason he'd be indebted to Mariana for the rest of his life.

He didn't mind in the least.

"Come on in, Michael." Logan brushed past Angel, unable to prevent himself from touching her shoulder, then he pulled back the netting.

"Oooh, awesome!" Michael bounced in—of course—and picked up the crystal sculpture Mariana had given them for a wedding present.

"Awesome? What happened to 'cool'?" Logan said, rustling his son's hair. The hat had been left back in Florida on Rocky's head. Michael had decided it wasn't proper wedding attire, and Logan liked the symbolism that change represented. His son was willing to accept Angel in Christine's place.

"'Cool' is a little kid's word. Since I swam with sharks and dolphins in a whirlpool, I'm all growed up."

Logan put his arm around Michael's shoulders and tugged his son against him. He didn't want Michael to be all "growed up"; he'd barely had any time to enjoy his son as a child.

But he definitely would enjoy the children he and Angel made together.

The look in her eyes said she was thinking the same thing—and couldn't wait to get back to *practicing* any more than he could.

He stepped out onto the patio to check the angle of the sun. A few more hours until his in-laws took Michael for a "cool"—no, make that "awesome"—underwater vacation, while he and Angel began a week's worth of uninterrupted, deserted island honeymoon. Sounded like heaven to him, though Zeus had assured him after the ceremony that the deserted island was nothing like Olympus.

Logan didn't care. Anywhere Angel was, was heaven for him.

"Oh, look! A rainbow!"

Michael darted out of the cabana, a finger pointing toward the beach.

Just offshore, a full rainbow arced across the ocean.

"Rainbow said I can remember her every time I see one, and she's right!" The little boy took off down the beach, kicking up sand behind him.

"Hi, Rainbow!" he called, running toward the water until Angel's sister rode a wave onto the beach, grabbed Michael around the waist, and sent him back to his father.

CATCH OF A LIFETIME

Not that Logan was worried about sharks anymore. Zeus had promised him there'd be no more of that in Michael's life, and Logan didn't want to ever drag Michael away from a rainbow. Not now, knowing what one represented. Christine's name choice was easy to understand.

"A cowrie for your thoughts." His wife—his *wife*—snuggled up under his arm in the beautiful peasant blouse and shirt Nadia had sent with Michael as a wedding gift. Someday he'd have to talk to his mother about her psychic abilities.

And find out how much she knew about Mers.

He kissed the top of Angel's head and nodded at the ocean. "Rainbow."

"Hey, Angel! Didya see it?" Michael bounced back onto the porch.

"I did, Michael. Isn't it beautiful?" She tilted her head back to look up at Logan, that gorgeous blonde hair flowing over his arm, her teal blue shirt the perfect foil for her hair and eyes. "Did you know that, in Mer mythology, a rainbow is said to represent the unity of heaven and earth? Over the ocean, it represents the unity of all three."

Logan reached out for Michael and drew him into a hug with Angel.

His wife and his son. Unity of all three.

A family.

As normal as any under the sun.

Or under the sea.

He could live with that.

~Fin~

Author's Note

Research is one of the best parts about writing, and I find myself getting lost in it on occasion, which opens up whole new worlds and possibilities—a gift for any writer. What I also like about research is that sometimes I need something to be a certain way for the story and *voilà*! I find the history, facts, or location I need. Sometimes, though, I have to tweak it, so enjoy the factoids but know that some might be tweaked to fit the story. I added the "over the ocean" part to the Greek mythology about rainbows, and I also played around with the Miami Dolphins' preseason game schedule.

I apologize to the players for having them suit up a few weeks early in the Florida heat so Logan could turn down the fifty-yard line seats, but I needed to make the story timeline work.

Enjoy the few extra weeks of practice, guys.

Acknowledgments

My editor, Deb Werksman. It is a true pleasure to work with you, and you make it all so much better.

My agent, Jennifer Schober, for the pep talks, enthusiasm, and sage advice.

Sue Grimshaw. Again. Because. ☺

Sia McKye, for the marketing/blog wonderfulness.

Hawk, for all the enthusiasm and help in spreading the word.

Carla, for the promotion, you sneaky thing!

Sharyn (and Vince, too), for all your Florida and bird information, as well as the perfect pre-RT stay at "VFRW South"!

Ann "Twinkles" LaBar Russek, for all things poetic.

Dana Marton, for the Hungarian help.

Tracy Garrett, for *The Princess Bride* reference at PASIC.

Jamie Chapman, for naming A.C.'s girlfriend. I can't believe I couldn't come up with that one on my own, and thank you for doing so! Utterly perfect!

Tailgate Russ and his Tailgate Nation, for all the votes. Every time.

Bob Hitchner at All Seasons Marina in Marmora, New Jersey, for painstakingly crawling over every boat in inventory with me to see where a mermaid could possibly hide. And not cracking a joke when telling people what we were doing (though we did get some funny looks).

The usual list of suspects: The Writing Wombats; all the supporters on Gather; my fellow VFRWers and AT3ers; The Survivor Girls; The SoonToBes; The "Jens:" Jenny G. and Jen T.; Robin K.; Val A.; Chris S.; Cindy S.; Julie P.; Mom and Dad; Nan; and of course, my own family—I'm so glad you love pizza!

My publisher, Dominique Raccah, and the team at Sourcebooks: Danielle, Sarah, Susie, the marketing department, and everyone else involved with the stories—thank you all for bringing my dreams to fruition. Especially to Anne Cain for the utterly gorgeous covers that really capture my world.

And to the readers who have embraced that world, I thank you for your emails. As much as you've said I've helped or amused you, you've given it back tenfold to me and make all of this fun and worthwhile.

About the Author

Judi Fennell is an award-winning author whose romance novels have been finalists in Gather.com's First Chapters and First Chapters Romance contests, as well as in the third American Title contest. She lives in suburban Philadelphia, Pennsylvania, and spends family vacations at the Jersey Shore, the setting for some of her paranormal romance series.

Author of *In Over Her Head* and *Wild Blue Under*, Judi has enjoyed the reader feedback she's received and would love to hear what you think about her Mer series. Check out her website at www.JudiFennell.com for excerpts, reviews, contests, deleted scenes, and pictures from reader and writer conferences, as well as the chance to "dive in" to her stories.

Read all of Judi Fennell's Mer trilogy

Now available from Sourcebooks Casablanca

From

IN OVER HER HEAD

Reel carried the woman toward his home. Had he done the right thing? The Powers-That-Be were not going to be happy. There was going to be Hades to pay.

"So where are her fins?" Chum swam up on his right.

"I told you. She doesn't get any."

"But I thought when you turned a Human, they—"

"Their lungs are able to breathe oxygen from water, Chum. Just like me and the rest of the Mers. That and they get the ability to see, speak, and hear underwater. But she doesn't get fins." If he couldn't have them, it'd be really unfair for turned Humans to get them.

Reel blew through a school of herring, their silver scales sparkling like a burst of moon-glow around them.

"Seems kinda unfair. They can't keep up with the rest of you if, say, Harry gets a hankering for a tasty meal."

"Harry's going to keep his rectangular head out of my territory, if he knows what's good for him." He angled down to a lower trench, skimming above a family of starfish out for a slow slink across a rusted ship anchor.

Those earlier Humans hadn't been too bright about sailing. His great-great-grandfather had told him hundreds of stories about drowning people being saved by dolphins. Well, what they'd *thought* had been dolphins.

"So, now what are you going to do with her? When she wakes up, she's going to have a ton of questions."

"And whose brilliant idea was it to turn her?" Reel glanced at her face, now restful in sleep rather than death, her chest rising and falling like his own. Her lungs were working perfectly.

"Hey, don't look at me. You could have let her drown."

"Like that had been a choice." But, oh, was he in for it when The Council heard about this. Turning a Human was expressly forbidden. No one had turned any since the massive sea-serpent hunts two hundred *selinos* ago.

A Human had changed his mind about living under the waters and told his kind about Mers, which caused the Great Exodus from coastlines. Before that, they'd enjoyed hanging out on nice sunny beaches among the seals, swimming in the surf, and passing themselves off as dolphins for the local legged folk, but that mass hunting of his kind had sent them to the ocean depths.

Then Humans had come up with all sorts of gadgets for exploring the sea bottom. Massive trolling nets, submarines, sonar, scuba gear… it was difficult to live a normal life anymore. No late-night jumping contests in the shoreline surfs—not unless they were uninhabited islands, and where was the fun in that? And even though he physically looked like a Human, his parents had grounded him for risking such exposure at their crowded beaches.

And for good reason. No Human could know Mers existed, or they'd be out on their ships in no time. With the technology they had today, an intensive hunt could lead to an intensive slaughter.

And he'd just brought one of their kind over.

He must be out of his brain-coral mind.

She exhaled and moved slightly in his arms. Her

eyelashes were the same seal brown as her hair. They swept her cheeks where the sun had lingered a bit too long, leaving a sprinkling of sun-dots on her nose, but even those were adorable. He wondered if her eyes were as Caribbean blue as he remembered.

Fish, she was so tiny. Her legs were in proportion to what he'd expect to see on a small Mer of her size, but to be so slight! His people were full of muscle to battle the roiling waves in storms, to swim downstream in the strong currents of the North Atlantic, to outrun a hungry white or orca...

She'd never be able to survive the rigors of his world. Maybe he should have let her die or taken the chance of rushing her to the surface...

"Dude, what's done is done. She's turned. Now you get to keep her."

"She's not a pet, Chum."

"It's sure going to feel that way until you get her used to her new home away from home."

"You know, I could use a little more confidence at the moment. A little more help. You were all full of advice while she died. 'Turn her, Reel. No big deal.'"

"Hey, that rhymed."

Reel rounded a *guyot*. Behind the rise in the ocean floor yawned the gutted hull of a once-proud U.S. battleship behind the gates he'd salvaged, complete with guards. No one entered his lair without permission. That included chatty remoras.

"I'll catch up with you later, Chum." He sped through the gates, nodding to the monkfish on duty.

"But—"

Reel turned back, the woman's hair wrapping

around his waist like a trawling net, only now he didn't mind being snared. "When she wakes up, she's going to freak out seeing me. We don't need to add talking fish to the equation."

"But every fish talks."

"She doesn't know that." He turned back and headed inside. "Yet."

WILD BLUE UNDER

Rod ran his fingers over Valerie's smooth leg, down the curve of her calf, around the heel, and gently probed the indentation below the anklebone.

"I don't think it's broken." Zeus, there were so many little bones in there.

And if he focused on that, instead of the soft puffs of breath brushing his cheek and the scent of flowers clinging to her skin, he might be able to ignore the heat radiating from her like the volcanic rock that lit his world.

Then he touched another spot that made her flinch and she grabbed his arm. Electricity raced from her fingers straight to his groin.

There was no ignoring that.

But he had a job to do, not to mention a throne to inherit by doing it, and he'd focus on that, and not the fact that her shell-fillers—breasts, Reel said Humans called them—were mere inches from him.

He shifted another inch or two away from her just to ensure he stayed focused, which also ensured that she'd remove her fingers from his arm.

A High Councilman *did* have to make sacrifices for his people.

"Rod, I'll be fine." She tried to stand and nibbled her upper lip again, an action so insignificant it shouldn't have caught his attention—but did.

Especially when she did it again.

Chum's words about falling in love with her came back to taunt him.

But that was ridiculous. He wasn't falling in love with her because she was beautiful. He'd been around beautiful women before. Hades, all Mer women were beautiful.

It was just that Humans *weren't* beautiful, and he hadn't expected her to be.

Her Mer blood must be shining through. Just like her eyes, blue as the Tyrrhenian Sea, shone beneath the jumble of blonde curls that framed her face with those adorable sun-dots bridging her nose.

"Um… Rod?" She tapped his shoulder this time, and, clothing or not, it had the same effect as when she'd touched his bare skin.

Not a thought he needed at the moment.

"Yes?" He cleared his throat and willed his body to simmer down. This attraction was odd. Stronger than he'd had to anyone before. Must have something to do with the air…

"Could you help me up? The shirts… they're too soft to push off of."

Then she nibbled her lip again. *Good gods.*

But what could he say? No?

So instead, he prepared himself to touch her again, stood up, and held out his hand. "Uh, certainly."

Her fingers rested in his palm. Yeah, there was no preparation for *that*…

"Thanks. I'm sorry for knocking you down—"

"It was nothing, Valerie."

She arched an eyebrow at him, steadying herself with yet another touch to his shoulder. "Really? You have women bowling you over all the time, do you?"

None before her, and he didn't mean the incident on the floor.

Zeus. What was wrong with him? She was just another female. Half-Human at that, and he was the next High Councilman. He needed to back off.

But then she stumbled as she tried to take a step, and he instead swung her up in his arms. Big mistake. It was as big a gesture on land as his brother had said.

He deposited her on top of the counter. "You should stay off that leg." And out of his arms.

Valerie looked up at him with those beautiful blue eyes, startled wide now, and a blush tinged her cheeks before she quickly lowered her golden lashes. "Um, thanks, but I have work to do. This mess has got to go."

And she had to go, too; that was the thing.

That bird, whoever he was, had a lot of explaining to do, and Rod would put out a call to Air Security to follow up once he and Val were on their way to the ocean. But right now, Val had something more pressing to deal with.

"Don't worry about it, Valerie. You have your father's estate to concern yourself with now."

She licked her lips, moistening their soft pink sheen, then nibbled one again. He still found the action mesmerizing.

"Right. My father's estate. Um, listen. I appreciate you coming here to tell me about it, Rod, but I'm going to pass."

"What?" That statement got his eyes off those perfect lips. "You can't."

"Yes, I can. I don't want it. At all." She slid to the edge of the counter. "Thank you for stopping by, but as

you can see, I've got my work cut out for me, so if you
don't mind…"

She was refusing?

No. That wasn't possible. She *had* to accompany him.

"Valerie, you don't understand. You must accept this
inheritance. And soon. Time's running out. Just come with
me to New Jersey, and the estate will be all yours."

In Rod's experience, the words "legacy," "inheritance," and "dreams come true" brought people swimming—make that, running. The Council had fabricated
this story for that very reason.

He'd hated the thought of lying to her. Oh, there *was*
an estate. But it wasn't a cherished memento or a bag
of currency he could hand over. No, Valerie stood to
inherit the governorship of the Southern Ocean. They'd
all agreed, however, that spouting off about Mers and
Atlantis to an unsuspecting Human would damage
Rod's credibility and risk her refusal. Not to mention
break that rule again—and *that* was not an option.

Hades, they'd gone to the trouble of manufactur-
ing those papers to make the story seem legitimate in
Human terms. All he needed to do was get her to the
ocean where one drop of seawater would begin her
transformation so she could learn—and believe—the
truth. A tail was very convincing. But if he couldn't
even get her to come with him…

No. That was not even a consideration.

"Thanks, really, Rod, but I want nothing from that
man. Just take the inheritance and… I don't know, donate it to a children's hospital or something."

"Donate it?" An entire ocean and the fact that she was
the salvation of their world? Right.

The gods had to have gotten this wrong. She couldn't be the answer to The Prophecy.

He felt a rumble beneath the store. Ah, they'd followed him even here.

"Yes. Donate it. Let him do good for *somebody's* kids before it's too late, but he missed the boat with me."

Rod stared at her. No one had seen this coming. What person—Mer or Human—wouldn't want wealth?

Valerie, apparently, as she picked up the papers, rolled them, and tapped them against her lips.

"Seriously, Rod, pretend you didn't find me. Let it revert to the state, or whatever happens to unclaimed inheritances. Give it to the kids, a college… I don't care. I don't want to see any part of it. I'll stay here and run Mom's shop, and Lance can do with his inheritance what he's done for me my whole life." She slid off the counter, making him back up, and handed him the papers.

"Absolutely nothing."

Hex Appeal

BY LINDA WISDOM

**"Kudos to Linda Wisdom for a
series that's pure magic!"**

—Vicki Lewis Thompson,
New York Times bestselling author of *Wild & Hexy*

**JAZZ AND NICK'S DREAM ROMANCE HAS
TURNED INTO A NIGHTMARE...**

FEISTY WITCH JASMINE TREMAINE AND DROP-DEAD GORGEOUS vampire cop Nikolai Gregorovich have a hot thing going, but it's tough to keep it together when nightmare visions turn their passion into bickering.

With a little help from their friends, Nick and Jazz are in a race against time to uncover whoever it is that's poisoning their dreams, and their relationship...

978-1-4022-1400-4 • $6.99 U.S. / $7.99 CAN

Wicked by Any Other Name

BY LINDA WISDOM

"Do not miss this wickedly
entertaining treat."

—Annette Blair,
Sex and the Psychic Witch

STASI ROMANOV USES A LITTLE WITCH MAGIC IN HER LINGERIE shop, running a brisk side business in love charms. A disgruntled customer threatening to sue over a failed spell brings wizard attorney Trevor Barnes to town—and witches and wizards make a volatile combination. The sparks fly, almost everyone's getting singed, and the whole town seems on the verge of a witch hunt.

Can the feisty witch and the gorgeous wizard overcome their objections and settle out of court—and in the bedroom?

978-1-4022-1773-9 • $6.99 U.S. / $7.99 CAN

Hex in High Heels

BY LINDA WISDOM

Can a Witch and a Were find happiness?

Feisty witch Blair Fitzpatrick has had a crush on hunky carpenter Jake Harrison forever—he's one hot shape-shifter. But Jake's nasty mother and brother are after him to return to his pack, and Blair is trying hard not to unleash the ultimate revenge spell. When Jake's enemies try to force him away from her, Blair is pushed over the edge. No one messes with her boyfriend-to-be, even if he does shed on the furniture!

Praise for Linda Wisdom's Hex series:

"Fan-fave Wisdom… continues to delight."
—*Romantic Times*

"Highly entertaining, sexy, and imaginative."
—*Star Crossed Romance*

"It's a five star, feel-good ride!" —*Crave More Romance*

"Something fresh and new."
—*Paranormal Romance Review*

978-1-4022-1895-8 •$6.99 U.S. / $8.99 CAN

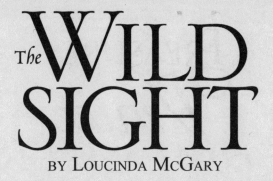

The WILD SIGHT

BY LOUCINDA MCGARY

"A magical tale of romance and intrigue. I couldn't put it down!" —Pamela Palmer, author of *Dark Deceiver* and *The Dark Gate*

◇◇◇◇◇

HE WAS CURSED WITH A "GIFT"

Born with the clairvoyance known to the Irish as "The Sight," Donovan O'Shea fled to America to escape his visions. On a return trip to Ireland to see his ailing father, staggering family secrets threaten to turn his world upside down. And then beautiful, sensual Rylie Powell shows up, claiming to be his half-sister...

SHE'S LOOKING FOR THE FAMILY SHE NEVER KNEW...

After her mother's death, Rylie journeys to Ireland to find her mysterious father. She needs the truth—but how can she and Donovan be brother and sister when the chemistry between them is nearly irresistible?

UNCOVERING THE PAST LEADS THEM DANGEROUSLY CLOSE TO MADNESS...

◇◇◇◇◇

"A richly drawn love story and riveting romantic suspense!" —Karin Tabke, author of *What You Can't See*

978-1-4022-1394-6 • $6.99 U.S. / $8.99 CAN

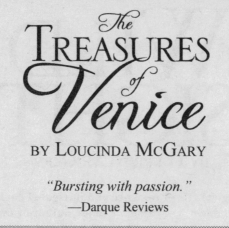

The TREASURES of Venice

BY LOUCINDA MCGARY

"Bursting with passion."
—Darque Reviews

An Irish rogue who never met a lock he couldn't pick…

With danger at every corner and time running out, Keirnan Fitzgerald must use whatever means possible to uncover the missing Jewels of the Madonna. Samantha Lewis is shocked when Keirnan approaches her, but she throws caution to the wind and accompanies the Irish charmer into his dangerous world of intrigue, theft, and betrayal. As the centuries-old story behind the Jewels' disappearance is revealed, Samantha must decide whether Keirnan is her soul mate from a previous life, or if they are merely pawns in a relentless quest for a priceless treasure…

"Lost jewels, a sexy Irish hero, and an exotic locale make for a wonderful escape. Don't miss this charming story."
—Brenda Novak, *New York Times* bestselling author of *Watch Me*

"A brilliant novel that looks to the past, entwines it in the present, and makes you wonder at every twist and turn if the hero and heroine will get out alive. Snap this one up, it's a keeper!" —Jeanne Adams, author of *Dark and Deadly*

978-1-4022-2670-0 •$6.99 U.S. / $8.99 CAN